BY LAURA ANDERSEN

The Boleyn King

The Boleyn Deceit

The Boleyn Reckoning

The Virgin's Daughter

The Virgin's Spy

THE
VIRGIN'S SPY

THE VIRGIN'S SPY

A TUDOR LEGACY NOVEL

Laura Andersen

BALLANTINE BOOKS

NEW YORK

A Ballantine Books Trade Paperback Original

Copyright © 2015 by Laura Andersen
Reading group guide copyright © 2015 by Penguin Random House LLC
Excerpt from *The Virgin's War* by Laura Andersen copyright © 2015 by Laura Andersen

Published in the United States by Ballantine Books, an imprint of Random House, a division of Penguin Random House LLC, New York.

BALLANTINE and the HOUSE colophon are registered trademarks of Penguin Random House LLC.
RANDOM HOUSE READER'S CIRCLE & Design is a registered trademark of Penguin Random House LLC.

This book contains an excerpt from the forthcoming book *The Virgin's War* by Laura Andersen. This excerpt has been set for this edition only and may not reflect the final content of the forthcoming edition.

Library of Congress Cataloging-in-Publication Data
Andersen, Laura.
The virgin's spy : a Tudor legacy novel / Laura Andersen.
pages ; cm
ISBN 978-0-8041-7938-6 (hardcover : alk. paper)—ISBN 978-0-8041-7939-3 (eBook)
1. Elizabeth I, Queen of England, 1533–1603—Fiction. 2. Queens—Great Britain—Fiction. 3. Inheritance and succession—Fiction. 4. Great Britain—Kings and rulers—Succession—Fiction. 5. Great Britain—History—Tudors, 1485–1603—Fiction. I. Title.
PS3601.N437V58 2015
813'.6—dc23
2015022848

Printed in the United States of America on acid-free paper

randomhousebooks.com
randomhousereaderscircle.com

2 4 6 8 9 7 5 3 1

Book design by Caroline Cunningham

To Katie,
as necessary to me
as air and water
and Diet Coke

THE
VIRGIN'S SPY

PRELUDE

March 1570

"How in the name of heaven above did FitzMaurice take Kilmallock with only one hundred and twenty men?"

Elizabeth, Queen of England and Ireland (that last clearly in some doubt in the minds of her Irish subjects), whirled furiously on Walsingham and Burghley, the only two men in England whom she would allow to see the touch of fear in her fury.

Lord Burghley might be her Secretary of State and principal advisor, but he was also a man who had known her since she was a girl. In all those years, he had learned when to speak gently. "The rebels were aided from within the town itself. Humphrey Gilbert did not endear himself to those he lived among. I'm afraid his policy of instilling fear into the populace was useful only so long as he was in residence. Since he returned to England last month?" Burghley shrugged. "The Irish were only too willing to turn on the English garrison."

"Now what?" the queen demanded. Oh, but she was tired of Ireland. The land sucked up men and arms and money and spat back nothing but rebellion and ingratitude. "FitzMaurice will not keep still long enough for us to catch him."

Indeed, the rebel leader of what was rapidly becoming known as the Desmond War had so begrudged losing the critical town of Kilmallock to the English once already that this time he had not stayed longer than three days, stripping the town of all valuables before burning it to the ground. Now he was back in the forests of Aherlow, unreachable and infuriating.

Burghley, as was his nature, pleaded caution. "Your Majesty, we must consider negotiation. James FitzMaurice is not without reason. As long as he keeps to the forests and mountains, his small forces can strike and move on before our troops can come to grips with them. It is a losing proposition for England."

"Not with enough men and money," Walsingham disagreed. His official position was somewhat fluid, being most often called upon to act as Elizabeth's chief intelligencer. "Your Majesty must accept that the Irish rebellion is not crushed, but in fact growing. Ireland must be brought to heel before the Spanish seize the chance to exploit the rebels for their own ends."

Elizabeth had long mastered the art of the quizzical eyebrow. "You believe King Philip would actively oppose the forces of his own wife?" she asked acidly.

"I believe that Spain is exceedingly interested in supplanting religious reformation in your kingdom by any means necessary. Ireland is easily manipulated. King Philip may not involve himself personally, but no doubt any number of Spanish nobles and Church officers scent Protestant blood. They will eagerly aid in shedding more of it."

Walsingham had never approved of Elizabeth's pragmatic marriage to the King of Spain nearly ten years ago. Burghley, however, both understood and continued to approve. "Her Majesty will of course write to King Philip in sharp protest. But threat of Catholic support from Spain only underscores the need for negotiations."

"Enough!" Elizabeth let the two men settle into silence before pronouncing the last word. For now. "Send for Sir John Perrot. Pull him away from his Pembrokeshire estates and tell him the queen has need of him."

"Perrot?" Walsingham said skeptically. "He is too old for active campaigning."

"And too fat," Elizabeth added. "But neither will stop him. And unlike Humphrey Gilbert, he will not scorch Ireland to the ground simply on principle. At least with Perrot I will have both loyalty and an honest assessment of the situation."

She looked at each man pointedly. "Does that answer, gentlemen?"

What could they say? The kingdom was hers. Walsingham could not bring himself to gladly agree, but he bowed grudgingly as Burghley said, "It will be done, Your Majesty. Kilmallock's destruction is a loss, but one we can afford. We will not lose you Ireland."

James FitzMaurice, Captain of Desmond, groaned inwardly when told one of the Kavanaughs demanded to see him. Tired, filthy, living on the run for months now, FitzMaurice would have sent the man away if he could. But a captain could only command while men obeyed, and governing people's petty squabbles and complaints was a necessary component of his command.

"Five minutes," he told his guard. "That's all the time he has."

No one had mentioned the girl.

She came in at Finian Kavanaugh's side, cloaked and hooded and head bowed so nothing of her could be seen except a lock of black hair fallen free from beneath her gray hood.

Finian, a broad and bristle-bearded man nearing fifty, had a voice that sounded suspicious no matter the topic. "What's to be done about the lass, that's what I want to know," he launched in at once, as though FitzMaurice knew what he was talking about.

"Why should anything be done?" FitzMaurice asked. "I don't even know who she is."

The girl kept her head down, as though she weren't the topic of this strange discussion.

"In Kilmallock, she was," Finian announced, "my niece. My brother wasn't quick enough to send her away when the English came. He died in the attack, but she survived. Been there all these months of the English garrison. My men found her just before you put the town to flames."

"I am sorry for your troubles," FitzMaurice said gently to the silent figure.

The girl raised her head, and two things struck him: first, that she was very young, and second, that she viewed him with cool disinterest. Whoever expected recompense for any harm done her, it was not this girl herself.

"What is your name, child?"

"Ailis." Her voice was soft but distinct.

"How old are you, Ailis?"

"Fourteen."

She and FitzMaurice studied each other in equal measure, until he blinked first. Then, to Finian, he said gruffly, "Surely any help the girl requires can be handled within your family and clan?"

"Help, aye. But vengeance—that will take more than just the men of our clan."

"Vengeance for what?"

When Finian reached for her cloak, Ailis made a single convulsive gesture of protest, but she stood still enough as her uncle swept off the enveloping garment and revealed her pregnancy for all Irish eyes to see and understand.

FitzMaurice narrowed his eyes. "Who?" he demanded of her. "Gilbert himself?"

Finian answered for her. "One of the English dogs under his command. She won't say."

"Why not?" FitzMaurice demanded. "You know who I am, girl. The Captain of Desmond. I would see your shame avenged."

With those clear, uncompromising eyes, Ailis answered, "Vengeance belongs to me."

With a shake of his head, but a grudging respect, FitzMaurice conceded. "If my men had half your focus, Ailis Kavanaugh, we should put the English to rout in a month's time. Go then, and seek your vengeance. If you find you would like my aid at any time, you have only to ask."

When she smiled, cold as it was, FitzMaurice could see the great beauty that she would one day become. "I can destroy one Englishman without any man's aid," she promised.

FitzMaurice believed her.

ONE

June 1581

Elizabeth loved weddings. At least those weddings in which she could appear the benign good fairy, generously bestowing her favour upon a couple and, as always, claiming the spotlight for herself. Most families fortunate enough to draw the queen's attention to such an occasion fell over themselves to get out of her way and let her run things in the manner she wanted them.

Not the Courtenay family.

At this wedding, Elizabeth was little more than a guest. For one thing, she had wanted the wedding to take place in London. As the bride was both the eldest daughter of the Duke of Exeter and Elizabeth's own goddaughter, the queen had graciously offered any number of royal chapels for the ceremony, from private ones such as Hampton Court to more public parishes like St. Margaret's at Westminster.

But Lucette Courtenay had her mother's stubbornness when her own wishes were at stake, and so Elizabeth herself had to travel northwest to participate in the wedding of the English lady and her French Catholic spy.

Elizabeth did not stay at Wynfield Mote with the Courtenay family, but in Warwick Castle ten miles northeast. After the castle's forfeit to the crown upon the Duke of Northumberland's death, Elizabeth had bestowed it upon one of the duke's surviving sons, Ambrose Dudley. In gratitude for the queen's generosity, Ambrose gave her the run of the castle whenever she wished. A queen had no release from ruling, so Elizabeth filled hours of each day with letters and papers and in meeting with the men who rode back and forth between the monarch and Walsingham in London. Though her Lord Secretary (and chief spymaster) had once used both the bride and groom in his intelligence web, Walsingham had not been invited to the wedding.

The ceremony itself went off beautifully. Conducted at Holy Trinity Church in Stratford-upon-Avon—and in the language of the Prayer Book issued by Elizabeth's government in the first year of her reign—Lucette Courtenay and Julien LeClerc pledged themselves to love and honour, to worship with their bodies, and remain loyal to their deaths. Elizabeth herself had not been married to quite those words. Indeed, the working out of her marriage more than twenty years ago to Philip of Spain had required nearly a month of exhaustive debates on how precisely to balance their vows as Catholic and Protestant. But as Julien LeClerc had willingly adopted the Protestant faith for his bride, there was no trouble about words today.

They at least allowed the queen to host a banquet for them afterward at Warwick Castle. Elizabeth had rather hoped that Lucette would wear the Tudor rose necklace she had once given her, but the dark-haired bride was adorned instead with another necklace familiar to the queen: pearls and sapphires, with a single filigree star pendant.

When the bride's mother joined her, Elizabeth said acerbically, "Don't tell me you have handed over your prized possession, Minuette. Whatever does Dominic say?"

Though nearly forty-five, Minuette Courtenay was recognizably still the young woman who had once captured the King of England's heart. If there were strands of gray in her honey-gold hair, they did not show, and her gown of leaf-green damask fit as neatly as when she was young. There were times, looking at her friend, when Elizabeth could almost believe the last twenty-five years a dream.

Minuette returned her to the subject of the necklace. "It is only lent for now," she replied with equal tartness. "And Dominic would say that we ourselves are our prized possessions, not any material goods."

"Do you never tire of your husband's practical perfection?" Not that there wasn't a grain of envy in Elizabeth's soul at her friend's long-lived and loving marriage.

Minuette turned the conversation with the ease of a woman who had known her queen since childhood—indeed, still knew her rather better than made Elizabeth comfortable. "Anabel tells us you intend to invest her formally as Princess of Wales. She is very proud—and, to your credit, taking the responsibility seriously. Dominic says her spoken Welsh has become quite good."

Instinctively, Elizabeth darted a look to where her only child sat in merry companionship with Minuette's twins. Kit and Pippa Courtenay were on either side of the princess, their matching honey-gold heads (like their mother's) bent inward as the three of them talked in no doubt scurrilous terms about the guests. The tableau tugged painfully at long-ago memories. "The Holy Quartet," Robert Dudley had called them: Dominic, Minuette, Elizabeth . . . and her brother, William. She could only hope there was less pain in these young ones' futures.

"The investiture," Elizabeth acknowledged. "Of course it is only a formality. A ritual I never had. But it will be useful just now to remind the Welsh of our power. That is why I have chosen Ludlow Castle for the investiture, rather than simply doing it before Parliament. Anabel will make a charming figure to the Welsh."

"She says the council has invited a representative from the Duc d'Anjou to attend the investiture."

"As well as an envoy from Scotland. France is prepared to give us a large measure of what we want now that Mary Stuart has wed Philip. I will see what I can get from them, but it is Scotland that is most desperate for an alliance."

"What is Anabel's preference?"

Elizabeth huffed in exasperation. "You know better than that, Minuette. With my divorce from Philip and his recent marriage to Mary Stuart, all Europe is on edge. Mary wants Scotland back, make no mistake, and if she can persuade my former husband to give her Spanish troops, then our island is in serious danger. If Anabel were at all prone to romance—and I'm not certain that she is—she would have to give over for hard, cold reality. England and Scotland must stand together or we will fall separately to the Catholics."

Minuette held her silence almost to the point of discomfort, but finally said, "I wasn't criticizing, Elizabeth. Not intentionally. It is only that you were my friend before you were my queen, and at times I wish you unencumbered by the burdens of ruling. You and Anabel both."

It was my choice to rule, Elizabeth thought, but would never say. I just didn't have a clear idea of what it would mean, the years of weariness and care and doubt. And always, the waiting for the next crisis.

She didn't have long to wait. Before the wedding party had quite broken up, a courier arrived from London with a curt message written in Walsingham's hand, the message Elizabeth had been fearing since the Scots queen had escaped her English imprisonment last year and then married the King of Spain.

Mary Stuart is four months gone with child.

The morning after his sister's wedding, Stephen Courtenay woke late and for nearly the first time in his life was reluctant to leave his bed. (His empty bed, at least, and at home it was always empty.) But with Lucie's wedding out of the way, he couldn't put off what came next. The queen had offered him a command, and would not long await an answer.

Command was one thing—he had been raised to expect it. Command in Ireland was something else entirely. And convincing his parents to accept it when he himself was ambivalent? No wonder he'd rather stay in bed.

But he was twenty-one years old and could hardly hide from trouble. So he flung himself out of bed and dressed in record time in the belief that he might as well get unpleasant things done quickly. If he were Kit, he would dawdle his way through, putting it off as long as he could, but irresponsibility was not a trait an eldest son and heir could afford. That was the province of younger brothers.

On this particular morning, Kit was long gone on a ride with Pippa and Anabel. Lucie and her husband had spent the night at their new home, Compton Wynyates, and from there meant to go north and spend the next few weeks in Yorkshire, since the French-born Julien thought it sounded exotic. From the way Lucie and Julien had been looking at each other last night, Stephen supposed they would hardly notice their surroundings, as long as they had a bed.

And that was a disturbing image of one's sister. Stephen shook it off as he swiped bread and cheese from the Wynfield Mote kitchens and headed for the fount of all certain knowledge where his family was concerned—Carrie Harrington.

Just turned sixty, Carrie had been in his mother's service for twenty-five years, and in Minuette's mother's service before that. After she'd lost her first husband and both their children to illness early in life, she had remarried the large, silent Edward Harrington, who'd served Dominic Courtenay since before he was the Duke of Exeter. Carrie had personally delivered Stephen and each of his siblings and could always be counted on for good advice.

And also a certain amount of mind reading.

"Looking for your parents?" she asked, squinting up at him from her comfortable chair in the sunlit solar. "Or looking to avoid them?"

Stephen smiled. "Which should it be?"

Her hair was a soft gray-brown and her face lined, but her hands were steady on her needlework. "Don't look to me to sort your problems. Go to Ireland or not—it is your decision. And that, for what it's worth, is what your parents will tell you."

"I know. Sometimes I wish they were more autocratic."

"No, you don't. You only appear submissive in comparison to your brother. If ever you are commanded against your wishes, Stephen, you will balk authority as surely as Kit does."

"Then let us hope I am never commanded against my wishes. There can only be one Kit."

"Your parents walked in the direction of the old church," Carrie said, dismissing him and returning to her sewing.

Stephen met them coming back toward the house, halfway between Wynfield Mote and the Norman church that had stood empty since Henry VIII's reformation. Dominic and Minuette Courtenay had been married in that empty chapel—married in a Catholic ceremony, surprisingly. Every now and then Stephen remembered that his parents had not only had a life before their children, but a rather complicated and dangerous life. They were so very . . . stable. But today, remembering that his father had once been enough of a rebel to land in the Tower gave Stephen courage to speak the whole of his conflicted mind.

As ever, his mother went right to the heart of the matter. "The queen is demanding an answer to Ireland, is she not? I could feel the weight of her attention on you yesterday."

"I've put her off as long as possible. If I'm taking a force to Ireland, it must be before summer's end."

"Are you seeking counsel, or approval?" his father asked.

"I'm always seeking both." Stephen smiled briefly. "Partly I feel I don't want anything to do with the mess in Ireland—and partly I feel that very reluctance means I should go."

His mother laughed. "So like your father, making everything ten times more difficult than it need be. Go to Ireland or don't, Stephen, but stop flaying yourself alive over the decision."

But Dominic Courtenay knew his son as he knew himself, and so he added what the young man craved—an opinion. "If it were myself, I would go. I was your age when I commanded men along the March of Wales, and it was a critical experience in my life. You are a good leader with good men from your Somerset lands who will follow you. Let them. What they learn of you in Ireland will shape their lives and yours. Besides," and here he cast a rueful glance at his wife, "military service is the least demanding request a monarch can make. Be glad if that is all the queen wants of you, son."

Stephen laughed as he was meant to, and he did feel lighter when he wrote to the queen later that day to accept her offer of command in Ireland.

But beneath the lightness of a decision made was a brittle unease. Because military service was not the only thing wanted of him. His second letter was addressed to Francis Walsingham. Though officially the queen's principal secretary, Walsingham had never given over his role as her chief intelligencer. Last year, Stephen had served him from within the imprisoned household of the exiled Scots queen, Mary Stuart. Walsingham was a man to exploit what advantages he could, and having a spy he trusted in Ireland would be a definite advantage.

I will be in Ireland by mid-August, Stephen wrote.

He expected Walsingham would have requests of his own to add to the queen's orders.

Anne Isabella, Princess of Wales, had learned from her earliest years that she could nearly always get her way. Not many people had the power to say no to the daughter of two reigning monarchs, and so nineteen-year-old Anabel, when she was being particularly honest with herself, admitted that she was a bit spoiled.

The trouble was, one only tended to realize that when one didn't get one's way. As now, with Kit Courtenay staring her down in refusal.

"What do you mean, 'No'?" she demanded. "I have appointed you my Master of Horse. It wasn't a request."

"Unless you mean me to operate in chains, then I am telling you that I very kindly decline the appointment."

"What is wrong with you, Kit? You've been irritable and difficult for months."

"Because I have a mind of my own and a wish to do more with my life than follow you around and offer you compliments? 'How lovely you are today, Your Highness,'" he said in deadly mimicry of court sycophants. "'The very image of your royal mother, but is that a touch of Spanish flair in your dress?'"

Anabel's temper went from raging to white-hot in a moment. In a chilly tone reminiscent of her father's Spanish hauteur, she said, "Long acquaintance does not give you the right to insult me to my face."

Most unusually, Kit did not immediately respond. Anabel was used to his ready tongue and quick wit, which could spin any conversation a dozen dizzying directions without warning. But in the last months, his irritability had been accompanied by these bouts of reflection before speech.

Kit did not apologize; she had not expected him to. But he offered something of an explanation. "I am growing older, just as you are. I do not have a throne waiting for me, nor even a title. Stephen inherits my father's riches. I must make my own path. And I would prefer to do it without undue favouritism."

"And what of due favouritism? Do you expect me to appoint strangers to serve in my household?"

"I am not insensible of the great honour, Your Highness. But I have made other plans. The Earl of Leicester is bound for Dublin and has appointed me his secretary. I leave for Ireland in two weeks."

"You're going to Ireland with Brandon Dudley? To be a *secretary*?" Anabel laughed in disbelief. "Why not at least go as part of Stephen's forces?"

"If I'm not going to accept your favours, Anabel, I'm hardly likely to go begging to my brother."

That at least sounded like the Kit she had always known— irreverent and occasionally insolent. Although Anabel was as close to the Courtenay children as anyone, the princess occasionally studied their relationships as an outsider and wondered if the pleasures of siblings outweighed the resentments.

"I don't suppose there's any chance you would reconsider?" There was a wistfulness to her plea she had not expected.

His quick, rueful grin was answer in itself. "You'll be happier with someone more biddable, Your Highness. You and I should only spend our days arguing."

But those are the best parts of my days, Anabel thought forlornly. Arguing with you.

She was still fretting about his uncharacteristic refusal that night when Pippa helped her change for bed. There were two other ladies moving silently about with her gown and kirtle and ruff, but Anabel ignored them.

"What is wrong with Kit?" she demanded of his twin.

Pippa continued to brush Anabel's hair as she answered. "Kit told you the truth. For all his mischief, he is ambitious and proud. Is it truly a surprise he should wish to make his way independently?"

Pippa had her twin's sharp cheekbones and eyes that tilted up on the outer corner. They both had their mother's thick, wavy hair the colour of sun-warmed honey, but Pippa's had a streak of black in it that framed the right side of her face. It made her look—not exotic, exactly, but otherworldly. It was not the only otherworldly aspect to her character.

But at the moment, Pippa did not seem interested in sharing any of her unique knowledge, so Anabel contented herself with logical argument. "Being Master of Horse for the Princess of Wales would be an independent position. I don't mean to tell him how to perform his responsibilities."

"Kit does not wish to take your gifts."

"Because he does not wish to waste time in my company?"

Pippa laid down the brush and, when Anabel made no objection, pulled a stool alongside her friend. Her voice was kind but implacable. "You know better than that. Anabel, what is truly bothering you?"

Your damned twin with his arrogance and pride and sudden wish to cut himself off from me. Kit was hers, as much as Pippa. What was the point of being royal if one could not keep hold of the people one wanted?

But not even to Pippa was she prepared to share the full turmoil of her thoughts, because beneath them lurked something that frightened her. An image—a memory—that came to her at night as she drifted between waking and sleep.

The expression in Kit's eyes when he'd walked into Wynfield Mote a year ago to negotiate her out of the hands of a violent man.

Anabel had not seen that expression in the months since. Instead, Kit had been moody and unpredictable. And now he seemed so determined to get away from her that he was willing to go to godforsaken Ireland.

When it must have become clear that Anabel would not speak further, Pippa sighed. "Someday you will have to learn to trust yourself, Your Highness. I cannot do it for you."

30 June 1581

Dearest Lucie,

When you traveled to France last year, I teased you about coming home with a Frenchman. Or half teased. I did not know—I never know for certain—how events would play out. I knew there was danger and pain and loss all tied together with your happiness . . . but is that not the nature of life itself? One cannot untangle only the parts one wants. They are woven together too tightly.

How do I tell Anabel that? She is not prepared to admit, even to her-

self, that she knows perfectly well why Kit is leaving England. Having had the shock of confronting his own feelings for her so suddenly last August, Kit cannot go on taking her favours as nothing more than the friend he has always been. But nor will he press on her a love she is not prepared to accept. To serve in her household would be a daily insult to his pride, especially with the looming visits of the French and Scots representatives coming to vie for her hand. Kit knows perfectly well that Anabel is not meant for him.

What do I know? Only a tangle of paths and choices and troubles that lie ahead. England's future is no more secure than Elizabeth's or her daughter's. If I knew how it would all turn out, I would truly be the witch some might fear me of being.

But I am only a girl who knows more than I wish.

Oh dear, only days away from you and already I am slipping into melodrama. In your great happiness, Lucie, steal a few minutes away to write to me with your mix of sisterly compassion and common sense. I need it.

Love,
Pippa

5 July 1581

Pippa,

Stop being melodramatic! The world is not yours to order or decipher, only to live in as we all must do. If you had tried to tell me that I would fall in love with Julien, I would likely have refused to do so out of sheer stubbornness. There's no use fretting over Anabel and Kit—I have never known two people more certain to do precisely as they please. Getting in their way will only aggravate the issue.

I feel quite certain now that York is the most beautiful city in England. Though probably I should feel that way about Bristol or Leeds or Carlisle if I happened to be passing these days in any of those towns. It is

Julien that makes all beautiful, especially at night when we can shut the door and there is nothing in this world but the two of us. And a fine cambric shift. And a bed.

It is a state I highly recommend.

Your most lovingly contented sister,
Lucie

TWO

"And how are you feeling today, Maria?" Philip asked from polite habit. He could see perfectly well that his wife continued in the good health she had enjoyed since the earliest days of her pregnancy. It was a blessing he did not lightly discount, for Mary Stuart was thirty-eight years old and had not borne a living child since James of Scotland fourteen years ago.

Pregnancy agreed with her. Mary, unlike her cousin and Philip's previous wife, Elizabeth, was entirely feminine and she glowed with the sheen of contented womanhood.

But, very much like Elizabeth, there were times when the queen outshone the woman.

"Why," Mary replied tartly, "has there been no aid sent to Ireland? The Earl of Desmond desperately needs men and arms and food."

Desmond also, in Philip's opinion, needed better tactics and a country worth fighting for. But his wife knew she was on secure ground, for he would not quarrel openly while she carried what could only be hoped was the future King of Spain.

"Maria," Philip said with the lightest warning, "you should not trouble yourself with the politics of Ireland at such a time." Or any time, he thought wryly. Ireland was nothing but a wasteland of men and money.

But it was also Catholic, nominally controlled by England, and Mary sought any outlet that allowed her to strike at the queen who had kept her captive for a dozen years.

"I am not troubling myself about the politics of Ireland. I am troubling myself about my husband keeping his word. Spain has promised aid. And do not speak to me of legalities and councils and the fine details of such a promise. Tell me what the most powerful king in Christendom intends to do in the next four weeks to aid his brothers in Christ."

"Sit down," Philip said flatly. And when she opened her mouth to protest, repeated a touch louder, "Sit down, Maria. I will speak to you, but I will not keep the mother of my heir on her feet while I do so."

She sat and studied him with a suspicious arrogance that was an uncomfortable trait in one's wife. Not that Elizabeth Tudor could ever be outmatched in terms of arrogance, but she possessed in addition the saving graces of a first-rate mind and a mischievous sense of humour. Neither of which Mary Stuart could claim. Mary's intelligence was instinctive rather than cultivated, narrow rather than wide, and she distrusted anyone who might be laughing at her.

"As a queen all your life," he began, "you know perfectly well the limitations even royalty must work around. Yes, Spain is Holy Church's most zealous defender, but that means we must always look at the wider view. Ireland is but one piece, and because of her geography and culture, a minor piece at that."

"But—"

"Let me finish." Once, Philip would never have talked over a woman. But queens, at times, had to be an exception. "Since your escape from England and our divorce from Elizabeth, Ireland has become a pivotal piece, for all that it is minor. We are sending men and arms and gold. They will reach the west coast of Ireland by the end of July."

No need to give details, for Mary would only complain that the numbers were not enough. Probably she was right. But Philip trusted his military men more than his wife. They had chosen what they thought an optimal number—enough to tip the balance if the stars aligned for the Earl of Desmond, but not so many that Philip could not afford to lose them. More importantly—if they did lose them, Spain's prestige would not be touched.

Ireland might yet prove fertile ground to attack Elizabeth's fragile empire. But not for certain, not yet. And Philip gambled only on certainties.

"If you're going to gamble, Kit, don't wager more than you can afford to lose."

Kit choked back a curse and rounded on his twin. "First, don't sneak up on me. Second, you sounded scarily like Mother just then. And third, don't twit me, Pippa. I am not in the mood."

Mimicking his tone, she said, "First, pay attention to your surroundings. Second, I know what mood you're in before you do. And third, I don't care. The privilege of older siblings, Kit—to speak to you how and when we choose."

"You're older by five minutes. And I don't need you to play Stephen's part any more than Mother's—"

He only stopped when he caught the flash of true concern from his twin. It was there and gone too swiftly for anyone else to have noticed, but Kit knew Pippa as well as he knew anyone in the world. Better. It wasn't just that they had the same colouring, the same thick waves of dark gold hair, the same wide smile used to deflect others as much as to charm them. Their bond was more than physical, encompassing a queer double sense of the world and of each other. Because of that bond, Kit could feel that Pippa's concern about his state ran deep—and her intentions to keep at him until he was at least partly truthful ran even deeper.

"Come on," he sighed, and pulled her away from the public galleries of Greenwich Palace into the more secluded corridors where only royalty and their closest councilors and friends ventured. He would allow Pippa much, but airing his most private thoughts for anyone to hear went too far.

When they were as alone as could be managed, Kit folded his arms and leaned against the wall. "Talk," he commanded Pippa.

But his twin only smiled with deadly sweetness. "I believe that's my order for you."

He would have liked to make her press and pry and work for every concession she meant to wring from him. But it would have been pointless. The talking was not to satisfy her curiosity; it was to force him to come to terms with things that, in her opinion, he had kept too long even from himself.

There were times when Pippa looked at him that Kit felt as though they were two parts of one whole. And other times when she seemed as foreign to him as an ancient Roman would have been.

Today, he felt only that she was his sister and dearest friend. That there was nothing about him she didn't already know and forgive. And so, less grudgingly than he'd intended, Kit began to talk.

"I can't do it," he confessed. "I cannot sit around Anabel's household and watch the parade of men hoping to claim her. Don't ask it of me."

"I wouldn't. I know you need to go."

"But she doesn't." As Kit spoke, he felt hollow at the truth of his words. "And that's the hardest part of all—that Anabel does not know why I'm going. She thinks I'm merely being difficult."

"You could tell her the truth."

"To what purpose? You know better than anyone, Pippa—Anabel is not meant for me. I'll get over it. I'm not stupid enough to stay hopelessly in love with a woman I cannot have."

It was as blatant a lie as he'd ever told, for he and his siblings lived daily with a father who had only ever loved one woman, one who had remained steadfast at the cost of his honour, his left hand, and very nearly his life. Did Kit's siblings ever feel, as he did, that such a love was both a hope and a dreadful burden?

"Yes," Pippa said, and Kit thought for a moment he'd heard her only in his head. It happened from time to time, this silent communication—mostly in moments of strong emotion—but no, just now her mouth was moving, although she was answering the question he had not uttered aloud. "We are not Mother and Father, Kit. You must rule your own life and your own heart. Go to Ireland. Work hard and be yourself. You were not wrong when you said you needed to discover your own path. Go and find it."

"And you?" he tried to tease, but it came out more wistful than light. "Pippa, must your path always parallel the princess? Do you not wish for independence?"

"What makes you think I don't have it? Independence is not a matter of situation but choice. I am where I choose. You can always trust me for that."

And then, as Pippa so often did, she walked away, leaving her brother to try and decipher another of her cryptic statements. So he did what he usually did—ignored it and went about his own business.

There was plenty to do in preparation for Ireland, and Kit threw himself into filling requisition lists and planning supply routes for the Earl of Leicester's trip. On his last day at court he was walking abstractedly through the halls of Greenwich calculating the weight of horses on board ship when a woman—blonde, beautiful, experienced—called his name.

And suddenly abstraction gave way to wariness, for Eleanor Percy fixed him with an amused expression that promised a playfulness he had no patience for. She was of an age with his mother, but behaved as though any man would be grateful for her attention. It was an effort wasted on the Courtenay men, but that did not stop her from trying.

"Where are you off to with such a distracted expression, Lord Christopher?" Eleanor was one of those women who purred rather than spoke, her words a caress that made his hackles rise. She went on without pause. "Oh, that's right . . . you're going to Ireland. I suppose you must be sulking at being forced to leave the princess. But then royalty does tire of their lapdogs so quickly. Just ask your parents."

Or I could ask you, he thought ungraciously. How long did *you* keep the last king entertained before he pushed you out of his bed?

Kit shuffled mentally through the various marriages in Eleanor Percy's past, trying to pin down the right name to give her at the moment. Finally he gave up and said simply, "My lady." He bowed, and began to walk once more.

She stepped in his path, so that he could not continue without absolute rudeness. Stoically, he waited for her to say whatever it was she'd stopped him for. "I imagine we'll cross paths from time to time in Dublin. Lord Leicester seemed quite pleased at the prospect of my company."

"You're coming to Dublin?" was all Kit could manage.

"Oh, yes. And a little further. An invitation to Kilkenny from the Earl of Ormond, you know. And there will be so many of our eligible young men in Ireland this autumn, how could I deprive Nora of their company?"

And there it was. Kit wanted to swear aloud, but stifled the impulse. Now he knew why Eleanor had stopped him. Her daughter Nora, despite being the acknowledged daughter of Henry IX, remained unmarried at the age of twenty-seven. Either because Nora was naturally shy and resisted being courted for her blood or because her mother was considerably less than shy, and few men wanted Eleanor Percy as a mother-in-law.

Eleanor would settle for no less than an earl for her daughter, and would prefer a duke. And if she could spite her former antagonists through matchmaking, all the better. Eleanor wasn't talking to Kit for his own sake, but because his older brother, Stephen, was Earl of

Somerset and would one day be Duke of Exeter. What better vengeance on Minuette than to trap her son for Eleanor's daughter?

Sure enough, Eleanor said, "You must persuade your brother to come to Dublin, or at least Kilkenny, during our visit. The Earl of Somerset should not be spending all his time in the wastelands beyond the Pale."

There was little Kit liked less than being courted solely for his relationship to his older, wealthier brother. "As you pointed out, I will be mostly in Dublin. If you have Lord Leicester's promise to see you, then I'm afraid the company of one Courtenay brother will have to suffice."

Derision lit the edges of her smile. "As long as it is the right brother."

Rude or not, Kit stepped around her and went on his way. But not before he heard her call after him, "I expect the princess would not be so ready to part from your older brother as she is from you. It's a pity there is not another title to go around in your family—perhaps Princess Anne is merely using you to get to Stephen."

Stephen spent the month of July on his lands in Somerset, mustering a handpicked force of able and willing men who had been trained by his father, often alongside Stephen himself. Two weeks into training Edward Harrington arrived to act as Stephen's second in command. Harrington had been the Duke of Exeter's seneschal/steward/man-at-arms for years before Stephen's birth, with a taciturnity surpassed only by his battlefield skills. After the expected period of discomfort in feeling that his father was watching over his shoulder, Stephen relaxed into the new relationship. A commander could not afford to scorn men of skill, and he knew Harrington would be invaluable in Ireland.

The company rode out on the first day of August. When they left Stephen's castle at Farleigh Hungerford, it was with laughter and teasing from those left behind, a sense of adventure among those marching, and Stephen was confident in the abilities of his 150 soldiers and glad to be finally on his way.

His father had appeared at Farleigh Hungerford the last day, asking if he might ride with them to Bristol. In another man it might have been awkward and caused Stephen's force a sense of split loyalties. But no one knew better than Dominic Courtenay how authority could be as much a matter of expectation as ability, and he would never interfere in his son's command. At least not publicly.

In the end, Stephen discovered, his father's topic of discussion had little to do with military matters. They reached Bristol the afternoon of August first, with a ship prepared to take them on board the very next day. Stephen allowed his men to disperse with orders to be returned to their encampment by dark. Then he walked with his father along the Severn Estuary.

"Any last words of advice?" Stephen was quick to ask. Better than having it offered without asking.

"Be careful with Oliver Dane. He's an old Irish hand who dislikes English interlopers as much as he does the Irish rebels. As long as you make clear you are not interested in encroaching on his Irish lands or rights, you should be all right."

Stephen huffed a laugh. "I hardly feel I deserve what I have in England—I shall make clear to Captain Dane that Ireland is not in my ambitions."

"What are your ambitions?"

"Personally or professionally?"

"There is little difference between them for a belted earl. Since you were twelve we've received many overtures of interest from good families with daughters."

"You're not planning to marry me off already, are you?"

"And if we were? I must confess, Stephen, I haven't the slightest idea how you would take it if I announced one day that I had secured you a marriage."

How *would* he take it? Stephen wondered. He hadn't spent a lot of time thinking of marriage—twenty-one was indeed young. "I suppose I would thank you for your concern."

"Don't look so stricken, son. Surely you don't seriously expect your mother and me to arrange you a marriage without your knowledge or consent."

No, he supposed not. Other sons of dukes would expect to be dutifully wed wherever their family required. But the children of the Duke and Duchess of Exeter were, first and foremost, the children of a love match, one that had defied royalty and endured prison. They would not balk at the thought of love—after all, Lucie had married her French Catholic spy against all good sense. But his sister had also walked through a valley of pain and sorrow to get there. Stephen wasn't sure it was worth it.

"Honestly, Father, it might be simpler if you chose for me. And don't tell me Mother doesn't have some very specific ideas of her own," he teased.

"It's not marriage we're concerned with at the moment, Stephen. It's the women that you will encounter in Ireland. I have campaigned more than once in my lifetime. I know what happens in the camps of soldiers."

How on earth was he supposed to respond to that? *Do tell, Father, what were you like on campaign?* Surely there had been women before his mother—she was five years younger than her husband, after all. But Stephen didn't want to know, he didn't even want to guess. Why on earth bring it up?

As though he could read his son's embarrassment, Dominic asked wryly, "Would you prefer to have had this discussion with your mother? If I hadn't promised to address the matter myself, she would have taken it in hand."

Stephen choked. "In that case, say what you must."

"It might not be what you fear, Stephen. I simply want you to consider this—never take what is not freely offered, and then only if you are certain you will not leave pain behind. That is poor payment for any woman, whoever she may be."

"No virgins, no wives, and no force? I remember. I promise not to shame myself or you, Father." To lighten the subject, and because he was feeling unfairly singled out, he added, "I presume Kit has already been given the same lecture for his time in Dublin?"

With hooded eyes, his father said simply, "Kit's lectures will never be the same as yours."

Because you are the eldest, ran the unspoken words, *and my heir. Because your life and honour must be impeccable if you ever hope to live up to me.*

There were times when Stephen envied his younger brother so much that he could hardly see straight.

In all her years as queen, Elizabeth had never met so subtle and capable a negotiator as her own daughter. Though Anabel was only nineteen, she possessed her father's certainty and her mother's stubbornness, traits that she ably employed in negotiating her immediate future as Princess of Wales.

"In addition to Ludlow, I need a home rather closer to London," Anabel said. Not for the first time.

Elizabeth had been admittedly dragging her feet on the issue, not so much because she disagreed as because she wanted to remind her daughter that there was only one queen in England. But when even Burghley backed the princess, Elizabeth knew her daughter was in the right.

That didn't mean she would make it easy. "And which palace would you like your queen to abandon?" she asked tartly. "Windsor? St. James? Perhaps I should simply move out of Whitehall and pass the seat of government into your hands."

Anabel didn't—quite—roll her eyes. "The point of me being near but somewhat independent is to learn from you, Your Majesty, and to learn how to run my own royal household in a controlled environment where I cannot do too much damage. Of course I do not want to run England. Not for many long years."

Sometimes, it was like speaking to herself, Elizabeth thought.

Other times, it was like speaking to Anne Boleyn. And every now and then, just for a flash, it was like speaking to William.

With a heavy sigh meant to convey giving in with weariness (though Anabel would correctly read it as assumed), Elizabeth capitulated with the decision that had already been taken in her privy council more than a fortnight ago. "In addition to Ludlow Castle, you will also be given Syon House and Charterhouse. Does that meet with your approval?"

How could it not? Syon House would not come as a great surprise, for Anabel herself had suggested it months ago. Once an abbey, Elizabeth's father had granted the lands to John Dudley, Duke of Northumberland. Upon his execution in 1556, the land and beautiful house Northumberland had built had passed back to crown control. But Elizabeth never made use of the house that had once been a prison for her half sister, Mary Tudor. Because Syon House came with ghosts, and one of those was Northumberland's fifth son, Robert.

Situated very near Richmond Palace, it would make a gracious home for the Princess of Wales when she wished to be more central than the Welsh borderlands could afford. And when she wished to be at the very heart of things? No place better than Charterhouse.

Just a mile from Whitehall (itself the largest palace complex in Europe), Charterhouse had been the London home of Elizabeth's uncle, George Boleyn. As Duke of Rochford and both regent and chancellor in his time, he had commanded more power than any man in England, save the king. Charterhouse had been witness to ambassadors and foreign royals, to negotiations and threats and careful deploying of English power. Charterhouse was also the site of Lord Rochford's assassination. In the twenty-five years since, it had been used primarily as a temporary residence for visiting dignitaries and those wealthy Continental merchants whom England needed to impress.

Anabel looked suitably surprised, which pleased Elizabeth enough for her to add graciously, "If you want to learn how to rule, nowhere better than in my uncle's home. I expect the very walls are soaked in Lord Rochford's genius."

"Thank you, Your Majesty." Then, after a moment, Anabel added, "Mother."

"Now," Elizabeth continued briskly, "more important than the physical residence is the makeup of your own household. Philippa Courtenay, naturally, will be chief of your ladies, but you need an older, more experienced woman to take charge."

"I can think of no one better than Lady Leighton as the public face. Of course, Madalena will take care of the details, as she always has."

Madalena Arias had been a gift to Anabel from her father, a lady-in-waiting who had come to England at the age of ten and firmly attached herself to the five years' younger princess. Her grand-mother had been a *converso* Moor, making Madalena darker than the usual Spaniard and, Elizabeth conceded, extremely attractive. She served Anabel faithfully, though Elizabeth was always watchful, afraid of Philip using any tactic against his daughter.

"I approve your chaplain and steward. That leaves you two posts to fill—Master of the Horse and household treasurer." Elizabeth spoke casually, knowing how insulted her daughter had been by Kit Courtenay's refusal to accept the former post.

But, like her mother, she had mastered the art of moving on, and if not feeling indifference, at least feigning it well. "What do you think of Robert Cecil for Master of the Horse? Lord Burghley might be pleased to have his son expand his experience in public service."

It was an astute choice. "He'll do very well. And treasurer?"

For the first time, Anabel looked a touch defiant, as though an-ticipating a refusal. "I should like Matthew Harrington."

She had sense enough not to say more, for Elizabeth knew per-fectly well who Matthew was. His parents had been Minuette and Dominic's loyal companions through their disgrace and exile, and their only son had been rewarded with an education to match that of the Courtenay sons. Matthew had studied law and, for the last year, been part of Lord Burghley's staff in his role as Lord High Treasurer.

Young, yes, but so was Anabel. And Pippa. As Elizabeth had once been young, with Minuette and Dominic and Will . . . Youth had its faults, but also its strengths. And with his bloodline and upbringing, Matthew Harrington would be the most faithful of servants.

She nodded once. "I think Matthew is quite a good choice. Provided you can persuade Lord Burghley to part with both his son and his protégé."

Her daughter's smile was blindingly confident. "Pippa says Lord Burghley has been training Matthew specifically for my household. He will be glad to have him with me."

"And Philippa would know," Elizabeth retorted wryly. "Very well. We shall make all the necessary arrangements and announcements before leaving for Wales next week."

Where Anabel would be formally invested as Princess of Wales and begin her public tasks, meant to bind the hearts of England as firmly to herself as to her mother.

And where she would meet for the first time the French representatives of Francis, the Duc d'Anjou, and begin the delicate formal dance of possible betrothal.

THREE

6 August 1581

Dearest Lucie,

We arrived in Chester earlier today. It has been more than two weeks since we left London, in slow procession north and west to this town once so precariously held by the English on the very doorstep of Wales. Now, of course, the divide is cultural rather than political and it is from here that Anabel takes center stage. Over the next two weeks we will travel through northern Wales, freely crisscrossing what was once such a hotly contested border, making our way as far west as Caernarfon and thus onto Wrexham, Oswestry, and Shrewsbury before riding in triumph into Ludlow, where Anabel will be formally invested as Princess of Wales.

She has made me study Welsh with her, though her language talents far outstrip mine. I might just be able to ask for a loaf of bread if left alone, but Anabel is capable of conducting quite broad conversations. She is rightly proud of her talents, and of the work she has put into them. I think the Welsh will be celebratory enough to please even her.

The queen will meet us in Ludlow. I suspect it is not easy for her to launch Anabel on her own, but what makes her such a good ruler is that she does not put personal feelings above the good of the realm. England needs Anabel.

And Anabel needs me. For now, at least.

You are coming to Ludlow, aren't you, Lucie? Or has joy—and newly-wed nights—turned your mind enough that you have decided to live in York forever?

Pippa

11 August 1581

Pippa,

Julien and I returned to Compton Wynyates two weeks ago, as you know perfectly well since that is where you directed your letter. I still don't feel I can call it home—I suspect that will always be Wynfield Mote—but I am not one to take against a perfectly good house and land merely because it's new. Besides, the queen would be insulted. Yes, I know, Compton Wynyates was Father's gift to us, but I also know that it was the queen who made the suggestion to him and might even, I suspect, have paid for some of it. How could I not be touched? Both by her unexpected parting with money, as well as the even more unexpected humility in doing so in secret.

And don't lecture me about what I owe her. The queen and I understand each other perfectly well since last summer.

Do you miss Kit very much? It is hardly fair that you should be caught between him and Anabel. Now that one of them has been enlightened, how long before the other follows? Queen Elizabeth may have had her Robert Dudley (though we have only stories of their love), but I do not imagine she will remember that if ever she is forced to deal with a defiant daughter in love.

How very glad I am to be out of all that uncertainty! And yet, despite my perfect happiness, we will indeed be in Ludlow for the investiture. Julien and I can only stay locked away for so long before it becomes a scandal, even if we are married.

I wish you well in managing your absent twin and temperamental princess.

Lucie

After just one week in Ireland, Stephen was good and ready to take a ship straight back to England. Except he couldn't, because they were well into the interior by now. His company had landed in Waterford on the fourth of August and marched out again just forty-eight hours later, for rumours of Spanish troops along the west coast were rampant and Sir William Pelham and Captain Oliver Dane needed as many men in the field as fast as they could get them.

It wasn't especially fast. Waterford was an English town, but its hold on the coast was tenuous, and within five miles the landscape itself seemed to turn against the English soldiers. There had been no recent fighting, but the countryside could hardly be called easy. They were shadowed along their way—Stephen could feel the watching eyes even when he had no idea where the watchers were hiding. He and Harrington marched the men at a pitch of wary preparedness that was exhausting. He knew ambushes were the favoured method of the Irish fighters and wondered how he was supposed to avoid them. It would take him years to learn the land half as well as those born in it, which left all the momentum in the rebels' favour.

From tension and exhaustion, everyone in the company was in a foul mood by the time they met up with Oliver Dane's troops. Stephen left his men settling under Harrington's direction and went directly to Dane's tent.

It was serviceable and stripped down, the tent of a man accustomed to rough campaigning and who had little use for ornament.

By reputation, Captain Dane also had little use for idle noblemen who came to Ireland simply for the sport of it.

In appearance, Oliver Dane seemed a man designed not to stand out. Of medium height and build, he had brown hair shorn close to his skull and was as clean-shaven as could be managed in a military encampment. Other than the red and gold boar badge that marked his jerkin, his clothes were as serviceable as the rest of him.

He had maps spread before him on a table, and after a quick glance in Stephen's direction when he was introduced, kept his eyes on his work.

But it was clear whom he was addressing. "How are your men?"

"Wet and hungry, but fit enough."

Dane grunted. "Can't control the weather, and supply lines are a bitch throughout Munster. Fields and crops are nonexistent here and that old biddy of a queen won't loosen her purse strings sufficient to feed us as she should."

Stephen guessed that Dane wanted to see how he'd react to the offensive remarks about Queen Elizabeth. Of course, Dane would know the Courtenay family's ties to the throne. He was trying to goad Stephen into a display of temper that he would no doubt slap down as hard as he could. Stephen might be a titled earl, but in the field he answered to a commanding officer.

Fortunately, the queen needed no defense from him. Stephen had never known a woman more able to look after herself than Elizabeth Tudor—except possibly his own mother. So his tone was level when he replied. "We've brought our own supplies along, and used them sparingly on the road. We will not be an additional burden to your forces."

Finally, Dane straightened from the maps and, crossing his arms on his sturdy chest, studied Stephen. His eyes were an icy blue that seemed designed for no emotion warmer than contempt. "Not completely useless, then. Good to know. But bloody hell, boy, I hope not all your men are as wet behind the ears as you. What are you—sixteen?"

Another offensive strike, for Dane would know perfectly well his age. "Looks can be deceiving. I am twenty-one, and yes, that makes me considerably younger than most of the men of my company."

With a twist to his mouth that might have been amusement or grudging respect, Dane replied, "Well said, Courtenay. Which is what I'll be calling you, mind, at least as long as we're marching. I have no patience to coddle English lordlings when every day might be your last—or, more importantly, my last. I've been in Ireland twenty years now and I know my job. Your job is to obey. Is that clear?"

"Perfectly clear."

Dane flicked his hand in dismissal. "Take an hour to see your men are settled and your camp in order. Then come back and we'll talk strategy while we eat."

Stephen nodded once and turned.

"And Courtenay? I've a rough tongue but that doesn't mean I'm not glad enough to have you and your men. Any son of Dominic Courtenay is always welcome as a fighting man."

And that was perhaps the most offensive thing Dane had said yet, though no doubt the man had meant it as a compliment. How was he to guess that Stephen was growing awfully tired of being known simply as Dominic's son and heir?

"How many men?" Elizabeth asked Walsingham. The Lord Secretary had just brought her the unwelcome—if not entirely unexpected—news that Spanish ships were headed for the west coast of Ireland.

"Not more than five hundred," Walsingham answered, and he looked almost unhappy about the small number. If only Philip would commit once and for all in Ireland, then Walsingham might get the support he needed to wage wholesale war and crush the Irish. But Philip was nearly as cautious as Elizabeth. The Spanish king probably wanted war in the far-flung island as little as she did.

Burghley, at least, was relieved. "Enough to cause increased trouble in Munster, but not enough to reach beyond. And there's no indication that Desmond himself is committing to join them."

Gerald FitzGerald, rebellious Earl of Desmond, had been proclaimed traitor by Elizabeth's government in Dublin two years earlier. And he deserved it, for he had offered aid and comfort to the rebels in his county and never turned out with troops or support for Elizabeth's army. But nor had he fired upon English soldiers, and in her most contemplative moments Elizabeth knew that Desmond was in a desperately difficult position. Besides, wasn't it she herself who had pointed out to Pelham the idiocy of publicly proclaiming Desmond a traitor before they had managed to lay hands on him? As she had predicted, the proclamation served only to drive the earl further into rebellion.

Walsingham had never been hesitant to push his Irish policy. "Pelham and Dane are on the move to Carrigafoyle. The Spanish will not break out from the coast. And when Carrigafoyle is taken, Your Majesty, your soldiers should move against Askeaton."

Her refusal was swift and uncompromising. "No."

"As long as Desmond remains in Askeaton, he will continue to be the center of resistance in Munster. And as long as Munster is in open rebellion, all our Irish holdings are at risk. Before we know it, the Pale will shrink to merely the streets of Dublin itself. Are you so certain of the Earl of Ormond that you cannot envision him taking advantage of an English retreat to consolidate his own power?"

"The Earl of Ormond," Elizabeth said chillily, "is to be trusted. He has shown it often and I will not suspect my own kinsman of so lightly moving against our throne."

"It is imperative that you suspect *everyone*!"

Being shouted at was not a common experience for a queen—in the handful of times it had happened in the last few years, it was certain to be either Walsingham or Anabel doing the shouting.

And when Walsingham shouted, it was almost always about Ireland. Or Spain. Catholics, at least.

There were two ways to deal with it—shout back or cloak herself in royal hauteur. Elizabeth chose the latter this time. "Perhaps I should suspect *you* of wanting to bleed England dry of both money and men in advance of a concerted Spanish attack, so that we are vulnerable when the ships are pointing at our island rather than Ireland."

Burghley, always and ever the mediator, spoke swiftly into the appalled silence. "The point is to avoid matters coming to such a head. Which is why we must pursue negotiation."

"You mean conciliation," Walsingham spat.

"If necessary. We can afford, to some degree, Ireland in turmoil. We cannot afford that same turmoil to strike our own shores. What if it were the Midlands scorched to the ground, her people starving? What if it were the Earl of Arundel pressing his newfound Catholic conversion in open defiance? We have just arrested Lady Stonor and her son for harboring Jesuits!" Burghley pressed his lips together and made an effort to control himself. At last, he said firmly, "England must have peace."

"At what cost?"

"Enough!" Elizabeth used the most impressive of her public voices, the one that mingled Henry VIII's righteousness with Anne Boleyn's pride. With just that word, Burghley and Walsingham were brought to heel. For the moment.

"Pelham and Dane will deal with the Spanish landing at Carrigafoyle," Elizabeth stated. "They have our leave to crush anyone in their reach at that time. The Spanish must not break out—and just as critically, neither must any of their supplies. Weaken the Irish with hunger this winter and perhaps they will be more amenable in the spring. But by no means are our troops to launch headlong against Askeaton. Is that clear?"

"Yes, Your Majesty." Burghley answered for both men, probably because Walsingham was still fuming at her restraint.

Elizabeth turned her back. "That is all."

Only when they had left did she allow herself to sigh and rub her forehead. Would to God she could solve the Catholic problem. She had been so certain, taking the throne twenty-three years ago, that navigating a middle path between the torrent of religious fanatics on either side was the only way to keep England afloat.

She still believed it was England's only hope—she just didn't know if there was any chance of success.

Kilkenny Castle was an impressive fortress that had controlled the fording point of the River Nore for more than four hundred years, and the town that had sprung up near its walls was one of the largest in Ireland. Chartered by the Lord of Leinster in 1207, the burghers of the town had long profited from the protection of the Butler family.

Awed, as he was meant to be, Kit approached the walls of Kilkenny with Brandon Dudley and fifty of the Earl of Leicester's men for a courtesy meeting with the Earl of Ormond. Though Leicester's assignment was primarily in Dublin, maintaining close ties with Ormond was a very close second.

There was a flurry of building work within the castle's outer walls. It took only moments to identify Thomas Butler, black-haired and fierce in the midst of a swirl of people from rough-garbed workmen to sober clerks. Kit was hardly a stranger to castles and palaces but had seen few as impressively medieval as Kilkenny Castle. With its four enormous circular towers and massive defensive ditch, it looked like a place prepared to withstand Viking raiders.

With a shout, Black Tom hailed Brandon Dudley. "What's this, Robert Dudley risen from the dead? For sure, boy, you have your uncle's very aspect."

"But not his arrogance, or I'd have something less flattering to say about your own aspect, Ormond." Brandon swung down from his horse and submitted good-naturedly to his fellow earl's thumps on the back.

Kit was prepared to be overlooked entirely, but Brandon Dudley pulled him quickly into the circle. "And here's Lord Exeter's younger son, Christopher. He's my secretary while in Ireland."

"Dominic Courtenay's boy. But with the look of your mother, all the better for you. The Duchess of Exeter is, as I recall, an uncommonly beautiful woman."

"She is, my lord."

"Call me Ormond. We do not stand on ceremony so much in Ireland, save against our fellow landowners. Come." Ormond gestured to the two men to follow him, leaving the others of their escort in the capable hands of his own men. They followed Ormond into Kilkenny Castle. Though built as a Norman stronghold, it had been more recently opened to the light and air with Tudor windows set into the medieval walls, and the interior was now almost as much elegant manor as military fortress.

Kit found the castle a good backdrop for Black Tom. The earl was fifty years old, the same age as Kit's father, and like him had retained the figure and bearing of a serving soldier. Ormond's abundant black hair had less silver to it than Dominic Courtenay's and there was something definitely, restlessly, Irish to him despite his Norman heritage. He was cousin to Queen Elizabeth from several generations back, for Anne Boleyn's grandmother, Margaret Butler, had been born in this very castle more than a hundred years ago. There had even been a time in Anne Boleyn's youth (Pippa had told him these stories) when she was nearly married back into the Irish Butler family. What a change that would have wrought—no Queen Anne to give Henry VIII a son, no Elizabeth Tudor to reign now.

Ormond took them into a long gallery flooded with light pouring through the open diamond-paned windows and overlooking a meticulously planned ornamental garden. Despite its comforts, the chamber lacked the indefinable touches that reminded Kit that Ormond had been single for nearly twenty years. He'd separated from his wife long years ago with no legitimate children and had not remarried. Yet.

"Tell me about the roads," Ormond said when he'd passed around wine and the three were seated casually before a stone fireplace.

"Quieter than we'd feared," Brandon answered. "But not quiet in a good way. More in the manner of being watched and weighed."

"I wish I could say your unease is unwarranted, but you're no fools. Kilkenny is safe enough, but best you stick to Dublin this autumn. Unless Pelham and Dane are pulling you into the mess of Munster?"

Brandon shook his head. "We're not a fighting force. Her Majesty wants us in Dublin and to be seen supporting you in the east. The west is not our affair."

"Will Desmond throw in with the rebels openly?" Kit asked bluntly.

For a measuring gaze, Ormond seemed likely to slap him down for interrupting. But then a spark flashed through his eyes. "That's right—the Earl of Somerset has men with Oliver Dane's forces. Your older brother. Why aren't you marching with him?"

"I wasn't invited."

Ormond laughed heartily. "Ah, to be young and so easily offended. Fear not, little brother. If Philip of Spain manages to land forces sufficient to break free from the west coast, there will be fighting enough for all Her Majesty's men in Ireland. Pray that it does not come to that."

As far as Kit had gathered, Ormond himself was desperately praying for it not to come to that. He was Elizabeth's man through and through—not only by the blood of cousinship, but in temperament. Black Tom Butler wanted to preserve what he had, not see it scorched to the ground as so much of southern Ireland had been. And, after all, Gerald FitzGerald was not only a fellow Irish earl but had been married to Ormond's mother after the death of his father. Family ties marched hand in hand with family resentments, and Ireland provided fertile ground for such a disastrous mix. Another of Pippa's stories popped into Kit's head: That when English troops had last laid siege to Desmond's castle at Askeaton, they had destroyed the neighboring abbey and wantonly flung corpses out of their crypts. Including that of Desmond's second wife—who had been Tom Butler's mother.

Into the silence of men contemplating the complexities of war as they drank came the trill of feminine voices. One voice clearly dominated—one that made Kit swear to himself softly when he recognized it.

How had he not known that Eleanor Percy was currently resident at Kilkenny? He had noted her absence from Dublin during their brief stay and been glad of it, without bothering to wonder where she had gone. He really must learn to think ahead, as Pippa was always counseling him.

"What need have I to think ahead when you do it for the both of us so neatly?" he usually teased. But Pippa wasn't here and so Kit met the lady unprepared.

He'd never seen a woman so thoroughly able to take charge of a room outside his mother and the queen. Eleanor did it not through position or warmth or natural respect, however, but by wielding her considerable physical charms. Past childbearing she might be, but everything about her was cultivated for best display. Even Kit grudgingly conceded her appeal to that part of a man interested only in pleasure.

"Such a delight!" she trilled in overdone rapture. "To have three such handsome men in attendance tonight. Nora and I could never have dreamed such good fortune."

She had her daughter by the elbow, holding on to her as she might a horse prepared to bolt. Nora was objectively as lovely as her mother but had none of Eleanor's instinct for presenting herself. She usually looked either shy or bored. Today, however, there was a stain of colour on her cheeks and she spoke without being urged.

"It is a pleasure to see you again, my lord."

Ormond's gaze slid sideways, for she was not addressing him, but

Brandon Dudley. Brandon was too well-practiced a courtier for Kit to tell if he was merely being polite when he answered, "The pleasure must always be mine."

From the way Nora lit up when Brandon spoke, it was clear that if it was up to her, Stephen Courtenay was not the earl she would be trying to land. It unaccountably cheered Kit, though he doubted his brother had ever looked at Nora Percy with anything like personal interest. Perhaps he just liked being reminded that not everything in the world revolved around Stephen.

"I must see to the men," Kit said before Brandon could beat him to it. The Earl of Leicester had an expression of well-bred forbearance, but what protest could he make? It was Kit's duty to see after such matters. And if he managed to avoid dining with the nobles later, all the better.

"Such a pity." Eleanor pretended to pout. "If only your brother were here in your stead."

If only he were, Kit thought grimly as he escaped the now-cloying chamber. He had nothing against Nora Percy, and wondered if her mother were setting her sights on Brandon as a possible replacement in case Stephen proved reluctant. Or even Ormond—the man was vigorous despite his age, and despite his long solitude would surely be eager to get legitimate children on a young wife. And Nora was the queen's niece. It made her attractive, despite her difficult mother.

As Kit strode through the noisy, busy courtyard in search of the Earl of Leicester's men, a closed carriage clattered in through the gates. In the immediate absence of Ormond, Kilkenny's steward—in his red Butler badge marked with three gold cups—hurried to greet the new visitors.

"Who is it?" Kit asked curiously of one of the clerks who looked slightly less frantic than the others in sight.

"Scots girl, granddaughter of William Sinclair in Edinburgh."

Kit nodded, for everyone knew the name. William Sinclair owned one of the largest banking and merchant concerns in Europe and was at least twice as wealthy as Queen Elizabeth. Or he had been— for the old man died earlier that year.

"What's she doing in Kilkenny?"

"On her way to marry old Finian Kavanaugh. Lord Ormond is to remind her that Scots money best not be used to finance Irish rebels. No worry, really. Her brother gave her a dowry, but not enough to tempt Kavanaugh into open fighting. He'll get sons on her and that's all."

The steward handed out a lady from the interior of the carriage. She was small, almost a child in size, and she looked up at the steward with a tilt to her head that had something of a child's curiosity in it. After greeting the steward, she cast a glance around the courtyard and faltered slightly at seeing Kit.

Seeing her hesitation, the steward must have decided it indicated interest, for he at once led her toward Kit.

"Lord Christopher Courtenay," he said to the girl as they neared. "Youngest son of the Duke of Exeter, here briefly from Dublin in the company of the Earl of Leicester. Mistress Mariota Sinclair."

"Maisie," she corrected. "What an illustrious guest list I have come upon! I am quite abashed."

Kit bowed to the girl, who must have been nearly a child in age, as well as size. If she was more than fourteen he'd be surprised. Not a beauty, either, though she had good cheekbones and arched brows over wide-set gray eyes. There was a glint of fair hair from beneath her hood. And despite her words, she did not look at all abashed.

After a few banal words of welcome, Kit made his escape, deter- mined more than ever to keep with the men tonight. Better to eat in the stables than sit at a table with ambitious earls and cunning women and child-brides.

Poor child. He wouldn't wish an Irish marriage on any girl out- side this island. He spared a moment's pity for Maisie Sinclair, then cleared his head of her with a shake and followed the clerk to the lodgings set aside for Brandon's men.

FOUR

By August 17 the combined forces of Oliver Dane and Stephen Courtenay had arrived in Shannon and they could see Carrigafoyle standing defiantly on the small rock in the estuary. They made separate but adjoining encampments several miles off to await orders from Pelham. They'd had reports as they marched that two Spanish ships had landed five hundred men a week ago who were now in the fortress along with the local Irish. Including women and children—a development Stephen did not like at all.

But Dane merely grunted at the news. "Don't get squeamish on me. Irish women are not like ours. They'll cut your throat as soon as look at you. It's the women they send to torture their prisoners. If they're holed up with their men—well, that's their choice and they must stand by it."

In Stephen's opinion their choices had been few, for he had traveled through a wasteland to reach here. The earth looked as though it had been salted and burned, to ensure that no crops could grow this year or any year in the near future. The few Irish they'd seen were gaunt and hollow-cheeked with hunger.

Dane noted Stephen's unease and seemed equal parts surprised and amused by it. "Don't get me wrong, Courtenay. Before she slits your throat, she will give you pleasure you've never dreamed of. Bed an Irish girl—the *right* Irish girl—and you'll never be contented with a polite Englishwoman again. But in the end, best kill her before she kills you."

It was getting harder and harder to respect the man from whom he must take orders. Stephen jerked his head in what could charitably be called a nod and stalked off to his own tent. Only the tiny part of him that still responded to every situation with mordant humour noted that perhaps part of his irritation was actually the lack of women. Not necessarily to take to bed—though he wouldn't have said no, whatever his father's counsel—but simply as part of his life. Raised by an involved and clever mother, with two sisters who could rival any woman in Europe for wit and learning, accustomed to a court ruled by a queen of uncommon intelligence and strength . . . well, slogging through the razed fields and sullen populace of Ireland was only made worse by the lack of feminine company.

His mood did not improve the next morning when summoned for a meeting with Dane and William Pelham, Lord Justice of Ireland. Pelham had been tempered by Ireland, a rigid man made harder by previous failure and the impossible task he'd now been given. His high forehead sloped back to close-cropped hair, his fierce mustache and beard bristling with restrained nerves.

"English ships under Admiral Winter's command sailed into the estuary yesterday. If Spain were serious about supporting the rebels, they'd never have drawn off their own ships. But they have, and with Winter on the water, Carrigafoyle will not last more than three days."

"Bombardment begins tomorrow?" Dane asked, as casually as if inquiring about dinner.

"Yes," Pelham said curtly. Stephen had the impression that the Lord Justice resented having Dane here, perhaps because the man had greater experience in Ireland even though Pelham outranked him. When the fighting ended, Pelham would answer for the results to the queen, while Dane remained in Ireland and expanded his own lands as a result of the English troops sacrificed here.

Stephen cleared his throat. "Where will we be positioned?" he asked neutrally, as though addressing both of them. It was the kind of tactic he'd learned, not from his plainspoken father, but from his more politically subtle mother.

"My men will form the first landing parties," Pelham answered. "Once we've established a hold on the island, they can be relieved or reinforced as needed. Captain Dane, your men will pour across when the walls begin to collapse. Lord Somerset, your force will guard the perimeters to ensure no one comes at us from behind."

Dane's next question surprised with its apparent randomness. "No sign of any Kavanaughs coming to fight?"

"From Carlow Castle?" Pelham asked with slight surprise. "No. Just like the Earl of Desmond, they're keeping their peace and sitting it out as long as they can manage. Finian Kavanaugh's no fool—he's arranged to get himself married tomorrow as a reasonable excuse not to commit to anything just now."

"Hoping for new heirs?" Dane's neutrality seemed forced. It was the first time Stephen had ever heard him sound stiff, and he wondered what interest Dane had in the Kavanaughs.

"Seems likely. The only heir he has now is a niece who refuses to marry. The new bride is young enough—and rich. A Sinclair from Edinburgh. We'll have to keep an eye on Kavanaugh, see if his wife's money seems primed to outfit a force of gallowglass."

As Stephen walked away to prepare his men to move out, his mind spun with possibilities. For Finian Kavanaugh was a name he knew, one dropped to him in a letter from London. And any name dropped by Francis Walsingham, however apparently casual, was a name to look out for.

———

The wedding of Finian Kavanaugh and Mariota Sinclair occurred beneath lowering skies that occasionally spit rain and, even more occasionally, let through fitful hints of sun. But the party was as raucous as if the weather were perfect, for the Irish had never given much account to the skies. One took pleasure when one could in this world, and did not wait for the world to return the favour.

Ailis Kavanaugh, Finian's niece and, through a long toll of death and misfortune, her uncle's only heir, helped make ready the bride. Not that there was much to it—the Scots girl was as straightforward in her dress as in her speech, and seemed to survey the world from a vantage of perfect equanimity. An unexpected quality in a girl of only fifteen; odder still in this staunch Protestant foreigner being married off to an Irish clan chief more than four times her age. Maisie, as she had cheerfully told all to address her, might have been only a fool, of course—but Ailis, who was not a fool, had caught the sparks of steel in both her mind and her spirit in the three days she'd been here. A girl, perhaps, but the woman would be one to reckon with. As was Ailis herself.

"Will I do?" Maisie asked her intended's niece, nearly ten years older than herself, and stood with unusual stillness while Ailis studied her. Most people squirmed when Ailis studied them. It was a talent of which she was proud.

Maisie was quite a bit shorter than Ailis, just above five feet, and nearly as slim as a boy. Wide cheekbones and a strong chin, her eyes the gray-blue of the winter seas. Her only truly beautiful feature was her hair, a unique shade like silver gilt, which fell straight nearly to her waist. Her dress was blue silk, its fineness owing more to its weight and colour than any decoration. But then, Maisie came from the wealthiest trading family in Edinburgh—she knew how to judge her audience. She was being married for her money, but she would acknowledge it discreetly, not flaunt it in front of the proud Irish Catholics who would consider her, at best, a necessary evil.

And so Ailis had been prepared to consider her. But to her surprise, she had found that there were aspects of Maisie Sinclair she almost liked.

"You will do very well," she declared, and Maisie lit up in a smile that combined surpassing sweetness with a healthy dose of mischief.

"I want to look just like you when I'm married!" The exuberant cry came from Ailis's daughter, an eleven-year-old who would have thrown her arms around her new-claimed friend if Ailis had not stopped her.

Maisie laughed. "I'm afraid there's not much hope of that," she told the child. "And all the better for you, Liadan. You are the very image of your mother, and any woman in the world would sell her soul to look like either of you."

"But you don't have a soul."

"Liadan!" Ailis exclaimed. "What a wicked thing to say."

"It's what Bridey said," Liadan insisted, not at all repressed. "Bridey said Protestants haven't souls like us."

"Bridey is a superstitious old woman," Ailis snapped.

"Never fret," Maisie intervened, and there was an impish hint to her smile as she summoned Liadan to hold her hands. "Protestants may lack many things in the eyes of Catholics, child, but souls we have. Besides, I was educated in France at a convent. I have heard enough Catholic prayers to work some sort of grace even on my Protestant soul."

With that sense of unwilling admiration the Scots girl had wrung from her all week, Ailis admitted that her uncle was getting much more than he'd bargained for in Maisie Sinclair. Finian Kavanaugh believed he'd be able to wheedle more money from her brother, with Maisie simply a means to an end.

Ailis had believed the same. She might have to readjust her own plans in light of who this girl had turned out to be.

For two days Carrigafoyle was savagely battered by English guns from both land and sea. At the end of the first hour, Stephen thought he would run mad from the roar. At the end of the first day, he couldn't understand why the outpost had not yet surrendered. But by the end of the second day, the guns had become merely a fact of life. He could hardly recall a time that he hadn't woken and slept and eaten and stood guard without the roar and rumble of heavy artillery.

On the first day, Pelham ordered men forward to take the sea wall, but they were pinned down by Spanish guns and boulders hurled at them from above. When the English attempted to raise siege ladders, the Spanish halbardiers flung them back until the sea wall ran dark with spilled blood. Stephen and his men were spared that, at least, for their orders were to stand ready with a company of lances outside the northern wall. That was where the English guns were expected to break through first. Pelham had ordered that none of the rebels be allowed to escape and make their way to the Earl of Desmond, now hunkered down forty miles away in Castleisland.

The conclusion of the battle was foregone. Even supported by Spanish troops, the Irish rebels could not hope to counter the largest English force ever assembled in western Ireland. There were near a thousand men between Pelham and Dane, and by late in the second day it was reckoned those inside the fortress had taken refuge in the great keep tower.

On the third day, the western wall of the keep collapsed under several direct hits from the ships' guns. Oliver Dane led his men inside the walls of Carrigafoyle to end the fighting and flush the survivors out.

Stephen and his men were charged with rounding up those rebels who managed to slip past Dane. In twos and threes, they could flit through the rubble and smoke and water, but could not long escape men on horseback. Stephen was not sorry when he found Captain Julian among them—the Italian engineer who had built up the keep and led the defenders within. And he didn't mind taking back the

Irishmen. When a man went to war, especially a rebel, he knew the price.

The women were another matter. Within four hours of the fall of Carrigafoyle, Stephen had under guard twenty-three men, women, and children, the youngest just ten years old. Frankly, he would have let more of them slip away if he hadn't seen the state of the countryside and knew they'd likely starve if left to their own devices. Better to be imprisoned and fed, he argued to himself.

It was oppressively silent as they approached Carrigafoyle. After the days of bombardment, there was something ominous about the lack of guns. Stephen could see where the western wall of the tower keep had collapsed and winced. Surely lives had been lost beneath the crushing stone. Wearily, he gave orders to Harrington to quarter the prisoners for now in their own camp until decisions were made about their destination. Soldiers in the flush of victory could not always be trusted, but at least Stephen knew Harrington would keep their men in order and the prisoners safe.

He rode into Oliver Dane's camp and found only a handful of men who had suffered injuries. When asked where their commander was, all Stephen got was a jerk of the head in the direction of the fallen keep and a curt, "Finishing off, they are."

Finishing off what? Stephen wondered. The keep was in English hands, which meant the whole of river and its approach to the port city of Limerick was secure. This defeat would be painful—perhaps fatal—to the rebellion in Munster. All that was left to finish was the diplomatic maneuvering to get to the Earl of Desmond himself, certainly nothing that could be accomplished on this battlefield.

Stephen had never been more wrong.

He crossed to the island and entered the keep, almost choking on the stench of smoke and rubble and—distinctively threaded through it all—blood. Every sense alert, as though he might be attacked, he kept one hand on the hilt of his sword and stepped cautiously past the outer walls into the courtyard where the rebels had made their final stand.

It was like no nightmare he'd ever suffered—the only thing his horrified mind could conjure were some of the more dismal ancient depictions of hell. He'd expected death, but what he found was slaughter. Everywhere he looked there were men wearing Dane's red and gold boar badge, with dripping swords and expressions either grimly purposeful or disturbingly casual. Behind and around them, heaped against walls, huddled in corners, lay the bodies of Carriga- foyle's defenders, hacked down in the moment of surrender. No, worse than that—in the hours *after* surrender, when tempers should have cooled and negotiations held sway. Even had the English meant to kill the rebels, these men should still have had a brief trial and been properly hung. But this?

This was nothing short of murder.

He might have talked himself into a cooler head—or at least a more prudent response—given time. It was Oliver Dane's bad for- tune to come swaggering up to Stephen while he was still trying to settle his stomach.

"Sorry to miss the fun?" Dane asked.

"What in the name of God have you done?" Stephen demanded, his voice low with fury. It almost scared him, how angry he was. His father never showed anger beyond a few cutting words, never let his temper roil through him and into violence. Stephen had spent his lifetime, all twenty-one years of it, trying to live up to Dominic Courtenay. That habit alone kept him from knocking the smirk off Dane's face with the hilt of his sword.

"I've done what needed doing," Dane said calmly, but the slight- est twitch around his left eye showed that he hadn't missed Stephen's insubordination. "Don't come into my country telling me how to win a war, English lordling. Ireland is not like anywhere else."

"And that justifies butchering unarmed men who have surren- dered? Like they were nothing more than cattle? Do you have any idea the folly you have wrought?"

"Killing my enemies? That is no folly."

"You haven't destroyed your enemies today, Dane. You have

strengthened them a hundredfold. Have you ever met King Philip of Spain? I have." Stephen felt the recklessness seize hold of his tongue and made no effort to restrain it. Damned with being controlled and sensible and cautious. "And I spent six months last year in close quarters with Mary Stuart. There is no pride like their Catholic righteousness, and I tell you that what you have done today has single-handedly ensured that Spain's support of the Irish rebels will no longer be halfhearted. Philip will send an army now—his wife will see to it—and what is left of Ireland will be razed to the ground. You stupid, stupid man."

Dane's fist didn't connect as hard as it might have, just hard enough to rock Stephen back several steps. "I don't like English lordlings," Dane spat at him, "and I don't like boys half my age telling me what to do. I've no more need of you now that Carrigafoyle has fallen. Take your men and go crawling back to that bitch of a queen. Tell her to leave us alone to bring the Irish to heel."

Stephen spun around, head ringing from the blow but his temper still burning bright enough to keep him moving without showing sign of it. Then Dane called after him, "I'll send guards for the prisoners you rounded up."

With foreboding, Stephen half turned back. "What will you do with them?"

"Don't worry, boy. I don't intend to run through a bunch of women with my sword."

Before Stephen could decide if he believed him, Dane added with a mocking edge to his tone, "I plan to hang the lot of them."

20 August 1581

Lucie,

I suppose I hardly need bother to write, as this letter will scarcely reach you before you are here. But habits are hard to break, and without Kit to talk to I need to spill out my thoughts in words of some sort.

We arrived in Ludlow in great state this morning. Sir Henry Sidney, newly appointed President of the Council of the Marches, spared no expense in welcoming the princess, who is, in some sense, displacing him. Sidney has built comfortable family apartments here, which they will continue to occupy, but whenever Anabel chooses, Ludlow will be first and foremost her home.

Fortunately for the Sidneys, Anabel is eminently reasonable. When she chooses to be. She has nothing to gain from being difficult at Ludlow, and everything to lose. So we swept into the town and castle with a flurry of graciousness and gratitude. All eyes were on Anabel, thanks to the queen's decision not to arrive until just before the investiture, and I think Anabel quite reveled in being the center of attention. She does it so well.

The Sidneys, while welcoming to Anabel, are less than excited about the prospect of a possible French marriage. I was politely cornered after dinner by Philip, their oldest son. In the gentlest, warmest manner possible, he grilled me about Anabel's wishes. Could the princess be brought to oppose the queen in the matter of the Duc d'Anjou?

Observers might have suspected Philip Sidney of having his own designs on Anabel—he is, after all, Robert Dudley's nephew and thus a favourite of the queen. Or they might have thought him interested in me. Even Anabel eyed me mischievously. She should know better. All the world knows that Philip is desperately in love with young Penelope Devereux—I say young, although she is only a year younger than I—but that is nine years younger than Philip, and with her father's death it does not seem likely a marriage will be ever made.

No, Philip's interest in me is only in how I am connected to Anabel. The Sidneys, nearly Puritan in their religious sentiments, are adamantly opposed to allying with France. Of course they will be, of necessity, polite to Anjou's personal representative while he is at Ludlow with the queen, but Philip at last asked me quite bluntly, "Can the princess be persuaded to look elsewhere for a husband?"

"Where would you suggest?" I asked, with my best impression of wide-eyed innocence. "Scotland? Rest assured that James's court will also be well represented at the investiture. Beyond that, I would never presume to oppose the royal family in matters of matrimony."

With a shrewd grin, Philip said, "Oh no, the Courtenays would never oppose the royals in such matters."

I've always liked Philip. But beneath his charm and his family's warmth is a stern conviction of their own righteousness. There are many in England who echo that. Puritans and militant Catholics—sometimes I think there is nothing to choose between them.

At least I am not Anabel, having to balance all those prying people wanting a say in my most intimate future.

Love,
Pippa

23 August 1851

Pippa,

This letter may not reach you until I do myself—but if you want to write, I have no objections. So Philip Sidney was flirting with you for information? How very wicked of him! If Kit were there, he'd never have been allowed to, so enjoy the experience while you can. Our brothers seem to believe our intelligence flies out the window the first time a good-looking man turns his attention our way.

Speaking of good-looking men . . . how is Matthew doing in Anabel's service? Conscientious, of course. He would hardly be Harrington's son if he were not. I am glad he, at least, is with you. It must pain Kit to be left out of the investiture—though it was more or less his choice. Have you heard from him? I've had one—annoyingly brief—letter. Our brother seems to be mostly intent on avoiding Eleanor Percy, who appears to have taken up residence at Kilkenny Castle as though staking a claim to the Earl of Ormond. I wonder how the queen feels about that!

Lucie

FIVE

In the end, Stephen had to resort to using all his birthright and position and family and royal connections to keep Oliver Dane from wresting every last Irish woman and child from his hands. He couldn't reasonably expect to hold onto the eight men among the prisoners and had hoped the chance to hang those—especially the engineer, Captain Julian—would satisfy Dane. But the man seemed almost as obsessed with slapping down Stephen as he was with destroying Irish rebels.

"Rebels?" Stephen had scoffed when Dane accused him of aiding the enemy. Casting a calculated, contemptuous eye over the thirteen women and two boys, he added, "If you are afraid of such, Dane, then you should not be in the field in Her Majesty's service."

It had very nearly come to blows then. It was only stopped, Stephen hated to admit, by Harrington's intervention, which consisted mostly of laying a hand on his dagger hilt and moving within arm's reach of Oliver Dane. Harrington might be well into his fifties, but Stephen had never met another man able to match him for sheer physical intimidation.

Dane had retreated then, and attempted to enlist Pelham's aid in the matter. But Ireland's Lord Justice, well aware of the Courtenay family's reach, had declined to intervene. At first light the next morning, Stephen and his men rode away from Carrigafoyle with the fifteen prisoners. Their destination was Kilkenny, where current intelligence placed the Earl of Ormond in residence. It seemed safest to get the prisoners into the hands of a local lord capable of resisting Dane and who also had a vested interest in keeping Ireland stable. What Ormond did with the women and boys then would be an Irish affair. As for himself, Stephen wanted nothing more than to go home.

But go home to what? He pondered the question as they made their way back across the ravaged landscape of Munster. No doubt Queen Elizabeth would be pleased by Carrigafoyle's fall, but she would also correctly assess the future dangers arising from the cruelty of her soldiers. No one knew Philip of Spain better than his former wife; Elizabeth would know how far he might be willing to go to placate his current wife. Mary of Scotland would press for retaliation of the cruelty in Ireland. Would Philip grant it? If he did, if Spain committed greater forces to Ireland, then England would require more men and weapons as well. Stephen had no other skills— what else could he do but fight?

Fight . . . or immerse himself more thoroughly into Walsingham's murky world of intelligence and lies. Stephen had proved himself quick and clever while embedded in Mary Stuart's English prison. He had gained the Scots queen's trust, even affection, and she had never guessed until the last that he had been spying on her. So it seemed he did have other skills: the ability to lie convincingly, to twist the trust of the gullible against them, to hide his true face behind a convincing mask. Yes, all that had been done in the interests of England. But that didn't stop him feeling guilty at being good at it. Dominic Courtenay couldn't tell a convincing lie to save his life— as evidenced by his past. Why was Stephen so conflicted? Wasn't he eager to prove himself apart from his name and birth? Why did the thought of proving himself a good spy feel second best?

But second best or not, Stephen thought he mightn't even mind that as long as it kept him out of Ireland's battles.

Their progress was excruciatingly slow. At the end of the third day, they'd gone barely thirty miles and Stephen's frustration had him snapping at his men. Harrington, always so careful not to over-step his bounds, also knew when and how to intervene. He got Stephen on his own and cautioned neutrally, "There's no way to move faster than ten miles a day with the prisoners walking."

"I know. You'll smooth things over with the men?" Stephen asked abruptly.

"They understand."

"It'll take us nearly two weeks to reach Kilkenny at this pace. And I don't . . ." Stephen rolled his shoulders, feeling the tight pull of tension. "The danger increases the longer we're out here."

"I agree."

To know that an experienced soldier like Harrington could also feel the dread that seemed to seep out of the very ground and air steadied Stephen and made it possible for him to make a decision.

"We'll split up," he announced. "Mount the prisoners, and that still leaves us two dozen men on horseback to ride with them. The rest of the men will march behind. Without the women slowing them down, they can make nearly as fast a time as we can. That should cut our trip to Kilkenny down to four days, five at the most."

Harrington nodded in agreement, possibly approval. "You want me with the other group?"

"No. I need you. Put Lewis in charge of those marching and see to the disposition of the horses. I'll let the women know."

The de facto leader of the small band of prisoners was only a few years older than Stephen, a wary redhead named Roisin. She wasn't the oldest of the women, nor the most hostile, and perhaps it was her even temperament that led the others to defer to her. When told they would ride from here, she studied Stephen briefly before asking, "You feel it, don't you?"

"Feel what?"

"Someone's coming for us."

He didn't know if she meant English or Irish—either way, it confirmed his belief that he'd best get them into Ormond's hands at Kilkenny as quickly as possible. With a curt nod, Stephen told her, "Prepare the others. We'll be riding as fast as we can go. It will not be comfortable."

"Comfort is not something we are raised to look for in Ireland."

Why did he feel the urge to apologize to her? Biting down on his own distaste and impulse to strike out in order to alleviate it, Stephen stalked away.

The prisoners were tough and uncomplaining riders. They more than doubled their pace from the previous walking and would have made it to Kilkenny by dark on the fourth day if a strong storm had not swept in. They made camp five miles from Ormond's castle, the women and boys housed in two tents and the men taking it in turn to watch. Stephen retreated to his own small space, having given his larger tent for the prisoners, and sat on a folding stool, head in his hands, hoping that the pounding he felt would ease tomorrow with the handing off of this unlooked-for responsibility.

That sense of responsibility, at least, was something he could trace directly from his father. Lucky Kit, he decided wryly, who seemed to have escaped that particular trait.

It was an hour or two past sunset—if they'd been able to see the sun through the rain—when Harrington announced himself outside. "Come in," Stephen called, rolling up the map he'd been studying at a table not much bigger than the stool. The only other objects in the tent were a pallet bed and his weapons.

Harrington did not enter alone. Behind him, perhaps half his size, was Roisin, a drenched cloak over the dress that still bore bloodstains from Carrigafoyle beneath the dirt of travel.

"Asked to speak with you," Harrington said without emphasis.

"About?"

Instead of a direct answer, Roisin said simply, "Alone."

Stephen raised an eyebrow. "Got a knife secreted somewhere to kill me with?"

"We were searched. Your men were thorough."

He did not want to be alone with her, and not out of fear. There was something about her direct gaze and the blaze of her hair ... it had been a long time since England. And despite hating himself for it, Stephen could hear Oliver Dane's taunt in his head, *Bed an Irish girl ... and you'll never be contented with a polite Englishwoman again.*

"Leave us, Harrington," he said, despite all the warnings of a young, healthy body strung too long at too high a pitch without release.

For the first time Stephen could remember, Harrington hesitated. "Stephen," he said, the fact that he had called him by name as much a caution as his expression. Harrington looked as though he meant to say more, but obedience and reticence were long habits. He shut his mouth and exited the tent with only a last inscrutable look at Stephen and the Irish girl.

"What can I do for you?" Stephen asked. He offered her his stool, the only place to sit.

She remained standing, facing him with that self-possession he'd noticed for days, and also a touch of curiosity. Her hair was plaited away from her face, then fell loosely across her shoulders. In the lamplight, her eyes were a shifting greenish blue that pulled at Stephen like the ocean waves they echoed.

He'd nearly forgotten his question when finally Roisin answered. "You can tell me why," she said.

"Why what?"

"Why have you gone to so much trouble for us? Splitting your force, marching us across Ireland—is it merely to spite Oliver Dane?"

"You know Dane?"

"Everyone in Munster knows him. A hard man. One it is wiser not to cross."

Stephen gave her a wintry smile. "I do not plan to be in Ireland long enough to need to worry about the consequences of crossing Dane. As soon as I've seen you all into the Earl of Ormond's hands, I'll be returning to England at the earliest opportunity."

"You do not care for Ireland?"

"I hardly know Ireland. And no, I cannot say I have any great wish to know it better. I would think you should be glad to see the last of any Englishman."

She shrugged. "One less or one hundred less makes little difference. Unless your queen cares to give up her claim, there will always be Englishmen in Ireland. And in the end, we will win. Not with weapons or soldiers . . . There is a Latin saying. 'Hibernia Hibernescit.' Ireland makes all things Irish."

"All the more reason for me to retreat while I can, then, for I rather like being English."

"There might be things here . . . people here . . . that would make your memories sweeter."

Had she moved closer? Stephen focused on breathing evenly. She most definitely had stepped nearer, so that he had to tilt his head down to meet her eyes. They were wide and wild, fathomless in a way he was afraid to recognize.

She was his prisoner. No virgins, no wives, no force . . . but she was the one leaning into him, tipping up her face until her lips were within inches of his own.

"I would give you one happy memory of Ireland," she whispered, and the warmth of her breath was like spiced wine, heady and sweet and tantalizing.

"Why?" he breathed out. When he should have said no, or simply stepped back firmly.

"Because you have been kind, Lord Somerset. There is not so much kindness in Ireland that it should go unrewarded."

Virtue is its own reward rang through his mind, but that platitude had little to do with the desire that had seized him until he could scarcely see straight. This is wrong, he thought frantically, this is wrong, I will not do this . . .

Stephen lowered his mouth the fraction needed and kissed her.

Her response was either genuine warmth or such an imitation of it that he would never know the difference. And he let himself not care. Stephen had always tried to bestow pleasure as well as take it, but nothing in his past was like the jumbled, stolen time that followed. He only came to himself, clear-headed, when he woke later with Roisin curled up next to him on the narrow pallet.

What a mess, was his first thought. But the second, on its heels, was, It was worth it.

He didn't know how long they'd been asleep, but he judged it was not past midnight yet. The rain had slowed. She could not stay here all night. As it was, every person in the camp would know what had happened in here—including, he realized with a chill, Harrington. Which meant his father would soon know it.

Time enough to deal with that when he reached England. For now, he had to wake her and thank her genuinely before sending her back. To be handed over to the Earl of Ormond in the morning.

Unless . . . what if he simply let them all go? They were far from Carrigafoyle, but no doubt they could slip away into the stones and hills of Ireland and make their way wherever they could. Some provisions from his stock—his men would do as ordered. And it would ease his conscience about tonight's lapse.

He slipped on a shirt and simple breeches and knelt down to touch Roisin on the shoulder. Even as he opened his mouth to wake her gently, there was an eruption of screams and hooves and the clash of arms.

Stephen jerked up, a swift moment of shock giving way to well-honed instinct. "Stay here," he commanded Roisin, who had sat up, eyes wide, and then he grabbed both sword and dagger on his way out of the tent.

The camp was engulfed with men on horseback, clothed in dark, rough fabric such as could be seen all over Ireland. They wore half masks to conceal their eyes, and the rain did the rest to cloak them effectively. Stephen's own men were as swift as he was, on their feet and armed, but they bore all the disadvantage of being surprised and on the ground against horses.

Harrington stood tall above the rest, but they were being forced away from the tents that held the prisoners. Was that the attackers' purpose—to free the women and boys? More power to them. If Stephen could have identified a leader, he would have told him to take them and go.

But whoever they were, they meant to shed blood. He saw two of his men fall and then a horseman was bearing down on him. He sidestepped at the last second, only to realize the man hadn't been riding for him. Roisin had come out of the tent behind him, dressed in only her shift, her hair darkened with rain. She put up her hands, in protest or surrender, but it didn't matter. The horseman ran her through with a sword, barely slowing to tug the weapon free.

Without awareness of having moved, Stephen was next to her where she'd fallen. The sword had been driven clean enough through her heart, and there was a bewildered expression on her face. Swearing, propelled by rage, Stephen launched himself into the fight.

The English stood no chance. The attackers had one very clear goal—to keep any aid from reaching the prisoners. It was like no fight Stephen had ever been in—messy, dirty, chaotic—with his men herded in one direction and prisoners in the other.

They fell one after another, the twelve remaining women and two boys, helpless before their killers. Stephen tried to get to them, but he was herded back and away without ever being allowed to come to grips with the enemy.

When the prisoners were all dead, the ring of horsemen broke away and began to retreat. Stephen lunged at the only one in his reach and managed to knock the man's horse sufficiently to jar the rider off. But the man was good and kicked himself free so that he landed on his feet facing Stephen, sword drawn.

"Want to die here, English lordling? I'll be happy to oblige." The voice was Irish, the words English, the venom unmistakable.

Stephen parried the man's first blow and ducked beneath the second. But barefooted, he slipped in the churned-up mud and stumbled as the man's sword point drove straight at him.

As Stephen's leg wrenched beneath him, Harrington slammed the Irishman with all his weight. But he, too, was off balance, and the man stepped out of it and then, terribly, thrust a dagger that seemed to come from nowhere up and under Harrington's half-laced brigandine.

Stephen's eyes had misted over, from pain and blood and water, but he could just make out the Irishman's outline as he leaned over and spat into the mud. "Remember this, lordling, and don't play games out of your depth again."

He raised his sword and Stephen waited for death. But it was the hilt, not the blade, that met Stephen's arm. He heard the crack of bone and then, mercifully, everything went white.

In his six weeks in Ireland, Kit had spent nearly as much time at Kilkenny as in Dublin. He would never have agreed to be the Earl of Leicester's secretary if he'd known how often it would throw him into social situations that he despised. Being at the English court was one thing—the endless protocols and rituals and social lies were all made bearable by Pippa and Anabel, as well as the usual outlets afforded a young man of good family. He was an outstanding rider, an excellent huntsman, and skilled in all forms of sport.

Ireland was not much for sport, unless killing one another counted. And having to play gracious courtier to Eleanor Percy was nothing short of galling. She stayed at Kilkenny as though expecting Stephen to arrive any day. Barring that, she seemed prepared to charm Ormond, though Kit still couldn't decide if it was for her daughter's sake or her own. Surely the Earl of Ormond, old as he was, would require a second wife able to bear him children. Then again, perhaps Eleanor wasn't interested in marriage. Her morals had proved to be elastic from an early age, when she had borne her daughter to the king.

The worst part of this latest visit at Kilkenny Castle was the absence of both Nora Percy and Brandon Dudley. Nora had received a personal invitation from Anabel—who was, after all, her cousin—to attend the investiture at Ludlow, and as Dudley had also been invited, he escorted her back to England. It was painful for Kit to watch them go. Anabel had not sent for him. Never mind that he had told her not to—it still stung.

Ormond was a man worth cultivating, at least, and one with a certain sense of humour and practicality that Kit found refreshing. The earl was not afraid of Elizabeth, having known her since childhood, and was thus not particularly impressed by Kit's connection to her and her court. And Kit was prepared to listen and learn from the older man.

He and Ormond were in the courtyard in late August, headed for a morning's ride along the River Nore, when the earl's men alerted them to riders approaching. Wariness was the order of the day when unexpected strangers appeared in Ireland, and Ormond took to the tower battlements to view for himself.

Just steps behind Ormond, Kit spotted the fairly sizable group moving with ragged slowness. Unusually, there were more horses than riders. As they drew nearer, Kit could make out that several of the riderless horses bore what looked like bodies draped over them. He felt a chill like hailstones striking the back of his neck, sudden and sharp, even before he saw the raised standard.

Quartered in gold and azure, with the torteaux and lions of their father, stars for their mother, and storks representing due filial piety from the eldest son—the arms of Stephen Courtenay, Earl of Somerset.

He was down the stone stairs and at the gatehouse before Ormond could stop him. The earl was quick enough to put together the signs; when he followed, he said simply, "Lord Somerset's men. Do you see your brother with them?"

Kit shook his head once, praying silently with a fervor that shocked him. Of course Stephen was all right. Stephen was the heir—blessed, adored, showered with all the gifts of a gracious creator. Nothing bad could ever happen to Stephen. Even when, as an oft-jealous child, Kit might have wished it.

He did not know the man who rode ahead of the small company, for Kit had hardly ever set foot on Stephen's Somerset lands. But the man looked as though he knew what he was about, early thirties with a lined face that spoke of experience. And also, Kit realized as he approached and dismounted, anger and grief.

"Lord Ormond," the man said, identifying Thomas Butler by his distinctive size and coloring.

Kit pushed his way forward. "Where's my brother?" he demanded.

A moment of confusion, then understanding. "You're Christopher. He said you might be at Kilkenny."

"Where's Stephen?"

"He's alive, but injured." He gestured to one of the horses bearing the less upright.

Kit took a step forward but Ormond's men were already moving, bearing down on those clattering up to the gatehouse.

"What happened?" Ormond demanded, though it looked rather clear to Kit.

"Set upon in the night. We had prisoners with us, women and children taken from Carrigafoyle, we were bringing them here. We thought at first they'd come to free the prisoners, but it was blood they wanted. Every last one of the prisoners, cut down. And four of our own men who tried to prevent it."

That was all Kit waited to hear. He'd had a good look at Stephen at last, unconscious and bruised spectacularly. One arm was strapped to his chest. Several grooms carefully eased him from the horse onto the ground. Already litters were appearing in the courtyard.

But Stephen was the only wounded man. The other four horses carried the bodies of the dead. Kit stumbled when he caught sight of a familiar, enormous form carefully strapped to the largest horse.

"Oh, no," Kit stuttered and prayed, "oh, God, please no."

But there was no man on earth who could be mistaken for Harrington. The Duke of Exeter's aide, steward, friend. As fiercely loyal a man as Dominic, and as fiercely loving of his own wife, Carrie. What on earth would the Courtenays do without Harrington?

Stephen was carried still unconscious to a spacious chamber and physicians summoned. Unable to do anything for his brother, Kit threw himself into doing what needed to be done for Stephen's men. The slightly injured were treated, then baths and food and beds. Kit spoke further with the sergeant, a sturdy man named Lewis, and with Ormond's permission sent a contingent of Kilkenny men to the campsite. "We covered the prisoners decently as we could, but didn't dare delay to bury them," Lewis had explained.

Kit wanted to see the site for himself, but knew that Ormond's men would be much better equipped to identify anomalies and evidence of the attackers. And there was one duty he could not delegate.

Harrington could not be allowed to lie in Irish ground. He must be taken home—and so must Stephen's other men. That meant embalming and coffins, carefully sealed and treated, and Ormond's own chaplain to speak over them in these first hours of their deaths. For all his careless, reckless attitude, Kit knew precisely what should be done and with what respect.

It was some hours later, afternoon squalls dimming what light there was, when Stephen awoke. Kit had been sitting in the chamber, waiting, and was on his feet at once when Stephen groaned.

His brother looked awful, and Kit was only too glad to tell him so. "I should let Eleanor Percy in here," he said lightly. "One look at you like this and she might finally give up on trying to catch you for Nora."

Stephen's eyelids fluttered shut, then opened again as though it pained him. It probably did, judging from the damage to his face. "Kilkenny," he rasped. "My men?"

"Safely here. And Ormond sent a company after those still marching. They'll be all right now."

"Not all of them."

"No."

"How many, Kit?"

"What do you remember?" Why was he hedging? He hated it when others did it to him—just tell him and be done with it. But he had never imagined his perfect older brother looking so . . . damaged. So vulnerable.

"I know Harrington is dead." If anything could have made Kit more anxious, it was the complete absence of emotion in Stephen's voice. As though his brother couldn't bear for that to matter and so nothing must matter ever again. "How many others?"

"Three." Without being asked, Kit recited the names the sergeant had given him.

Stephen did not close his eyes, but he didn't look at Kit, either. He seemed focused on some point outside the walls of the castle, a point that fixed and pained him at the same time.

"Your arm is broken in two places, and several ribs as well. Looks like you were kicked once you were down. And your face, of course. Ormond's physician says you should recover."

"Recover?" Only then did Stephen look at him, with a depth of resentment and rage Kit could never have imagined from his brother. "That's what I'm afraid of."

SIX

Elizabeth's journey to Ludlow was an exquisitely judged measure of pomp and practicality. She had welcomed Jehan de Simier, personal envoy of the Duc d'Anjou, at Hampton Court Palace, where they'd spent three days in semiformal affairs before setting out northwest to the Welsh border. Simier, Anjou's Master of Wardrobe, had something of a dubious reputation, but how could she not be impressed with a man who brought her twelve thousand crowns' worth of jewels?

Actually, Elizabeth found herself quite taken by Simier as they traveled; by the end of the first day on the road she had taken to calling him "my monkey" as a play on the Latin allusion of his surname. He had the qualities she most appreciated: intelligence, education, and wit. And he knew how to flatter, which she would never admit to craving. So adept was he at keeping her entertained as they traveled to Ludlow that a suspicious Walsingham murmured one night, "One would think the whoreson has come to court England for himself and not his master."

Dominic and Minuette joined the royal party as they passed

near Wynfield Mote, but they kept to themselves for the most part. That was the general condition for their presence at any royal event: do not force us to take part formally or use us against others, and we will be there. In this case, they were attending for Anabel's sake, not Elizabeth's. She tried not to take it personally.

The last night was spent at another Hampton Court, this one the medieval home of the Coningsby family. The quadrangular, castellated manor presented a pretty aspect with square towers echoing the shape of the three-story gatehouse. A pleasant spot and home, and as it had borne its name long before Elizabeth's palace was built, she refrained from comment on the matter. They were only fifteen miles from Ludlow, which allowed for a gentle pace tomorrow and a celebratory arrival into the town and castle by early afternoon. There were messengers awaiting her, and Elizabeth summoned Walsingham and Burghley. When she realized that one of them bore news from Ireland, she sent a courteous note to Dominic and Minuette asking if they would care for firsthand news of their sons.

She had dealt with the other reports—the questioning of Jesuit Edmund Campion in the Tower, a polite letter from Anabel reporting her arrival at Ludlow—by the time her friends appeared. Always their reverences would be different from those of others, their bows and curtsies more familiar, and Elizabeth quickly motioned them to sit. Then she nodded to Walsingham to report.

"Carrigafoyle has fallen," he said bluntly. "After several days of bombardment from our ships, Pelham and Dane led the assault on the tower. The Earl of Somerset"—a brief nod to Stephen's parents—"and his men were tasked with rounding up those who fled. No losses in his company, and only minor losses to the other English troops."

"The Irish and Spanish?" Burghley asked.

Walsingham did not blink. "We did not take prisoners."

Burghley raised a disapproving eyebrow. "A hundred or so Irish and five hundred Spaniards killed?"

"As for the numbers of Spanish . . . it seems not all of those who landed in Ireland were at Carrigafoyle. Pelham reports there are a hundred Spanish soldiers unaccounted for."

Elizabeth tapped her fingers on the arm of her chair. "Slipped away to meet the Earl of Desmond at Askeaton?" she pondered.

"Perhaps. You understand, this report was sent the very evening of Carrigafoyle's fall. More news will make its way to us quickly now."

Minuette rose without waiting to be dismissed. "But Stephen and his men were untouched in battle?"

"Yes."

She nodded. "Then we shall retire and leave you to your strategies and plans. You have no need of us for that."

Elizabeth's jaw tightened. "You are the best judge of what the Queen of England needs?"

Dominic rose with his wife. "Thank you, Your Majesty, for including us in the immediate report. We are grateful for Stephen's safety, and for the success of the English troops. If you have further need of us, you will command us as you choose."

When had Dominic learned to speak in fluent innuendos? *Command as you choose,* he meant, *but we will serve as we choose.*

Now was not the time for displays of temper. She would keep that weapon honed for its greatest need. And they were her friends, not adversaries. Perhaps she had taken their desire for independence too literally. Perhaps Minuette was simply exasperated with her.

"You are dismissed," she said. But then, in almost the same casual tone, she added, "Would you care to breakfast with me in the morning, Minuette?"

This time, when her friend curtsied, there was a teasing warmth in her smile. "With pleasure."

When the next morning came, it was indeed a true pleasure to sit alone with Minuette over a table with the most tempting foods the manor house could provide and simply talk. If the Coningsbys were at all put out at not being included, they were too wise to show it.

"I am glad that Stephen came out of this campaign well and

whole," Elizabeth began honestly. "If only because I would like to continue to have him serve the crown and I do not put it past you to spirit your son out of my reach if you are unhappy with what I demand."

"As if I could!" Minuette laughed. "Stephen is no child to be told where to go or what to do by his mother."

That wrung an answering laugh, tinged with cynicism, from Elizabeth. "Well spoken. Were we ever so hard to be persuaded when we were young?"

"I am certain both Queen Anne and Lord Rochford thought us the most stubborn of creatures. Now that I am older, I find that I have more sympathy with their point of view."

"I shall look forward to hearing directly from Stephen about Ireland. Your son has a good grasp of essentials for one so young."

"As does your daughter. We have had nothing but excellent reports about her conduct and reception along her way through Wales. Pippa may be fond of her, but she is not given to flattery. Anabel does you proud."

"Has she written to you? Anabel, I mean, not Philippa." Elizabeth fingered one of the heavy tassels at the edge of the damask table linen, reluctant to look at her friend as she asked.

There was a slight pause, as though Minuette were assessing and interpreting the question. "She has. It is kind of her."

"She doesn't do it to be kind. She writes to you because you matter to her."

"Anabel writes to me because I am *not* her mother. Because as much as she cares about me, I am not the one whose good opinion matters most to her. She can afford luxuries such as being imperfect with me."

"Is that pity speaking?" Elizabeth snapped.

"It is experience," Minuette retorted a touch sharply. "You are the one Lucette turned to, prickly as she was, during her years of uncertainty. Because our daughter loved us too well, and was afraid of being hurt by that love. Also, admittedly, a person at one remove can often see more clearly. You knew that Lucette needed the truth. Not that I will ever agree with the way you went about it. But you read rightly her need for facts."

"And what do you read rightly of Anabel's needs?"

"Her need to be useful. She will be a symbol on your behalf, as she must, but to be a symbol without a purpose will slowly kill her spirit. Let her be useful, and she will thrive."

"Fair enough. Then I will advise that, when Stephen returns from Ireland, you encourage him to take up residence in his Somerset holdings. He has been well trained, now he must be independent. He is not Dominic."

"I know that."

"But he must be made to feel that you know it. Everyone he ever meets is comparing him to his father—and Dominic is a most difficult man to live up to. I will let my daughter be useful if you will let your son be free."

"Since when does a queen make bargains?"

"Only with you, my friend. Don't let it go to your head."

The morning of Anabel's formal investiture as Princess of Wales began with Pippa dropping a letter and a package on her bed. "If you don't get up, it's entirely possible your mother will change her mind and keep all the honours for herself."

"Too late," Anabel yawned, propping herself up as Pippa, a brocade sleeveless gown over her nightdress, settled herself on the bed as well. "Now that I've been formally introduced to foreign representatives desiring my marriage, she can't put me back under lock and key."

"And what do we think of Jehan de Simier?" Pippa teased.

Anabel teased right back. "What should I think? Any guidance from my personal seer?"

"Nothing you cannot see for yourself. He's entertaining, but I suspect quite clever behind it. Make no mistake, he's taking notes for

Anjou. And for all his time spent with your mother, you are the one he's noting."

"Hmmm," Anabel mused. She had thought herself prepared for this business of suitors, approaching the matter as she did everything in her life—with study and preparation. But meeting Jehan de Simier and hearing stories of his friendship with the Duc d'Anjou had been a something of a jolt to her sensibilities. A reminder that this matter of political suitors would end in the most personal of ways—in the marriage bed.

Anabel shivered this morning as she thought of the more intimate matters of taking a husband ... and beneath the shivers, a memory of hazel eyes locked on hers across a chamber smoky with tension and threatened violence.

She shook her head and picked up the package. "What's this?"

"For luck."

It was a book, old and fragile in its binding. *De Libero Arbitrio—On Free Will*—by Erasmus. "An original edition from 1524," Pippa told her. "Lucie had Dr. Dee find it for you. Seems fitting for your future."

Anabel hugged her friend, wishing for a moment they were no more than friends, that there wasn't an entire kingdom holding its breath behind these doors waiting for her.

But the regret lasted only a moment. She would never give up her rights and responsibilities. Not for anyone.

Pippa handed her the sealed letter, raised and uneven as though enclosing something besides paper.

"Words of lavish praise?" Anabel asked. "Wise counsel for my new formal position?"

"I don't know. It's not from me."

Pippa said nothing else. She didn't have to. Anabel broke the anonymous seal and opened the pages. Out fell an oval badge, made to hang on a bracelet or ribbon around the neck. The white enamel was branded with a dark green panther in rampant position.

A panther for Anabel, Pippa had declared—more than ten years ago, wasn't it? A summer at Wynfield Mote as a child, at ease with the Courtenay children as she was never at ease elsewhere. *Fierce but loving.*

The three of them—and it was nearly always the three of them, as though Anabel were as much part of the twins as they were of each other—were assigning heraldic symbols to one another. Pippa chose Anabel's. Then Kit had chosen—what else?—an owl for his eerily wise sister. And then it was Anabel's turn to anoint Kit.

A raven, she pronounced, having spent time studying the meanings of various birds. She'd thought at first a cock, for what boy didn't want to be known for courage and readiness to fight? But then she'd come upon the raven. *One who makes his own fate, and is ever constant by nature.* Anabel was clever for nine years old, but mostly she just liked how it sounded.

Only half aware of Pippa silently next to her, Anabel picked up the sheet on which Kit had written in his surprisingly neat strokes.

A panther for fierceness, green for hope. May you have all that you have ever hoped for, Princess. Your raven stands ever constant at your command.

For one moment she let herself be tugged by memory—then fiercely shoved it back. Clearly Kit was not constant at her command, or he would be here today.

She dropped the badge and letter on the bed and shoved her way free of the covers. "Time to begin," she announced.

The day unfolded in a series of perfectly planned and executed moments. Anabel knew the power of symbols and the importance of ritual to a kingdom's people, and was somewhat surprised at her own peaks of emotion during their display. Draped in a mantle of crimson, long hair flowing loose down the back, she knelt before the Queen of England (the mother in Elizabeth held firmly in the background at this moment) and received the Honours of the Principality of Wales.

The gold ring for duty, the golden rod for good government, and the sword that symbolized justice. Then the coronet to herald her new, officially invested rank. It was old, by far the oldest item among the Honours. The Talaith Llywelyn had belonged to the last native Welsh prince; after Llewelyn's death in battle in 1284, Edward I had brought his crown to London and kept it with the other royal jewels and regalia. The iron coronet was of a curious design, more like a cap than a crown, the gold plating Edward had given it burnished and roughened by centuries, so that dark iron drew the eye beneath the old gold. It was heavy, but Anabel could swear it was not the weight of the iron she felt, but the very weight of her future as Elizabeth placed the coronet on her head.

Then, for just a moment, it was simply her mother looking at her with pride and complete and utter understanding. No one on earth could understand like Elizabeth the weight of ruling as a woman, and Anabel felt that there were only the two of them present as she spoke the formal words of fealty. "I, Anne Isabella, Princess of Wales, do become your liege of life and limb and of earthly worship, and faith and truth I will bear unto you to live and die against all manner of folks."

Speeches to the crowd followed, including Anabel's, delivered in flawless Welsh. No nerves at all, for she had prepared meticulously for all the moments of this day.

Except for those few that pulled at her heart. Such as when her mother, before the feast that evening, presented her with a locket ring of the same design she herself wore. The impossibly tiny minia-tures in the clasped oval on Elizabeth's thin gold band were of Eliza-beth and her mother, Anne Boleyn. Now, she presented Anabel with images of the two of them. Anabel blinked, surprised by gratitude and love, and her mother moved smoothly on so that the moment did not become uncomfortably emotional.

Then there were the embraces and whispered words of pride from Minuette Courtenay. Anabel could never think of her as Lady Exeter, however formally she might address her in public, and next to her mother there was no woman whose good opinion she cared more for in this world. Dominic did not embrace her, nor whisper.

Instead, he said clearly, "Even more than your mother's, I am yours to command, Your Highness."

Your raven stands ever constant at your command.

It was Kit who shadowed her through the day and into the night. Kit she kept turning to for comments, Kit whose honey-bronzed hair was like no one else's, Kit whose laughter and unfailing friendship Anabel missed so much she could hardly bear to think on it.

She wanted Kit back, whatever it took. Which meant she had to acknowledge the truth of why he'd left.

He'd left because of her. Because of what had happened at Wynfield Mote a year ago, when she and Lucette Courtenay had been held hostage by a Catholic troublemaker. It had been Kit who walked into the hall of his family home with the necessary information to have Anabel released. And when he'd walked in, those clear hazel eyes of his had locked on her with an intensity that stole her breath far more than fear ever had. It was the tension of . . .

Why balk at the word? The tension of love. Not the love of a childhood friend, or of a subject for his future queen. There was nothing political or calculated or planned to that emotion—it simply existed. Kit loved her. She had known it in her bones at that moment.

And ever since, she had been pretending not to know it.

Kit had made it easy for her, she could see that now. Kept his temper when she'd raged at him for not doing what she wanted, refusing to back down when she insisted he stay in England and serve her. She would never have guessed he could be so self-sacrificing. And while he said nothing, she had pretended to believe it did not lie between them.

Because if she once admitted Kit's love, then what might happen to her? If she once allowed herself to think of it, what might she feel?

There were some commands even a queen could not give. *Stop loving me,* for instance. *Stop getting in my head and making me remember your eyes and your laugh and how you are the one I look for a dozen times a day.*

Kit might be hers to command, but she was not his to love. Not ever.

For five days following her daughter's investiture, Elizabeth's government and court life was centered on Ludlow Castle. It was a testing period, to see how the Princess of Wales's household could work with the queen's without too wide an audience to comment on every moment of friction between them.

But some matters required still more privacy. Such as meeting with her niece, Nora Percy. Elizabeth welcomed the girl into an alcove off her bedchamber that had been set up for the queen to read and write in solitude.

It was always a bit of a shock to realize how much Nora looked like her mother. She might have been Eleanor reborn, with blonde hair and catlike brown eyes ... except that Nora had none of her mother's blatant sensuality and aggressive charm. Those traits had brought Eleanor into a king's bed when she was only eighteen and had kept her alive through multiple changes of fortune.

Elizabeth much preferred Nora's reserve, and she smiled now with a fondness few ever received from her. "Did you enjoy Ireland?" she asked.

"A little."

"Not sorry to leave your mother behind?"

Nora, whatever she felt, could never be brought to openly criticize Eleanor. "She will do well enough without me at Kilkenny."

"I assume that means your wishes are unchanged?" Elizabeth queried.

For the first time, Nora lost a little of her self-possession. "I do not ... No, Your Majesty. I have nothing to ask differently."

Nine years ago, the eighteen-year-old Nora had been a shy girl newly come to court after a quiet life with a musician uncle in Yorkshire. For the daughter of two such personalities as Eleanor Percy and William Tudor, Nora had kept to herself to a surprising degree and Elizabeth had quickly dismissed the girl as weak.

Until that weak girl had requested a private audience and asked the queen—her aunt—for a favor. "My mother has been matchmaking since I was little," Nora had said calmly. "She would have married me off long since if it were not that your consent is also required."

"And you have a particular young man to whom you would like me to give consent?" Elizabeth had asked, a little amused.

"I do not wish to marry, Your Majesty," Nora had answered. "I would ask you to refuse consent to all who might ask in the coming years."

And so Elizabeth had done, a little bemused but willing to grant what cost her nothing—and what displeased Eleanor in the bargain. Ten times in the last seven years Elizabeth had refused men who had wished to claim Nora.

Now Elizabeth studied the girl—woman, she corrected herself, for Nora was twenty-seven, though she looked younger—and wondered if she had finally met someone capable of changing her mind.

But if she did not wish to say, Elizabeth would not force the issue. "May I take it you are not interested in returning to Ireland?"

"I would prefer to return to York for a time, Your Majesty. My uncle Jonathan is ill. It would be a comfort to us both for me to go home."

"As you like," Elizabeth said. She did not add that Nora would be missed, for truthfully the woman moved through life with a delicacy that seemed to leave little imprint behind her. Though she had come to know this niece of hers well enough to recognize that was a deliberate choice on Nora's part.

With personal business completed, Elizabeth turned her attention to the more practical matter of judging how smoothly her daughter's household and council functioned. It did not take long to appreciate how well Anabel's treasurer worked as a liaison between households. Which made sense, since he'd been trained by Lord

Burghley. But Matthew Harrington also came from the Courtenay household. Elizabeth had known his mother, Carrie, since she'd become Minuette's personal lady almost thirty years ago. During those turbulent times, Elizabeth had often had cause to give thanks for Carrie's steadiness and loyalty when Minuette most needed it. Matthew's father, known to most simply as Harrington, had once been in Lord Rochford's service but took to Dominic Courtenay as though the two men had been meant to work together since birth. Elizabeth couldn't truly say she knew Harrington—she doubted anyone but Carrie and Dominic could say that—but he had been a godsend in keeping Minuette alive during the months William was determined to kill her.

Matthew Harrington, an only child, was twenty-two, brown-haired and calm-featured like his mother, tall and solid like his father. His mind had been well sharpened by his studies at Oxford and in Burghley's household this last year. Every morning at Ludlow, he attended upon Burghley and whichever council members were present that day for a sort of daily overview of events and expectations. Occasionally Elizabeth herself was present. As she was the day before their planned departure from Ludlow, when a breathless messenger interrupted their discussion on travel plans with a sealed missive for Walsingham.

Her chief secretary and spymaster had a face even Elizabeth had difficulty reading after all these years. But where a man could control his features, he could not always control his colour. Beneath the widow's peak and pointed black beard, Walsingham's skin grew ashen as he read.

"What?" Elizabeth demanded.

"Ireland," he said. "Word from the Earl of Ormond at Kilkenny."

"Surely the rebels have not so quickly regrouped as to be able to attack in the east."

"No, Your Majesty. This is of a more . . . personal nature."

She raised a single eyebrow. Walsingham was not usually so hesitant. "Do I need to read it myself?" she asked.

"I think, perhaps, we should excuse young Mr. Harrington first."

There were any number of reasons why a member of Anabel's household—and a young one at that—would be excused. Matthew took no offense, but there was a quizzical look in his dark brown eyes that Elizabeth felt mirrored in her own.

When it was just Elizabeth, Walsingham, and Burghley, she said simply, "Tell me."

"Stephen Courtenay has been injured and four of his men killed. Not at Carrigafoyle—they were heading to Kilkenny with women and children who'd been taken prisoner. They were ambushed."

"Will Stephen recover?" It was surprisingly difficult to ask. Life would be so much easier if sentiment were removed from the equation.

"It appears so. But one of the men killed was Edward Harrington."

She heard Burghley's indrawn breath and knew she was going to have to say something, but for just one moment she was twenty-four again and desperately trying to save her friend's life from her brother's wrath and there was Harrington, ready and willing to take orders from anyone as long as it meant doing what Dominic would have wanted. Elizabeth had ruled long enough to know how rare a quality that was.

Walsingham spoke again. "Shall I inform Lord Exeter?"

"No. Bring them to me, Dominic and Minuette both. I will tell them."

I will tell them their son who I sent to Ireland is damaged in body and soul. And that the man they sent with him to keep him safe is dead.

20 September 1581

Anabel,

Mother, Lucie, and I arrived at Wynfield Mote last night. Father has gone on to Bristol with Matthew; they are prepared to take ship to Ireland if the boys do not soon cross. I am worried about Matthew. I was there

when they told him and Carrie of Harrington's death and he behaved pre-
cisely as I would expect. Every thought now is for his mother's care and
comfort. But he must have sorrow of his own. He would not speak of it.
Not even to me.

Pippa

25 September 1581

Anabel,

We've had word that Stephen and Kit are expected in Bristol tomor-
row. Your mother has sent a contingent of royal guards to travel with
them as they bring Harrington home.

There was no question of him being laid to rest anywhere else. What-
ever family he had when young, I have never heard him speak of it. It was
from Wynfield that he set out all those years ago to protect my mother
when the king burned her home—and it is at Wynfield that he must lie.

Carrie is secluded, and sees only my mother.

Pippa

30 September 1581

Anabel,

Today Harrington came home for the last time. The queen's men
formed a guard of royal honour, but it was my father who rode before the
open wagon upon which the coffin rested. It was draped with the Exeter
coat of arms and a single spray of late white roses that I knew at once
Matthew had laid for his mother's sake.

Stephen rode next to Kit, both of them flanking my father, and my worst fears were realized when I looked at Stephen's face. It is not the physical injuries that are the trouble—though Kit confirmed that Stephen had only mounted a horse the last five miles, and that after a sharp disagreement with Father. By rights he should not be riding yet.

But it was the look of dread in his eyes that shattered me. He could hardly bring himself to look at Carrie. Thank heavens she knows him well enough to read his reticence for grief and pain rather than lack of caring. I don't know about the others, but Stephen's pain is as clear to me as though he were shouting it. As soon as the necessary business was accomplished, Stephen vanished to his chamber. Only Mother has been in there since.

I wanted to talk to Matthew, but other than a brief clasp of hands that I hope he felt as I intended, he has also vanished. So it was Kit and I, as it should be, who talked things out among Mother's roses.

"What happened to them?" I asked.

Kit shrugged. "Ambushed in the night. Raining and men on horses . . . I got all that from the soldiers, you understand. Stephen will not talk about it. I do not even think he has told Father anything."

It is a state of affairs that cannot continue. But for once, I am at a loss. Stephen has always been the self-sufficient one, even more so than Lucie. He is the most polite, well-bred young man, but he has very clear walls that he does not invite anyone to cross. Especially not his little sister.

I think it has shocked Kit to find that Stephen is vulnerable. I can see him trying to reorder his world in light of that fact, and in the end I think he will be better for it.

I miss you.

Pippa

SEVEN

The very day after being carried unconscious into Kilkenny Castle, Stephen had risen from his bed and demanded to begin planning his return to England. When Kit's protests achieved nothing, Tom Butler had stepped in to reason with his fellow—if much younger—earl, but even he had gotten nowhere fast. Kit could see that his brother's mind was made up. *Damn my injuries,* Stephen seemed to shout with every grim line of his body. So Kit acquiesced in making plans to get the bodies of Harrington and Stephen's men home as soon as possible.

They sailed from Waterford. Kit left behind his written resignation for Ormond to give Brandon Dudley in case Brandon returned to Ireland before they could cross paths in England. Then, with Stephen's sergeant, he set everything in motion and reported almost each hour to his brother. It was a situation he had long feared, never wanting to be officially subordinate to the older brother he simultaneously admired and envied. But Stephen hardly seemed to even know him. They might as well have been strangers.

Only once did Kit try to break Stephen's silence about the ambush. "Were there any identifying features of the attackers you could make out? It would help Ormond track them down."

"Gallowglass," Stephen said abruptly. "I've told Ormond as much. If he can find which lord paid this particular mercenary force, more power to him."

Encouraged by this slight responsiveness, Kit pressed, "Sergeant Lewis says you had mounted the women and boys because you were uneasy while crossing Munster. Did you have any sense that this might be coming?"

That was when Stephen turned on him a look more forbidding than even their father at his fiercest. "When you have spent weeks in hostile territory outside the luxury of castle walls, then you can ask me what mistakes I made in the field. Until then, I owe you nothing."

It had been a relief to reach Bristol and pass over responsibility for Stephen to their father. And an even greater relief to return to Wynfield Mote and the sympathy of his mother and sisters. Surely Stephen would talk to one of them.

The day after their return they laid Harrington to rest. Dressed in black, the entire household followed behind the Courtenay banners that preceded Harrington's coffin. Carrie wept a little at the graveside, as she and Matthew tossed in sprigs of rosemary for remembrance. But otherwise she was composed and gracious, taking care to speak to all at the funeral feast afterward.

At dawn the following day, Stephen left Wynfield Mote. Despite his mother's entreaties and physician's warnings, he insisted on setting off for his Somerset lands. Dominic went with him, though Kit thought his brother would have flat-out refused their father's presence if possible. But force of will alone could only lend so much strength. Probably Stephen was husbanding what he had in order to cope.

Probably Stephen was also running away. At first Kit instinctively rejected the thought. Stephen was the good brother, the one who did everything right. On the face of it, returning to Somerset while still badly injured argued an honourable care for his men and his own responsibility as a landowner. But there was a skittishness to Stephen's behaviour—an edginess around everyone—that forced Kit to realize his brother may not be as perfect as he'd thought.

Being who she was, Pippa insisted on talking about it as they rode out the next day to visit Lucette. Compton Wynyates, Lucette and Julien's manor house, was less than fifteen miles away across gentle farming country. When they had left Stratford-upon-Avon and its people behind, Pippa launched into questions.

"What is wrong with Stephen?" she demanded.

"You know as much I do, Pippa. I would have thought more, considering your talents."

She ignored Kit's hint at her intuitive abilities. "Of course you know more than I do, you were in Ireland with him."

"And he was just like he was at home! Wouldn't talk about it, all I know is what his men told me about the attack. I can see it, in a way. Stephen's always been the golden child. He was going to have to fail at some point. But this failure? To come through a battle with all of his men intact and then to lose them unexpectedly? To lose Harrington?" Kit broke off. They were all missing the big man, who had been as much a part of their childhood as anyone.

Kit went on bitterly, "Stephen doesn't know how to cope with failure. He should have asked me! At least he has somewhere to retreat to. I don't know what I'm supposed to do next. Do you want to tell me?"

Pippa turned on him sharply. "How long are you going to continue drifting through your life waiting for whatever wind takes you? I am not your personal star-teller, Kit. What do you want from me? You are young and rich and healthy. You can go anywhere and do anything. So do it."

Never in his life had his twin so thoroughly shot him down. They rode in uncomfortable silence for a long time, while Kit tried to distract himself with counting sheep. It was an impossible job, for they were everywhere, white shadows merging and blending against the green turf and those hardy flowers still blooming into this first week of October.

When in doubt, apologize. That was the first rule one learned dealing with royalty, so he supposed it would do for sisters. "Forgive me, Philippa," he said finally, reverting to formality to cover the awkwardness. "I suppose we all do that to you, looking to you to sort our problems. You just do it so well . . ." he hesitated, then barked a brief laugh. "So much like Mother. Do you suppose she ever loses her temper when people expect her to know everything?"

That wrung a small smile from his twin. "Undoubtedly."

"I suppose Anabel is anxious for you to return." For the first time in his life, Kit considered that Pippa's life must be even more circumscribed than his own. He, as she had caustically noted, could at the very least take his sword and his body and offer them for the use of whoever might pay at home or abroad. His sisters had not even that option. Pippa served at the pleasure of a temperamental Tudor royal. Was that enough for her?

Pippa said soberly, "I do not plan to return to Anabel just now. I shall stay at Wynfield Mote, and then spend the winter with the family at Tiverton."

"I'm sure Mother will appreciate having you home."

"I'm not doing it for Mother."

They locked eyes and, in that ineffable manner of twins, he felt a breath of words across his mind. He could never explain it—not so simple or straightforward as silent talking—but he knew now why she was staying.

For Matthew Harrington.

He should have guessed. Matthew had always been Pippa's friend, far more than either his or Stephen's. It wasn't that Matthew was awed or even much impressed by the Courtenay boys—Matthew was the one with the Oxford education, and birth would never be an impediment where Harrington and Carrie's son was concerned. It was simply that Pippa alone attracted him. In the manner of a magnet, as though he instinctively turned in whichever direction she did.

Kit had known Pippa cared about Matthew, but he hadn't guessed until this moment the nature and depth of that caring. The revelation left him feeling oddly lonely as they approached Compton Wynyates, the red-brick house as dark as raspberries, the castellated and turreted roofline jagged against the pale blue sky.

If he didn't have Pippa and couldn't have Anabel—what was left for him?

A week later he received a royal messenger commanding his presence in London as soon as possible to meet with Her Majesty, Queen Elizabeth.

In mid-October, Mary Stuart, Queen of Spain, retired to a lavishly appointed chamber in the Royal Alcazar of Madrid to await her confinement. Given her history, it was not an entire surprise when, just ten days later, she was delivered of twins. Not a stillborn boy and girl, as so long ago in Scotland, but two lusty boys.

Philip surveyed his sons with a pleased delight he had not expected to feel. An heir he needed, yes—and two sons was a luxury he had not looked for—but this marriage had been far more a political calculation than even his marriage to Elizabeth two decades ago. He had considered Mary's pregnancy in the light of a calculated risk. But what he felt now was more than the simple satisfaction of a risk paid off.

They were baptized two days later. Prince Charles, the elder by ten minutes, and Prince Alexander, a Scots name that gave the Spanish bishop difficulty. Afterward, Philip and Mary had a private interview.

"Are you well, Maria?" he asked with real solicitude. Her age, which had been such a real concern through the pregnancy, continued to keep the physicians watchful. Soon to be thirty-nine, but still with a luster to her fair skin and a light to her eyes. And a mind as dogged and certain as ever about what she wanted.

"I would be better without the slaughter wrought in Carrigafoyle. It haunts my dreams—the atrocities of the English to your soldiers."

"You should not be considering such things now. Think rather on your sons."

"I am thinking of my sons . . . of all my sons. And of your daughter, as well."

Her stubbornness was that of a limited viewpoint and self-righteous certainty. Not like Elizabeth's stubbornness, but irritating. And often successful, if only to keep from being worn down one frustrating drop at a time.

"I am sure both James and Anne will be pleased to hear of their new siblings."

"I am sure both James and Anne will be horrified. As will Elizabeth. They will guess what will follow from this."

Philip rubbed his face, an unusual sign of agitation. "Not now, Maria."

"You must avenge what was done to your soldiers in Ireland."

"I will discuss it later. With my council, as I should."

Her face flushed, not unattractively. "What more do you need from me to do what is right? You required a son—I have given you two. While you sit in your kingdom and count the earthly riches God has granted you, others of our faith are starving and dying beneath the hands of heretics!"

Philip had heard it all before. He knew the intensity of Mary's faith was equaled only by the intensity of her resentment of the English and Scots Protestants who had harried her from her kingdom and held her captive for years. But he also knew the practical realities of a fight in Ireland, details that Mary always brushed off.

So different from Elizabeth.

Despite Mary's complaints, Philip had not been idle since word of Carrigafoyle arrived. And he knew things his wife did not—for instance, the general location of the one hundred Spanish soldiers who had not been amidst the slaughter in Carrigafoyle.

But she did have a point. Who was he to refuse a crumb of comfort to a woman whose labours had brought such an abundance of joy this week? Philip raised her lovely, plump hand and kissed it. "I swear to you, I have not forgotten my responsibilities. And I will not forget what has been done to my men in Ireland. Trust me—because I hold my tongue does not mean that my mind is not ever working toward resolution of our political and religious splits. You cannot think I would so carelessly jeopardize my daughter's soul as to lightly consign her to hell."

Mary seemed mollified, but sniffed at mention of Anabel. "I hope your daughter will do you greater credit than my Scots son. Children or not, our first devotion must be to the truth."

Philip murmured what could be taken as agreement or mere comfort. There were times when Mary's resentments seemed likely to swallow up every other feeling she might have, affecting every decision. It was a mistake Elizabeth had never made.

It was early November before Christopher Courtenay answered Elizabeth's summons and presented himself to her at Whitehall Palace. She met him in a chamber with a high painted ceiling and linenfold paneling to shoulder height. Above that ran a frieze of Tudor roses picked out in ruby red and gold.

Elizabeth had always had a special fondness for Kit. He had the looks and personality of his mother—innately charming, mischievous, and amusing, with a warmth of affection so often absent in royal circles. Today, though, as he straightened from his bow, he looked subdued. Tired and worn, as though he were much older than nineteen.

Just as well, as her proposal was meant for an older man.

"How was Ireland?" she began after she'd seated herself and invited Kit to do the same. She had chosen not to use her canopy of estate, in order to lessen the formality, but her chair was still heavily carved and gilded. Though Kit had known her all his life, he did no more than perch on the edge of his seat as though ready to jump up at a moment's notice. Or perhaps he was only that eager to escape her.

In answer to her question, he began, "Stephen hasn't said much—"

"I don't mean Carrigafoyle or what followed with your brother. I meant yourself. Did you enjoy your time with Lord Leicester? Make yourself useful?"

"If you find it useful to parry wits with a woman like Eleanor Percy." Ah, there was the impulsive boy she knew and loved.

"Your mother used to do that very well—so well, in fact, I wager Eleanor has never forgotten it. You must watch yourself with her. She has no love for the Courtenays."

"She had no need to trouble herself with me in Ireland, not when she had an earl to charm."

"Eleanor Percy and my own Black Tom?" Elizabeth did not like that at all. Surely the Earl of Ormond was too canny a man to fall for Eleanor's tricks.

But men had been falling for her tricks ever since she'd charmed the late king. Elizabeth had thought her brother a fool then. Time had not changed her opinion of the woman.

This was not a subject to discuss with a curious boy. Elizabeth forcibly returned to the subject at hand. "I did not mean to inquire about women in Ireland. I meant your time as . . . what was your position? Seneschal? Clerk?"

"Secretary," he said stiffly. "I learned a great deal."

"And were bored out of your mind by three-quarters of it."

For the first time since entering, Kit's face brightened. "Closer to four-fifths."

"Then it's as well that what I need you for now is nothing like being a secretary."

He had his mother's lightheartedness—and his father's wariness. "Your Majesty, I cannot imagine any royal task for which I would be fitted—"

"I'm not asking you to imagine. I'm asking you to listen."

She could see the flicker of fear subsumed by stubbornness and knew he was afraid she was going to order him to Anabel's household. Elizabeth had a general awareness of why that would be troublesome—an awareness she had not wished to explore deeply— and wasn't bothered about using it against him.

"Some years ago—far longer ago than I truly care to examine—my uncle, Lord Rochford, trained your father as a personal envoy. Everyone thought Dominic a most unusual choice, considering that his strengths have always been of the straightforward variety. Your father despises politics and officials in almost equal measure. Which was precisely why he made such an effective envoy. People were blinded by what they knew of him, which made them careless. Expectations are such a useful tool."

If she had been anyone else, Elizabeth was certain Kit would have been on his feet by now, demanding that she either get to the point or leave him alone. But he managed to swallow his instinctive reactions. "What is it you expect of me, Your Majesty?"

"Mary Stuart, lately our reluctant guest, has given birth to twin sons to the King of Spain. I am preparing gifts, and I require envoys to present them."

"You have ambassadors for such a task."

"And intelligencers and diplomats ... of course I do. And of course those men are going. But I also need a friendly face for Philip to welcome. He is looking for something more personal from England, considering that his sons are also half brothers to the Princess of Wales. I propose you travel to Spain next spring, after spending the winter being trained as my envoy by Lord Burghley."

"You're using me to make King Philip think that his daughter is truly congratulatory."

"I am using you to make Philip think that his daughter truly misses him. He knows you, Christopher. He never forgets those who surround his daughter and he is perfectly aware of your particular closeness to Anabel." Using her pet name was a gamble, designed to make Kit soften. "Philip will expect that you are there simply to be friendly. And while he is blinded by your—innocence, shall we say?—some things might be let slip."

She'd expected one of two reactions. Either he would continue to protest his uselessness or he would flat-out refuse.

But Kit surprised her—which was probably why she liked him so much. "When do I report to Lord Burghley?" he asked, and his smile was a perfect match to his mother's most impulsive, most dangerous, smiles.

Anabel had expected to remain in Ludlow for some weeks after her investiture, but with the news from Ireland, she had chosen to follow her mother back to London. Taking up residence for the first time at Charterhouse—where Lord Rochford had both lived and died—she waited. Her household kept her very well informed; she knew to the day when Kit arrived at court and knew to the hour when he met with her mother. She even had a fairly good idea of what the queen was asking of him. And because she knew Kit, she knew he would say yes.

What Anabel didn't know was if he would come to see her of his own accord.

He did, a nicely judged two days after his audience with her mother. Though she considered herself nothing if not meticulously prepared for every eventuality, her heartbeat quickened a little when Madalena announced, "Lord Christopher Courtenay."

Madalena Arias had been part of Anabel's life as long as she could remember. At the age of ten, Madalena was chosen by King Philip to leave her native Spain and come to England to serve his young daughter. Raised in wealth and luxury in Seville, Madalena had grown into an exotic beauty thanks to her mixed heritage of aristocratic Spanish blood and a Moorish grandmother. But she seemed to have no life beyond serving Anabel, a fact that occasionally bothered the princess but just as quickly was pushed aside. If Madalena wanted anything, she had only to ask. It wasn't Anabel's job to pull ambition out of her.

The princess received Kit as no doubt her mother had, seated in royal state with her own coat of arms as Princess of Wales on the canopy over her chair. She always dressed with care, and was cross to catch herself wondering if Kit liked the peacock blue shade of her gown.

In just the few steps needed to stand before her and bow, Anabel thought Kit had aged far more than just the four months they'd been separated. For the first time she caught sight of him as a stranger might, rather than simply the boy she'd known all her life. She could also see the man he would be—in perhaps a far shorter time than she'd expected. Everyone thought him so like Minuette, but there was nothing soft or warm about his stance. Only his hazel eyes were familiar.

At least his voice had not changed. "You look well, Your Highness. Suitably royal."

"It's all stagecraft, you know that. The dress, the setting, the arrogance—"

"Oh, no. The arrogance is all yours."

And just like that they were grinning at each other as though nothing uncomfortable had ever happened between them. It made it easier for Anabel to ask, "So you've agreed to go to Spain at my mother's request?"

"The queen requested. But I did not agree for her sake. I did it for yours."

"You think I am so anxious to send you away? As I recall, you were the one who declined to serve in my household."

"I think that there might be things you would truly like to convey to your father that you would not feel comfortable confiding to professional diplomats. They see him only as the King of Spain. I see him, first and always, as your father."

Damn Kit. There was no one in the world who could burrow into her secrets half as easily. Except, of course, Pippa. Because being so easily read annoyed and agitated her in equal measure, Anabel rose from her seat and began to pace. Kit continued to stand solidly where he'd begun. Watching her. She could feel him watching her, as though his gaze were as tangible as silk.

When had he learned to be still?

"My father has two new children to concern himself with. Two new sons. It is surely what he wanted. Now he can safely consign me to the fiery Catholic hell awaiting."

"Your brothers," Kit said unexpectedly.

"What?"

"His sons are your half brothers, Anabel. Now you at last have siblings of your own. I know you always wished for them."

"Only until I was old enough to realize that I've had siblings all along. I've had you—all of you."

"Anabel—"

"I have no need to be loved by two babies who will be raised to hate me and all I stand for—if not by our mutual father, then certainly by their mother. Mary Stuart will never let her sons forget how England kept her prisoner. She will raise them to take vengeance."

"Is that the message you wish me to carry?"

"I have prepared gifts for the boys, and a personal letter to my father. I should like to ensure that he is given it without interference from any diplomats or clerics, English or Spanish." She turned to face him, startled to realize he'd moved closer without her hearing. She could see the ring of green that circled and bled into the gold of his eyes.

"Will you do that for me?" she asked, feeling more vulnerable than she liked.

He was close enough to touch, though he didn't. Quite. His hand came up and hovered at her throat, where she wore the enameled green panther on a black velvet ribbon, then dropped to his side. "I am yours to command."

"I'm not commanding. I am asking."

When the corners of his mouth tipped up, she had to stop herself from touching the dimples that formed. What was wrong with her? She was never this . . . whatever this was. She was always, perfectly and absolutely, in control of herself.

"I will go to Spain. For your sake, Anabel, no one else's."

It was the first time he'd called her by name since entering, and she thought she might cry from the tone of it. Or laugh. Or slap him on the arm to stop him from sounding so . . . intimate.

It was a very good thing, she decided at that moment, that Kit was going as far away from her as possible. That would give her time to flirt with the Duc d'Anjou and charm the Scots ambassador and, in general, do everything she could to remember that it was her hand and her future crown at stake in the marriage market.

Not her heart.

EIGHT

Somehow Stephen made it through the days by sheer force of will. He was disciplined and trained and self-controlled and his Somerset estates were run with care and efficiency. But force of will could not control the nights.

Only weeks after leaving Ireland did Stephen realize that he'd expected time to make it better. Surely he couldn't continue to dream night after night about what had happened, reliving his men's fall, the prisoners' slaughter, Roisin's death, Harrington . . .

But he did continue to dream. When winter arrived at Farleigh Hungerford in force in early December, Stephen had not slept more than two hours at a time since Ireland, with no sign of reprieve. He had left Wynfield Mote so his family wouldn't realize that his state of mind was much worse than the injuries to his body, hoping that being away from the living reminders of his failure—not having to see the widowed Carrie and fatherless Matthew every day—would allow him to grow numb. But again, numbness was only something he could control during the day.

So he did what countless men before him had done—he drank.

Heavily and indiscriminately. If his steward and household servants were concerned, he made sure they had no legitimate cause for complaint by concentrating ferociously on his work. The harvest was accomplished, the estate ledgers balanced, his tenants and servants healthy insofar as he could provide, and his soldiers well drilled. What could they say? That he looked unhappy? That where before he had been unfailingly polite, even kind, to those around him, now he was abrupt? Those were not sins, not even legitimate failings. His household said nothing to him, even when they must have been counting the number of bottles he got through in a week.

He was not afraid of his household or his men. And those he was afraid of kept well away from him. Until he received a letter from his sister, Lucette, announcing that she and Julien intended to spend Christmas at Farleigh Hungerford with him.

He stared at the letter for a long time, considering. Only Lucie would have dared to announce rather than ask. And unlike his other correspondents, she did not lace her letter with concerns about his health or well-being. She simply said that their parents, in an unprecedented move, had agreed to spend Christmas at court. "Because Pippa has been missing Anabel," she wrote, "and Kit is still in London preparing to sail to Spain in the spring."

As Julien, Lucette continued, was not comfortable with spending Christmas at the English court, they would come to Stephen instead.

Stephen might have forbidden her, if he hadn't known she would just go ahead and come anyway. And if this was the family's plan to see how he was doing, better Lucie on her own than all of them at once. He wrote back to his sister, just two lines, and said she would be made as welcome as a single man's household could make her.

That night he drained twice the usual amount of wine.

Lucette and Julien arrived five days before Christmas, and Stephen nearly lost control at his first sight of them. He watched from an upper window as Julien helped Lucie out of the coach. Instead of simply handing her out, he put his arms around her waist to swing her out and held her tightly to him so he could kiss her. Lucie's hands were in Julien's hair as he teased her with light kisses at the corner of her mouth and along the line of her jaw. Stephen could almost hear his sister's breathless laughter.

Their joy was sickening.

He allowed his steward to greet them and get them settled into the suite carefully prepared by his household. But he couldn't avoid them forever. Better to meet Lucie on his own terms rather than wait for her to waylay him. So he made his way to the Lady Tower, where he'd installed them at a safe distance from where he slept, and knocked twice for warning on the frame of the open door.

At least Lucie didn't fly to him, or hug him or stare at him or anything he could not have borne. But nor did she look abashed at inviting herself to Farleigh Hungerford; clearly her joy ran too deep for anything but surface concern. All the better for him.

Julien, on the other hand, watched him warily, and Stephen wondered what the Frenchman thought he might do. Yell at Lucie? Order them to leave? There was protectiveness in every line of his body, and Stephen didn't relish coming up against Julien in a dispute.

But there would be no disputes. If there was one thing the Courtenays knew how to do, it was behave properly.

Stephen took the first step, striding to his sister and lifting her hand for a light kiss. "I hope your journey was not too taxing."

"The cold at least makes the roads easier to navigate. You look . . ." She could not bring herself to openly lie and say *You look well,* and settled instead for the ambiguous, "better . . . You have healed?"

"I can breathe without feeling my ribs piercing my insides. The arm is still a little weak—the arms master has ordered me to switch sword hands for a while in order to strengthen it."

"I can help with that," Julien offered. "It's a handy skill, in any case, being able to use both hands."

Before there could be any awkward silences, Stephen said

smoothly, "I'll leave you to rest and change. My cook is overjoyed to have visitors—no doubt the kitchens will provide enough food for twenty. I'll see you then."

He escaped to his own chamber, hands trembling. This was going to be harder than he'd thought. Just two minutes with his sister and part of his mind was shouting that he couldn't do this, she would see right through him, how was he ever going to cope for a fortnight or more without drinking? His household might hold their peace, but Lucie would not be so circumspect. She would task him with it, and then, more likely than not, would go straight to their parents.

He forced himself to breathe in and out slowly, the chaos of his mind forced back into the shadowy corners where his memories usually lurked during the day. Then he poured himself a drink from the bottle of malmsey. He relished the sweet, sharp taste and told himself, *I don't have to stop drinking entirely. Just control it better.*

Only at dinner did he realize he might not have struck quite the balance he'd meant to. He wasn't drunk, but he wasn't entirely sober, either. That was not a mistake he'd made before, as he'd previously confined drinking to nighttime. But it did help, otherwise he'd never have been able to sit through a meal with someone who knew him as well as Lucie did. She had always been, rather of necessity, the closest to him—for who could be expected to break into the charmed twin-ship of Kit and Pippa? And if her tone tonight was mild, her eyes were sharp.

Julien did much to carry the conversation, which tended to the general, such as the weather and the state of the roads and the scandalous behaviour of one of Elizabeth's women who had been discovered six months pregnant with no husband in sight. Stephen gave a silent sigh of relief when they rose to disband. One evening down. Only thirteen more to go without giving something away.

But Lucette knew how to choose her moments. As Julien started up the stairs of the tower, she lingered near her brother. He braced himself for whatever she meant to say—but not well enough.

"You have not asked about Carrie."

His vision swam and he swore he could hear the clash of arms and the screams of the dying, smell the copper tang of blood . . .

Lucette touched his arm, and Stephen flinched away as though she'd struck him. His voice was harsh. "What is there to ask? She has been left desolate because of my mistake. Because of me, Carrie is bereft. Because of me, Matthew has no father. If I thought asking after either of them would make it better, then I would ask. But the only service I can imagine they want from me is not to be reminded of my existence."

He felt Lucie watching him as he stalked away, and prayed that she would not follow. He could not swear he would not strike her if she did.

As Christmas approached at Carlow Castle, Finian Kavanaugh's splinter of the clan settled in to make winter bearable. Dampness made the cold go straight to the bones, but the imposing castle could at least keep out the harshest of the winds, and much could be mitigated with fires, braziers, tapestries to cover the walls, and layers of clothing. The castle had been bought by Finian from the English crown thirty years before, and its location gave it the now precarious position of being within reach of the Pale. But as the Kavanaughs had no plans for active lawbreaking or rebellion this winter, it was as well to be seen to be blameless in comfort.

Ailis Kavanaugh knew Carlow Castle as well as she knew any other place. Hers had been a peripatetic childhood; her most stable home had been the convent at which she'd been educated for several years in western Ireland (where the English policy of dissolution had encountered distinct opposition). She was glad enough to have been itinerant, if only because it meant she was free of that dangerous attachment to specific places that often clouded the judgment of men in staking their claims. As far as she was concerned, Ireland as a whole was her home, and it was for Ireland as a whole that she resented the invaders.

Four months into his third marriage, Finian Kavanaugh himself was newly sleek and satisfied, though Ailis suspected that had more to do with pride of possession than any overwhelming passion. No surprise—he was more than sixty and his new bride was not a figure to inspire rampant desire. Not that Ailis didn't like Maisie. Frankly, she was glad not to have competition as the most desirable female in the clan, and however small and unremarkable Maisie might be physically, she had a keen mind and cynical humour that Ailis appreciated.

She'd never had a female friendship. It was a bit of a shock to realize she might have stumbled into one without meaning to.

Two days before Christmas, a nondescript rider on a sturdy pony of the kind often found in Ireland's more mountainous regions rode into Carlow. Divesting himself of a muddy, well-patched woolen cloak, the upright, gray-haired figure of Father Byrne was revealed.

Ailis, as always in the last four years, met the Kavanaughs' household priest on equal footing with her uncle Finian. "Followed?" Finian asked.

Father Byrne snorted. "I was noted coming out of Wicklow. But even the English don't care to stir too far from their warm fires in December. They'll watch for me coming back. It's not as if they don't know I was coming here. They'll only move if they think I'm staying too long."

Waving him to a thickly padded settle, Finian took his own seat near the fire roaring in the medieval, five-foot-high fireplace and poured Father Byrne a drink from the table set to hand. Ailis sat straight-backed and sober where she could watch them both. It was always wise to watch Irishmen when drink was involved.

"And how are our guests?" Ailis asked the priest.

"Complaining. About the cold. The clouds. The rain. The poverty. The lack of cathedrals and church gold. God knows we need the Spanish. But if they don't learn to shut their mouths, some of our men might do it for them."

Ailis waved off that expected issue. "Work them all hard enough and both sides will be too tired to fight. We're most curious about how quiet their location has been kept. We know the English are aware of the vanished Spanish soldiers."

"Aware, but in disagreement as to the why," Finian corrected. "A fair number of the English think they simply miscounted. And with the blood Pelham and Dane shed at Carrigafoyle, no one can be absolutely certain that the supposed missing soldiers weren't among the slaughter victims. It was all set fire to after, so who's to say for sure?"

Ailis made an impatient noise; she and her uncle had been disagreeing about this for months. "All it takes is one canny, careful Englishman who doesn't trust to the easiest answer and has the wits to use his eyes and mind to undo all of that. But of course, we don't intend to keep the secret forever. We would simply prefer to keep the advantage of surprise on our side until summer. Can the Spanish be controlled in the Wicklow Mountains until then?"

"They'll be controlled," Byrne promised, directly to her. He was smart enough to realize that, however nontraditional, Ailis was the strategist of Clan Kavanaugh. It was a position she had wormed her way to with a combination of native talent and careful exploitation of the injuries done to her in Kilmallock. No one could ever doubt the purity of her enmity, and she had given enough good counsel in the last years to earn her place at Finian's side. And as his heir, more or less, whenever he died. That position she would have to fight for—and almost certainly she would have to finally choose the right Irish husband in order to hold onto it. But not just yet.

When talk of tactics for next summer had drifted into the laughter and stories of the two old men, Ailis left them to it and joined her daughter in the warmest part of the castle. This chamber was small and snug, low-ceilinged to keep in the heat, with heavy velvet curtains on the casement windows to add to the warmth. It was a luxury not found often in native Irish households, but the Kavanaughs had been fortunate in navigating the tricky political waters these last decades and had some of the English comforts to prove it.

And Finian had received a hefty dowry from Maisie's brother in

Edinburgh. Ailis suspected it was less that the brother valued his
sister and more as a means to get her out of Scotland and off his
hands with relative ease. If Maisie resented that fact, she never
showed it. She never showed anything except a determinedly cheerful nature and an ease with every member of the household, which
Ailis would never have expected.

But no one in the household was more taken with Mariota Sinclair Kavanaugh than Ailis's daughter, Liadan. The girl had claimed
Maisie as her own particular friend and companion from the first.
Tonight, Ailis found the two of them at a round table in the—for
lack of a better word—schoolroom, Maisie tutoring Liadan in the
science of bookkeeping. It might seem an odd choice for an eleven-
year-old, but Maisie herself was only fifteen and numbers and business and trade were in her blood. The Sinclairs of Edinburgh had
been one of the wealthiest merchant families of Scotland for the last
hundred years, and, female or not, Maisie had inherited the gifts of
her forbears. Ailis respected that, being herself an unusual female.

"Mama!" Liadan crowed. "Maisie says if I study hard I could be a
merchant like her when I grow up." Her daughter jumped up from
her chair, the child's enthusiasm not yet constrained by the demands
of young womanhood. Liadan had Ailis's own black hair and deep
blue-purple eyes, and showed promise of having her mother's height
as well. If there was anything of her father about Liadan, it was in the
contemptuous twist of her mouth when she was in a temper.

"Is Maisie a merchant?" Ailis asked mildly. "I thought she was
Uncle Finian's wife."

She repressed a smile when Liadan gave her a disdainful look that
was a copy of her own. Her words were also repeated from her
mother. "Being a wife is not an exclusive role."

"Well said," Maisie praised in her light voice that touched the
Irish Gaelic with an occasional Scots inflection. "Do you know what
exclusive means?"

Liadan said loftily, "It means I can do what I want, because I am
of Clan Kavanaugh."

"Close enough," Ailis said. "Go and see Bridey, pet. You've had enough numbers for tonight."

She took her daughter's seat and scanned the paper before her. "You really are teaching her to trade," she said to Maisie.

"Teaching her to stretch her mind, rather. At this age, it doesn't much matter how it's stretched, as long as she absorbs the tenets of how to learn. Then she can turn her mind to whatever she wishes in future."

"And is this your wish? Being married to a man four times your age? Being exiled to a backwater country far away from all you've known?"

Maisie's smile was all youth and openness. "No one in this world, man or woman, always gets everything the way they want when they want. A wise person takes to any circumstance with an open mind."

"Are you sure you don't want to become a military tactician?" Ailis laughed. "I think you'd do very well planning field maneuvers."

"I don't think battlefields are to my taste." Maisie, too, laughed. "Too dirty."

Only much later that night did Ailis suspect that she had been neatly deflected.

Christmas Day passed quietly in church service and subdued feasting. If Stephen had been capable of feeling glad, he would have been glad to have Lucie there for the feast. Left to himself, he wouldn't have known what to say or how to behave with his household and their families, but Lucie could be charming when she wished, and Julien never seemed to have any trouble talking to people. It made his own reticence barely noticeable, Stephen decided. He'd never been at Farleigh Castle for Christmas before, so it wasn't as though his people had any great expectations of what he would do.

In the days that followed, Stephen accepted Julien's offer to train with him and strengthen the left arm that had been broken. Julien was good, in an eccentric, street-fighting manner grounded in the essential principles, a style Stephen had not encountered before. He could also be demanding. "One has to know the rules before one can break them," Julien explained.

It was the second day of January, glassy cold and clear in the practice yard, when Stephen realized that, for the last half hour, his mind had been blessedly silent while his body twisted and lunged and broke many of the rules his father had taught him about fighting. He was not yet as adept at switching hands as Julien, but his broken arm no longer ached—or at least no more than the rest of him did after a demanding bout.

But in that very moment of noticing his quiet mind, a thought tumbled out clear and mocking: *This would have been a useful skill in Ireland.*

Stephen stumbled. Julien's sword came at him from the left and he parried it, but then he could hardly see and it didn't feel like he was in his own practice yard any longer, but in a landscape wasted beyond repair, and then there was the stink and taste of blood, so thick in his throat he gagged, and men were dying and women . . . not even women, really, just girls they were . . . and two boys who would never grow up . . . and he couldn't get to them to stop it, there were too many in his way . . .

He came back to himself trying to fight free of the men who held him back. His own men, he slowly realized, restraining him from attacking, not an enemy, but his sister's husband. Julien's sword pointed out and away at the ground with his hands spread wide as though approaching a spooked horse.

Julien was speaking. Just one word, over and over. "Stephen," he said softly. "Stephen."

Stephen met his eyes and forced his clenched hand to open and allow the sword to drop. Julien jerked his chin, and the men holding Stephen released him. "Stephen," Julien said warily once more.

But Stephen didn't stay to hear the rest. He bolted from the practice yard. It was a flight of another kind he made now, a flight from his senses, pursued by the cries of the dead, but even when he slammed shut the door to his chamber they wouldn't stop. He tried to pour wine into a glass but the bottle slipped from his hands and smashed on the floor.

He crouched instinctively to clean it up. But his hands seemed divorced from his thoughts. Instead of carefully picking up one shard at a time, his fingers clenched themselves around the broken glass. He could feel each prick, each edge, each jagged piece where it tore into his skin. And where it pierced his hands, there was an almost physical sense of relief. Like bedding a woman, he thought hazily, only pain rather than pleasure.

He loosed his hands, letting the shards fall, then picked up the longest, sharpest piece of glass he could find. Standing, he contemplated his arms, and imagined the relief of one long cut rather than dozens of small pricks. He breathed in . . .

And from behind him, a strong hand clamped onto his wrist.

"Don't," Julien said quietly.

They held like that for a seeming eternity.

"Don't," Julien repeated.

Stephen dropped the glass. Julien let go and Stephen swung round to face him. "Aren't you going to ask me what the hell I think I'm doing?" At least the interruption had served to subdue the noise in his head.

"I know what you were doing. Having spent weeks drinking to dull the pain, that remedy has begun to lose its power. At the same time, you have your sister—who knows and loves you too well—living entirely too close and with entirely too much natural curiosity. And so the pain and guilt are beginning to spill out of the cracks in your control and maybe, you think, just maybe if you widen those cracks in your very skin, the pain and guilt will pour out enough to give you relief and let you breathe."

Stephen turned his back. He would not let Julien get to him. No one could get to him.

But Julien kept talking. "I understand your guilt—"

"Every leader loses men," Stephen interrupted sharply. "Guilt is the price of leadership."

"That's not why you feel guilty. This is not the expected guilt of a man who has lost those under his command. This is the corrosive, soul-destroying guilt of absolute personal failure. I know the look and feel of it, believe me. Drinking won't cure it. Neither will self-destruction. There are only two remedies I know of. The second remedy is appropriate vengeance."

Despite himself, Stephen asked, "And what is the first remedy?"

"Telling the truth of what happened."

"Talking won't change things."

"It might change you."

Stephen snorted. "I don't need to be changed."

"You don't *deserve* to be changed—that's what you mean. Stephen, I spent eight long years believing that of myself. But it was all based on a lie. If talking won't change things, neither will punishing yourself."

Even with his back turned, Stephen supposed that Julien could read the lines of his shoulders and knew how close he was to tears. He had not cried for any of it. He would not start now.

"Stephen, why did you miss the attack on your camp?"

"It was the middle of the night!"

"But you still think it's your fault," Julien noted, not without compassion.

"It's always the commander's fault."

"Where were you when they came?"

"In my tent. I'd been asleep." It was like the words wanted to come out despite his fighting it. Maybe he was just too tired to fight it any longer.

"Had you set up guards and watches through the night?" Julien demanded.

"Of course."

"Then why do you feel guilty for being in bed? Even a commander must sleep."

Stephen had no idea what he was going to say until he said it. "My father wouldn't have been there."

"In bed? Look, I'm as awed by your father as any man living, believe me, but despite that I'm quite sure the man sleeps. Even in the field."

"He would not have been there," Stephen repeated, each word like a hammer to his heart.

A long, thoughtful silence . . .

Then, as kindly as he'd ever spoken before, Julien asked, "Stephen, who else was in your bed?"

3 January 1582

Mother,

Julien has finally broken through to Stephen. He has not even told me the whole of it, and although I agree that it would be best for Stephen to share as and when he chooses, I'll admit to being slightly put out at being on the outside. In the last twenty-four hours Stephen has eaten more than he had in the previous ten days and he is sleeping without too much wine. So Julien reports. Yes, I have lent my husband to my brother even at nights—Julien stays on a pallet bed to ensure Stephen is not lost in the dark.

This is why we came. And here we will stay as long as Stephen wants us. Until spring, perhaps? Julien thinks it might be wise. I shall try and get Stephen home after that.

Lucette

NINE

When Cardinal Granvelle told him who would be heading the spring visit from England, Philip of Spain had to blink several times before he could speak. "The Duke of Exeter himself? Are you certain?"

"Very certain. It appears the Princess of Wales requested that the delegation include her close friends, Christopher and Philippa Courtenay. Lord Exeter seems to think his personal presence is required to ensure his children's safety."

"To be fair," Philip noted drily, "his children were caught in the Nightingale web. I don't suppose he trusts my new wife in the slightest. Let them come—but it will make for some interesting dynamics between us all."

That was an understatement. The Nightingale Plot, which ended with Mary Stuart's release from her English prison, had also involved a violent hostage situation at the Courtenay home of Wynfield Mote. Philip did not imagine that Dominic Courtenay would have forgotten. He did not know the Duke of Exeter well—he doubted anyone other than his family and Elizabeth knew him well—but Philip respected him for an experienced soldier and an honest man. They would have to be extremely careful while the Courtenays were in Spain not to reveal their Irish plans.

Which meant keeping Mary on a tight leash. When Philip told her that the Courtenays would be chief among the visiting English party, his wife sneered as only a queen can. "As long as it is not Stephen Courtenay. I could not bear to be reminded of his treachery."

Philip thought that an overreaction. The treachery of reporting on an imprisoned queen's behaviour and movements to her captor? Stephen Courtenay was English—what had Mary expected? But Philip simply made noncommittal noises she could interpret as agreement if she chose.

Fortunately, Mary's satisfaction at having produced two princes who continued each week to thrive, and neither of whom showed any incipient signs of the Hapsburg jaw, meant that she was more easily deflected from matters of state. As long as he assured her that Ireland was never far from his mind, she seemed content not to know the details.

Philip himself had designed much of the plan that, thus far, was proceeding without incident. Part one had been the landing of Spanish soldiers at Carrigafoyle. Because not every soldier who landed had remained there—one hundred well-trained and well-equipped men marched away into the interior well in advance of the fighting and were now cloistered in the impassable Wicklow Mountains.

In the spring, the Irish clans would begin to send out strike forces against English targets. While they kept the English busy riding hither and yon to deal with their gallowglass—the hired soldiers who were the backbone of the disorganized Irish military—the Spanish would march to the relief of Askeaton. Gerald FitzGerald, Earl of Desmond, had been holed up in his last remaining stronghold for many long months now. The Spanish troops would free him up to venture beyond reach of Askeaton and once more harry the west of Munster.

And a year from now, just before next winter closed the seas, at a time when Elizabeth would have difficulty finding more men to send after a season's campaigning, Spanish ships would land troops in force. With five thousand Spanish troops, the Irish rebels would be able to press against the English as never before. Drive them back into the Pale, perhaps all the way to Dublin. Manage to lay hands on one or two of Elizabeth's loyal earls—Thomas Butler, for choice— and the initiative would swing all the way to the Catholics.

And as figurehead of the Catholic peoples? The second son of their Most Catholic Majesties, Philip and Mary. Their firstborn, Prince Charles, would one day follow his father as King of Spain. But by the time the four-month-old twins were talking, Philip intended to give Prince Alexander a country of his own to rule as well.

It was the longest, coldest, hardest winter of Stephen Courtenay's life, but by the time the first flowers began to bud, he had been rebuilt. Not to who he was before, for that innocence could never be reclaimed, but as someone who could cope without strong drink. Someone who could sleep most nights. Someone darker, yes, but also stronger.

Lucette and Julien remained until late March. He wasn't sure what Lucie did with all her time—she had always been busy with books and ledgers and equations and long letters back and forth with scholars—but Julien made it his business to mold Stephen into a fighter of his own kind. Quick, unconventional, solitary. The lessons bled into more than just his weapons training. Julien had operated for eight years in enemy territory—his adversaries might have been his fellow Frenchmen, but they would have killed him in a heartbeat if they'd known what he was doing—and he couldn't help but teach Stephen how to rely on himself, how to trust his instincts for peril, how to hold onto the essence of who he was through the masks of secrecy and lies.

Only near the end did Stephen acknowledge what he was training for.

The day before Lucette's departure, she claimed her brother for a stroll through the box-hedge garden. Between the squares of evergreen, bright crocuses and sunny narcissus braved the chilly air. Stephen allowed Lucette to take his arm and waited for her to say what she'd kept inside all winter.

He expected questions or gentle reproofs or inquiries as to his future. Instead, she said, "I was thinking about the time you and I ran away from home. Do you remember?"

For the first time since Ireland, laughter bubbled out of Stephen. He remembered, all right. They had taken their ponies from the Tiverton stable and headed northeast. For some reason, lost to the mists of time, their parents had gone to Wynfield Mote without them and Lucette decided to take matters into her own hands.

"It was your fault," Stephen said, recalling. "I was simply following my grown-up sister."

"I was ten," Lucette pointed out caustically.

"To an eight-year-old, that's very grown up. I suppose it's surprising we got as far as we did."

"Do you think so? I think we were humoured. Harrington followed us, Stephen, without hurting our pride by letting us know it. He let us ride for three hours and only when it began to rain did he intervene to bring us back."

Stephen's breath caught in his throat at Harrington's name. But after a moment he realized it did not hurt as bitterly as he'd braced for. There was pain, yes, but mellowed by memories of love and care. Lucette let him walk in silence for a time, her fingers tightening a little on his arm.

At last Stephen said, "Thank you, Lucie. I can't imagine you wanted to spend your first winter with your husband stuck out here."

"Make it worth my while, Stephen. Don't slip back, don't hide, don't run away. Make the amends you feel necessary, and then move on. Your life is not wholly your own; it belongs to those who love you as well. Do you hear me?"

Stephen stopped walking and turned his sister to face him. She looked fierce and vulnerable at the same time, with those blue eyes that she alone of the Courtenays possessed. "Lucie," he said softly. "I swear that I will not give you cause to save me again." Then he hugged her.

Lucette and Julien departed the next day. One week later, Stephen also left Farleigh Hungerford. He packed thoughtfully but not extravagantly. He held long meetings with his steward setting forth plans and then delegating to him responsibility for at least a year. Then he traveled to London.

His family was at Whitehall. He met with his parents first, alone, and told them the whole of what had happened in Ireland—from the massacre at Carrigafoyle, to the dispute over the prisoners, to the slaughter near Kilkenny. He told them where he'd been and with whom and that Harrington's last words to him were a warning against misbehaviour.

When he was finished, his mother said, "When you are ready, it is something you should tell Carrie. For your own sake, as much as hers."

His father said, "You are not the first man, nor the last, to take to bed the wrong woman at the wrong time. Try not to do it again."

Stephen could not imagine ever wanting to take any woman to bed again, and wondered if he'd been permanently scarred by the bloodshed. With his mother looking at him, now was not the time to worry about it.

And then his father asked the pertinent question, the one to which Stephen had taken far too long to turn his attention. "Who do you think set the gallowglass on your prisoners?"

For that was the operative point, was it not? Any Irish force, mercenary or not, might gladly have attacked an English force too far from its own lines. Killing English soldiers was what they did. But prisoners? Irish women and boys? Even in the dark, a gallowglass force was too well-trained not to at least have hesitated at the women. But they hadn't. Indeed, in Stephen's memory, it seemed they headed straight for the larger tents, as if they knew who was housed there.

But it was not his father he wanted to discuss the matter with. Not that his father couldn't be helpful, but he was on his way shortly to Spain with Kit and Pippa. And Stephen knew this was his own matter to deal with. No more worrying about how he appeared to others. No more fears that he wouldn't live up to expectations. Time to be his own man. *Appropriate vengeance,* Julien had advised. For that, he needed to be in Ireland.

So the morning after half of his family headed to Portsmouth, Stephen sat down for a private conversation with Francis Walsingham. Not in his role as Elizabeth's Lord Secretary, but as the queen's intelligencer. Long before Elizabeth had come to the throne, Walsingham had been her man, ensuring that she always had all the information necessary to run her kingdom and protect her life.

Stephen had worked peripherally and briefly for Walsingham in the spring and summer of 1580, dancing attendance on Mary Stuart while keeping eyes and ears open for any mention of the Nightingale Plot. He'd gained the Scots queen's trust, and some of her secrets, but not enough to stop the plot in its tracks. Still, Walsingham seemed to think Stephen was worth cultivating, as he'd sent him to Ireland last summer with a watching brief to pay attention for any mention of the Kavanaugh clan.

When Stephen was shown into Walsingham's study, neither man wasted time. "What can I do for you, Lord Somerset?" the Lord Secretary asked.

"Send me back to Ireland."

"Her Majesty is always grateful for soldiers—"

"Not as a soldier."

"Then in what role? Your name is rather . . . restrictive. What use could the Earl of Somerset be in Ireland if not fighting?"

"You have men of many names and identities and stories working for you—let me be one of those. Under any name you choose."

Walsingham steepled his fingers, eyes that were as black as his clothes fixed and cautious. "To what end?"

"To the end of stopping the fighting in Ireland. If Philip and Mary gain serious hold there, Ireland will drown in blood. Even more than it already has. And Mary will never cease troubling the Spanish king to aid the rebels. I suspect that, for both of them, pride is at stake. And I know about the hundred missing Spanish troops from last summer."

With a deep sigh, Walsingham leaned back in his chair. "Do you remember the name Kavanaugh?"

"I do. The splintered clan, one faction led by Finian Kavanaugh. With the aid of his unexpectedly canny niece, they have orchestrated several victories in Ireland."

"Correct. Matters in that direction are somewhat . . . unsettled at present. Finian Kavanaugh died last month, leaving his clan under the tenuous hold of his niece. Finian also left an even younger widow—the only granddaughter of William Sinclair."

Stephen cast through his mind. "Edinburgh. The merchant family."

"The extraordinarily clever and influential and wealthy merchant family. William Sinclair's estate at his death was valued at five times the queen's personal wealth."

Stephen blinked. "How much of it came to the girl? Wasn't there some question about the settlements . . ." Lucie would know, or Pippa. That was always the sort of thing his sisters knew.

"Sinclair also left a single grandson, who is titular head of the merchant concerns. A young man of dubious reputation and worse financial sense. He's being restrained as much as possible by the board of the company. But they couldn't stop him auctioning off his sister to an Irish clan chief at a cut-rate price."

"But now you fear some of that merchant wealth might find its way to the Kavanaughs. Is the girl pregnant?"

"Does not appear to be. But she has made no move to return to

Scotland. Perhaps only because she is estranged from her brother, or would prefer to stay out of his hands and any plans for another bargain marriage. But perhaps not."

Stephen pondered. "A household and clan headed by two women. Two young women. That's where you want me?"

"You did well in Mary Stuart's household." Meaning Stephen had used his looks and his manners to ingratiate himself with the former Scots queen.

"Neither of these women are likely to be charmed by an Englishman. I can hide my name—I can't hide my tongue or country of birth."

Walsingham smiled, a singularly disconcerting sight. "There are ways around that. If you don't mind a little pain?"

Stephen gave a wolfish grin in return. "I would expect no less of Ireland."

22 April 1582

My dear Lucie,

I had my suspicions when I saw how many trunks Father loaded for our travels to Spain. I kept waiting for someone to say something . . . but it seems the secret was well kept until now. When it is too late for a furious queen to interfere.

Mother is coming to Spain with us.

She wrote four letters tonight, carefully sealed with her signature star badge, and gave them into the hands of Lord Burghley's son, Robert Cecil, who rode with us to Portsmouth. We have been here two nights, but the weather is perfect and we set sail tomorrow morning in the great galley built during the days of the last king, the Elizabeth Rose. *The Duke and Duchess of Exeter, and their two younger children—I wonder what the Spanish king will make of that. I wouldn't put it past Mother to task Philip to his face with taking you and Anabel hostage at Wynfield Mote.*

Poor Robert Cecil. He was no match for Mother. She smiled at him warmly and said, "Don't fret—no one will have expected this. Just deliver my letters."

One for you, of course, and one for Stephen. One for Carrie at Wynfield Mote . . . and one for the queen. It is that last one I wish I could read!

Pippa

22 April 1582

Dear Elizabeth,

Yes, I address you as my friend rather than my queen. Because my friend will understand why I am doing this rather better than the queen will. You have always been prone to quick offense, Elizabeth, but you know me too well to let resentment linger.

I did not ask your permission to go to Spain because I knew you would not give it. But I made a vow all those years ago, when I returned from France and then learned Dominic had survived. I vowed that I would never again cross the sea without him. And he feels the same. I know your arguments—that we should not trust so many of our family to a single ship, that illness could lay waste to all of us . . . I don't care. Where Dominic goes, I go, at least when it involves oceans and months of separation.

We will be fine! I promise to hold my tongue in front of Philip and Mary—though if I am given a private audience with the Scots queen, I may possibly find a few things to say. Somehow, I do not think you would mind that.

Promise me that, if anything does happen to us against my blithe belief in my indestructibility, that you will care for my Lucette and Stephen. As I have always cared for your Anabel.

Your most loving, impetuous friend,
Minuette Courtenay

TEN

The last thing Stephen did before abandoning his name and title in favour of going undercover to Ireland was to visit Wynfield Mote. It looked its best in the late April sun, showing its outer face of mellow stone to the world. But the true beauty of Wynfield was hidden—it only revealed itself fully once one crossed the moat and passed through the gatehouse. The house had been rebuilt to its original medieval design, around a central courtyard, and as he dismounted, Carrie appeared at the entrance to the hall.

Stephen swallowed once, then handed over his horse to a waiting groom and went straight to Carrie. He didn't quite know how he was going to greet her—With formality? Begging forgiveness at her feet?—but she took the matter into her own hands. As he reached the top of the steps, she pulled him into an embrace. He might have been a child again, going to Carrie for both comfort and dry wisdom. For only the second time since Kilkenny, Stephen felt the relief of tears.

Her own eyes were damp when she dropped her arms, but her expression was a familiar mix of affection and forbearance.

"It took you long enough," she said tartly. "I nearly came to Farleigh Hungerford myself to shake you out of it."

"Out of what?"

"Out of feeling sorry for yourself."

"That wasn't . . . I didn't mean . . ." he stuttered.

"Hush, now." She put a hand to his cheek and smiled. "Come inside and rest. You can tell me all about it over food."

As when he was a child, Stephen did precisely as Carrie said. He rested and changed and joined her in the painted breakfast chamber for a meal of spinach pie and toasted cheese. And then he told her all of it—not even leaving out Roisin and his own poor judgment—and when he was finished, they sat in silence for some minutes.

"And so," she said finally. "Have you spent all this time away afraid to ask for my forgiveness, Stephen?"

"I . . . yes, I suppose I have."

"Then you are a fool, for I would have offered it long since. Even supposing it were a matter for forgiveness, which it is not. It sounds to me as though it was simply the fortunes of war. And those are not your responsibility."

He drew a deep breath and let it out, a little shakily. "Thank you, Carrie."

"Now that we've settled that—you are leaving England for a time."

"I am."

"Somewhere you don't want people asking questions about. Well, I won't ask, either. I will only say to be careful. It would be poor repayment of my husband's life to lose yours in the bargain. Do you hear me?"

Stephen smiled, and it was the truest smile he'd offered in almost a year. "I hear you. I will come back, Carrie."

She sniffed. "See that you do."

———

When Elizabeth learned that Minuette had boarded the ship for Spain with her family, she was incandescent with rage. If she could have gotten her hands on any member of that rebellious, proud family, she might well have locked them up in the Tower purely for spite. But Lucette and Stephen were well out of her reach, and so, as usual, it was Walsingham and Burghley who bore the brunt of her temper.

"Damned proud woman will ruin everything!" Elizabeth stalked the perimeter of her blue-and-silver privy chamber, clenching her hands to keep from hurling various breakables to the floor. "And how Philip and Mary will mock that I cannot even control one woman! If Minuette's plan was to fatally weaken me abroad, then she has already succeeded beyond her wildest dreams."

Only when her anger had reduced itself to a low simmer did Lord Burghley venture to say, "Lady Exeter is strong-minded but not stupid. She will do nothing to weaken you. I daresay she was not thinking of you at all."

"Of course not! She was thinking of her precious Dominic and how she could not bear to be separated—that woman could not live a day on her own if required to!" Even as she shouted, Elizabeth knew she was being unfair. Minuette was highly capable of living on her own if required. *Why do I resent her so much when I don't have to?* Elizabeth asked herself. *It is not Minuette's fault that I am queen.*

Although, come to think of it, if Minuette had only done William's bidding and married him, then it would be Minuette with the crown, and Elizabeth herself would be . . . elsewhere.

Fine. Minuette had taken advantage of their friendship, and she planned to lecture her friend severely when she returned, but Burghley was right. Minuette would make a success of this visit. Truth be told, probably rather more successful than if Dominic were leading it alone. Dominic did not do gracious diplomacy. Minuette would smooth his edges and, with the twins, ensure that Philip was reassured as to his daughter's state of mind.

Speaking of which . . . "The Duc d'Anjou is committed?"

"He is," Walsingham answered gravely. He was opposed to any consideration of a French marriage for Anabel. "He will sail before month's end and stay 'as long as is amenable to Her Royal Highness.'"

"Charming, if disingenuous. It is my pleasure he must watch out for. Being French, I suppose he can make himself agreeable to whomever he must."

"What of Scotland?" Walsingham probed.

"There's no use extending an invitation to James—they would never let him come in person. The last monarch who left Scotland spent twelve years imprisoned, and pity for us it wasn't longer. They will never risk it."

"And you will not agree to Princess Anne going north?"

"To Scotland? Absolutely not. It is for James to court her. He needs us far more than we need him. I will not send my daughter traipsing to Scotland to beg for a husband."

"They are willing to send Esmé Stewart in place of James. He is Duke of Lennox now, and his credentials are impeccable."

"And he grew up in France—and also he is Catholic," Elizabeth countered. "Still, I hear that he is engaging and very good-looking. Perhaps it's as well he is already married or Anabel might have her head turned by a completely unsuitable man. But as he is King James's favourite, we must take it as the compliment it's meant to be and do our best to welcome him. Arrange it, Burghley."

"For after Anjou's departure?"

"It wouldn't hurt them to overlap a little. Does Anjou know Stewart from his years in France? Even if not, they will no doubt share acquaintances. Let each man size up the competition. It will be entertaining."

Burghley did not look convinced. But he had long ago learned when to argue and when to hold his peace. On the subject of eligible men courting Anabel rather than Elizabeth, he wisely held his peace.

DIARY OF MINUETTE COURTENAY

> 24 April 1582
> At Sea

There have been moments these last two days when I have nearly regretted my rash insistence on accompanying Dominic. It has been some years since last I crossed the sea and I am not as easy with it as I once was. But never mind, what is a little discomfort in the cause of my family and my queen?

There have been clouds, but the captain is confident we will sail into the Bay of Biscay tomorrow.

> 25 April 1582
> Bilbao, Spain

We landed—and none too soon, as we were chased by high winds and rain the fourteen miles from the Bay of Biscay to this merchant city grown wealthy from its port. We were met by a dozen men and two women of King Philip's personal household and they managed to accept my unexpected appearance with aplomb, though I gather there was some concern that two women courtiers would not be sufficient. I assured them neither Pippa nor myself are accustomed to constant attendance and we could keep each other company just as well.

They smiled their lovely, unreadable smiles beneath their serene black eyes, and have not left us alone for a moment until bedtime. I suppose it is to be expected. They will be watching for our unspoken messages as well as our words.

I can play that game, for I was taught it by more than one master.

30 April 1582
Valladolid, Spain

I must say that King Philip has extended himself and his country to show its best face. We have ridden horses with the most exquisite lines and perfect gaits, we have feasted each night in elaborately decorated homes and courtyards that serve as way stations from the north coast, and everywhere we see beautiful people and gorgeous churches.

After all my lifetime, there is still a faint call in my blood for the faith of my mother. For all her friendship with Anne Boleyn, Marie Hilaire Wyatt never abandoned the Latin rituals. I can dimly recall hearing her recite the rosary, fingers clicking on the jet beads. I have that rosary still, though I myself have never prayed it.

And when I see the plethora of priests and the sternness of their countenances and obvious discomfort with our—one might infer, contaminating—presence in Spain, I am grateful for England's precarious balance between old and new. For the most part, our Spanish attendants have refrained from conversation of a religious nature. Though Pippa says that one of the women asked her if Princess Anne ever reads the religious books the Spanish priests send her through her father.

Pippa wisely did not tell her the truth.

Of the children, it is Kit who is surprisingly most at ease. I am accustomed to Pippa being the one to lead the way among others, to subtly show her brother how to behave in new situations. But Kit has grown up when I wasn't looking. Every now and then I catch a glimpse of Dominic in his expressions. Of course Kit could not stay young and carefree forever, but I am disquieted at this new intensity.

And, uncharacteristically, I am almost afraid to ask him why.

3 May 1582
Torrelodones, Spain

Tomorrow we enter Madrid, where King Philip and Queen Mary await us at the Royal Alcazar. Considering the state of luxury in which we have thus far traveled, I can only imagine the beauties that await us.

Fortunately, we are English. We are not easily seduced by beauty.

From the moment they'd landed near Bilbao, Kit had been making notes of the many things he wanted to tell Anabel. At night he penned disjointed phrases and descriptions and partial stories to serve as an aid to his memory when he could sit with her in future and paint her a vivid picture of her father's homeland.

It was almost painful, to be experiencing all this while knowing that Anabel herself never could. She would never witness the colours and sounds and tastes of the country that, by blood, was half hers. Did she feel the loss of it? Kit wondered. Beneath the English culture and education, were there strains that called to her in whiffs of incense and whispers of chants and hints of exotic spices? Was there a seductive Spanish beauty beneath the impeccable red-haired princess? He imagined being in Spain with Anabel, and then he couldn't bear to imagine it. Instead he took his careful notes so that he could share it with her later as best he could.

It was illuminating traveling overseas with his parents. He was so accustomed to being with them at Wynfield or Tiverton or the English court that he hadn't realized there might be new things to learn about his parents elsewhere. But there were, if not all of them entirely surprising. Dominic traveled like a soldier: every moment of the day accounted for beforehand and always alert to subtle shifts in behaviour or surroundings. Kit didn't know if his father truly expected a physical attack on Spanish soil, but if it came, he would certainly be prepared.

Not that he was hostile. Just, as always, contained. Quiet. Remote, even harsh, one might think—if one didn't consider how he behaved with his wife. Again, Kit was now of an age to appreciate how unusual his parents' marriage truly was. The Spanish, even more so than the English, were rigid in their hierarchies and their expectations of behaviour from men and women. Their women—especially the most aristocratic—almost seemed to inhabit a different, parallel world to that of the men. Kit could only suppose Pippa would be paying attention to those things he could not by virtue of his sex.

Not that one or two Spanish women along their route to Madrid hadn't offered to pay him rather closer attention, but Kit would have said no simply because he was here on the business of queen and court even if he hadn't been traveling with his parents. Also, how could he make an accurate report to Anabel if he left out something as significant as his first . . . He was uncomfortable phrasing it even in his own head. Put it this way—he didn't intend his first woman to be one who couldn't even understand what he said in his native tongue.

He hadn't set out to reach the age of twenty a virgin. He hadn't really thought about it at all. Well, no, that was hardly right. Of course he thought about it. He wasn't maimed or dead. And he had some experience. Just not *the* experience. Stephen, Kit knew, had somehow crossed that line without any great soul-searching that he was aware of. Shouldn't it have been the older, responsible, perfect brother who kept himself pure, and the younger, charming, reckless brother who behaved badly?

Only in the last year had Kit sometimes dreamed of a specific woman. The fact that the woman was Anabel might, he knew, have some bearing on his present state of chastity. But he refused to consider that puzzle deeply, because it could not possibly end well. He would simply have to get over it at some point.

Just not on this visit to Spain.

Taken in all, Kit's mind and senses were already overflowing with impressions and emotions by the time they reached Madrid. Philip had moved his court from Toledo to Madrid twenty years before, and the city's architecture was a mix of foreign influences and the restrained aesthetic of Catholic Spain. The gray slate spires and red brick of the buildings around Plaza Mayor were distinctly, unmistakably, Spanish.

The English party entered the city with a guard wearing the royal badge with its three crowns—for Castile, Aragon, and Portugal—and its Latin motto, *Non Sufficit Orbis*—"The World Is Not Enough." That motto encapsulated all that most worried England about Spain, for it meant the Spanish made decisions based on a certitude of faith that overrode the autonomy of even its own people. Hence the Inquisition, in force in Spain for nearly a hundred years now, whose sole purpose was to protect the purity of the Catholic faith—even at the cost of destroying its own citizens.

Although their attendants had tried to put Kit next to his father near the front of the line, his parents had subtly resisted the segregation. They rode together, beautifully paired, with Kit and Pippa matched behind them. Kit knew they were an attractive family, though it would have been better to have Stephen and Lucie to complete the look—three dark-haired, three golden—as though they were chess pieces perfectly balanced.

Then Pippa turned her head toward him and Kit amended the thought. Almost balanced—with only Pippa's streak of black hair framing her face to disrupt the match.

The Royal Alcazar of Madrid had once been a Moorish fort, built seven hundred years ago on a high point to overlook the Manzanares River. As they approached, Kit could see the semicircular turrets along one facade of the palace that were likely Muslim remnants from the ancient fort. The newly built Tower of Gold dominated the horizon with the same slate roof as elsewhere in the city; all unlike anything in Britain that Kit felt a rush of pure adventure.

That rush was tempered the moment they rode into the courtyard of the King and were met by two regal figures.

Philip, King of Spain and all its imperial holdings beyond the seas, stood at the top of a short flight of steps, clothed in his typical rich but somber attire. One would think that in a country much warmer than England, black would not be the fabric of choice.

Two steps below Philip—thus equalizing their heights—stood Mary Stuart, a rare triple queen. Infant Queen of Scotland, briefly Queen Consort of France, and now through another marriage Queen of Spain. She was tall enough to carry the extra weight of age and motherhood with elegance, her hair a darker version of Queen Elizabeth's red-gold. Mary Stuart wore a Spanish-style gown of rich brown thickly embroidered with gold thread and had a fortune of rubies around her neck. Kit had met her only once before—two summers ago, when he spent several impatient, awful days in her company as they rode from her prison at Tutbury to the French ship that spirited her out of England. Seeing her here, triumphant after her blithe disregard of Anabel's life—not to mention that of Kit's older sister—made him straighten, and the frisson he felt this time was not excitement, but fear.

There was so very much at stake in all this delicate web of personal and familial relationships. He would not fail Anabel or England by letting his dislike get the better of his behaviour.

He felt a hand slide into his and almost smiled in relief as Pippa twined their fingers together. A quick glance to his twin, an even quicker wink, and then the two moved behind their parents as they were presented to the royal couple.

Kit had met the Spanish king many times before—as recently as two summers ago—but always in England, where Philip was little more than the barely tolerated husband of the ruling queen. Meeting King Philip in his own palace, in his own capital city—with another than Elizabeth at his side—was a much more intimidating experience.

"Lady Exeter," Philip said, coming down the steps in a show of friendliness. If initially nonplussed by news of her unexpected arrival on his shores, he'd clearly had time to accommodate the thought. "What an unlooked-for pleasure! I hardly dared dream that you would grace my humble alcazar."

Humble, Kit thought cynically. Right. Though alcazar was the Moorish word for fort, it was centuries ago and plenty of gold spent since this had been anything but a palace. The courtyard they stood in was porticoed with gothic arches, and the May sun, so much warmer in Spain than England, picked out the lines and shadows of the carved stone frieze. A riot of vivid flowers tumbled out of planters and against pillars.

Philip welcomed Dominic with less open friendliness, but what Kit perceived as genuine respect. Though that might only be his own filial pride for a father he was beginning to think he could be a little bit like if he tried.

The Spanish king was less wary with Kit and Pippa, and promised he would spend time in the days to come pressing them for every detail they could share of his daughter.

Then came Mary Stuart. From what little he knew of her personally, Kit was somewhat surprised that the queen had managed to keep still and hold her tongue this long. Was she regretting having married a king? Her first husband had been Dauphin—and then King—of France, but she had only been a girl then, and was widowed almost as quickly. Her next two husbands had been her own subjects. Now once more, Mary was not simply a queen by birth but also by marriage. Surely that had only increased her sense of importance?

What he had not experienced during those tense days riding to the coast two years ago was Mary's famous glamour. It was turned full force on them now. She allowed Dominic to touch her hand with his own, though Kit thought she was disappointed that he didn't kiss it. Minuette she did not quite embrace; his mother met Mary's wide smile with one of her own. Were they *both* false smiles?

"Lady Exeter, you look hardly older than when we met in France all those years ago."

"Your Majesty is as royal as ever." Kit had never heard that tone from his mother. It could have matched Queen Elizabeth for its ability to cut glass.

"Of course, none of us are as young as we once were. Your own twins are quite grown." Mary moved to Kit and Pippa. Kit did not dare refuse to kiss her hand as his father had, but nor could he smile like his mother.

Mary seemed not to notice, for she was still speaking to Minuette. "Though, God be good, I have proved young enough to bring twins of my own into the world. A great gift."

And a subtle taunt, to the absent English queen who had been divorced half for her religion and half for her age and inability to bear Philip further children.

"I cannot wait for you to meet my sons," Mary finished triumphantly, thus underscoring her victory. Where Elizabeth had given Philip only a daughter, Mary had given him two perfect male heirs.

Kit had a flash of understanding in that moment, for if Mary were so assured of her triumph, why did she have to underscore it so carefully? No, as far as Mary Stuart was concerned, the battle between the two queens was not over. It had, perhaps, scarcely begun.

Stephen's return to Ireland was effected under much different circumstances than his first visit. Rather than landing in Waterford in open daylight, his men marching serious and disciplined through the English-held town, he came ashore alone out of a fishing boat and was met by a rather dubious character whose speech was nearly unintelligible but who led him straightaway to a small farm.

Where, incongruously, awaited Thomas Butler, Earl of Ormond.

The older earl, dressed inconspicuously beneath a cloak of rough homespun, surveyed Stephen critically from head to foot. "Well, you look better than when last I laid eyes on you. Sure you want to do this? Ireland didn't treat you so well the last time."

"That's precisely why I'm back. To reset the balance."

"Better you than me," Ormond grunted. "Don't know why Walsingham's taking such a risk."

"Because I asked him."

"You know, son, once you're in—that's it. You're on your own. No visits, no messages direct . . . we can't risk blowing your cover."

"I'm quite clear on that, yes. Walsingham went into detail."

Ormond did not smile at the, admittedly weak, jest. "Does your father know the details as well?"

"It's none of his business—or yours."

That did wring a smile from Ormond. "And here I thought you were nothing like your little brother." He rubbed the back of his neck, arms strong and thick. Ormond was a working earl, as Stephen thought of it. A man of action more comfortable with his men than paying court in softer surroundings. Finally, Ormond nodded. "Fine. You're off at dawn to meet up with Walsingham's contact. Don't ask me who it is—I don't know. Until dawn, keep your head down in here."

After an uncomfortable night in the straw, the guide roused Stephen at dawn. Their journey served as a physical progression into his new role. With each mile his title and privileges receded further, until Stephen Courtenay began to seem like an entirely different person. The last time he rode across this landscape, he had been in command, living on the edge of his nerves with the responsibility of prisoners and soldiers. He felt those memories reaching for him— the anxiety and panic threatening to undo his hard-won control— and kept it all at bay by reciting the Catholic prayers he had labored to learn as cover for his new identity.

The guide left him finally in a crofter's hut a mile up a hill off the rough track that served as a road. Stephen hoped his new contact would make it to him before he finished the last of the bread— nothing in the landscape promised easy access to food.

The contact did make it before the end of the bread, but barely. A day and a half after Stephen arrived at the hut, a man strode up the hill leading a shaggy pony.

In educated English with a hint of Irish melody beneath it, the man greeted him by his new name. "Stephen Wyatt, is it?"

Wyatt had been his mother's father, a name less laden with aristocratic Norman overtones than Courtenay. Jonathan Wyatt had been a scholar and gentleman farmer, of no particular account or note, ideal for Stephen's cover.

The man, who was younger than he'd at first looked, said, "I'm Peter Martin."

"Directly from England?" Stephen asked.

"From France, most recently. I spent two years at the English College in Douai, but stopped short of taking orders."

The seminary whose primary purpose was training men to go undercover to England to, first, succor English Catholics and, second, topple Queen Elizabeth. Though Stephen knew Walsingham had spies everywhere, just the name of the place made his hands tense. "Right," he said suspiciously.

Martin read his suspicion rightly and gave a fleeting, grim smile. "I report to Walsingham, same as you. I don't suppose either one of us cares to explain why—and that's the last time his name will be spoken between us."

"Right." Stephen relaxed slightly.

Tethering the pony, which bore light packs, Martin said, "We'll leave in the morning. A quick meal now, while I give you the layout of the household and what to expect and to ensure our stories match. And then I'm going to beat you."

It was Walsingham's idea: Stephen as an English deserter, a gentleman's bastard with no love for English authority and a liking for an Irish lass who'd been killed (it was easy to slide his memories of Roisin into that) ... in short, an Englishman who'd opened his mouth once too often and was beaten and flung out to starve in the wastelands of Ireland for trying to help the locals. Peter Martin would bear witness to the story.

But none of it would matter if Stephen's body didn't bear the marks of his supposed insubordination.

"Just try to avoid the arm they broke last time I was in Ireland," he told Peter resignedly. "And if you have to kick me, there are some areas I'd prefer you avoid."

After all, there might come a day when the thought of taking a woman to bed filled him with something other than guilt and grief.

ELEVEN

By mid-May the Kavanaughs had moved from Carlow to Cahir Castle, farther west. Cahir had the distinction of being built on an island in the River Suir. Almost a peninsula, really, for though it was surrounded by water on three sides, the fourth side nearly touched the riverbank. But the causeway was easily defended and walls encircled both the castle and outer courtyards.

As the party clattered across to the island, Ailis thought how odd it was to arrive without Finian. His death had been more of a shock than Ailis had anticipated. He'd been sixty-one, but a big, bluff man who had never been ill and hardly ever injured. Then in February he was struck with fever and flux that gradually turned bloody and left him bedridden and wasting away so rapidly he seemed to grow smaller each day. After three excruciating weeks, he had died with his wife at his bedside.

Although unexpected, he had lingered long enough for Ailis to be prepared. The transition period to her leadership would be the most delicate time, but she had Father Byrne on her side and the support of the rebels in the Wicklow Mountains. She was the one who had determined to get the hundred Spanish soldiers away from the coast. She was the one who had come up with the daring plans for this summer. All she had to do now was keep a cool head, refuse to be cowed by any bluff Irishman who thought his body made him a better leader than a woman, and ensure her schemes were followed. If she succeeded this summer, her leadership would be unassailable.

As they entered the castle, Liadan took charge of Maisie. "I want you to stay by me," the child announced. "Right next door."

Ailis interposed. "Maisie will have Uncle Finian's chamber, as she should."

It was a calculated move. Ailis had watched Maisie closely during her uncle's illness, but the Scots girl managed herself so neatly that perhaps no one would have been able to read her intentions. Maisie had cared for her dying husband with kindness, and conducted herself as a new widow with perfect gravity that gave nothing away. She had come to Ailis three weeks after Finian's death to inform her there was no chance she was with child—Ailis was not surprised— and ever since, all the household had been waiting for Maisie to announce her intentions. Return to Scotland seemed likely, for why would she remain in Ireland now?

But here she still was. Without ever announcing anything, simply a serene part of the household whom Ailis was uncharacteristically hesitant about questioning too closely. The Holy Mother knew how desperately they could use Maisie's fortune—if she left Ireland, there would be no chance at all of any more forthcoming. Ailis controlled her curiosity. Instead, she began to compile an unwritten list of possible Irish husbands for Maisie. Young, this time, and handsome. Silver-tongued charm would not go amiss. Although come to think of it, Ailis had no idea if Maisie was at all susceptible to charm. Surely she must be. She was a girl just turned sixteen who had been married off to an old man. Find her the right young man now, and they could tie her to Ireland and its interests for the long future.

Maisie accepted the offered courtesy of taking up residence in her dead husband's usual chamber. Ailis didn't mind—she had never been easily moved by luxury. Far more important to have the power rather than merely its trappings. And the Kavanaugh plans would be run from her own chamber in the rectangular keep, with its narrow windows giving a far distant view of the Rock of Cashel in clear weather. She had settled herself beneath those windows at the long table that served as her desk, reviewing the household accounts for the move from Carlow, when Maisie knocked on her door.

"Come in." Ailis angled her chair away from the table and waited for Maisie to draw up a low padded stool near her. The Scots girl wore a black Italian-style bodice gown, silver buttons running from waist to high neck, with an underskirt of dark gray that echoed her eyes. Her extraordinarily pale hair was severely parted in the middle and contained in a silk caul at the back of her head. The colours of mourning suited her fairness.

Ailis didn't often smile, but she did now. "How are you settling in?"

"Very easily. I was hoping, now that we have something of a new beginning, that we could talk about my role in the household."

Interesting. Was Maisie going to make a power play? She'd never get away with it, not without a child of Finian's to her name, but it could prove entertaining. Not that Ailis had time for entertainment this year.

So she said neutrally, "How do you envision your role?" Always let the opposition speak first. The more you knew of their minds, the better you could anticipate and block them.

"I had thought I could take over Liadan's education. That would remove some of the pressure from your clerks. I know you were convent-educated, as was I, and if you are not yet prepared to send Liadan away, I could be useful for the interim. She is a very bright girl. She should not be neglected."

It was the closest thing to a criticism Maisie had ever made. It narrowed Ailis's eyes as she answered, "No, I am not prepared to send Liadan away." Certainly not this year or next, for Liadan lay at the very heart of her ultimate plans. "And I do agree, of course, that she is very bright. Do you think I had not noticed?"

Maisie managed to apologize without backtracking, a rare feat. "I think you notice everything and everyone. I only thought I might be useful in this. As far as the rest of your tasks are concerned, I suspect only you could accomplish them half so well. If I could ease your mind about Liadan's education—and even some of the domestic details of the household—then you would be freer to use your talents where they will have the greatest effect."

"How much do you know of the effects I intend?"

"Finian was my husband. If it was not precisely a marriage of true minds, he did speak to me a little. Mostly of you, and always with admiration. I know something of the Spanish soldiers, and something less of how you intend to use them. As I say, I doubt I could be helpful in those plans. But why not use the talents I do have to make your life easier?"

"Why?" Ailis asked abruptly. "Why do you care to make my life easier? Why do you care to stay in Ireland at all? How do I know I won't turn over Liadan's education to you, only to have you decide on a whim to return to Scotland? My daughter is exceedingly fond of you. I would not encourage that attachment if it will only lead to her disappointment when you leave."

"It is my intention for the foreseeable future, certainly for the next year, to remain in Ireland. My brother would not welcome my return to Scotland. If I were to return, he would no doubt once more arrange to marry me off to the first convenient suitor. I would prefer to make my own choices for now. I had thought that was a viewpoint you might understand."

Ailis stared at Maisie, who stared right back without a trace of being flustered. She was such a small thing, and young. Ten years younger than herself. But there was, as Ailis had noted from the beginning, a steadiness in her eyes and a diamond-sharp quality to her mind that belied her appearance. If she were to be completely honest, she would have admitted that part of her wanted Maisie to stay merely for the company. There were so few she had trusted since she was younger than Maisie.

With the smile that she used as one of her finely honed assets, Ailis put out her hands to Maisie and said, "Liadan will be beside herself with joy to have you stay. And indeed, the household would be the poorer without you."

"Then I shall gladly make myself as useful as I am able. With whatever you care to entrust me."

"For now, that is Liadan. Sharpen that mind of hers so that she might grow up to do honour to our clan."

Everything that sharpened Liadan made her more valuable . . . and more useful. Ailis knew how to deploy every one of her advantages. And finally, after ten long years, her revenge was beginning to be in sight.

Despite his own wariness, Philip discovered that he actually enjoyed having the English visitors at his court. Usually the only English that came to Spain were professionals—diplomats and ambassadors and cautious churchmen of the heretical variety—all of whom came primarily as Elizabeth's messengers and were not interested in anything other than their own points of view.

The Courtenays were a different matter. Philip had known them fairly well during his stays in England and found the Duke of Exeter to be a man of good sense, if little patience. His wife, of course, would have been worth cultivating by any measure, as she was undoubtedly Elizabeth's closest personal friend. The Duchess of Exeter could get away with saying things to the English queen that no one else could, not even Philip when he'd been her husband. But Minuette Courtenay made it a pleasure to cultivate her, for she was warm and witty and effortlessly charming.

Philip's present queen did not like her at all.

But Philip's truest interest among the guests were the children: Christopher and Philippa, whom his daughter, Anne, seemed to consider as siblings. A less intelligent observer might think, as Mary said to him the third night after the party's arrival, that he was "wasting his time and efforts with those too young to be influential."

Those observers would be missing the longer view. Elizabeth was a remarkable woman, but even she could not live forever. When their daughter inherited England, it was her friends who would wield influence. And that meant paying them attention while they were young.

Besides, whatever his other purposes, Philip was always a father. If he could not have Anne in Spain, then her friends were the next best thing. Philip craved their stories of Anne, and he hoped they would return to her with good impressions of him and his kingdom.

After five days of lavish feasts and receptions in Madrid, the royal party escorted their English guests to Philip's pride and joy, the royal complex at El Escorial. Situated at the foot of Mount Abantos thirty miles from the capital, the monastery and royal residence had been begun twenty years ago as a burial place for his father. Charles V had added a codicil to his will to establish a religious foundation in which he could be buried with his wife and Philip's mother, Isabella of Portugal.

Philip had overseen every step of the design and decoration of the complex himself and, though only the chapel and monastery were completely finished, he felt an almost unholy sense of pride at its appearance. To bring the Courtenays here was a way to highlight his artistic, spiritual side as opposed to merely his formal religious opinions.

They toured the basilica, two stories high at the facade, the interior with its Greek cross originally modeled on St. Peter's Basilica in Rome. To the south of the church were the austerely decorated royal apartments. The Patio de los Mascarones, surrounded on three sides by a gallery, led to the queen's apartments, in which, for this visit, the

Courtenay family would be quartered. They seemed appropriately impressed with their surroundings, though none of them were given to lavish praise.

Leaving the family in their suite of high-ceilinged chambers, Philip spent two hours in council with Cardinal Granvelle and others. All were cautiously optimistic about the Irish project, but it was still a relatively minor matter. From the high mountains of the New World to the sultry tropics of Manila, the Spanish empire had both problems and opportunities enough for three monarchs to handle.

When matters of business were concluded and his councilors withdrew, Philip walked silently through El Escorial. The monks were accustomed to him, and he slipped unaccosted into the church for vespers. There, he was surprised to find Philippa Courtenay sitting in the far back of the public chapel, the monks' voices wafting from behind the sail vaults.

"Like angels," Philip said softly, seating himself near her. "Heard and felt, but never seen."

She smiled, a shade more warmly than mere politeness dictated, and Philip smiled in return. "How do you like Spain, *dama*?"

"Very well, Your Majesty." She spoke Spanish with near fluency, a point of pride for Philip, as he knew she had learned it with his daughter. "I am only sorry that you must make do with us, rather than the visitor you would most prefer."

"But Anne would not be a visitor. Spain is her heritage as much as England." That was disingenuous, for he knew that heritage must be nurtured over time, and time was a luxury Anne would never have for her father's country. Philip sighed. "Can you tell me, *dama*, of my daughter? Those things not easily found in ambassadorial reports."

"She was most anxious that we convey to you her love and care. She rejoices in her new young half brothers and hopes they will bring you great joy."

"That is no more nor less than might be written in a report."

When she wanted, Philippa Courtenay had her mother's smile,

one that lit up wherever she was. Her next words were much less formal. "Anabel is your daughter. She will always choose her words with care. But privately? She is as dear to me as my own sister. So you will not accuse me of lack of love when I say that she has a temper and a way with words to rival Queen Elizabeth for wit and sharpness."

Philip surprised himself by laughing.

Then Philippa added, "She has considered that the birth of your sons will ease the pressures on you, and thus on her. She hopes that in these new circumstances, your attitude to England might soften. She has no wish for her young brothers to be raised to think of her as an enemy. Whatever the politics, families should behave generously."

"I hope I will never fail in my generosity to my only daughter," Philip said, suddenly less amused. "But Anne, like her mother—and myself—is responsible for far more than her own life. These two women have the souls of all England in their charge. And they fail them every day in which they hunt down innocent priests and continue to defy God by setting themselves above his earthly representatives."

Philippa Courtenay, for all that she had her mother's looks, had her father's ability to make her expression completely neutral. "Anabel has never once failed to remember the lives of the people that will one day be in her charge. She will do what she must for England." She rose, without genuflecting toward the altar, and said, "I am sure Your Majesty is aware that the Duc d'Anjou will soon be in England to pay court to your daughter. I know that was your wish, that she consider marrying a man of your faith."

It had once been his wish, and he still thought it the most likely match, for England needed a counter to Spain's increasing hostility. Now he was not so certain.

As if she could read his indecision, Philippa Courtenay added as a parting shot, "I understand that Esmé Stewart has also been invited to court. He will come with full authority from King James of Scotland to treat for Anabel's hand as well. I wonder how Her Majesty, Queen Mary, will feel about that possibility?"

Perhaps not so much a girl after all, Philip thought, but a clear-eyed, sharp-tongued female such as only England seemed to produce. Why could they not keep their women reserved and restrained like the Spanish?

The journey from the isolated crofter's hut to the Kavanaugh manor in Cahir was a nightmare for Stephen, jolting along on the pony Peter Martin had brought along. The pony was sure-footed but bony, and Stephen ached clear through with every jolt. Martin had done a dispassionately thorough job of beating him, though he had avoided the once-broken arm and anything too difficult to heal. That didn't make Stephen's head or jaw ache less, or stop parts of him from being covered in spectacular bruises.

It all went to the authenticity of his cover, as did his hair, allowed to grow past the collar of his doublet, and his rough growth of beard. His clothes had been carefully procured in England to reinforce the picture of a young man born bastard to a gentleman who had only carelessly provided bits and pieces for his unnecessary son. The Courtenays were a conservative family by royal court standards, so Stephen only realized how accustomed he was to the luxury of expensive—if sober—fabrics and soft linen when forced to change to coarser weaves.

It felt like penance, which was a very Catholic thought. That also played into his cover, for in his new role he was a recusant, born of a mother devout in her faith if not her behaviour. That was something else Julien had provided him with—an attempt at understanding Catholicism that only one born and raised in that faith could grasp. Stephen didn't need to be word perfect; he need only have another plausible reason for loathing the ruling English authorities.

Not a problem, with ruling authorities like Oliver Dane.

That was the only thing Stephen had kept wholly to himself—his certainty that the gallowglass force that attacked them outside Kilkenny had been sent by Oliver Dane. It was the only answer that made sense. Who else had wanted those prisoners dead? Pelham might have hanged them at Carrigafoyle if he'd cared to, but he had made no move to reinforce Dane in trying to wrest them from Stephen's hands. Pelham, he was quite sure, was essentially law-abiding. Dane, on the other hand, had a malicious streak a mile wide. He was the one who had engineered the massacre at Carrigafoyle after the surrender, the one who had spoken almost casually to Stephen about killing women for nothing more than being Irish. After using them to his satisfaction, no doubt.

And once his head had cleared from the fog of physical pain and emotional turmoil, Stephen remembered one tiny, telling detail from that horrific night: the masked man who, before breaking his arm, had sneered at him. *English lordling,* the man called him. A phrase Stephen had first been called in Ireland—on the day he met Oliver Dane.

Not absolute, but telling. And a detail Stephen did not intend to share with anyone.

Appropriate vengeance, Julien had counseled. Stephen was in Ireland primarily to keep the Spanish and their new queen from exploiting the situation—but he intended to exploit whatever opportunities came his way for bringing down Oliver Dane. No need to share that with Walsingham, who might not like the thought of removing an important—if sadistic—English landholder from the shaky balance of power. Stephen would not let Ireland fall to Spain if he could help it, but nor would he overlook any opportunity to strike at Dane.

They reached Cahir in a sodden spring rain that had them huddled beneath cloaks and blowing on cramped fingers for warmth. Martin walked, with Stephen on the pony, his hands tied together to complete the picture of a sullen Englishman half refugee, half prisoner. They were stopped at the causeway to Cahir Castle, secure on its little island, challenged by men of sturdy build and sharp eyes.

The men knew Peter Martin, of course, but declined to let Stephen enter or even dismount on the cleric's authority. So Martin went ahead while Stephen shivered in the rain under the scrutiny of the wary Kavanaugh guards.

He expected the thin, ascetic man who returned with Martin and recognized him immediately from description, as well as the priestly robes he wore, as Father Byrne. With Finian Kavanaugh's death, the priest was the chief voice of male authority in the household.

But Byrne and Martin did not return alone. Walking a little ahead of them was a tall, striking woman with black hair and cheekbones that set off a face of rare beauty. He knew she must be Ailis Kavanaugh, the niece who now ruled by tacit consent, the strategist who had planned her uncle's small but significant victories of the last five years. Martin had prepared Stephen for Ailis's authority—he had not prepared him for the intensity of her presence.

Ailis drew near, the guards in protective stances beside her, and tipped her head up to study Stephen. She did not rush to speak, but slowly considered every aspect of his appearance, from wet hair to bruised face to stiff posture indicating discomfort.

"Why are you here, Englishman?" Her voice was as alluring as the rest of her, the kind of voice a siren might use to lure sailors to their deaths.

"It was come with the priest or starve to death. I was left in the wilderness to die by my own people."

"Why?"

With the touch of insolence that was part of his cover, Stephen replied, "For daring to have an opinion of my own, and the stupidity to voice it. There is nothing you can tell me about English contempt that I do not know for myself."

Nothing in her exquisite face revealed what she might be thinking. "Martin tells me you might be worth our while. I respect his opinion, but the final decisions are always mine. For your English blood alone I would cheerfully leave you to die, but if there is a possibility of you being useful? I am not vindictive enough to overlook any advantage fate offers."

Then she addressed the guards. "Take him to Father Byrne's rooms. Untie his hands and lock him in."

Looking up at Stephen once more with eyes like violets—particularly sharp and predatory violets—she said, "Consider yourself a prisoner for now. Whether that changes will be up to you. Do you understand?"

Suppressing the surprising lift of relief, Stephen said, "I understand. And I will give you no cause to regret it."

It was just the first of many lies he would be telling this woman in the months to come.

TWELVE

27 May 1582
El Escorial, Spain

We have spent the last week at King Philip's austerely beautiful compound that is half religious house, half royal palace. Like Hampton Court or Richmond, it is set just far enough from the capital city to be both healthful and relaxing. It has the stamp of Philip everywhere I look—I understand that he deliberately restricted the number of artists invited to participate so that there might be unity of theme and effect. It is when I consider such things that I know why Elizabeth married him. Yes, it was a political match. Yes, he offered her a necessary counterweight to stabilize England from within while not having to worry overmuch about threats from abroad.

But the Elizabeth I know might still have found reason to refuse—if there had not been something in Philip that attracted both her heart and her head. I have long recognized her reasons for respecting him. As he now shows us his heart poured out into architecture and devotional worship, I begin to see what caught and held fast her own heart all these years.

It frightens me. Enemies who respect one another are one thing. Enemies who resent having been made to love are far more dangerous.

4 June 1582
Toledo, Spain

After the rarefied atmosphere of El Escorial, we have traveled to the more domestically mundane household of the young Spanish/Scots princes. It was the primary stated purpose of our journey, of course—to personally lay eyes on Charles and Alexander that we might provide an unbiased report of their apparent health. That is easy enough, for they both appear to be thriving. Despite the multiple purposes of our journey, it was easy to forget ourselves during the hour we spent in the princes' nursery. The pleasures of fat babies are universal. Kit and Pippa presented their fellow twins with the wooden dolls Anabel sent for them; while Pippa held Prince Charles with natural ease, Kit and Prince Alexander regarded each other with similar wariness.

Unfortunately, babies do not exist apart from their parents—in this case, their mother. Mary Stuart personally supervised our visit and, when it was over, asked me with gracious condescension to walk with her in the gardens. I was tempted to pull a face behind her back at Dominic, but was afraid Kit might laugh and give me away. So my family went one direction, and I went another, determined to hold my tongue for England's sake.

That resolve lasted not even a minute. For Mary opened with the worst possible statement. "Your children are quite charming. I remember that from your oldest son at Tutbury. Pity that charm can only go so far."

It went far enough on you, I thought uncharitably. Mary continued, either royally oblivious or cruelly pointed, "Though I believe our dear cousin Elizabeth is susceptible to charm from young and handsome men. Perhaps fatally susceptible. In such an atmosphere, no doubt your Stephen will rise high enough to satisfy even you."

"That my children live and are happy has always been the highest satisfaction I could hope for," I told her. "If only Your Majesty could say the same, what an awful lot of trouble could be avoided."

We were past politeness now. Mary's eyes were steely with resolve and tainted with hatred. Of me, of Elizabeth, of England—she has an abundance of hate. "My children are royal. They have no need to rise, for they have been born to the highest positions. James may have usurped his position too early—I will not make those mistakes with my new sons. And England will long have cause to regret that I left its shores alive."

I told no one of her words except Dominic. When we return to England, we shall pass on all we heard and observed and guessed to Elizabeth and her ministers. That is why we are here.

15 June 1582
Seville, Spain

Thankfully, after my last encounter with Mary Stuart, we left her and her children behind and traveled with Philip to Seville in the south. We will remain here until we sail in six weeks. As the only port city authorized to trade with the New World, Seville is at the center of the magnificent riches being brought from Spain's overseas empire. No doubt Philip intends our stay here to impress us with the weight of Spanish gold and Spanish ships and Spanish resolve. For Seville is also the home of the Inquisition in Spain.

Pippa seems particularly struck by the city. With her fluent Spanish, honed in long years with Anabel, she has struck up friendships among the women who joined us in Madrid and, with appropriate

*guards, has been touring the city. With Kit, of course. He is almost
more protective of her than Dominic is. And Spain has unsettled him
in an entirely different way than the rest of us.*

Because of Anabel.

And that is a puzzle beyond my skills to solve.

A week after their arrival in Seville, Kit and Pippa set out from
the fantastical Royal Alcazar to pay a promised visit to the grandmother of Madalena Arias. It was Pippa's errand, but she would
never have been allowed out without one of the males of her family.
The siblings were surrounded by royal guards—six of them with
their red and gold badges—and Pippa had two women of the Spanish court as well. Philip had chosen older women to attend on the
Courtenay females—frankly, they had not met very many young
women and even fewer single women. Spain kept their females in
closer hold than England.

Kit had thought himself prepared for Madalena's grandmother.
He knew that she was of pure Moorish blood—her family one of the
conversos in the days of Ferdinand and Isabella—but still it was something of a shock when he and Pippa were introduced to Catalina
Duran. Madalena was such a warm and generous woman, it was hard
to connect her to this silver-haired, aristocratic woman who looked
as though she had stepped straight out of a royal court of fifty years
ago. A foreign royal court.

She remained seated as the twins bowed and curtsied. In a voice
like molten iron, she said, "Doña Philippa, my granddaughter has
written much of you and the princess you both serve. It is kind of
you to visit."

Her tone was more one of "of course you would visit, but I shall
be polite as long as I choose."

Then Doña Catalina turned a severe eye on Kit. "And this is
Christopher, of whom also I have heard."

Somewhat at a loss, Kit said, "We are very fond of Madalena."

"Do not bother trying to impress me, young man. I am too old for such tricks. You may wait quietly in the corner. It is your sister I have agreed to speak with."

What protest could he make? It wasn't as though he could believe Pippa in any danger from a woman approaching eighty with royal guards within shouting distance. Kit made another, ironic, bow and withdrew to the far end of the chamber, where he leaned against the edge of a tiled windowsill and listened.

Doña Catalina waved a long-fingered, gnarled hand, and Pippa perched on a priceless-looking chair embroidered with gold thread. Then the doña stared at her for a long time without speaking. Pippa did not move nor make any attempt to break the silence, and Kit tried to follow her example. Being still did not come naturally to him.

"Do you know what Madalena wrote to me of you?" Doña Catalina finally asked.

"I do not," Pippa replied smoothly.

"And yet you know so many things, that some would consider . . . unusual."

"Madalena said that you have some experience in unusual knowledge."

"And is that why you have come to see me, young Philippa? An interesting name for an English girl born in the time of an unwelcome Spanish consort in your country."

"I was not named for King Philip, but for my grandmother. She died shortly before my birth."

Doña Catalina tipped her head, a youthful gesture that called to Kit's mind the image of her elegant granddaughter. "A woman of troubled mind, was she not? Is that the fear that stalks you? For fear I see, like a stain on your soul. Do you fear the loss of your mind?"

"I do not. I am not my grandmother."

With a smile that could only be called cynical, Doña Catalina said, "So proud to announce your independence . . . so it is fate that you fear. I cannot help you with that."

Kit felt Pippa's instinctive resistance to being handled. "That is not why I came."

"So you did come for reasons other than politeness."

Had she? If Pippa wanted something from this woman, she hadn't said as much to him. Intrigued, and a little annoyed, Kit sharpened his focus. Since they were little, he could access his twin's emotions and thoughts if he tried hard to shut out everything else.

Letting his awareness of the physical surroundings fade, Kit narrowed in on the intangible thread that bound him to his sister. It was as delicate as silk and as durable as diamonds, the finest, brightest part of him. Through it now, his senses were doubled and he felt Pippa's inner trembling inside his own skin.

If Doña Catalina could sense it, she gave no quarter. "Give me your hand, child," she commanded.

Kit raised his eyebrows as he felt Pippa's shock magnify his own. Chiromancy, the art of palmistry, had been classified by the Roman Catholic Church as one of the seven forbidden arts of magic. Doña Catalina, who must always be viewed with some suspicion because of her *converso* status, could easily attract the unwelcome attention of the Inquisition for practicing chiromancy.

She did not seem bothered by the possibility. Pippa extended her right hand, but Doña Catalina waved it away. "The left, if you please. It is your unrealized life that troubles you."

Kit clenched his own left hand as he fleetingly wondered if his palm would yield the same information as his twin's.

"A woman so severely in control of herself often runs riot in her own heart," Doña Catalina said, running her fingertips across the lines on Pippa's palm, and Kit felt a shiver of that touch himself. "Passion you have, no surprise for one young and lovely, but you submerge your own passions in serving others. Such service, though admirable, cannot compensate for your own desires. What is it you wish, Doña Philippa? Your body knows, for our bodies cannot lie as our thoughts can."

Kit felt on the edge of some revelation and then, suddenly, Pippa pushed back against their bond. Whatever had risen instinctively in her mind, she did not want Kit to know.

"Child," Doña Catalina continued, "you have been seeking an answer you already possess. Simply because you do not like the answer does not mean you can force someone to give you another. Your life is your life. Each hour given to you by God is to be lived as you yourself choose. Do not look to others—not even the stars—to make those choices for you."

"What if I choose wrong? What if my choices lead others to suffer?"

With an impatient shake of her head, Doña Catalina answered, "You think too much, child. And you take too much on yourself. You will light the beacon, but your princess will command the flames. Those you love are stronger than you give them credit for. You must stop feeling superior."

"I don't feel superior!" Pippa pulled her hand away, and behind her Kit felt the sting of the insult.

But Doña Catalina gave her the sort of look that Carrie might give, when the children had been caught in an egregious act of mischief. "The first step to knowing yourself is knowing your faults. And that, child, is the best advice an old woman can give you. You may go now. Thank Madalena for sending you to me."

The doña looked across the length of the chamber to Kit. "As for you, Lord Christopher, pay attention to that princess of yours. You may not know her mind as well as you think you do. And royalty with minds of their own are unpredictable."

Anabel spent early summer at Syon House, the former abbey turned into a gracious home by the late Duke of Northumberland. The gardens were the specialty of Syon House, and June sent them into spectacular bloom. From the upper floor windows, one could admire the intricacies of the parterres and knot gardens below. Lavender softened the outer brick walls and within the small square beds bloomed daisies and hollyhocks and herbs such as marjoram and mint.

The interior of the house, left mostly untouched since the 1550s, was slowly being modernized, and Anabel enjoyed making design decisions, from fabric for the windows to which royal tapestries to borrow from her mother's collection. Her grandfather, Henry VIII, had possessed perhaps the largest collection of tapestries in Europe during his day and there was no shortage of themes or styles to choose from.

On this particular day, she was studying the ledger detailing various tapestries, trying to decide on a theme for her updated privy chamber. With her was Lucette Courtenay—no, Lucette LeClerc now—who had agreed to come to Syon House and continue on to court with Anabel during the French and Scots visits. The queen had encouraged Anabel's request, since Lucette's husband was French and might prove useful with the Duc d'Anjou. Though Julien had spent eight years secretly spying for Walsingham on his own countrymen, that fact was not widely known. Most people assumed that his move to England had been entirely for the love of Lucette—as indeed it had. Both Julien and Lucette had since declined further offers from Walsingham to aid in his intelligence work.

But Lucette had been Anabel's friend long before she was anything official at court, and with Pippa and Kit absent in Spain, she seemed to accept Anabel's need to have someone familiar about her.

"What do you think?" Anabel mused aloud. "The Labors of Hercules? Or Persephone and Demeter?"

"The myth of the Queen of the Underworld and her mother? That could set quite the tone for visitors to your privy chamber." Lucette had the trick of her mother and Kit, to infuse her words with an innocent mischief that inspired laughter.

"As my father already thinks of England as on our way to hell, I might as well claim my place as queen forthwith. Persephone it is."

She shut the ledger decisively. "What next? We have Syon House's reconstruction well under way—what is the program for reconstructing me to impress the Duc d'Anjou and Esmé Stewart?"

"I am the wrong woman to ask about impressing men."

"With a husband that every single female in my household cannot stop talking about? I'd tell you to keep a close watch on him if it weren't so obvious that he has eyes for no woman but you. If I thought all Frenchmen were built like Julien, I'd say yes to Francis right now."

Lucette rolled her eyes. "You are the least sentimental person I know, Anabel. And that includes your mother. You will never have your head turned by a handsome face."

Was that true? Perhaps. For all her sharp wits and cynical outlook, Elizabeth had her one great love in Robert Dudley. Not that her mother talked about him. But Minuette would, if you asked her, though Anabel had always wondered how accurate her image was. After all, Robert had died in the cause of helping to save Minuette's life from the last king.

But Elizabeth had not been born to be a queen; not like Anabel. She'd had a little room for implausible dreams. Anabel did not.

Except . . .

As though she could read her wayward thoughts, Lucette asked, "What did Kit have to say in his last letter?"

"He wrote to you as well."

"Three lines, scrawled in a hurry, that told me nothing except he likes the sunshine and the food. Kit is not one for writing—at least not to his older sister."

"He wrote little more than that to me," Anabel said. "A bit more expansive about the quality of the wine, though."

Why did she lie to Lucette? In truth, Kit's letter had been . . . what? Not intimate, for he wrote nothing that could not have been openly read by anyone. But it had felt intimate. It felt as though they were in Spain together, and that he was merely commenting on things as they went along, as though he were always engaged in conversation with her, whether she happened to be with him or not. It was how she often felt herself.

"Well," Anabel continued brightly, "they have their tasks in Spain, and I have mine here. If only I were certain which country my mother wants me to snare, I would have no qualms about the coming visits. But trying to balance France and Scotland without giving either one false hope? That will be a trick."

"But a trick these men will be prepared for. They know, Anabel, that the decisions will not be made by the two of you alone. If there is danger there, at least it is not personal."

Her words were flavoured with the faintest hint of bitterness and guilt, in a way that made Anabel vividly recall the days she and Lucette had spent imprisoned together in Wynfield Mote. Their captor had been Julien's older brother, Nicolas, who for all his apparent political motivation had been obviously captivated by Lucette. And who had hated both her and his brother for ruining any hopes he might have had.

Their eyes met, and Anabel could see that Lucette was thinking the same thing. Tenderly, Anabel touched the back of her friend's hand and said, "You are quite right. Whatever happens, there will be no real harm done."

Except to England if I choose wrong, she thought. And to Kit.

"He's in?" Elizabeth asked Walsingham. Two days before Anabel's arrival at court—four days before that of the Duc d'Anjou—and they had just had the first word about Stephen in Ireland. The queen and her spymaster spoke alone in one of Greenwich's old-fashioned chambers, essentially untouched since the early days of her father's reign. The box-beamed ceiling was punctuated by whitewashed plaster, and the mullioned windows let in far less light than in the newer palaces.

"According to my source," Walsingham said, "Stephen was admitted to the Kavanaugh household in Cahir three weeks ago. You understand that we will not receive regular updates. Stephen himself will maintain silence for as long as he deems fit. And my source is not always with the Kavanaughs. He travels, which makes it possible for him to send messages."

"What if Stephen gets into trouble?" Elizabeth fingered her long string of pearls, letting each smooth oval slip through her touch as though it were a rosary.

"Then he will get himself out of it. He is very resourceful, Your Majesty. And committed. Though not perhaps in quite the way he wants us to believe."

Elizabeth's hands stilled. "If you are about to tell me that you think Stephen Courtenay will turn against England, then I shall have to remove you as my Secretary of State since clearly you will have lost your mind. Didn't we have this discussion when he was assigned to Mary Stuart at Tutbury? Where Stephen behaved with perfect correctness in our cause."

Walsingham, characteristically, took his time answering. It was one of the qualities she most appreciated in her spymaster—his thoughtfulness. That didn't mean he always gave her the answers she wanted. Which, when she was honest with herself, was the other quality she appreciated.

"Stephen Courtenay is a young man of principle," Walsingham agreed. "Most of those I work with are more . . . predictable in their motivations. A man who can be bought—I know where I stand with such a man, and precisely how far I can trust him. I do not know young Courtenay's limits, and that makes me uneasy. Particularly when we are talking about leaving him undercover for an extended period of time."

Elizabeth began to pace, her wide skirts brushing the bare brick floor. There was not even a rug, and she made a note to herself to speak sharply to someone about that. "How long do you think?"

"At minimum, through the summer. Perhaps longer. It will take time for him to find his feet among the Kavanaughs. There is no point inserting him there if we are not willing to be patient to see if it pays off. We set up some things with the Earl of Ormond for early summer—English forays that Stephen can share with the Irish. Ormond is agreed with the necessity of losing some land and cattle—hopefully no lives—as the price for future intelligence from Stephen."

"This had better work, Walsingham," Elizabeth warned once more. "Last time Stephen was in Ireland, he came back bloodied and near broken. Minuette may say she does not blame me, but if worse happens to her son in my service? I do not wish to bear her that message."

"Stephen is more canny and careful than I think you recognize, Your Majesty."

And something in Walsingham's tone as he said it alerted Elizabeth. "And that is why you are wary—you're afraid of what he might do on his own."

"My lot in life," Walsingham agreed wryly. "For twenty years and more I've been afraid of what *you* might do on your own. It's why I fuss so much."

"Like I do with Anabel? I suppose none of us is free from the impulse to control and worry. For now, let us focus on France and Scotland. There is quite enough to fuss about this next month without adding in things beyond our immediate control."

Wise words—and Elizabeth didn't believe them in the slightest. She was queen. Everything should be in her immediate control.

THIRTEEN

Ailis Kavanaugh was not a woman lightly given to trusting any man—and Englishmen not at all. She had learned that lesson in the hardest way possible twelve years ago in Kilmallock. That said, as the days of his imprisonment at Cahir Castle grew to weeks, she watched Stephen Wyatt thoughtfully.

He was generally patient, and when he lost patience at his confined situation, he was neither cruel nor harsh. He seemed to grasp the necessity of being locked up. He answered the questions put to him with only the slight hesitations that might be expected of any man unsure of his future in enemy hands.

Most intriguingly of all, he spoke Gaelic.

Not fluently, by any means, but in a lifetime of rubbing up against the English in Ireland, Ailis had found few not born here who troubled. It made sense if you were an Anglo-Norman lord like Ormond or Desmond to learn the language of the estates you ruled—but Stephen was not one of those. When asked why he'd bothered, Stephen had said simply, "It seemed only fair. We expect travelers to France or Spain to speak the language—or at least Latin as a last resort. Why not Ireland?"

"Because England does not consider us a separate nation. We are their vassals, and as such our language is inferior."

"I thought, Hibernia Hibernescit."

Ireland makes all things Irish. "Where did you hear that?" she asked suspiciously. He'd been here just short of a month now, and they had progressed to the point where she would visit with him seated in the chamber poor Father Byrne had sacrificed to the prisoner, with the door open and guards within sound of her voice. She was not afraid of Stephen Wyatt. But she was growing increasingly curious.

For a heartbeat, he hesitated, and there was a flicker of pain in the way his eyes tightened at the corners. "I heard it from a woman. An Irish woman."

"The Irish woman put to death by your company for a traitor?" she asked bluntly. He had not told her that story directly yet—that had come through Father Byrne, who had borne the brunt of early weeks of questioning their prisoner.

To her surprise, he corrected her. "The Irish woman put to death for nothing more than being unhappily in my company. Her name was Roisin."

Something in the way he said it, the pain that was still raw when touched, told Ailis that this, at the very least, was the truth.

"So when you protested, you were beaten for your insolence. And when you continued to rail at your commander and at general English policy in Ireland, you were put out into the wilderness to starve."

"Or to land with the Irish Catholic trash whose company I craved. So said my commander."

"Lots of Englishmen use Irish women. Why were you different?"

She didn't think she'd faltered in her tone, but something sharpened in Stephen's eyes, as though he could guess at how she had once been used. "Bedding the girl was not my crime. Refusing to believe that every word out of her mouth from the moment we met was a lie? That was my sin. I believed her innocent of treachery."

Stephen leaned forward, hands clasped and arms resting on his legs. He looked deadly serious, as though he needed to impress her with whatever he said next. "And even if I was wrong—even if Roisin was using me for reasons of her own—she did not deserve to die for it. Ireland was her country, far more than it is mine. It does not take a scholar to see what damage we have wrought here. I was already beginning to think that we English are not as interested in controlling Ireland as we are in razing it—and all its people—to the ground. Simply because we can."

"That is what kingdoms do," she reminded him sharply. "Assert their power wherever possible. Because England cannot fight France or Spain, it uses Ireland as an outlet for its aggression. All we have ever wanted, for four hundred years, is to be left alone."

Stephen sat back, thoughtful. "Unfortunately for you, England is not the only power eager to use Ireland for its own purposes. With the English queen's divorce from King Philip, the Spanish must be looking to Ireland to drive a wedge into a Protestant kingdom they despise."

That was verging entirely too close to secrets he could not be allowed to discover. Ailis changed the subject, with an abruptness that might have dizzied a less focused man. "Tell me why I should keep you alive."

"Because my own people wanted me dead. And because you have no interest in doing English dirty work for them." He twitched a smile, there and gone again, then said, "No, sorry, this is not the time for lightness. Why is it, in the time you've had me here, no one has asked me what I might know about English forces and plans?"

She answered truthfully. "We wanted to get a sense of what sort of pressure might be necessary—and if your answers would be worth expending that pressure."

"You might simply try asking."

"How could I know that you wouldn't be setting us a trap?"

"You don't, not the first time. But being duly cautioned by your own highly developed sense of self-preservation, you can take precautions not to be caught unawares. And when the first information I provide proves useful, you might be more willing to trust me the second time."

Englishmen lie. It was a truism Ailis had learned from the time she was old enough to walk. She wanted to believe Stephen—which in itself was a warning. When was the last time she'd cared whether a man told her the truth? In the end, it was all about assessing risk. Did the risk of Stephen lying outweigh the benefits that would accrue if he were telling the truth?

There was only one way to find out, as he had so astutely highlighted. She must ask, and risk at least one action on whatever he told them.

"Very well, Stephen Wyatt," she said in Gaelic. "Tell me something useful that I can use against the English you claim to so despise."

Two weeks after he told Ailis when and where she would find the Earl of Ormond's men patrolling into Munster lands, Stephen was released from his confinement in the priest's chamber. The guard who motioned him out gave no explanation, so Stephen was left to follow thinking mordantly, *Either she's decided to trust me or she's decided to execute me.* It almost didn't matter which, as long as he was free of that spartan priest's chamber.

He had always thought himself a self-contained, controlled man, but confinement—however light—had worn on him, turning his thoughts back in on themselves. He'd tried to break the cycle by reciting poetry, composing letters in his head to his family that would go unwritten for the indefinite future, and obsessively checking and further embellishing his cover so that by the time he was released, he could almost believe he was Stephen Wyatt. Wynfield Mote, Tiverton, the estates of Somerset, the memories of court and family—all shoved far beneath the surface.

Ailis waited for him at a table in a small chamber off the Great Hall, over which she leaned, studying a map. She wore her usual outfit of scarlet broadcloth kirtle with bodice, her linen smock finely blackworked. Father Byrne was next to her, a kindly looking man for all his asceticism, and the captain of her guards, a distant relative named Diarmid mac Briain, glaring balefully at Stephen. His heartbeat sped up. If the Kavanaughs had lost men on this raid, his fate was sealed.

Every man there waited on Ailis—and Stephen thought she knew and used that to perfection. When she straightened, studying him without speaking, he was rather forcibly reminded of Queen Elizabeth, another woman who ruled using every advantage she held. Not excluding her femininity.

He declined to ask, and finally, with a ghost of a smile, Ailis spoke. "Your information was correct. We took Ormond's patrol by surprise and came away with half a dozen horses and a not insufficient store of food. Not a great battle, but pricking the English here and there is a strategy we have long embraced."

"None injured?" Stephen asked coolly.

"Not among us," she answered, just as cool. "Ormond's men took some injuries."

He could only pray none of those injuries were great or fatal. The Earl of Ormond had not struck Stephen as a greatly patient man; his willingness to abide by Walsingham's instructions would probably not outlast serious cost to his own men.

"Well," Ailis said after another long silence, "you have passed your first test. There will be others, and not always set out on your terms. But for tonight, I thought you might enjoy eating with the household. At night, I'm afraid, I will continue to lock you in. You understand."

"Perfectly." When their eyes met, Stephen felt a spark leap between them.

If Ailis felt the same challenge and response, she did not show it. "Diarmid or one of his men will be watching you, but you are otherwise free among the public spaces of the castle." Then, with real laughter in her voice, she suggested, "Beyond the hall is a makeshift schoolroom. There is at least one member of my household who has been consumed by curiosity about our unexpected English guest. Perhaps you might quench that curiosity to a degree."

Stephen took the suggestion as an order, which it had been, and did his best to ignore the Irish guard tasked with following him. Through the hall, a space elegant in its lines and clean medieval feel, to a door left ajar at the base of a tower. The schoolroom, as Ailis had termed it, was round and with only small windows set high near the ceiling. There were two tables in the chamber, one piled high with books and ledgers and heaps of paper and ink, the other a study space where two children sat together working.

No, Stephen corrected himself as he got a better look, *one child and one young woman.* He knew their names and some of their history from Walsingham—that is, Stephen Courtenay knew those things. Stephen Wyatt did not, and so he said courteously, "Forgive me for intruding. I was told there was someone here who wanted to meet me."

The child flew out of her seat and planted herself in front of Stephen. Even if he hadn't known who she was, he'd have been able to guess, for she was a miniature of Ailis. Black braids swung past her shoulders, and her light green dress showed the snags and stains of a child who liked playing outdoor games. "My mother let you out!" she exclaimed, as though Stephen had been a horse confined to pasture.

"If Ailis Kavanaugh is your mother, then yes, she let me out."

"I'm Liadan," the girl declared. "I'm eleven years old and someday I will lead Clan Kavanaugh like my mother. And this is Maisie."

She spoke in staccato bursts of enthusiasm, her braids bouncing as she moved. Behind her, Mariota Sinclair Kavanaugh rose with a little more restraint but an equally wide smile. Standing, she was only an inch taller than the eleven-year-old.

"We are glad to finally meet our mysterious guest," Maisie said.

Her sober attire as a widow contrasted sharply with her obvious youth. She had turned sixteen a month before her husband's death, but the overwhelming impression as Stephen greeted her was calculated intelligence. She spoke Gaelic much more fluently than he did, though with a slightly different accent than the native Irish.

Then she switched to English. "I am very glad you have come, because Liadan needs to practice her English and she does not trust mine, seeing that I am Scots."

Liadan pulled a face, but obediently said in very good English, "That is an excuse. Mostly we just wanted someone new to talk to. Have you ever been to London?"

From there, the interrogation was conducted with rapid force and with dizzying changes of subject that left Stephen mildly amused and thinking that maybe this was Ailis's secret weapon in disarming prisoners. He admitted to having been in London and even to having seen Queen Elizabeth—at a distance, on a festival day. He told them about the supposed household he'd grown up in, the illegitimate son of a carelessly affectionate knight who'd let him be trained as a soldier. While he and Liadan batted words back and forth, he noted that Maisie watched them both with a benign expression that suggested either idiocy or careful masking of attention. He favored the latter. Probably she had been tasked by Ailis with listening for inconsistencies in his story compared to what he had already told the other interrogators.

There would be none. Stephen was flawlessly prepared and beginning to enjoy himself. Liadan finally stopped questioning and, with a crease between her brows, remarked, "You are nicer than I thought you'd be."

"I don't suppose you have any good opinion of Englishmen. I don't blame you."

"My father's an Englishman," she said, unexpectedly. Though Stephen knew that much, he didn't have to feign surprise at her easy admission. "Father Byrne says I should not want to kill him for it, because then how would I have been born? But I think I should at least like to slap him for what he did to my mother."

"I'm sorry to hear it," Stephen replied carefully. "Not all men, of any country, are good men. I am sorry that Ireland has had to learn that lesson over and over."

"Liadan," Maisie said abruptly, softened by a smile, "go and see how long before dinner."

When the girl had vanished, after bestowing an affectionate hug on the previously stone-faced guard standing in the open doorway, Maisie stepped in front of Stephen and tipped her head up. A long ways. She was a foot shorter than he was, her heart-shaped face bland and unremarkable save for the intensity in her gray eyes. The linen wimple covering her hair had slipped a little and he could see that her hair was astonishingly pale, reminiscent of silver gilt.

Stephen mentally raced through what he knew about the Sinclairs: wealthy, but because of their cleverness and business acumen rather than birth or position. Old William Sinclair had died a year and a half ago, leaving only two grandchildren, Maisie and her brother. From what he'd heard from Walsingham, Maisie's brother had inherited his grandfather's business but not his intelligence. From the way she was studying him, Stephen suspected that legacy had gone to Maisie instead.

But how dangerous could a sixteen-year-old girl be?

Her first question was unexpected but not especially dangerous. "Do you have a brother, Mr. Wyatt?"

"Call me Stephen," he replied instinctively, to keep from flinching. "I have no siblings, as I told Liadan—an only child, just like her. Just like I told Ailis and every man of hers she's had question me. Did she ask you to try and trip me up? But then I suppose the Scots have as little reason to trust the English as the Irish do."

He focused on Maisie's intent face, refusing to let anything rise to the surface of his mind: Lucie, Pippa, Kit. No siblings. No attachments.

Maisie smiled, quick and mischievous. "Just as well. Siblings can be difficult—especially brothers."

The guard shifted as Liadan came darting back in. "We can go to dinner now! I'm to bring our guest."

Stephen gallantly offered the girl his arm and, giggling, she put her hand in the crook of his elbow. Both Maisie and the guard followed them out. But it was Maisie's gray eyes Stephen could feel focused on him. Assessing.

Francis de Valois, Duc d'Anjou and heir presumptive to the throne of France, arrived at Greenwich Palace the last week in June to royal fanfare, beneath which atmosphere mingled calculation, mistrust, and hope. Elizabeth and Burghley stood with Sir Henry Lee, who had arranged the ceremonious arrival to the last footstep, and everything—even the weather—cooperated.

Elizabeth chose to greet Anjou dockside, where the royal barge she had lent him pulled alongside. She wore an elaborate gown of purple and cloth-of-silver, and atop her closely curled red wig perched an arrangement of jewels and stiffened silver lace like butterfly wings. Behind her, Greenwich was at its best in its summer colours, and it was a real pleasure to once more greet Jehan de Simier.

"My monkey!" Elizabeth said delightedly. Simier kissed her hand, then made way for his royal prince, Duc Francis of Anjou. The French royal equalled—if not surpassed—Elizabeth for sartorial flamboyance. His doublet and trunk hose were made of gold damask, with stiffly embroidered silk set in the trunk-hose panes. He wore rubies on his fingers and had an enormous diamond in his hat.

Like both Elizabeth and her late brother, Francis had suffered a bout of smallpox when younger. The scarring had left him far short of handsome, but the twenty-seven-year-old prince had merry eyes and thick hair and an intelligent good humour about him that was attractive in its way.

"*Madame la reine,*" he said graciously, and kissed Elizabeth's offered hand. She was still vainly proud of her white hands and long fingers, even if age had begun to slowly creep into her joints.

Francis straightened and said in charmingly accented English, "I bring with me the well wishes of my brother, the king, and of my mother. It has been too long since France and England have been friends. We would remedy that in whatever manner seems best to both our countries."

Oh, how glad Catherine de Medici must be to have Spain no longer allied to England, Elizabeth thought. She wondered if the French queen mother was quite as glad to have Mary Stuart replace her as Philip's wife. Catherine did not like her deceased oldest son's bride at all and had been only too glad to get rid of Mary to Scotland. During her years of trouble at home and confinement in England, the French crown had made no move to intervene. Probably Catherine was most disappointed with Elizabeth for not having gotten rid of Mary and saved all of them this trouble.

For if Mary Stuart had not wed Philip, the Spanish king might well have turned instead to the French nobility for a young Catholic bride.

But he hadn't, and so here they were. Elizabeth bestowed a dazzling smile on Francis and said, "Our wish for friendship could not be greater. Come in, and meet the jewel of England. My daughter, Anne."

Anabel, by her mother's design, was seated in the hall on the smaller of two thrones. Hers bore the embroidered canopy of the Princess of Wales, and she rose, cool and remote, as her mother and her possible future husband approached with the rest of the court officers behind.

Elizabeth had overseen the design of her daughter's gown in every detail. To accent her youth and virginity, Anabel wore an ivory silk damask that emphasized her pale skin. The ruff was mostly lace, to delicately frame the face, and her red-gold hair was dressed in loose waves pulled into a chignon at the back of her neck. She wore no jewels, save the locket ring Elizabeth had given her at the investiture.

Naturally, Anabel spoke fluent French to their guest. "Welcome to England, dear brother of France. It is a great joy to my heart to meet at last."

Elizabeth continued to her own throne and sat where she could watch Francis's face. He had been sent portraits of Anabel, and of course had the reports of many ambassadors and visitors over the years. Despite all that, she thought she detected a quiver of surprise at how truly beautiful her daughter was. Portraits could exaggerate, after all, and men's tales could be embellished. But Anabel herself was perfect.

Francis bowed low to Anabel—who did not extend her hand to be kissed—and when he straightened said simply, "I had thought I had anticipated all that this visit would bring. I confess that I severely underestimated the joy of it."

Though she kept a straight face, Elizabeth's eyes briefly darted to Burghley, standing a little behind Francis. She knew they were thinking the same thing. *If Anjou has his way, he'll be wed to Anabel before ever he leaves England.*

Good. That meant they held all the cards. And that was the only way Elizabeth liked playing.

The formal reception for the Duc d'Anjou flowed in a steady progression through the afternoon: introductions to England's leading nobility and councilors, a tour of Greenwich, a feast nicely balanced between impressive and welcoming, and finally musicians. There was no real dancing tonight, but lots of opportunities for private conversations between two or three as people mingled inside and out.

Anabel took the first chance that offered to steer Lucette and Julien LeClerc into a garden alcove for their opinion.

Lucette spoke first. "And what do we think of Francis de Valois?"

"I don't know, what do we think? Any guidance from my personal Frenchman and his wife?" But though Anabel nominally addressed Julien, it was Lucette's opinion she wanted. Of the man, not the position.

Her friend understood her at once. "Nothing you cannot see for yourself. He's smart and cautious and principled—and masks it all with a French insouciance that he can turn on and off at will, I imagine."

Julien breathed out a laugh, and Lucette's teasing smile at her husband made Anabel's heart ache. She had thought herself prepared for this business of personal suitors, approaching the matter as she did everything in her life—with ferocious study and flawless focus. She had thought she'd known all she needed to of Francis. Right up until the moment she met him and realized that there was a physical being behind all the reports and letters and political considerations.

It wasn't that she found him repulsive. They were of a height and his fine dark eyes went a long ways to balance his slightly crooked posture and scarred face. But his flattery had left her cold. She could never imagine looking at him as Lucette was now looking at Julien.

"Well," she said brightly, suddenly anxious to escape, "at least he will not be boring. We are riding tomorrow—would you both come?"

This time it was Julien who spoke, though it was more to her previous concerns than the question asked. "Your Highness, the Valois family can be . . . prickly. Prideful. But Francis is among the best of them. He is not given to quick judgment or narrow views. I think you might like him well enough."

She forced a smile. "If he is half as astute as you are, I shall like him very well. What more could I wish for?"

Hazel eyes and golden hair, a mind that matched hers beat for beat . . .

Anabel shook off that fantasy and headed inside to flirt with Anjou.

FOURTEEN

Over the next three weeks, Stephen Wyatt provided information on two more planned English patrols. Ailis's men brought home success each time, including finding a small cache of weapons during the second raid. Her guards were well-trained and well-disciplined, not always usual for Irish forces, and Diarmid mac Briain kept them on task. After the third raid, she and her captain of the guard discussed the immediate future of their prisoner.

"He seems genuinely interested in opposing his former countrymen," Ailis mused. "Though his motive seems a little thin to me. All for a woman? I've never known any man to be that fond of any woman."

"Perhaps you aren't looking at the right men," Diarmid answered neutrally enough, but Ailis caught the twitch of his jaw.

She ignored it. "I lend more weight to his recusant Catholicism, and most weight of all to the beating and the savaging of his pride. He strikes me as a very proud man—in himself, mind you, not just because he's English—and I believe he has a genuine thirst for revenge. How far can we harness it?"

"Not far enough that I'd stop locking him in at night," Diarmid warned.

How well he knew her. She smiled. "What, you don't trust your men if he sleeps among them? I think we might learn more of Stephen the more we give him his head. I've no doubt you will continue to have eyes on him at all times."

Diarmid grunted but would not argue. There were advantages to his feelings for her, and Ailis used them skillfully.

"Our overseas guests are on the move?" she asked. Even alone, they spoke elliptically of the Spanish soldiers. Surprise was their greatest weapon, and it could not be wasted.

"They are. We've had word from Fiach O'Toole. The guests moved out of Glenmalure two days ago and are marching fast and dressed as locals toward Askeaton. The English might see them, but only from a distance. They will expect it is only more Irish coming to defend the Earl of Desmond."

"And the earl? He is prepared to make his stand?"

Gerald FitzGerald was a chancy man at best, having long had to balance his family inheritance and land of birth against the English crown that ratified his title. He'd never cut the dashing figure of his cousin James FitzMaurice, who had romped through Ireland twelve years ago and come very close to driving the English out of Munster entirely.

Then they'd caught him, and James FitzMaurice had died either a traitor or a martyr, depending on which side of the impassable divide you stood. Ailis remembered FitzMaurice and his kind words to her after Kilmallock. For his sake—and because they could not do without Desmond at this juncture—she would support FitzGerald.

As for Stephen Wyatt, she was prepared to give him his head to some degree. With the Spanish finally on the move, her part in the plan was to wait for word from Askeaton. Diarmid and her men would ride if FitzGerald called for aid, but for now she would stay in Cahir. She would not stray too far from here, in such easy reach of

Templemore and the man upon whom she had vowed vengeance a dozen years ago.

Only one man living knew the name of Liadan's father. She had never even told Finian, despite her uncle's shrewd guesses. Father Byrne alone knew her secret, for telling him carried with it the seal of the confessional and he would never divulge it. Ailis never talked about her months in Kilmallock as a fourteen-year-old Irish girl in an English-garrisoned town, for she had learned cunning and caution at the hands of the very man who had stolen her childhood. From him she had learned to school her expressions, not to flinch or show fear, to never admit weakness.

The English were enemies. He was *the* enemy. The object of long years of planning to bring him within her reach. Soon, very soon, thanks to the Spanish soldiers and the relief of Askeaton, the man at Templemore would have to move at a time and place of her choosing. And with Stephen Wyatt resident with the Kavanaughs, Ailis had a new plan to bring her enemy within reach.

She began to lay the groundwork that very evening, when she asked Stephen if he would join her to discuss his immediate future in Ireland. Diarmid made to follow her—and even Father Byrne moved slightly—but she waved them off. She was not afraid of this Englishman.

Actually, she found him far more engaging than was comfortable. Bastard son he might be, but he'd clearly been educated and had a quick sense of humour and a gentleness with Liadan that had not gone unnoticed. Ailis knew how to read the characters of men, and despite her native caution, she felt certain that Stephen Wyatt was not given to cruelty or attacks on women.

Stephen followed her to her chamber, which served for both sleeping and study, and took the proffered seat across the table from her. Stretched across it, as she usually had, was a map of Ireland. Dublin, Cork, Waterford, and Galway were lightly shaded, fading out around the cities to indicate the Pale, those areas under direct English control. Ailis hardly needed the map any longer, for she could see the details imprinted on her mind every time she closed her eyes. But this map had become something of a talisman. She had drawn this map—and others like it—herself over a number of years, and each hour spent with parchment and ink was a symbol of her control.

Ailis pointed to Askeaton, fifty miles northwest of Cahir. "You know the Earl of Desmond?"

"Not personally."

"The English think he cannot hold at Askeaton any longer. We are expecting an English siege this summer, which would force Desmond to run for the hills as his cousin FitzMaurice did ten years ago. He could last some years in the wilderness, but that's hardly likely to advance our cause and roll back English control. Desmond must hold Askeaton."

"'Our' cause?"

She met his eyes, a shifting greenish-gold fringed by dark, thick lashes. His hair was almost as black as hers. Though he'd had it cut since reaching Cahir, it was still unruly, and he'd not shaved his beard completely, letting it shadow the angles of his face and jaw. For the first time in her life, Ailis was swept by the desire to touch a man's hair, to feel it slip between her fingers where it clung to his neck.

It was such a surprising sensation that she almost lost the thread of what she'd been saying. She cleared her throat and looked down at the map without seeing it. "I will never trust you wholly—I cannot afford to. But you have proved useful and I find I can believe in your need for revenge. In that, we are very similar."

"Are we?"

His voice was neutral, but Ailis thought there was a suppressed energy to it. "You know that Liadan's father is English—no doubt she told you herself. I have never tried to hide it. I was fourteen when Kilmallock fell to Humphrey Gilbert and the English. By the time FitzMaurice retook and burned the town, I was five months gone with child. I have not spoken of the man responsible, not all these years, because it is no one's business but mine. Until now. Now, he is almost within my reach. There are plans within plans afoot in Munster just now—and one of those plans is my vengeance."

"Why are you telling me this?"

Because you are surprisingly easy to talk to, because you are not Irish and not family, because even though you are English, you do not have that smug air of everything belonging to you, because I believe that you wept when the Roisin you spoke of was murdered . . .

"Because I believe you could be of use to me. I don't intend to set you against your own countrymen in general. Too much risk of your native honour staying your hand or making you hesitate at the worst possible moment. But I think you might understand the nature of vengeance. And be willing to aid me in trapping one particular Englishman."

He was silent a long time, those deep hazel eyes shaded as he considered. Finally, he raised his head. "Tell me who we're trapping."

With a tremulous breath and a sensation as though she were falling, Ailis spoke her enemy's name. "Oliver Dane."

Only long experience of mimicking his father's blank expression kept Stephen from flinching when Ailis pronounced Dane's name.

It did not keep his mind from leaping into a whirlwind of shock and questions. *Dane?* Oliver Dane was Liadan's father?

Bed an Irish girl—the right Irish girl—and you'll never be contented with an Englishwoman again. Dane had spoken with perfect accuracy when choosing the word "girl"—Ailis had been but fourteen inside Carrigafoyle.

In that turmoil of thoughts, Stephen instinctively chose the right emotion to show—disgust. With a twist of her beautiful mouth, Ailis said, "I assume your expression means you've heard of him."

"I have." He forced his mind under his control, because just now he needed to think quickly and decisively. "It was under his orders that I was punished and Roisin killed."

Her eyebrows shot up. "Indeed? You did not say so before."

"I did not think it mattered. It wasn't Dane himself, you understand"—Stephen let the tiniest memory of that night outside Kilkenny leak into his voice—"but I'd met him. And I know it was by his orders that violence was done."

She propped her chin in one hand, her eyes dark and liquid. "You sound as though you care for him almost as little as I do."

"It cannot be compared. What he did to me, though abhorrent, is at least just excusable in the bounds of warfare. What he did to you—what he has done to other women and children—there is no excuse. I meant only to say that I will have very little trouble in helping you destroy him."

"Good." Ailis smiled, and Stephen thought dizzily that he would gladly agree to anything this woman wanted so long as it made her look at him like this.

His pulse beat loud and fast, and he was almost light-headed from this swift turnaround. God must be watching over him, to present this opportunity so neatly in his path. There was only one sticking point. However Ailis meant to trap Dane, Stephen could not allow himself to be seen. He wanted vengeance, but not at the cost of losing his place in this household. He wasn't ready to leave. Not yet.

Fortunately, Ailis did not press for specific plans just then. Perhaps uncomfortable with how personal she'd allowed herself to be, she dismissed him a little abruptly and said they would talk more later. He sent in Father Byrne and Diarmid, as she'd asked him to, ignoring the baleful glare of the captain of the guards. Stephen had worked out the first week that the man was in love with Ailis. Picking a fight with Diarmid would not help.

Liadan called to him from where she and Maisie were playing chess at the end of a long trestle table previously set for dinner. "Maisie cheats!" she announced energetically, as she announced everything. "So it's only fair that you help me."

"I'm not really sure it's possible to cheat at chess," Stephen answered, swinging a leg over the bench so he straddled it next to the exuberant child. "Even if it is, I'll be of no use to you. I'm no good at chess. That's all my—"

He swallowed hard, almost choking back the damning word. *That's all my sister,* he'd nearly said. But Stephen Wyatt did not have a sister. Could he really be so easily thrown by the smile of a beautiful woman and the promise of revenge on Oliver Dane?

Liadan didn't seem to notice, but Maisie glanced at him curiously. "That's all what?" she asked.

"That's all my own fault," he retorted, hoping he didn't sound as shaken as he felt. "I could never concentrate long enough."

"It's not concentration so much as the ability to see the wider picture," Maisie countered. "It's all a matter of patterns and probabilities—rather like business."

Liadan, impatient, cried, "It's your move."

With scarcely a glance at the board, Maisie moved a knight and took one of Liadan's pawns. The pieces were pewter, not the ivory or marble or jewel-inlaid pieces Stephen was accustomed to seeing. He had dozens of memories of Lucette and his mother, playing each other mostly to spend time together, since Lucie had been able to beat everyone in the household by the time she was eight.

While Liadan pursed her rosebud lips in a mock ferocity of focus, Maisie said to Stephen, "Peter Martin is supposed to be back here in the next few days. I imagine he'll be glad to see you on your feet and out of your locked room."

"Do you think he'll care? He did his Christian duty when he kept me from starving alone, but he has no other interest in me than that. It's been eight weeks. He mightn't even remember me."

That was a mistake, he knew it the instant he spoke. For he would need to speak with Martin during his time in Cahir, to pass information both ways. Better to paint a picture of a man who would be very interested in his welfare.

Liadan jogged his arm with her elbow and asked, "Do you think this move is right?"

He looked at her small hand hovering over a rook, then shrugged.

"I wasn't lying, I'm useless when it comes to chess." Shoving himself up from the table, he said as casually as he could manage, "I'm off to bed. Trying to keep up with the conversations of the women of this household is exhausting."

He was off to bed, but not to sleep. Far into the night he lay awake veering in his mind between Oliver Dane, Peter Martin, and—most disturbingly—Ailis Kavanaugh. When Walsingham had proposed sending him to the Kavanaughs, he'd assumed it was to take advantage of a young woman in a precarious leadership position. He had planned to insinuate himself into her good graces, much as he had with Mary Stuart at Tutbury, but from the first he'd realized Ailis was a different matter. Not because—strangely enough—she was a hundred times warier than the Scots queen, and not because her hatred of Englishmen ran deep.

It was because he cared.

Only because he hadn't cared about Mary Stuart had Stephen been able to flirt with her—to use the charm he'd borrowed liberally from Kit's example to flatter her and twist her impressions so she found him a sympathetic and ready listener. But then, Mary Stuart had been a job to him . . . right up to the moment he discovered that she'd put her life above that of his sister's. And then she had become a more personal enemy.

But Ailis was not just a job. The most successful covers, Julien had taught him, were those that hewed most closely to the truth of a man's soul. And truth be told, Stephen had serious qualms about English policy in Ireland. He'd been appalled at the poverty and hunger, made many times worse by English soldiers burning crops and destroying livestock solely to deprive the Irish of a means to live. If a man couldn't eat, ran the reasoning, then he sure as hell couldn't fight. But where was the valour and honour in that?

The slaughter at Carrigafoyle might have been masterminded by Oliver Dane, but Pelham had done nothing to stop him, and he had not even been reprimanded by the English authorities. And then, of course, came the slaughter of prisoners outside Kilkenny. Though

Stephen knew that act was beyond the pale of what even the most staunchly loyal lords like Ormond could stomach, the fact remained that it had mostly been shrugged off. Buried and forgotten.

The truth was, he sympathized with Ailis. Especially now that he knew it was Oliver Dane who had so abused her when she was not much older than Liadan. How many Irish women had borne children to Englishmen who'd used them carelessly and then moved on? How could he possibly justify his countrymen in that? How could he not look at Ailis and want to help her seek vengeance?

And how could he look Peter Martin in the eye in the next few days and lie? Even if by omission. For Stephen already knew that he would not breathe a word about Oliver Dane that might make its way back to Walsingham. He did not want to be ordered off that scent.

Because if he was, he could not swear he would obey that order.

Despite her reservations, Anabel thoroughly enjoyed herself the first three weeks of the Duc d'Anjou's visit. Whatever his physical drawbacks, Francis was witty and clever and knew how to make her laugh. Not, perhaps, as easily as Kit could, but it was a welcome respite all the same. She and Anjou each took to composing scurrilous verses about various members of the English court, striving to see who could outdo the other. Francis usually won, because he didn't have Anabel's innate respect for men and women she'd known most of her life, but every now and then that very familiarity meant she could go devastatingly to the heart of pomposity or vanity.

Pippa would have scolded her. Kit would have joined her. Lucette, in her siblings' place, merely rolled her eyes like the nominal older sister she was.

Anabel worked hard to keep the rest of the Courtenays out of her thoughts. Whatever they were doing in Spain was beyond her reach and there was little information coming in other than official reports. The personal letters were few and far between. At last, three

months after they had sailed from Portsmouth, two insightful letters
arrived from Spain.

10 July 1582

Dearest Anabel,

*Are you surviving Lucie's attentions? Although, truth be told, since she
met Julien she has very little attention for anything else.*

*No, that is not true. There is no man in the world who could make
Lucie stop solving puzzles and immersing herself in mathematics and logic.
But Julien has tempered her previous desire to be seen to be perfect. Though
perhaps you know that even better than I do, seeing as the two of you were
confined at Wynfield together. Stress, I believe, can forge strong bonds.*

*Seville is my favourite of the Spanish cities we have seen. Perhaps be-
cause it is the least insular, its port being the gateway to a world far beyond any we have ever dreamt of. I watch the ships coming and going
from the New World and a small part of me longs to wing my way to the
ends of our earth. To see the jungles and savage coastlines, to hear lan-
guages never before imagined, to meet people who have not the slightest
idea who we are—or care!*

*But that is just fancy. I promise I will not leave you like that. We shall
be back in a month or so, Anabel. With enough stories to satisfy even you.*

Love,
Pippa

Beneath Pippa's carefully composed letter were two lines scrawled
in a familiar hand.

*Every sight, every sound, every taste of Spain reminds me of you. I will
have lots to tell you when we return.*

Kit

The second letter wasn't even for Anabel. Madalena, while helping string pearls through Anabel's hair for an evening reception of London's mayor and guild leaders, said matter-of-factly, "My grandmother writes that Lady Philippa and Lord Christopher came to see her in Seville."

Anabel flinched against Madalena's hands, then stilled. "Did they? I presume they are well."

Of course they were well. Illness or difficulty would surely have been reported to her mother.

She could never deceive Madalena. "She thought Lord Christopher more astute than she would have expected from such a pretty younger son."

Pretty? Anabel choked back a laugh. She would never have used that word, but had to admit it fit. At least on the surface.

"Lady Philippa, my grandmother wrote, is troubled. And taking care to hide it from those around her."

"Did she elaborate on the nature of that trouble?"

"She did not."

They had been speaking English; now Anabel switched to Spanish just in case one of her other women came into the chamber. "Why are you telling me this?"

"Because you are also troubled, and like Lady Philippa choose to hide it rather than face it. My grandmother thought it strange that two young women so closely knit would choose to keep their secrets from each other."

Just how canny was Madalena's grandmother? Anabel wondered. Could she read her secret from across the seas? A secret she was keeping from herself almost as much as from Pippa.

How do you know when you're in love? Anabel had asked that question when she was twelve—not of her mother, whom she could not imagine ever having been in love, but of Minuette. It had seemed a very pressing question then, when she was just old enough to realize that love was possible, while still young enough to believe such a question would matter in her life.

Minuette did not laugh it off, or turn her away with a teasing answer. Perhaps she had sensed the trouble behind the question, from a girl who had watched her parents and knew that, whatever they felt, love was not the motivating factor of their relationship.

Only now, at the age of twenty, did Anabel realize how Minuette must have paused at the question—for surely it had brought a flood of memories about a man who had loved her to violent distraction. Anabel's uncle, the late King of England.

"I can only speak for myself," Minuette had warned her, "but there were two things that told me I was in love. First, that there was no one else I would rather be with for every moment of my day—not just the romantic moments."

"And second?" Anabel had prompted, only slightly unsettled by the thought of grown-ups being romantic.

"Second, because he made me want to be better. Not by lecturing me or ordering me—trust me, the few times he tried that ended disastrously!—but simply by being himself. The very fact that Dominic loved me precisely as I was made me want to give him the best person in return."

That had seemed an esoteric answer to a twelve-year-old, even a precocious princess with an impressive education. At the time, Anabel had been looking more for fireworks and breathless proclamations of an inability to breathe without each other.

But now, as Madalena silently pinned her hair, Anabel knew that Minuette had spoken true.

She had known Kit was in love with her since the crisis at Wynfield Mote. But only now could Anabel admit that she was as wholly in love with him as well.

FIFTEEN

Their final weeks in Spain passed in a whirlwind of official events and semiofficial discussions between Philip's councils and Elizabeth's envoys. Kit watched his father come and go from those discussions with his usual imperturbable expression and wondered what he thought of the current situation in Spain.

Kit was young, but one didn't have to be old to feel the undercurrents of tension and suspicion that had followed them through their travels. Indeed, perhaps he and Pippa had the advantage. People took less notice of the young—everyone, that is, except Philip himself.

The King of Spain might be the most powerful monarch in the Christian world, but he was also a loving father who had spent several afternoons in private consultation with Kit and Pippa, encouraging them to share as many stories of his only daughter as they could. And not just of the last year, but all the many years he had missed of her life. The king was particularly enchanted by stories of her stubbornness, and had laughed when Pippa did an accurate imitation of a ten-year-old Anabel using devastating logic to refute every argument her mother made as to why she had to learn Greek.

But other than by the king, the Courtenays had been received with surface courtesy and sideways glances. Kit had thought Seville might be less wary than Madrid or El Escorial, since the port city had such a constant influx of traders and contact with the New World. But there were undercurrents here as well. He was beginning to grow tired of politely shuttered faces and people who pretended not to understand his most basic questions.

He was also increasingly worried about Pippa. His twin had grown ever more inward since her visit to Madalena's grandmother. She would not talk about it, and only on reflection did Kit realize how much of their life had been defined by Pippa not talking. Or at least, not talking about herself. She was always the one giving advice and counsel and keeping her own interior life securely locked away. It was disconcerting to realize how little he knew about his twin.

All in all, by the time his father asked him to walk down to the harbor, he felt rather like one of the Arabian thoroughbreds the Spanish had in plenty. The day after tomorrow they would set sail on one of Philip's royal ships and hug the coast of Portugal north before returning to Portsmouth.

It was blazingly hot, in a way Kit had never known before. Even his parents had never been this far south, and the entire English party was amazed at just how thick the air could lay beneath the sun's rays. Kit couldn't believe that people managed to labor in this weather. But there were crowds aplenty as they strolled the bright streets.

If Dominic's stated reason for their route was to cast an eye over their ship, Kit quickly realized there was more to it than that. Of course there was. Dominic Courtenay did not lightly seek his children's company—or at least, not Kit's. He'd always had time for his daughters, and Stephen had naturally spent many hours alone with their father, being appropriately raised as heir to one of England's wealthiest estates.

Could it be his father had regrets? As they strolled into sight of the harbor—two of Philip's guards following at a discreet distance to ensure their well-being—his father said, "If I had known that going abroad was the surest way of getting to know you, I would have done it long ago."

Kit's first instinct, as always, was to tease. "What is there to know? I'm the simple one—no need to fret over the lighthearted younger son as long as I don't too openly smear the family name."

His father's reply was measured and grave. "The fact that you believe that tells me I have failed you in important ways. I am sorry for it."

What on earth was he supposed to say to that? Trying furiously to deflect the emotional undertones threatening to swamp him, Kit said, "Why would you apologize? You never do anything wrong." It didn't come out quite as teasing as he'd intended.

"And that tells me how very young you are." Dominic pushed his hand through his hair, threaded with silver but still abundantly black. "If you need me to, I can enumerate my many failures. But then we might be here awhile. All I can say in my defense is that I might have been much worse were it not for your mother. Believe it or not, I used to be even more rigid when younger."

They had stopped at an overlook of Seville's busy harbor, the guards keeping watch to—what? Ensure they didn't jump? Set fire to Philip's ships? Contaminate the population with their Protestant heresies?

Dominic had a naturally low voice, which he used to his advantage now. Kit was sure that he was the only one who heard his father when he said, "We've been in Spain for three months. Tell me what you see."

It was the kind of quizzing given to Stephen when younger—or even Lucette, with her brilliant, puzzle-solving mind. But this was not a quiz. This was the struggle of kingdoms.

As he had learned to do over the last year, Kit took his time answering. Once, he had rushed to speak, afraid if he did not keep people entertained they would lose interest in him. But his father was an eminently patient man and would prefer thought to impulse.

"I see a court glad enough to have twin boys to secure the inheritance . . . but uneasy with their new queen. Mary's pride is not meshing well with the Spanish. Perhaps it's her early years spent in France—she can't help but feel superior and distrustful. And vice versa."

Kit stretched, then leaned on the rock wall above the harbor. He could feel the rough texture of stone and mortar beneath his palms as he looked beyond the surface to what it might mean.

"There aren't enough ships," he observed finally, keeping his voice as low as his father's. Though it seemed folly to conduct this conversation in public, it was actually more private than in one of Philip's palaces with attendants around every corner. No doubt reporting on them.

His father nodded once, to show he'd heard, and Kit continued his analysis. "Seville is the sole port open to the New World. There should be more ships here. Which leads one to wonder—if the ships are not in Seville, where are they? There are too many missing to simply be accounted for by New World travel."

"Yes, there are."

"And we have not visited any other ports since we arrived. The Spanish have gone to some lengths to keep this secret."

With that rare smile of approval, his father said, "There's always another secret—so Henry VIII used to say. Philip knows we did not come simply—or even primarily—to present gifts to his new sons. He also knows we can count. It is the analysis they are trying to obscure. And fortunately, it is not dependent on you or I to make that analysis. We simply return with our observations to a court with men capable of seeing beneath obscurity."

"And then what?" Kit asked.

He meant what came next with the Spanish and English opposition, but his father answered a different question. One Kit hadn't been aware of asking. "Then you make up your mind to serve where you are best suited—and where you are needed. I would suggest intensive military training before all else, for I do not think the Spanish threat is neutralized. You have a talent for command, Kit, perhaps more even than Stephen or I. Your mother gave you gifts of warmth and interest and genuine care for other people. Men will follow a commander who cares."

Never in a hundred years would Kit believe he could ever be half the commander his father was. Dominic's men loved him, reticent as he was, and no man could command greater loyalty. Kit said wryly, once again deflecting, "Too bad I don't have any men to command."

"You do. When we return, I will settle Blessington and Upham Court on you. They come with a small contingent of experienced soldiers who will be happy to take you on and teach you leadership while giving you plenty of bruises and lessons in humility. And perhaps you might consider going abroad for a time. Renaud LeClerc would work you to a degree of high proficiency."

Kit didn't know if he could take any more surprises. Manors of his own? Training in France? But his father was not yet finished delivering surprising news. "You should also know that King Philip has offered you a Spanish bride. 'As a token of his esteem for his daughter's great friend,' he said. I think it is rather a token of His Majesty's concern."

His head was whirling so much he didn't know which sentence to address first. "Why is the king concerned with me?"

Now his father grew quiet, in a manner much more familiar to Kit. He seemed to be considering a great many things. Finally, he asked a question. The most humiliating question Kit had ever been asked. "How many women have you been with?"

He turned scarlet despite himself, and stuttered in reply. "I . . . What do you . . ." he stopped, wishing the earth would swallow him up. Was this the sort of conversation Stephen had with their father? If so, perhaps he preferred being overlooked.

"You haven't," his father concluded. "I didn't think so, but I'm not so old as to be convinced I know everything my children do. I'm afraid it's that fact—or, more truly, the motivation behind it—that has King Philip worried."

"Surely the King of Spain has more to worry about than my love life!"

"Did you not mark the number of women who, well, more or less offered themselves to you along the way? Spain is traditionally more conservative than England—these women would not have done it if they hadn't been steered in that direction."

This was growing too wild for reality. King Philip of Spain had been trying to lure him into a Spanish woman's bed? Why would he possibly care?

As though he'd spoken the last question aloud, his father answered. "Because of Anabel."

From scarlet, Kit's face turned white. He kept his eyes fixed on the horizon beyond the masts of the ships below.

His father continued, gently, "I do not wish to force you to speak of private things, but Kit? You're in dangerous waters if royalty is noticing your attentions and trying to find ways to break it. Philip is afraid of the hold you have on his daughter."

"And are you afraid of the same thing?" Kit asked bluntly.

"No. I'm afraid of the hold she has on you. I have always wished for my children to love as your mother and I do—but I had hoped it would come without the costs we had to pay. You and Anabel . . . I do not see an easy path there, son."

"Why do you think I went away?" he said forcefully.

His father sighed. "Does she feel the same about you?"

"No. Of course she doesn't. She's in England right this minute trying to decide between France and Scotland."

"I hope so, son. For both your sakes."

"Tell me, Walsingham, what am I do about William Catesby and this wild scheme for a Catholic English colony in the New World? The Spanish ambassador has his fingerprints all over this proposal. And I do not like them meddling with my subjects."

"Catesby should have remained in prison," Walsingham said severely. "He harbored Edmund Campion and has shown no eagerness to reform after the treasonous priest's execution. When you give the recusants so much room to maneuver, of course they will maneuver to your disadvantage."

"Better to let them leave, then?" Elizabeth demanded, piqued. Walsingham was nearly always proposing harsher measures. Sometimes she wondered if she opposed him merely from habit.

"I do not think any plan that involves the Spanish and English citizens is a good plan."

"Well, let us see what our envoys and Lord and Lady Exeter have to say about Spain when they return. It's only another ten days or so. I doubt Catesby and his ilk are preparing to sail on the next tide."

Walsingham nodded and his brother-in-law, Walter Mildmay, took the pause to redirect the conversation. "Esmé Stewart is expected to pass the night at Oxford and arrive at Hampton Court late tomorrow. Apparently the Duke of Lennox is coming with full plenipotentiary powers to treat for a marriage with Princess Anne."

"And no doubt the Duc d'Anjou is fully aware of the same," Walsingham continued. "You must make a decision, Your Majesty. You cannot continue to lead two countries on indefinitely. Her Highness is appealing, but these men have their pride."

"And I have mine!" she snapped. "England is not so poor that we must beg attention. But by all means, if you wish to please the French before Stewart's arrival, then send the Duc d'Anjou to me. The two of us will talk."

To his credit, Walsingham looked wary about that plan. Sometimes the man knew her entirely too well for comfort.

Anjou appeared a quarter hour later, neat and suave as though he'd simply been waiting for her summons. Truly, he had proven himself an intelligent and cultured prince as well as a pleasing one. He could debate, he could command, and he could charm. As perfect a prince as could be hoped.

As Elizabeth waved her ladies to the far end of the presence chamber where a lute player entertained, she remembered other moments when she'd sought the illusion of privacy in public spaces. When it had been Robert walking toward her with that assured grace bordering on arrogance that so captivated her. There had never been another like him—and Elizabeth had been feeling that loss keenly this last month. As she'd watched her beautiful and very young daughter captivate Anjou, she had felt moments of pure resentment that she was no longer the most desirable woman in England.

Perhaps, she thought mordantly, that is why my own mother and I had difficulties. Perhaps all mothers and daughters are destined to shipwreck on the shoals of aging and jealousy.

Still, Anabel did not possess the throne of England. Not yet. And thrones, in and of themselves, were very desirable.

"La belle reine," Anjou murmured, bending low in greeting. "To what do I owe this great honour?"

"To the tediousness of ruling," Elizabeth retorted. "Sit, and relieve me of my boredom."

"How can a queen of such accomplishments ever be bored?" Anjou sat with the kind of graceful ease that did much to compensate for his physical drawbacks. And one could not take exception with his manners. "The court of England draws men of the highest scholarship and adventure, like moths to a flame. You have only to snap your fingers to command whom you wish."

"And at this moment, I snap my fingers for you. Entertain me with news from France—not the dispassionate accounts of diplomats. Give me rumour and gossip. Truly, how did your mother take the news of Mary Stuart's escape and marriage?"

Anjou laughed, and Elizabeth could swear it was unprompted and genuine. "You do go right to the heart of the matter," he said. "You have met my mother, yes?"

"I had that honour." So many years ago that Elizabeth did not care to mention it to Anjou. He'd scarcely been born when she had gone to France as Princess of Wales. No, she would not remind him of that.

"My mother, the Queen Dowager, reacted precisely as you would expect: fury at Spain for not only taking Mary Stuart in but wedding her. And, I'm afraid, a great deal of contempt directed at you for letting her slip away."

"Then perhaps she should have taken care with your brother's subjects not to let them plot against my daughter! I doubt even Catherine de Medici would lightly sacrifice one of you." Although, perhaps, maybe she would. Catherine had an excess of children, after all. Unlike herself.

Anjou was quick enough to read Elizabeth, and said smoothly, "My mother and I are hardly a model of agreeing with one another."

That did make her laugh. "I imagine if Catherine found my release of Mary Stuart contemptible, then the Edict of Beaulieu must continue to drive her to distraction." For it was Francis, this younger son of whom no one had expected much, who championed the Huguenots and negotiated the peace six years ago that, at least nominally, allowed French Protestants to worship without fear of massacre. A slap at the policies of his brother and the French queen mother who had ordered the St. Bartholomew's Day Massacre.

"Your Majesty," Anjou went on, his keen eyes unwavering, "surely you know how deep my hopes run to ally with England. We need each other. I know that the Scots envoy will say much the same thing. And I know Esmé Stewart." Anjou grinned. "He will say it more handsomely than I can manage. But if my face is imperfect, my sincerity is not. I will offer anything within my power to be wed to England."

Anything in his power? An idea, that had before been but a half-formed dream and shadow, was beginning to take root in Elizabeth's mind. Why should England not have everything it needed? Alliance with France, and union with Scotland. Appease the Catholics and reinforce the Protestant ascendancy on this island. And, not least of all, infuriate both Philip and Mary Stuart in equal measure.

With her most seductive smile, honed all these years on more men than Robert Dudley, Elizabeth briefly touched the back of Anjou's hand with her beautiful long fingers. Her locket ring glinted, less showy than the sapphires and rubies on her other fingers, but it seemed to convey Anne Boleyn's approval. If anyone would have understood finding pleasure while also doing what one must, it would have been the much-maligned Queen Anne.

"Francis," Elizabeth murmured. "Why make it a contest? I have never been one for doing what others expect me to do. And so I think that perhaps you and I might come to an arrangement that benefits both France and Scotland."

Anjou was quick and intuitive. If there was a moment's surprise, he covered it neatly as his mind leaped to follow hers. She thought she saw a brief flash of wry regret in his eyes, but he conquered it almost at once as he lifted her hand to kiss it. "I like the way you think, Your Majesty."

Peter Martin duly arrived in Cahir and, after completing his round of messages and information for the Kavanaughs, had a cursory interview with Stephen. He appeared content to see Stephen's improved standing in the household as work well done for the time. There were no new instructions from England, but Martin was able to tell him a few things thanks to his travels around Ireland.

"Ormond is keeping close to his own lands," Martin reported. "Resisting calls from England to move on Askeaton. Pelham is facing outbreaks of violence in Dublin and may not be able to move, either."

"So who is going to Askeaton?"

Martin shrugged. "Not my area. I'm just an itinerant messenger who knows rather more Latin than is good for him. Anything at this end? If you wanted to write to someone, I could get it through."

Stephen wouldn't risk it. His family knew only the barest bones of where he was, and he had nothing to say to Walsingham. Yet. Besides, Ailis had already offered to send any letters he cared to write. Maisie sent letters by the dozens—she spent hours each day writing

copiously to various people in Scotland and received almost as many
in reply. No doubt any missive of his would have been read before
being sent, but he had an innocuous code and cover for a letter that
would mean something only to the spymaster. That he hadn't written was due mostly to his own reluctance.

Martin's last words were a warning, a message from Walsingham.
"Our master says there have been a few inquiries about your where-
abouts in London. Among the city classes and the foreign merchants.
He says to keep your head down in case a lady of your acquaintance
might be trying to track you."

Mary Stuart? Despite her exalted status, Stephen wouldn't put it
past the queen to be trying to trace him. Mary had left him in no
doubt of her contempt when she'd left England.

Before Martin left Cahir, he spent several hours closeted with
Ailis and her chief advisors. There was clearly something in the air—
something the Kavanaugh household was waiting upon. Stephen
knew it had something to do with Askeaton. He didn't try too hard
to find out after being verbally slapped down by Diarmid mac Briain
for asking artless questions. Diarmid did not like him in the slightest, but Stephen thought that had as much to do with Ailis as anything. Mac Briain was besotted with her and did not like anything
that turned her attention elsewhere.

And these days, her attention was fixed on Stephen. Even Liadan
commented on it one afternoon as he watched her riding astride a
horse that could easily have crushed her. "Mother must like you very
much or she'd never let you near the horses."

"She lets me near *you*—surely that's a greater sign of trust."

"No. Because you could use the horses to escape Cahir if that's
what you wanted. What could you possibly use *me* for?"

Stephen laughed even as a chill ran down his spine. Before she
knew it, Liadan would no longer be a child—and a beautiful woman
in Ireland could be put to all sorts of uses by unscrupulous men.

He knew he was well on his way to being besotted himself with

Ailis, in a manner he'd never expected. All his previous women—not as many as all that—had been of a more professional nature, the affairs conducted at one remove from his daily life. All save Roisin, whom he carried with him like a little spark of fury to remind him what he most wanted in Ireland. But it meant that he'd never had the experience of being attracted—such a mild word for such a dangerous emotion—to a woman whom he saw every day in all manner of situations.

Before now he'd never guessed that breathless desire could strike so strongly when watching a woman poring over maps or snapping orders to her guards. Half a dozen times a day Stephen had to force himself to stand straight and breathe normally, to not let his eyes follow Ailis like a puppy with a new master. It was an insane, impossible proposition. One he would never, ever make. He could never bed a woman who didn't know his name—and if Ailis knew his name, she would stick a dagger in his chest.

If only she would kiss him first, it might be worth it.

He'd not been this long without a woman since he was eighteen. Ironically, instead of making him hunger for bed, it increased his hunger for any touch. However slight. Even the right kind of sideways glance from Ailis left him dizzy.

He was behaving precisely like a lovestruck girl, alert to her every movement and expression. And there was just enough of intimacy in both to keep him in suspense.

In which state he remained until the first Thursday in August when the household at Cahir erupted in triumphant victory. Stephen, teaching Liadan how to handle a wooden small sword, had watched a dusty outrider exchange terse nods with Diarmid in the courtyard and then the two men vanished inside. Not two minutes later the shouting began, of a cheerful tone that made Maisie, watching from her seat on the steps—a partially written letter on a board across her lap—look up and say, "Well, at least we know it's good news."

"What is?" Liadan dropped her wooden sword and scampered in the direction of the activity.

Stephen caught at her arm and held her back. "A soldier must always keep focus."

"I'm not a soldier."

"But you are learning to handle a sword. That makes you responsible while you hold that weapon. Would your mother go running off at the first excitement?" When Liadan scowled, Stephen promised, "If no one comes to tell us in five minutes, we'll go in together."

It was only three minutes before Ailis appeared, Diarmid a pace behind at her shoulder. Their shared lineage was obvious in the sharpness of their cheekbones and the fierceness of their dark eyes. Just now, both of them seemed lit up like candles from within.

"Askeaton is fortified," she called to the three of them, and there was no mistaking the triumph in her voice. "One hundred Spanish soldiers have marched to its relief. The Earl of Desmond has already begun sending raiding parties out to reinforce his borders."

One hundred Spanish soldiers . . . so the missing soldiers had finally revealed themselves. Stephen spared a moment in considering Walsingham's dismay at the news, but then Ailis came closer. "Will you ride with me, Stephen? This news brings forward some of the plans we have spoken of." She kindled like a flame, and Stephen felt his blood pulse to meet her.

"Ride?" he repeated, at the same moment as a furious Diarmid fumed, "You can't be serious!"

"I'm always serious," Ailis replied serenely. "I think it's time I show Stephen the Rock of Cashel. Alone. If we are not back by dark, by all means send a scouting party after us."

She stared at her captain, daring him to openly disobey her. But the success at Askeaton gave her enough sway for Diarmid to mutteringly agree.

Stephen mounted a horse and followed Ailis, for the first time since his arrival, outside the walls of Cahir Castle.

————

With Stephen riding at her side, Ailis felt the tension of the last months—all that time hoping the Spanish soldiers would remain concealed and their plan unnoticed—slip away like the scudding clouds overhead. It was little more than ten miles to the Rock of Cashel, and during their leisurely ride Ailis told the Englishman stories about the spot. From St. Patrick banishing the devil—thus blasting the entire enormous rock to its present location—to the Irish abbot in Germany who sent two of his carpenters to help build Cormac's Chapel.

Stephen said little, but he appeared to be listening closely. And as they approached the limestone plateau rising sharply against the level landscape, he whistled in appreciation.

They were allowed through the walls that encircled the plateau and found a boy to watch their horses for an Irish shilling. Then Ailis led Stephen around the complex of chapel, cathedral, castle, and graveyard.

"St. Patrick came here?" Stephen asked. "After he blasted the devil, I mean."

"Converted the King of Munster on this spot. The buildings are mostly from the twelfth and thirteenth centuries. Cormac's Chapel is quite beautiful. We could attend service, if you like?" she teased.

He answered in kind, with a smile that only just tipped up the corners of his mouth. "I quite like worshipping God outdoors. With you."

Ailis felt her tension return—but of a kind she had never known. She had not played these sorts of games before, but her instincts seemed to know where to lead her. She laid her hand on his arm and let it slip into a hold. "Then come see the round tower. It's nearly five hundred years old."

The drystone tower looked as it had for centuries, its entrance high aboveground so that church treasures might be hidden when Viking invaders swarmed the land. Pity, the Normans and the English had not been so easily dealt with. Ailis ran a hand along the stones, almost feeling the pulse of her country beneath her palm.

Stephen watched her. "You said our plans have been brought for-ward?"

"I don't want to talk about plans," she said. "Not just yet. I want to celebrate what we have already achieved."

Ailis watched Stephen survey the church towers and stone out-buildings around them. Though there were people living within the walls of the rock, the Round Tower was deserted. She had chosen her spot well.

"I thought the Irish preferred people and music and drink for celebration," Stephen observed.

Ailis released his arm and did something she'd wanted to do for weeks—moved her hand to the back of his neck so she could feel his hair brushing against her fingers.

"Stephen," she said, amazed at her own daring, but it was as if the triumph at Askeaton had loosed something in her, something liquid and warm. She had not been afraid of Englishmen since she was a child—she would not be afraid of this one. "I never knew what it is to want a man. I never had the chance to know. All my thoughts since I was fourteen have been bent on destruction, not desire. I did not think I had it in me."

He eyed her warily, as Ailis had seen men watch a wild animal to see which way it would bolt, but beneath his wariness were other signs. She might not have personal experience of female desire, but she knew all about men's. Stephen wanted her. But unlike most men, he would be a gentleman about it.

Had he guessed that his English reticence would force her to be so bold?

"Do you not wish to celebrate with me?" She hadn't even known that she knew how to tease a man. Some things must be instinctive.

He had the most glorious smile and his voice had gone low and husky. "Tell me how."

"Do they not celebrate in England?" One step at a time, drawing ever nearer so that Stephen had to angle his head down to continue looking at her. She was tall, but he was taller. She liked that about him.

"I thought we English were a cold, suspicious race, not given to celebration."

"Then I shall have to teach you." Her breath caught as she finished, and she thought she heard his hitch as well. Still he would not move. Fine. As he was still—technically—her prisoner, then she would dare the leap for both of them.

Ailis kissed him.

It was like storm clouds and lightning, freshening sea winds and bursts of spring colours. For half a heartbeat she thought Stephen was merely enduring her touch, but then his arms came around her and everything was wonderfully, vividly alive. She had been a man's mistress when she was barely a woman, had given birth to a child now verging on womanhood herself—and never had she imagined this.

His kisses—nothing at all like Dane's—started at her lips and then trailed along her cheek to her throat. She gasped and he paused.

"Ailis, tell me to stop if—"

"Do you want to stop?"

He groaned. "Not ever."

"Neither do I." She wound her fingers through his hair. "Teach me, Stephen. Teach me about joy."

SIXTEEN

Just as Anabel had grown accustomed to entertaining Anjou, the new player on the stage arrived from Scotland. Esmé Stewart, Duke of Lennox and favourite of the young King James, was an impressive figure from the moment of his arrival at Hampton Court. Forty years old, born and raised in France, Stewart was at the height of his power and attraction. From the first moment, he cast even the royal Anjou into the shade. He was built along elegant lines, slender and fine-boned, but there was no mistaking his masculine appeal. His dark eyes gleamed with appreciation as he bent over Anabel's hand in greeting.

"Your Highness," he said in a honeyed tone that once would have had Anabel exchanging eye rolls with Kit, "I fear my king will never forgive me for laying eyes on you before he could. But be assured that I am here wholly to speak for James himself."

"Wholly?" Anabel teased. She had learned the trick of it these last weeks.

"I could not swear that one or two compliments of my own might not slip through. Don't tell my wife," he added with a conspiratorial wink.

With a laugh, Anabel passed Stewart over to her mother's councilors, who were less likely to be impressed by his manners. They would want to know what was being offered for their princess in terms of cold, hard advantage.

Anabel spent the next few hours attending to her own business matters. Matthew Harrington had proved the wisest choice possible as her treasurer—like Burghley, he had the knack of tying together seemingly unrelated matters and making the most complex transactions clearly understandable in a wider context. They worked well together, and even her mother had commented on how profitably Anabel's investments and estates were faring.

Matthew also had the knack of sticking to essentials. He did not engage in small talk or gossip. So Anabel was taken by surprise when he said at the end of their workday, "I hear that Esmé Stewart is an appealing man."

"Would you like an introduction?"

His mouth twitched up and Anabel realized how it suddenly lightened her heart to see any sign of happiness. Matthew had always been reserved, but since his father's death there had been an unmistakable oppression to his spirits. "Lady Philippa said that you would like him. That if it were Stewart himself being offered, you might be tempted."

"She said that? Before or after she went to Spain?"

"Before."

"Well, unless Pippa offered to find a way to divest Esmé Stewart of his wife and four—or is it five?—children, then there is only James on offer from Scotland. A sixteen-year-old Protestant king, or a twenty-four-year-old French Catholic prince? Which one would be best for my account books, do you think?"

"That I cannot tell you, Your Highness."

"I suppose I shall have to wait for Pippa's return for guidance. It cannot come soon enough."

His answer was so quick and fervent, she almost didn't recognize his voice. "I agree."

Oh dear. How many romantic secrets were being kept around court just now? At least the best that could be said of her situation was that no one in France or Scotland was likely to be brokenhearted whatever choice England made.

The morning after Esmé Stewart's arrival, the queen summoned her daughter for a private tête-à-tête. Anabel had been enjoying the last few weeks so much that she was slow to recognize the purpose behind this particular conversation. They settled into cushioned seats embroidered in a riot of flowers and vines, a table with ginger-bread and pear cider in easy reach.

"And how do you like the Duke of Lennox?" her mother asked.

"Does it matter? I am not on offer to Esmé Stewart, but to the king who is young enough to be his son."

Her mother merely blinked and waited. Anabel sighed. "I would say he is a very good man. Having met him, I believe that his conver-sion to the Protestant faith is sincere, and not politically motivated. He serves his king well."

"So he does. And just now, there is no one in Scotland better situ-ated than the Duke of Lennox to offer us the truth of James's inten-tions. And the truth is, James refuses to discuss any possible bride except you."

Anabel didn't think she quite matched her mother's air of disin-terest. "Of course not. He is determined to have England."

"Marrying you does not give him England," her mother pointed out sharply. "There is no question of any husband of yours receiving the crown matrimonial. It will be a marriage of rulers, not kingdoms. Only if you have a son together might the question arise of a united kingdom."

"Pity for my own father I wasn't a son, then."

Did that make her mother flinch? Elizabeth had never shown any sign of wishing Anabel had been a boy, but then the queen was excel-lent at hiding her true feelings.

"It would not have mattered. England and Spain could never be reasonably combined, whatever your sex. But England and Scotland? I suspect that is inevitable."

"It sounds as though you are decided. I will be betrothed to James, and the Duc d'Anjou will go home. Disappointed in his ambitions." As for her, Anabel hardly knew what she felt.

"Not so disappointed," her mother disagreed.

The queen reached for a cup of cider, then drew her hand back. In any other woman, Anabel would have thought it a sign of nerves.

But her mother's expression was one of disinterest as she continued. "I do you the courtesy of informing you first of what I will discuss in council later today. When we announce your betrothal to King James of Scotland, we shall simultaneously announce my own betrothal to Francis, Duc d'Anjou."

Surprise made Anabel indelicate. "You are twice his age!"

"And has that ever been an issue for a king taking a wife?"

"You are not a king."

In the furious snap of her eyes, the Queen of England subsumed the mother. "Of course I am! And so must you be. If you are determined to play the child, then you will never be fit to rule."

All at once Anabel knew precisely what she was feeling. Cold, hard fury. She had controlled her own impulses. She had put Kit out of her mind as best she could. She had submitted to being paraded like a broodmare, to setting her mind to accept men she had no personal attraction to, had allowed herself to believe that sentiment had no place in affairs of royal matrimony. But what was her mother doing if not behaving sentimentally?

With an inward snap that could almost be heard, Anabel completely and thoroughly lost her temper.

"If this is what ruling is," she said with controlled venom, "then I want no part of it. Announce whatever you wish. With the decision made, you have no need of me to pretend to flirt with men who are not interested in anything other than power. I shall go to Ludlow.

When my body is required to seal this arrangement, you will let me know."

The Courtenay family landed at Portsmouth the first week of August and spent one night at Southsea Castle, where, two years ago, Kit had watched Anabel say goodbye to King Philip for good. It was more of a relief than Kit had expected to set foot on English soil once again, to be surrounded by voices he didn't have to try to understand. Only then did his body relax and he realized how tense he'd been while in Spain. As they rode out the next morning, he whistled a jaunty tune, earning an answering grin from Pippa.

"Feels good to breathe again," she said. "You were making me nervous all those weeks in Spain."

"Me?"

"I kept waiting for you to snap at King Philip every time he asked about Anabel. You were like a dog defending its territory—all laid-back ears and bared teeth."

"What? I didn't . . ." He floundered, then shrugged his shoulders and asked simply, "Was I that obvious?"

"Only if one were looking for it. And King Philip *was* looking for it, I'm afraid. He might even welcome Anabel's marriage to Scotland or France as long as it keeps you out of the picture."

"Well, she's not going to marry me, so I'd say Spain has nothing to worry about."

"Spain has plenty to worry about, almost as much as England. Sometimes I wonder what might have happened if King Philip and Queen Elizabeth had never married each other. I doubt the two countries could ever be friends, but perhaps their enmity would be a little less barbed without the personal aspects."

Kit shrugged. "What might have happened is of no matter. Only what is. Spain and England are on a collision course. The only question is when and how sharply they collide."

"Not the only question."

"What else is there?"

"How prepared we are for the collision. War is coming, Kit. Anyone who's paying attention can see that. All eyes are on Elizabeth and Philip. Anabel is considered little more than a pawn in her parents' games. But I think . . ." Pippa's voice trailed away, and Kit, turning sharply on his horse to see her face, marked the faraway gaze. The one that always gave him chills.

Then Pippa snapped back into the moment. She met her twin's eyes and said, "Anabel is no one's pawn. She is not simply a piece on the game board—she *is* the game. I have seen it."

Rarely did Pippa speak so plainly. Kit opened his mouth to question her, but his sister urged her horse forward until she was riding next to their mother. Leaving Kit to wonder just how plain Pippa's visions were.

They spent the second night in Haslemere. News of their arrival had been spurred ahead by faster riders, and they were met along their route the next morning by an anonymous rider carrying a private message from the queen. They encountered him at a hamlet, no more than six houses and a tiny church, and read the message practically on the side of the road.

Kit knew it couldn't be good—the queen would not go to such trouble merely to welcome them back when they were expected at court shortly—and was relieved when the first part proved simply to be word that they'd found the missing Spanish soldiers in Ireland when they'd marched to the relief of Askeaton.

He wasn't sure what that meant for Stephen, but there didn't seem to be any immediate danger to his position.

But it was the last part that made the world collapse inward, two lines that his mother refused to read aloud but mutely passed to her husband and then to the twins.

Anabel has fallen seriously ill with fever. Don't spread the word, but come straight to Hampton Court.

Kit was allowed to ride ahead with a single guard as fast as he could push, while his parents and Pippa followed at a more reasonable rate. He was glad to have his parents' agreement to the plan, but he would have gone on without it. It was not possible to hold back when Anabel was ill. Kit had paused just long enough to pull Pippa aside and ask, "What should I know?"

He probably didn't have to put it to words, for no doubt she could feel his fear as her own, beating through both their bodies like a flood. He couldn't feel her to the same degree, so he needed her to speak.

She wasn't as comforting as he'd hoped, nowhere near as certain as she'd been yesterday. "I don't know, Kit. I think it will be all right, but everything's . . . I don't know. There's too much in the way."

The remaining twenty miles to Hampton Court passed in a blur of speed and barely controlled imagination. It wouldn't be smallpox, would it? The queen had fallen ill with smallpox when Anabel was a baby and nearly died from it. Wouldn't she have said if it was smallpox? But no—the queen would not have put anything that inflammatory into writing. The government was controlling the flow of information. That was probably what scared him more than anything. If they were controlling information, it was because they didn't trust people with the truth. Not yet. And that augured ill. The last time information about Anabel had been controlled was when she was held captive at Wynfield Mote two years ago.

He clattered into Hampton Court in as much of a lather as his horse and darted through courtyards and up staircases that were less populated than usual, a fact that increased his tension. Finally he spotted someone who could direct him—Lord Burghley's son Robert—and hailed him.

"We had word from the queen," Kit said.

Robert, a year younger than Kit, nodded once. "I'll take you in."

Not, as it turned out, to Anabel or the queen, but to Burghley himself. He did not look surprised to see Kit. "You came on fast," he observed. "Your family is with you?"

"A few hours behind."

"Good. Anabel has been asking for your sister."

Only for Pippa? "Tell me how she is."

"Sit down," Burghley said gently. And when Kit didn't move, added, "You won't do her any good looming over me."

Kit sat abruptly, like a marionette with all its strings cut.

"Good." Burghley always had an air of calm about him and he seemed to be trying to communicate it to Kit now. "Four days ago Her Majesty and the Princess of Wales had something of a disagreement. Not to put too fine a point upon it, the princess was in a raging temper and determined to leave court at once. She put her household in motion to ride to Ludlow the next day. But by dawn she had been stricken with fever and other symptoms."

"Tertian fever? Flux? What's wrong with her?"

"The physicians have diagnosed scarlatina. It is an illness more common in children. It began with a fever and sore throat, and some stomach distress. This morning a rash appeared."

Kit didn't like the sound of that. "Spots? They're certain it's not smallpox?"

"They're certain. At this point, it is the fever that is the greatest concern. It's remained high and she seems to be suffering from side effects."

Was he going to have to drag everything out of the damned man? With tight jaw, Kit said, "Just tell me the worst."

For a moment there was an entirely too knowledgeable look of compassion on Burghley's face. Then the politician returned. "Anabel is seeing things that aren't there. And she has taken a violent dislike to some of her attendants, accusing them of wanting her to die. The only one she has been completely at ease with is your sister, Lucette. And as I said, she has been asking for Lady Philippa." Burghley paused. "And you."

"Then I'm going to her." Kit stood.

"I don't think so."

"You can't stop me."

"The queen can, and she will."

Even while Burghley was speaking, Kit shoved his way out the door, into the corridors that would lead him to Anabel's chambers. Burghley followed, trying to hold him back.

"Lord Christopher, if you would only listen—"

He wouldn't listen and he wouldn't slow. Two guards stood outside Anabel's door. At Burghley's resigned signal they allowed Kit through. He stepped into Anabel's presence chamber and hesitated, disoriented. The high-ceilinged chamber, usually flooded with light from the windows overlooking Clock Court, was shrouded in gloom. Heavy velvet curtains of emerald green gave the space a claustrophobic feel, as though one were trapped underwater. At any given time Kit would have expected to find a dozen or more clerks and courtiers waiting upon Anabel, but today there were only two people— Queen Elizabeth and Lucie's husband Julien.

Without a word, Kit strode across the presence chamber toward the inner door that would lead him nearer to Anabel. By the time he reached it, Julien blocked his way.

"Sorry," Julien said.

Kit whirled on Queen Elizabeth. "She wants me," he said flatly. "I'm going in."

"Lord Burghley," she ordered, "summon Lucette to speak to her brother."

"Lucie can't stop me any more than you can," Kit warned. "Burghley told me she's scared and seeing things—if she wants me, why in God's name won't you let me in?"

"Because you haven't had scarlatina," Lucette said, easing through the privy chamber door to stand next to her husband. "It's contagious."

"I don't give a damn. And if it's so contagious, why are you in there? Didn't your husband try and stop you?"

"I have had scarlatina," Lucette answered calmly. "So have Stephen and Pippa. I was nine years old—you were five. It was the spring you broke your ankle, remember? You stayed at Tiverton with Father and Carrie while Mother took the rest of us to Wynfield

Mote. While the three of us were there, we all had scarlatina to-gether. There's little danger to me now, but quite a lot to you."

"I don't bloody care!"

Not unkindly, Lucie said, "When Mother and Father are here, you can take it up with them. But not now, Kit. I'm sorry. And hon-estly, I don't think Anabel would even know you were there."

Kit looked from his sister's compassionate and weary face to Ju-lien, who stared back at Kit as though daring him to make a move. Julien's loyalties were entirely with Lucie—he would keep her brother out by force if she wanted him to.

"Fine." He forced himself to speak. "I should change anyway after the ride. But the minute Mother and Father arrive, I'm going in there. Is that clear?"

He had forgotten that Queen Elizabeth was in the room until she said, rather drily, "You make yourself very clear."

"Kit?" Lucie looked as though she wanted to touch him but wouldn't because of whatever risk she imagined. "Scarlatina is not smallpox or the plague—so long as we can keep her fever controlled, she should recover just fine."

"'Should' isn't good enough." He whirled on his heel and left the presence chamber without making any obeisance to his queen, and stalked furiously away to bathe and change. His family should be here within two hours. He would wait that long. Then, if he had to, he would fight his way into Anabel's room.

In the end, he didn't have to. Surprisingly, it was not his gentle, softhearted mother who decreed he be allowed in, but his father. They were all gathered in Anabel's presence chamber—the queen and the entire Courtenay family save Stephen.

His father took one look at Kit's furious, fearful face and said, "Let him go in."

Elizabeth narrowed her eyes. "Do you really want three of your four children in there? Even if the girls have had scarlatina?"

"There was a night," his father said slowly, eyes locked on the queen, "many years ago in this very chamber, where I would have cheerfully sold whatever remained of my life to be allowed into a sickroom."

"I remember. And that is what frightens me."

"It's too late for that, Elizabeth." Kit had never heard his father speak to the queen so personally; that was generally reserved for their mother. "They must find their own way."

Elizabeth's expression tightened as she turned away from Dominic's burning gaze. "Go in," she told Kit.

He didn't trouble to decipher all the undertones of that cryptic exchange, but shot through the privy chamber with its physicians and nursing ladies and on into Anabel's bedchamber.

At the threshold of the open door he halted. He'd never been in here before. But there was Anabel on the bed and protocol didn't matter.

Kit ignored everyone else, including his sisters, who'd followed him, and went straight to the bed. From behind he heard Lucie say, "It's not a good idea to touch her."

He wasn't afraid of infection—but he was afraid of people changing their mind and forcing him from the chamber. So he refrained from touching.

Her cheeks and forehead were covered in a bright red rash, with a ring of white skin left around her mouth. Her lips were dry and cracked, and her hands and her eyelids moved restlessly as though dreaming. Most shockingly, her hair had been shorn.

Pippa, reading him with her usual ease, murmured, "It's to help with the fever, Kit. It will grow back."

He had never seen Anabel vulnerable. Even as children, she'd had an innate self-possession that marked her as much as her red hair. She looked very young and very ill indeed.

Her eyelids in their fluttering opened enough to look at him. He wasn't sure she was aware of anything until she whispered, "Kit?"

"I'm here," he said, smiling a little, as though that would have the power to heal her.

"I always think you're here." She sounded deeply drugged, and profoundly weary. "But it's just a dream. You're not here. You left me."

To hell with warnings. Kit leaned over and cupped her fevered cheeks in his hands. "I am here now, Anabel. It's really me. And you're going to be well. I promise."

Remarkably, she managed to move her right hand and touch his arm. "You came back," she said.

If his sisters hadn't been standing right behind him, he might have kissed her then. Instead, he leaned closer and murmured in her ear, "I will always come back for you, *mi corazon*."

SEVENTEEN

The summer weeks passed for Stephen in a blur of activity, punctuated by the clarity of his time alone with Ailis. He hadn't lost the ability to think—he knew this interlude couldn't last, and not just because he was lying to her about his identity. From the day they'd returned from their stolen hour at the Rock of Cashel, Diarmid mac Briain had tracked their every movement with a resentment that was all the more dangerous for being swallowed. The captain of the guard only refrained from open hostility because of his own deep feelings for Ailis. But the rest of the guards were not so disciplined. With every evening that Stephen and Ailis went off alone, the restlessness of Clan Kavanaugh increased.

One mid-August night, the air cool and damp with days of rain and fog, Stephen lay stretched full-length on Ailis's bed. Since she also used the chamber as her study, they could preserve the illusion that they were only talking strategy behind closed doors. They *did* talk strategy—the scattered maps and reports across the table bore witness to it—but it was never long before the bed beckoned.

Tonight, Stephen wondered aloud, "Are we taking too many chances with your household's trust?"

"They will hold," Ailis assured him, trailing one hand down his chest beneath the unlaced doublet and open shirt. "I have led them to successes enough over the years to have earned their trust."

Rolling onto his side, Stephen pondered her exquisite face, framed by the black hair falling over her shoulders. She wore a sleeveless gown dyed madder red, ribbons loosely laced so the shift beneath was all that covered her in places. Stephen resisted the impulse to remove the gown completely.

"But they do not trust me," he pointed out. "And what happens if Father Byrne and Diarmid decide to withdraw their support from your leadership? It could get ugly."

"I know what I'm doing," she said confidently, leaning in to kiss him as a reminder that she did, indeed, know what she was doing.

They were not lovers, whatever the rest of the household assumed. Near enough, but Stephen would not go that far while lying to her, and Ailis seemed happy to take her time with a man she liked. He didn't press and neither did she. But that did not make their time alone any the less joyful. Ailis seemed capable of endless delight in discovering that not all men thought only of their own pleasure.

The only one in the household who didn't seem to mind the change in Stephen's status was Liadan—mostly because she hardly seemed to remark upon it. Maisie did, though, and Stephen would have bet that behind her careful face was a mind whirling through the possible complications. But he wasn't worried about Maisie.

He *was* worried about Diarmid. Stephen didn't pass entire nights in Ailis's chamber—even she would not press Father Byrne's principles so far—but she had long since removed any pretense of keeping him guarded. He spent his nights with the other men in an outbuilding, wishing he had a dagger to sleep with. How long before Diarmid's patience snapped and he found himself at the end of an unfriendly blade?

He and Ailis did not spend all their time exploring their growing passion. They also made plans for Oliver Dane. And one month after Askeaton's fortification with the hundred Spanish soldiers, they were ready to put those plans in motion.

The council summoned was a small one—only Ailis herself, Stephen, Father Byrne, Diarmid and his second-in-command, and Maisie. Stephen listened with admiration as Ailis laid out the deceptively simple operation. They knew that Dane, like all English landholders, was in constant need of money. Thanks to Maisie's merchant connections and constant letter-writing, they knew precisely how bad that need currently was. So, from the shadows, the Kavanaughs had arranged a meeting for him with a banker in Limerick. Maisie possessed not only a copy of the banker's seal—Stephen didn't ask how she'd obtained it—but a surprising talent for forgery in imitating the man's handwriting. The forged letter instructed Dane to travel with no more than four men, so as not to draw the attention of rebels.

"And we," Ailis announced in her cool, decisive manner, "will be waiting near Tipperary with five times that number of men and sweep him off the road."

"Killing?" Diarmid asked. Beneath his black mustache and beard, he seemed as pleased as he ever did. Which meant a small loosening of his tightly held mouth.

"No. At least, you can kill his men if they make it necessary. But Dane is to be taken alive—and brought here."

"Why?" Again it was Diarmid who asked. Father Byrne shot a look at Ailis but did not otherwise intervene. It was her choice how much to tell.

She was ready. "It is time Oliver Dane was brought to answer for his crimes in Kilmallock twelve years ago."

As her meaning sank in, the reaction around the table varied. Father Byrne studied his linked hands. Diarmid's quiet second-in-command opened his mouth, then shut it firmly. To Stephen's eye,

Maisie looked inscrutable as always. He wondered if she had already guessed it. She seemed to have a store of unguessable knowledge.

"Dane is Liadan's father." Diarmid's voice had lost all inflection.

Ailis lowered her head in acknowledgment. Diarmid rubbed his chin, clearly trying to control his immediate—probably violent— reaction.

At last he jerked his head, as though deliberately placing that information behind him. "Right, then. I'll get the men ready. We should ride out tomorrow to make sure we're in place near Tipperary well ahead of Dane."

Ailis had one final command to issue. "Take Stephen with you."

Stephen's jaw dropped. So much for believing he knew everything in Ailis's mind. How the hell was he supposed to get out of this? He could not possibly risk being seen by Oliver Dane.

Diarmid seemed nearly as shocked. "I don't think so!"

"I'm not asking."

"May I speak to you alone?" Diarmid ground out.

"No need. Everyone here can guess what you are going to say."

Diarmid said it anyway. "He is English. No way in hell I'll trust him with a weapon in my company. Nor do I trust him here without me. You must lock him up while my men and I are gone."

"Absolutely not!" Ailis snapped.

Maisie's voice was like a dash of cold water in the overheated room. "May I make a suggestion?"

Diarmid almost growled at the interruption, but Ailis kept visible hold of her temper and narrowed her eyes. "What?" she asked.

"I suggest allowing them to settle the matter as they're both clearly dying to do—with violence. Controlled, naturally, in a fair fight."

Once again Stephen's jaw dropped. He shut it with an audible click as Diarmid laughed nastily. "Englishmen aren't interested in fair fights."

Stephen bared his teeth in a smile. "Afraid I can't handle myself?"

"Afraid you'll stick a blade in my back," Diarmid spat back.

"I think we all know it's the other way round."

"Enough!" Ailis ordered. She was still angry, but thoughtful with it. "Diarmid, since you seem determined to come to blows with Stephen, have at it. An hour from now in the courtyard. Blunted daggers and hand-to-hand. Pummel each other until your aggression is spent. If you win, Stephen remains at Cahir. Locked up. If he wins, he rides with you. Unless you don't like your chances against him?"

Diarmid could hardly admit to that. And no doubt the thought of getting to hit Stephen mollified him enough to agree. "One hour it is."

He shoved his way out of the room as if the door were a personal enemy. Stephen watched his furious retreat, and caught Maisie's dry murmur next to him. "Who says that women are the dramatic sex?"

The courtyard fight was as vicious and drawn out as the two of them could make it. Diarmid was clearly surprised by Stephen's unorthodox tactics, but the Irishman had been fighting unconventionally since he was fifteen and they were well matched. Stephen had cause more than once to silently bless Julien for training him to take a hit as well as give them out.

Stephen had gone into the fight planning to let Diarmid win, despite the fact that he did not relish being locked up while the men were gone. He hoped Ailis would be pliable on that point. Losing was certainly the sensible thing to do. But once in the thick of it, sensible flew out the window. All he knew was that here was a man who not only despised him, but underestimated him, and it gave Stephen enormous satisfaction to prove Diarmid wrong.

In the end, the damage they were doing to each other proved too much for Ailis to ignore. Her voice carried high and clear above the practice yard as she ordered them to stop.

Stephen bent over, hands on his knees, trying to catch his breath. His knuckles were split and bleeding and his mouth was already swelling. As he straightened, it gave him pleasure to note the damage he'd wrought in return to Diarmid's face.

"Satisfied?" Ailis said drily to the two men. "We shall call it a draw. Stephen does not ride out with you, Diarmid, but nor is he locked up in the interim. He has proved himself and I trust him. That should be enough for every man here."

And that smote Stephen with the sharpest pain yet. All his relief at avoiding Oliver Dane for now was swamped by the knowledge that he continued to betray Ailis with every day that he lied to her.

For three days the entirety of Cahir Castle lived on a knife's edge of anticipation and fear. Ailis knew the word had spread from the council chamber, and when their two dozen best men—a third of their force—rode out armed to the teeth, there was a distinctly Irish fatality in the minds of those left behind. What if Dane didn't come? What if he came but in greater force than he'd been cautioned to bring? What if, worst of all, he'd seen through their ruse and waited only to slaughter the Kavanaugh men?

Knowing how swiftly word would spread through the household—and the nature of Bridey, Liadan's gossipy nurse—Ailis had summoned her daughter and told her herself who Oliver Dane was and why she was bringing him to Cahir. Liadan behaved as her mother had hoped: no tears, no curiosity except the most basic, and no arguments. She asked only one question.

"Will I see him?"

"For a moment. With me and whatever guards you choose. You will not need to speak to him or listen. And afterward, you will never need to think on him again."

The only difference in Liadan was that she left that conversation thoughtful and a little subdued. It could not be helped. Maisie would see to it that the child had whatever comfort she required.

Ailis hardly slept the nights her men were gone. Without Diarmid in the household, she took to keeping Stephen with her most hours of the day. She wanted him at night, as well—wanted him in a manner she thought Oliver Dane had destroyed before it could bud—but Father Byrne was watching. She did not think the priest would challenge her, but she couldn't risk it. Without the support of Byrne and Diarmid, Ailis knew she would have a difficult time keeping control. But once Oliver Dane had been dealt with? That success would give her a stature no one would dare challenge.

Stephen was excellent at reading her moods, or perhaps he was merely suffering the same agonies of waiting as she was. In the late morning of the fourth day, he suggested that she ride. "Perhaps you'll meet them as they return," he said.

"Come with me," she said impulsively. They had not ridden alone together since their visit to the Rock of Cashel.

He hesitated, which surprised her. Ailis asked, "Do you not want to see Dane in our hands as much as I do? I know you were not lying about how much you hate him."

Without answering the question, he smiled. "I'll come."

They raced their horses at the beginning—not long, not enough to tire them too early—before settling to a slower pace along the Suir River. As Ailis watched the play of silver water, she felt her nerves begin to settle. She had fantasized about this for so long it hardly felt real. No, not fantasized. Planned for. Worked toward. Sometimes she thought every decision she'd made in the last twelve years had been aimed solely at Oliver Dane. What would she do when it was over?

Impulsively, she repeated that last question to Stephen. He had a blunt answer. "What will you do? You will live, Ailis. In whatever manner you find best."

She drew her horse level with his, at a walking pace that allowed them to look at each other. "I think I know the first thing I shall do when it is over. It will require you, I'm afraid. Though perhaps the activity will be to your liking as well."

The corner of his eye twitched. She had learned to read those twitches of his. They usually meant he was more moved than he cared to admit. Englishmen, she mused. So painfully polite and reserved.

But this particular Englishman was also painfully honest. "There is nothing in the world I want more," he said simply. "But perhaps we can also talk. When the business with Dane is over. There are things I would say to you before . . ."

Her eyebrows shot up in amusement at his fumbling. "Before bedding me? Talk was not quite what I had in mind—but I suppose I can endure the conversation for anticipation of what will follow."

Stephen looked away—odd, since it was usually she who broke contact between them. She almost asked him why. Then she saw his chin come up and his body straighten in alert. "Riders," he said.

Instantly, she swung her gaze to where he looked across the river and saw, as he did, the outlines of men and the dust they kicked up on the road. She held unnaturally still, straining to catch details . . .

Ailis was the first to be certain. And why not? She had spent a lifetime watching the riders of Clan Kavanaugh. "It's Diarmid," she said, surprised that her voice sounded so flat. Normal. As though this were nothing more than another raid. "And I count the same number of men he rode out with. Doesn't look as though we lost anyone."

There was, however, one additional rider. Kept in the middle of her horsemen, riding upright but, Ailis wagered, with hands tied and reins in the control of one of her own men. They had got him. Oliver Dane.

Stephen had seen the same things. "Go and meet them," he said urgently. "I'll ride back and alert the castle."

"Come with me," she said. "I thought that's why we rode out."

"That is why I brought you out. This is for you, Ailis. This is all your clever doing. I came in rather late to the Dane vendetta—all I need to know is that he is punished. I don't need to do it myself. Not the way you do."

She tried to read his face but failed. As for herself, she felt as though every bone in her body was ready to leap through her skin in anticipation of facing her enemy. What other man would give her this gift?

If she could have reached him for a kiss, she would have. Instead, she blazed a smile of triumph and said, "Tell Father Byrne to have the chains ready."

Stephen turned his horse and was gone. Ailis took a moment to steady her hands, trembling on the reins, then set off to meet her men.

Diarmid hailed her, his expressive face plainly glad to see her alone. He must have marked the rider at her side in the distance and guessed it was Stephen. "No difficulty?" she called as she approached.

"None. Worked just as you said. Killed one of his men in the fight, brought him in."

"Let me through," Ailis commanded.

Her men obeyed, and Ailis and her mount picked their way through the guards until she was facing Oliver Dane for the first time in twelve years.

He had aged, naturally, but the figure was the same. Rough-hewn and suspicious, the brown hair salted with gray and the deep-set eyes surrounded by more lines. Ailis felt an instinctive flood of revulsion and, disturbingly, terror. She swallowed it down. *He can't touch me, he can't hurt me, I have all the power now . . .*

Astonishingly, Dane smiled. The same mocking expression she had seen from him a hundred times. "Little Ailis." His voice had not changed at all, gravelly and deep with contempt threaded through it. "You've grown up even more marvelous than I expected."

One of her guards moved to strike him, but Ailis raised a hand of restraint. She did not need to be protected. "As I recall, you are not overfond of grown women. You like them young."

"So much more pliable," Dane agreed. "Like you. Never a complaint, never a word but what I taught you—and such an apt pupil. How many men have had cause to thank me these last years for my well-tutored concubine?"

This time she did not restrain her men. He was struck from both sides before Ailis called them off. "You should know Irish women better," she said conversationally to the bruised but stubbornly upright Dane. "We may hold our tongues, but only to plot more creatively. Vengeance is best served cold . . . and I've had many wintry years to hone mine."

She jerked her horse around and moved to the front with Diarmid. "Let's go."

It had begun.

With Oliver Dane at Cahir, the very air of the castle felt aflame. It was as though each person in it moved with a keyed up awareness of what was at stake. It could not have been easy for Ailis to allow her personal secret to be aired; Stephen heard only the edges of whispers, but he knew it was all over the household that here was the man who had fathered Liadan.

He had expected to feel, at the least, nervous—not to say frantic—at the knowledge that a man who could so easily unmask him lay within the castle walls. But calm had settled over him as he'd watched Ailis's men returning with their prisoner. All had gone according to plan. The only thing he had to do was stay out of Dane's way—which shouldn't be a problem considering the man was locked up. Not in a dungeon or even belowground, for Father Byrne had insisted he be kept with at least the barest courtesies of a prisoner held for ransom. Only Byrne himself and Ailis held a key to the windowless chamber where Dane was confined.

The trouble began that very first night. Stephen had been telling stories to Liadan of the Green Man and the Wild Hunt and he finally left her in the hands of her excitable Irish nurse. Maisie asked if she could walk with him toward the Great Hall.

"Something on your mind?" he asked, surprised.

"Peter Martin arrived an hour ago."

Stephen blinked. "Did he?" he asked blandly. "Interesting timing."

"Isn't it?"

What was it about this slip of a girl that kept him so off balance?

He covered it, he hoped, by saying, "I imagine he'll be sent away as soon as it's light. Perhaps he'll even be used to take the ransom demands."

She hesitated, but he'd known her long enough to know that propriety would never stop her observations. Sure enough, she asked, "Are you certain Ailis will hold Dane to ransom?"

"Considering she already has him in hold . . ." He trailed off, for what had started as a teasing answer was stopped by Maisie's serious expression. "You think she won't?"

"I think she wanted Dane in her hands. I'm not sure even she knew for certain why until now."

"That's taking enigmatic a bit far."

"Is it?" Maisie quirked her lips, not so much a smile as a marker of her argument as she tipped her head down the last few stairs. "Listen."

Stephen stopped and listened. Damn it, Maisie was right. There was shouting coming from a nearby chamber. He would have known the quality of Ailis's voice anywhere. Biting off a curse, he strode to the half-open door through which could be heard both Ailis and, shockingly with a similar raised voice, Father Byrne.

Maisie did not follow.

He pushed open the door, which was blocked by Diarmid. The captain of the guard scowled and tried to shove Stephen back out, but Ailis commanded, "Let him in. And shut the door this time!"

Stephen had never seen Father Byrne flushed and ruffled. The priest's thick white hair looked as though he'd been running his hands through it in frustration; it stood up in tufts around his ears. Behind him, leaning against a deep windowsill, lounged Peter Martin. Walsingham's spy met Stephen's eyes, then looked away.

"What's going on?" Stephen asked warily.

"We are having a debate on the nature and quality of leadership." Ailis's voice was uneven, a rare sign of emotion. "Father Byrne seems to be under the illusion that I lead only with his gracious acquiescence. I, naturally, dispute that position."

Since that told him little of substance, Stephen turned to Father Byrne. "What is going on?"

"There have been no terms set for ransom of the prisoner. And no plans, as I have just discovered, for doing so."

Despite himself, Stephen shot a glance at Peter Martin once more. They should not be having this conversation in front of a man who could betray them all with a word. But there was no help for it.

"We have to ransom Dane," Stephen insisted. "Make his life miserable in the meantime, but you can't afford to hold him indefinitely. Someone will come looking." Sooner rather than later, if Martin had his way. Could Stephen possibly make Ailis keep the spy at Cahir Castle until this was over without betraying either of them?

"That someone will be disappointed, for there will be no Oliver Dane to find," Ailis said. "At least, not living."

Damn it all to hell. Stephen closed his eyes to gather himself, then looked at Ailis and spoke to her as though they were alone. "You cannot kill him. You know you cannot."

"Who are you to tell me what to do, Englishman?" she spat. "I thought you wanted him dead as well."

"And if we lived in an ideal world, we could kill him. But we live in this world, Ailis. If you kill a man like Oliver Dane, you will bring down wrath upon your head you cannot imagine."

"We can deal with Ormond."

Father Byrne snorted, clearly about to dispute her blithe assessment of their military readiness.

Stephen spoke over him. "I don't just mean the Earl of Ormond. You're mad if you don't realize that killing one of her landowners, one of her captains, will bring Queen Elizabeth's fury down upon you in full force. She will send her finest soldiers to destroy you for the slap to her pride."

Eyes bright and cheeks flushed, Ailis laughed. "I think you're imagining things."

I wish I were, he swore silently. *I wish I could tell you that I know this queen, know her well enough to predict her rage. And Walsing-*

ham will encourage it. Killing Dane will be the spark that will see Clan Kavanaugh burned to bare earth.

Ailis was confident of her position. "Father Byrne, I appreciate your concerns. But there can only be one voice at the end of the day. And that voice is mine. Are we clear?"

Byrne shot a glance at Diarmid, standing behind Stephen. His point was self-evident: Ailis ruled only so long as she had the support of armed men. And though Stephen had no cause to like Diarmid and knew that Ailis's plan was self-destructive, he felt a moment's relief at the pleasure on Ailis's face when the captain of the guard said solidly, "I do as she commands."

Knowing when he had been beaten, at least for the moment, Father Byrne pleaded, "Promise to do nothing precipitate. Allow tempers to cool before going forward."

"Don't fret, Father. Killing him immediately would be too kind. I have plans for Dane before that."

The priest's lips tightened, but he managed to nod before escaping the chamber. Peter Martin eyed each of them thoughtfully before following. At least, Stephen thought, Martin left under the impression that his fellow spy had been arguing on the English side.

With Byrne gone, Ailis said, "Thank you, Diarmid. I will remember this."

Then, as though Diarmid were not still standing there, Ailis came to Stephen, her face blazing in joy. "Don't worry," she told him. "I know what I'm doing. When Dane is dead, then I will be free."

She kissed him then and there, with Diarmid glowering behind them so hard Stephen imagined he could feel the fire in the Irishman's eyes boring through him.

We are all going to regret this. Stephen knew it, but he couldn't bring himself to care. Much.

EIGHTEEN

13 August 1582
Hampton Court

Anabel has passed through the worst of the fever. The rash contin-
ues, but I am confident now in her healing. At least in the immedi-
ate sense. She seems to have been—frightened? humbled?—by this
illness. Perhaps it is only that she is still so weak. It takes time to
recover, as I recall all too well from my own desperate illness so
long ago at Hampton Court. Of course, mine was due to poison,
but perhaps that made it easier for me. I had an actual enemy to
focus on. Anabel has only fate, or God.

Elizabeth allowed us to take charge of the sickroom. Both Lu-
cette and Pippa are capable nurses, not prone to hysterics or dis-
taste at any task, and it comforted Anabel to have them near her.

But it was Kit's presence that made all the difference. Of course
he could not stay in the sickroom, but I let him in twice a day to see

*her. Even when she wandered in fever hallucinations those first two
days, Kit could always calm her. She would fix her eyes on him as
though he were the only constant in a dangerously shifting world.*

*I know that expression. It is the one I first gave Dominic when I
was not much younger than Anabel.*

The stalemate between Ailis and Father Byrne did not abate over
the course of three days. As long as Diarmid's loyalty held, Ailis
knew she would get her way. Stephen, after his first disagreement
with her position, kept his mouth shut on the matter. Despite his
ability to keep his emotions off his face, Ailis knew he thought her
wrong. But no Englishman, not even one as surprising and appealing
as Stephen Wyatt, was going to come to Ireland and tell her how to
avenge her honour.

With Dane at Cahir Castle, her private hours with Stephen in her
chamber came to an end. She was wholly absorbed in her enemy.

At first it was enough simply to know she had him in chains. She
did not see him the first days, content to let Diarmid in once a day
with bread and ale. If Diarmid took out his resentments on Dane,
she didn't ask. He knew her—he knew how far he could abuse the
prisoner without going too far

Finally, Ailis was ready. Stephen didn't say a word at her announcement, but Diarmid followed her to the makeshift prison
chamber with the intention of following her in. When Ailis forbid
it, he scowled impressively.

"It's not safe," he said bluntly.

"Is he in chains?" she asked.

"He is."

"And as I understand, only I and Father Byrne hold a key to those
chains. As long as you put them on correctly, all I need do is stay out
of his reach."

Diarmid gave in with bad grace, particularly when she insisted on shutting the door behind her. Just because word of what Dane had done to her had circled through her household didn't mean she wanted details shared with all and sundry. And who could guess what Dane would say?

She could guess it would be offensive; he did not disappoint. "Your men are loyal. How many of my tricks have you used to keep them that way?"

"Perhaps Englishmen need inducements to loyalty—Irishmen are different."

His smile . . . she had forgotten how that smile could crawl beneath her skin. "Not so very different. If you were ugly or old, these men would not be so quick to listen. Certainly not that thick-headed captain of the guard. He wants from you what any man wants."

They had no true prison cells at Cahir, at least none that were in proper repair. The chamber that held Dane was little more than an empty storeroom on the top floor of the rectangular central castle. The outer wall was stone and had no window. To the right of the door—well out of his chained reach—a small torch flared in its bracket. Other than a bucket for his sanitary needs, the chamber was empty. Dane sat on the bare floorboards, back against the wall, wrists and ankles circled with iron and chains fixed firmly to the wall. He would be able to stand—just—but could not move more than a foot in any direction.

Still, he managed to look at her with amusement and contempt, and to control the conversation as he always had. "Come to see your handiwork?" he asked. "Or to engage in a battle of wits? You may be too old now for my tastes, but your mind seems keen enough. I wouldn't mind engaging in a debate."

"I don't care what you want. I care about what you owe. There is someone at Cahir Castle who merits an introduction to you."

He raised a skeptical eyebrow. "Some man you have your eye on? You wish me to provide a testimonial as to your skills?"

"Your daughter."

That shut him up . . . for all of five seconds. "You couldn't even manage a son?"

"Would you have cared?"

"No. Irish brats are of no interest to me."

"Good. Because I consider the only claim in play here is hers. She is owed the chance to meet her English father. Once."

"I'm not going anywhere just now." He rattled his wrist chains and smiled.

"She will come with guards of her choosing. The moment you insult her or say anything to distress her, those men will do more than blacken your jaw."

He leaned his head against the wall behind him, eyes closed. "I liked you better when you kept your mouth shut and your legs open," he murmured.

She swept out, refusing to be baited. "Stay here," she commanded Diarmid outside the door.

Liadan and Maisie had claimed one of the tower chambers just off the Great Hall for their schoolroom. Once as bare as Dane's prison cell, the two of them had softened and warmed the space with carpets and tapestries scavenged from around the castle. With the stacks of books and parchment and ink scattered across the round table, it was by far the coziest space in the castle.

It was a pity to disturb them, but Ailis didn't hesitate. Nor did she try to dismiss the Scots girl—she was fairly certain Liadan would insist on Maisie staying with her. Most nights, Maisie even slept in Liadan's chamber.

Her daughter looked up. "Is it time?" she asked simply.

"Only if you are ready."

As she'd predicted, Liadan looked to Maisie. "Will you come with me?"

"Of course, pet."

"Not you, Mother." Liadan's self-possession was so complete it took Ailis a moment to formulate a response. She could not deny that she was nearly as proud of the girl as she was dismayed by her order.

"Are you sure, Liadan?"

"It's better," she said, for all the world like a woman grown and tested rather than a girl just turned twelve. In the flickering light, the set of Liadan's mouth was very like Dane's. "You said I might have guards?"

"As many as you choose."

"I want Stephen. Just Stephen."

Ailis nodded. "I will fetch him for you, and meet you both outside the prison chamber."

Well, she thought wryly, if I don't decide to keep Stephen around after all this, Liadan might insist upon it. Ailis tried to ignore the thought that her daughter preferred a Scots girl and an Englishman to her own mother.

Stephen pretended to absorb himself in poring over Ailis's map of Ireland in the Great Hall—one marked with her careful notes about manpower and allegiances. Mostly it was to try and take his mind off Oliver Dane. He didn't know what he was going to do about that looming disaster.

Then, of a sudden, the disaster was no longer looming but imminent.

Ailis swept in and said, without preamble, "I need you to see Dane with my daughter."

He straightened, trying to keep the panic from showing in his movements. "You're letting Liadan in?"

"She has the right. I told her to take whomever she wished. She asked for Maisie—and you."

Only long years of practice at control kept Stephen from cracking. How the hell was he going to get out of this? The answer was that he couldn't, not without raising suspicion.

Then how to ensure that Dane didn't expose him?

As he assented to Ailis's request and followed her to the top-floor interior chamber—reinforced on the inside with stone walls and not a single window—Stephen thought frantically.

Liadan and Maisie were waiting outside Dane's prison door, with Diarmid scowling behind them. For just a moment Stephen forgot his own dilemma in the face of a twelve-year-old's bravery. Liadan's usual high spirits were subdued. She stood with hands crossed demurely against her yellow skirts.

The only thing Stephen had been able come up with was a matter-of-fact request to see Dane by himself. "Let me go in alone first," he said to Ailis and Diarmid with forced ease. "No doubt he's been well threatened, but as a fellow countryman, I might know a trick or two to ensure his politeness."

Please say yes, Stephen prayed, heart so thunderous he feared Liadan and Maisie heard it from where they stood. Maisie studied him with a curious expression.

"Very well," Ailis agreed abruptly. "Go ahead and vent your own displeasure at Dane beforehand. I want to ensure Liadan is not disturbed."

"Of course."

Diarmid unbolted the door, shooting Stephen a look of such loathing it might have shaken him if he wasn't already halfway to not breathing. Stephen pulled the door firmly shut behind him and hoped the thickness of the wood would keep them from being heard. He thought they were safe to talk—as long as neither of them shouted.

Dane had been beaten, but not so badly as Stephen himself had been in Ireland. Twice. The man sat with head bowed—possibly dozing—but even so it was possible to see the bruising and cuts along the side of his cheek and jaw. Then his head jerked up and he blinked several times before he recognized Stephen.

"What the hell—" Dane began.

"Keep your mouth shut." Stephen displayed the dagger he'd been allowed to carry for the last week. "Your life is hanging in the balance, and if you tip it, I'll be the one to silence you."

"They can't afford to kill me."

"She doesn't care."

Dane furrowed his brow. "Ailis? She won't—"

"Don't say her name!" Stephen knew it was a mistake to give Dane anything to work with, but he couldn't help himself.

Slowly, understanding spread on Dane's face. Along with a leer that twisted his mouth. "Ah, so you took my advice on Irish women. Good choice. Ailis was a concubine worth cultivating. But skilled enough to sway the upright English lordling from the path of duty?" Dane whistled. "I'm a better teacher than I thought."

"If you ever want to leave this place alive, you will shut your mouth and listen. My name is Stephen Wyatt. We have never met. Remember that, and I'll see to it that you keep your filthy life."

Not for your sake, but for hers. Stephen could not let Ailis destroy herself by killing Dane.

The man was not stupid. He assessed correctly—more or less—Stephen's implication. "Walsingham?" Dane whistled. "So you've gained Clan Kavanaugh's trust in order to betray them. How cold-blooded of you."

"Don't get in my way."

"Then get me out of here."

"I'm working on it."

Dane leaned as far forward as he could in chains and snarled, "If they drag me out of here to die, then the last thing I'll do is make sure you go with me."

Stephen didn't flinch. "I'm supposed to be warning you to watch your words with Ailis's daughter. I'm bringing her in now. The moment you even *look* as though you'll insult her, I will kill you myself."

With a laugh, Dane sat back. "I shall be the proper English gentleman to his bastard daughter."

Stephen had reached for the door when Dane added, "If my men had not intervened outside Kilkenny last year, you might have had an Irish bastard of your own by now. I heard tell there was a woman in your tent that night."

Everything went red. From somewhere, Stephen heard screams. He didn't realize he had moved until his eyes cleared and he was standing over Dane with the dagger pointed at his chest.

With deliberate care, he turned the dagger in his hand and struck Dane on the jaw with its hilt. Not hard enough to knock him out, but it might have loosened a tooth or two.

Then he strode across the room and opened the door. He nodded once to Ailis, then said to Liadan, "Are you certain?"

Eerily like her mother, the child didn't even deign to answer, but swept past him into the prison chamber. Maisie followed, and Stephen closed the door behind the three of them.

From the moment she entered, Liadan controlled the room. She studied Dane like he was a species of wildlife. "Where are you from?" she finally asked abruptly, in flawless English.

"Templemore. I live at Blackcastle."

"I mean in England. You were not born here."

"No." He looked about to add an insult, but refrained, possibly because of the fresh pain blossoming through his jaw. "I'm from Yorkshire. Another forbidding landscape that shapes all who live there."

"Why did you come to Ireland?"

"For the opportunity. I had no inheritance, no skills except soldiering, and Ireland is a place where a man can carve out his own future."

"You are not married?"

"Tried it once. She died in childbed with the brat and there didn't seem any point in continuing on that path. What I've earned here is for me. No one left me anything—why should I breed merely to pass on my own hard work?"

"But you did," Liadan said, as calmly as though she were twenty years older. "Breed, I mean."

His mouth twisted. "You don't count."

Maisie laid a hand on Liadan's narrow shoulder, but in truth the girl had not recoiled. Stephen was filled with admiration for her. "I'm afraid," she told the man who could only be counted her father in the most basic sense, "that it is you who do not count. Not at Cahir. We are Irish here, and you are nothing but an interloper."

She turned away and said to Stephen, "I'm finished."

Only when Liadan passed him did Stephen see the fine tremble beneath her skin. He expected her to reach for her mother upon release, but it was Maisie who put her arm around Liadan's shoulder and murmured soft words to her as they walked away.

"Well?" Ailis asked him.

With a glance at Diarmid, hovering menacingly, Stephen said, "Let's walk."

They had not been wholly alone since Dane's arrival. His body, finely honed to every move and glimpse of her, urged him to sweep her into a quiet chamber and on into his arms.

But it was his mind that would keep him alive. And keep Ailis from a catastrophic mistake.

"There's no blood on your dagger, so I presume he minded his tongue with Liadan," she said.

"As well as he's able. Liadan was impressive. She has all your sense of self. I think it startled him."

"Good."

Stephen put his hand lightly on her arm, and she stopped. They were in an empty corridor, no one else to be heard or seen. "Ailis," he said softly, "you have to let him go. Hurt him as much as you like. Hell, I'll help you build a rack to put him on! But then send to the Earl of Ormond with ransom demands. Make it outrageous—so much that the English cannot hope to pay without sending to London first. Hold Dane and make his life miserable while you wait. And then take England's money, and let Dane go knowing that your enemies have paid for your next five years of fighting."

She pulled away, her predatory eyes blazing. "Do you know what I hate most about Englishmen? It is not your arrogance, that self-righteous sense of superiority. It is not even your cruelty, for we can be just as cruel. It is that you're so damned reasonable! Yes, reason says I should ransom Dane. Reason says I need the money. Reason says I should not risk English reprisals for killing him.

"But I am not reasonable. I am Irish, and a woman wronged. How often does a woman get the chance to answer the crimes against her? I have that chance—and I will not forsake it."

She took his head between her hands, harder than affection would dictate. "If you love me, you will not ask it of me."

Then she was gone, in a whirl of skirts and fury, and Stephen was left to wonder which principle he would land on: loyalty or love.

From behind him, footsteps sounded quick and soft. He jerked around and swore when he saw Peter Martin. How much had the man heard?

Enough, it seemed. "How are we going to get Dane out of here?" Martin asked.

Stephen had been waiting for this. Martin had kept away from him the last three days, which at least had given him time to consider his response. "I'm not risking my place here for Oliver Dane."

"Isn't this the very reason you're here—to protect England's interests?"

The two of them were speaking so softly it was barely words on their breath. "Dane doesn't matter," Stephen countered. "Not compared to the Spanish soldiers fighting with the Earl of Desmond. Dane threatens only this household—Desmond threatens all of England's interests in southern Ireland."

"And how much intelligence have you sent to Walsingham about Desmond's actions?" Martin asked shrewdly.

"I don't report to you."

"So you won't help me?"

"You want Dane released, find a way yourself." Stephen could not afford to be attached to it, even if he knew it was wise. He was not prepared to give up his place in this household.

He and Martin parted without further words. Stephen braced

himself for the storm that would follow when the spy either spirited Dane away or got caught in the act. He hoped not the latter—Martin might not keep his mouth shut if he were taken. But he told himself there was nothing more he could do.

The wait was not long. Just hours later, Stephen was awakened before dawn to the news that Oliver Dane had vanished.

And so had Liadan and Maisie.

Ailis had not expected to sleep at all that night. So when Diarmid woke her in the dark, it took precious minutes for what he was saying to penetrate her foggy mind. When she understood that not only was Oliver Dane gone, but the guard set outside his cell had his throat cut, Ailis came painfully awake. While Diarmid roused the men, Ailis went straight to Liadan's chamber, driven by an instinct she was afraid to name.

The bed was empty, the linens thrown back as though in haste, and on the floor before the fireplace lay Father Byrne. Ailis knelt, but hardly needed to check. Like the guard, the priest's throat had been cut nearly to the spine. Tossed on his limp body were the keys to Oliver Dane's chains.

Within three minutes the household was roused and searching. Ailis forced herself to wait in the Great Hall, terrified that at any moment someone would bring her word of her daughter's death. She paced the hall, afraid to stop moving because if she did, what she felt would break upon her, and she did not have time to give way to emotion. She would use it, instead, take all her rage and panic and distill it into a weapon with which to scorch her enemies. Wherever they might be.

The first to come was Stephen. He strode straight to her as though to take her in his arms, but Ailis could not allow any weakness. She stopped him with a statement. "Father Byrne is dead."

"Was it Byrne who released Dane?"

"And got his throat cut for his mercy. A typically English gesture."

The line of Stephen's jaw tightened. "Is anyone else gone?" he asked abruptly.

"Besides my daughter? Only Maisie. Must I now suspect that quiet girl of collaborating with the English to kidnap my daughter?"

"Of course not. I'm relieved Maisie's with her."

"With her where?" Ailis cried. "How did they get outside the walls?"

Diarmid entered at that moment with the answer. "They got out through the postern gate. They must have crossed the river."

"In what? We leave no boats outside the walls. Are you telling me Father Byrne went so far as to provide a boat for him?"

"Maybe not Byrne," Diarmid said bluntly. "Peter Martin is missing as well."

"Martin?" Her bewilderment swiftly hardened into outrage. "Bastard! Why couldn't he just stay out of it?"

Fury swirled with her terror, so that Ailis didn't know which way to turn. Before she could decide, a weeping Bridey pushed her way into the hall. "A note," the old nurse wailed. "Dropped in the wee girl's bedding." Bridey held out the note she couldn't read, then scuttled away.

Ailis moved faster than Diarmid and snatched it before he could. It was Dane's writing, she knew it at once. It had been scrawled on one of Liadan's translation sheets.

I will release her, but only to one negotiator. Send Lord Somerset to me, and you may have your bastard back.

After her first, silent, read, she repeated it aloud. Diarmid looked as confused as she was. "Somerset?" he said. "Must be English, but why would Dane involve someone we've never heard of? And it will take days—weeks—to get word to England and back."

"Liadan can't stay with him for weeks," Ailis insisted, a little of her desperation leaking through. Surely Dane wasn't so depraved as to use his own daughter? He was doing this to frighten her, to force her to comply . . .

"It won't be weeks." It was Stephen who spoke, his voice oddly blank. "It's not even a day's ride to Templemore. You can have Liadan back in less than two days."

She looked at him in surprise, and then concern. He had gone dead white, so that the black of his hair and the warm hazel of his eyes stood out like warning beacons. But warning of what? She had never seen Stephen look so remote, or so stern.

"What do you mean?" she asked. "Do you know this Lord Somerset? Is he in Ireland already?"

When Stephen swallowed, she could actually see the movement in his throat, he was so tightly wound. Then he answered, and everything went still. "My name is not Stephen Wyatt. It's Stephen Courtenay . . . the Earl of Somerset."

There was a hiss, then Diarmid lunged at Stephen, dagger drawn. "Stop!" Ailis commanded wildly.

"He's a traitor!"

"Diarmid, stop it. Leave us alone."

"Not a chance. He's just waiting to kill you."

"If he wanted to kill me, he'd have done so long before now." She felt unbelievably, icily calm. Stephen did not look away from her gaze. "Search him, Diarmid, then leave us be."

Diarmid was rougher than he needed to be in the search, for Stephen wore only a shirt and hose, and every line of the body she knew so well could be easily traced. The dagger she'd allowed him was removed by Diarmid, then he backhanded Stephen across the face with a cracking blow that made her wince.

"Out," she ordered Diarmid. "And keep your mouth shut. We cannot afford the household in more of a panic."

Then it was just the two of them.

"Why Wyatt?" she asked, softly, circling him where he stood straight and tall.

If he was surprised by the question, he did not show it. English reticence was written all over him. "My grandfather's name."

"So, you are not a gentleman's bastard with a Roman Catholic mother."

"I am not."

She stopped and stared at him, then shook her head, everything she knew about the English nobility coming to her as she sought for it. "No, you are Stephen Courtenay. *Courtenay,*" she spat. "Earl of Somerset and oldest son of the Duke of Exeter. When your father dies, you will inherit the richest dukedom in England."

He said nothing.

Prowling around him again, as though he were a zoological exhibit, she mused aloud. "Just how well do you know the English queen?"

"Ailis—"

"Don't! Every word you've said since coming to us was a lie. Designed to betray us into English hands. And when one of your countrymen was in danger . . . well, of course you had to argue to let him go. But why Liadan?"

"It wasn't me."

"How can you say that?"

"If I had helped to free Dane, I could have ridden out with him. As Peter Martin did. Dane wants me to come precisely because he couldn't get at me any other way."

"Are you telling me Dane is another intelligencer? Making sure his spy is safe?"

"No. There are things Dane has done . . . it doesn't matter at the moment. All that matters is getting Liadan home. You have to let me go."

She bit her lip so viciously she tasted blood, the terror sweeping back in as the first shock of betrayal faded. "How do I know I can trust you to free her?"

"You don't. Until I do. Then, whatever else you think of me— whatever I *deserve* you to think of me—perhaps you'll remember this:

since my arrival, I have done nothing to jeopardize your position in Ireland. Indeed, I have refrained from making reports I should have to England. There is reason to suspect Dane wants me for nothing more than to hand me over to the English as a traitor." He met her gaze squarely. "And he would be right."

"I don't care." She pronounced each word fully and distinctly. "I will let you go because I must. But if you do not bring back my daughter, I will see you suffer to the end of your days."

"If Liadan is harmed, you won't have to punish me. I'll do it my-self."

She glared at him and was shocked to realize that part of her still wanted to throw herself at him, to let him embrace her with all his strength and promise her everything would be all right.

Instead, she swept to the door and, finding Diarmid immediately outside as she'd expected, told her captain, "Find the Englishman a horse."

NINETEEN

They did not let Stephen go alone. Even if Diarmid had trusted him, it was far faster to lead him toward Templemore than leave him to find his own way. But they didn't get far, he and Diarmid, before they were intercepted by two men wearing Dane's red and gold boar badge.

"Just the Englishman," they said.

Diarmid glowered at them, then glowered even more heartily at Stephen. "I never liked you."

"Good to know."

"Get her back."

Stephen set his jaw and fell in with Dane's men. One of them he recognized; he'd last seen him with blood dripping from his sword as he methodically slaughtered prisoners at Carrigafoyle.

They weren't more than two or three hours behind Dane and the girls—his men must have been patrolling as close to Cahir Castle as they dared. Probably Peter Martin had sent word of what he planned, thus preparing Dane's men to aid them.

They rode through the kind of darkness that only Ireland produced—as though the air itself were alive and twisting its way inside Stephen's head. It was a seductive darkness, promising oblivion rather than pleasure, and Stephen had to fight to keep himself focused. No drifting back to regrets, no dwelling on Ailis's expression when she realized how he'd betrayed her. The only thing in the world that mattered was to get Liadan and Maisie out of Dane's hands as quickly as could be accomplished.

Blackcastle, as with so much else in this swath of Ireland, had long been owned by the Butler family. This particular property had been leased to Oliver Dane after the destruction of Kilmallock twelve years ago. The eastern sky was lit with the dawn as they approached, and Stephen noted the abbey—or Big Church, as the literal Irish form of Blackcastle translated—to their north. They turned west and there was the castle, looming black and stark against the sky as though untouched since 1450. They had to pass through three sets of armed guards before entering; some of them looked at Stephen with recognition and undisguised interest. They knew who he was— some, he had served with at Carrigafoyle—and Dane must have warned them of his imminent arrival. He wondered how Dane had described him today. Traitor? Coward? English lordling?

Stephen didn't care. He didn't give a damn about his reputation or his own well-being. Liadan and Maisie were innocents in this entire affair—he would see them clear of it. No matter the cost.

Clearly Dane was not domestically minded. The medieval lines of the castle looked uncomfortable, as though it knew itself foreign to this land, and there was little to dispel that immediate impression within its walls. All well-ordered, of course, for Dane was a methodical and successful campaigner who knew how to organize men and stores, but also bleak. This was a castle of invaders, who knew themselves to be in hostile territory. It was not where Stephen would have wanted to make his home. But then Dane had no family for which to make a home.

He dismounted in the courtyard and was disappointed, but not terribly surprised, when they did not take him directly to Dane. The man would want to punish him for last night's interview. So Stephen submitted to being locked in a cell—much less salubrious than the one at Cahir Castle—though at least he wasn't chained.

Then he waited.

His cell was belowground, with just a slit at the ceiling to give a little bit of light. Stephen dozed in short bursts on the stone floor—the pallet provided was stuffed with rank straw and had a colony of mice living in it—and otherwise watched the changing quality of that light, trying to judge the hours. He guessed it was late afternoon before anyone bothered to come for him.

It was Peter Martin.

Stephen, who had come to his feet when he heard the door being unlocked, subsided slowly onto the stool that was the only object in the cell besides the pallet and the unsavory bucket in the corner that had not been cleaned since the last prisoner. "What do you want?" he asked Martin.

"To make you see sense. Dane did you a favour, pulling you out of Cahir before it was too late."

"It was only too late because Dane made good and certain to blow my cover."

"You did that yourself—the moment you allowed Irish concerns to override your judgment."

"Not your affair."

"The hell it isn't!" Martin exploded. "Because of your refusal to act, I've blown my own cover. I can't stay in Ireland after this—because of you, I've lost years of work. Walsingham got good intelligence from me. Now what is he left with?"

"He's left with a man who would throw away the lives of two innocent girls to save one bloody wretched Englishman!" Could he manage to throttle Martin before the guards came running?

Martin blinked. "I didn't know Dane would take the girls. I had nothing to do with what happened inside the castle. I simply persuaded Father Byrne to release Dane and have him meet me outside the postern gate. I was bloody shocked when he dragged those two out with him!"

"Not shocked enough to force him to leave them behind. Did you even try? Or were they just two more impediments to your service?"

"Dane has not touched them. They are safely confined to the top floor of the castle, with myself the only man who goes up there."

"And if Dane wanted to go up there . . . you would stop him?"

Martin's silence was answer enough.

Stephen shook his head in contempt. "Two men are dead back at Cahir—Dane's guard, and Father Byrne himself. I imagine the priest, at least, was protesting Dane's attempt to remove the girls."

"It's no matter of mine. Not anymore. Wherever Walsingham sends me after this, I won't be able to return to Ireland."

"You'd better hope Walsingham sends you far away from me," Stephen countered. "Next time we meet, I'll kill you. Not for doing your job—but for being a coward about it."

Martin left without another word.

It was fully dark once more before the door opened again and Oliver Dane sauntered in. Stephen wasn't fooled by the apparent casual ease—he had studied Dane last year. He knew all too well how quickly the man could shift from repose to violence.

Dane had bathed and changed, although Stephen doubted he owned anything too luxurious. The man was not interested in luxury itself—a trait that Stephen had admired in the field. He liked soldiers who knew their job and did it well for its own sake, and not for the rewards it might bring. How could he feel otherwise, with the father he had?

Stephen shoved away thoughts of his father, knowing that would not help now. For all Dane's claim that Liadan would be released when he arrived, he didn't trust the man. They were embarked on a delicate dance of negotiation, with lives in the balance. This was nothing like shadowing Mary Stuart. Flirting with the Scots queen had been a lark compared to Ireland.

He should have confined himself to the battlefield.

Dane took the stool for himself, stretching out his legs and tipping back against the wall. "Sit," he commanded.

Stephen sat on the floor, braced arms resting on his knees. He could propel himself up quickly if necessary. Then he waited.

"It takes a lot to surprise me," Dane said musingly. "Especially in Ireland. I pride myself on expecting the unexpected. But nothing prepared me for seeing you at Cahir Castle. Last year, I took you for nothing more than a spoiled rich boy who came to Ireland for adventure and would gladly go home when it became uncomfortable."

Since there didn't seem to be any response required, Stephen kept quiet. That made Dane narrow his eyes and shake his head.

"Then came your protests at Carrigafoyle. You know who can afford to take the moral high ground? Men who have no vested interest in the outcome. You don't belong here, Courtenay, and you proved that the moment you defied me over the prisoners."

Stephen bit the inside of his mouth to provide a distraction from the mocking.

Dane's face lit with a knowing smile. "But Ireland sees to its own. You learned that lesson, didn't you? Outside Kilkenny? But not well enough. Because there you were last night, slipping into my cell at Cahir, giving me orders. Who would have guessed you had that in you?"

"Where's Liadan?" Stephen said abruptly.

"Safe. Along with her rather persistent nursemaid."

"She's not a nursemaid."

Dane waved away the issue of Maisie. "The Scots girl took a swipe at me with a dagger. I would have left her behind like the priest, but decided it would make things easier to bring her. I'm not meant to look after children."

"I couldn't agree more. So let Liadan and Maisie go and simplify your life."

"Don't you want to see them?"

"I'll be happy to watch them as they ride out of here."

Dane stretched, a disconcerting grin on his face. "So self-sacrificing! Don't you even want to know my plans for you?"

"Not really." He would not engage. He would not let his temper break. He would not think of Roisin and Harrington and all the prisoners falling at this man's orders . . .

With a thud, Dane let the stool thump back to the ground. He stood. "It's late. I've put the girls in a chamber well away from my men. No one can get to them except me and Martin. We'll let them sleep, shall we? Feed them well in the morning, then finish the affair."

Was it really going to be that easy? Stephen slowly levered himself up from the floor, watching Dane warily. "Can I see them in the morning before they go?" One last chance to send a message back to Ailis. If he could think of anything worth saying.

"Oh, I've a better idea than that. I'm sending you back to Cahir yourself."

Whistling, Dane let himself out, leaving Stephen dumbfounded behind him.

As the first streaks of morning crept through the narrow slit, a man brought him porridge and ale. Stephen ate gratefully, for yesterday had been a long ride and, if Dane could be believed, today would be the same.

The same guard who'd brought breakfast returned perhaps an hour later and motioned Stephen to follow him. He did, a bit stiffly, for the combination of stone floor and taut nerves had not contributed to rest. He took careful note of all he saw on the way—partly instinct, and partly a means of calming his nerves. There was little enough of use, for they were hardly going to parade him through the heart of the castle. Still, he counted the men that he saw passing in corridors or through windows once he was aboveground. He also noted that though the castle had not been much updated, it was well maintained. Medieval it might be, but nothing close to a ruin.

His nerves eased a bit when he reached the courtyard and caught sight of Liadan and Maisie. The child had grown since Stephen's arrival in Ireland, and now topped the older girl by an inch. But this morning Liadan looked younger, vulnerable in a way he'd never seen her at Cahir.

When no one tried to stop him, he went straight to her. "Are you all right?" he asked, leaning down.

"Of course." Liadan's voice wobbled. Frowning, she tried again. "I'm sorry to put you to all the trouble of riding after us."

"No trouble at all," he assured her. "Your mother is most anxious and would spare nothing to get you home at once."

She smiled, a miniature version of Ailis's blindingly beautiful smile, and said, "I am ready."

"So eager to leave your father's hospitality?" Dane strode into the courtyard, his mockery ringing through the air.

Stephen straightened while Maisie laid a hand on Liadan's arm—in warning or support. Perhaps both.

Liadan declined to answer, and Stephen bit back a grin at her obvious contempt. Here was a girl who would make her mother—her entire clan—proud.

There were two horses readied; either the girls would share or Stephen wasn't really leaving. Though in that case, surely Dane didn't mean to send two young girls on their own across the Irish countryside?

"What about you, Courtenay? Ready to leave English territory so soon?"

"Why? What was the point of bringing me here only to let me go?"

"Two reasons. First, you had to admit your true identity to Ailis to get here. I imagine that did not go over so well. I don't mind confessing I relish the thought of her taking out all that wild Irish anger on you rather than me."

Liadan was looking at him, confused. Maisie seemed as impassive as always. "And second?" Stephen ground out. He'd have to tell the girls the truth on the way back to Cahir. He did not relish having

Liadan's contempt turned toward him. He could not predict Maisie's reaction.

"Second," Dane repeated thoughtfully. "Well, I'll make you a deal on the second. You want to leave, there's a horse. Go with my blessing."

"Or?"

"Stay."

Again Stephen asked, "Why?"

"You stay here willingly, and return to England where you belong. Report to Walsingham and your queen and put Ireland behind you forever."

Dane moved in closer, fingering the hilt of the dagger in his belt. "But if you return to Cahir, then I send word to the English court that their favourite son has turned traitor. 'Gone native,' I believe the phrase is. You're not the first. It's a flaw the weak-minded are prone to, sympathizing with the enemy. I don't suppose it's a flaw your queen—or your father—will forgive."

Stephen's head spun. It was all too easy to imagine the black picture Dane painted. No, Elizabeth would not forgive. He knew her well enough to know ingratitude hurt her more than any other sin. And his father? Stephen tried to picture his father here—and came up blank. Dominic Courtenay did not belong to the murkiness of Ireland. In his father's eyes, loyalty was a matter of black and white.

But it wasn't. Because Liadan and Maisie were looking at him, and behind him, at Cahir, was a woman he had wronged. *Never take what is not freely offered,* his father had counseled, *and then only if you are certain you will not leave pain behind. That is poor payment for any woman.*

He had already repaid Ailis in pain.

"You should stay," Maisie said evenly. "I will make sure she understands."

Whether she meant Liadan or Ailis, he didn't know. And he didn't have a chance to figure it out before Dane continued.

"One more thing." Dane pulled his dagger free, a deceptively fine blade twelve inches long, honed to a wicked edge. "A message for Ailis and her clan—a reminder, if you like, that I cannot be black-mailed."

Without a word, without a warning, Dane seized Liadan around the shoulder and pulled her close. The blade went through her throat like the softest cheese. Dane was soaked in a spray of his daughter's blood, then let her limp body drop to the ground.

There was a roaring in Stephen's ears and the smell of blood assaulted his senses. At the edges of his vision ghosts crowded in, hungry to pull him back into their maelstrom of pain, Harrington and Roisin and the screams of girls in the blackest night . . .

But it was daylight and there was only one small, dead girl. Maisie dropped to her knees, making a keening noise that broke through Stephen's shock. He lunged for Dane.

And was brought up short by a guard with a loaded crossbow. But it was not pointed at him—it was pointed at Maisie.

"You promised to let them go!" Stephen shouted.

"I promised Ailis the return of her daughter. I did not specify in what condition. You have two minutes to decide," Dane added, casual despite the blood on his hands and clothes. "Take Ailis her daughter and you may have the Scots girl living. Or return to England and have one more dead girl on your conscience." He raised his hand at the bowman, ready to signal and let fly the bolt that would kill Maisie.

Stephen couldn't get her to move. He crouched, speaking low and urgent in her ear. "We have to go, Maisie, listen to me, we've got to go now . . ." a refrain that went on and on and did absolutely nothing to reach her.

"One minute," Dane said.

Stephen grabbed her by the shoulders, silently apologizing for his roughness, and pulled her to her feet. "Mariota," he said in as commanding a voice as he could manage. "Get on the horse."

It at least stopped her keening. He practically shoved her onto the larger of the horses. He couldn't mount that one on his own with a burden. They could rearrange themselves as needed once they were away from Blackcastle.

Hating Dane and Ireland and God and himself most of all, Stephen draped Liadan's limp body unceremoniously over his shoulder. Despite his anger with God, he prayed fervently that he could mount without dropping her. No way in hell was he letting Dane or one of his men touch her.

He managed, just, and when mounted subsequently managed to shift Liadan so she lay cradled before him with her head in the crook of one arm. Kicking his horse into movement, he was glad to see Maisie aware enough to follow.

As they went through the outer gate, Stephen heard Dane call, "Tell Ailis and her clan that the English will have Ireland. If we have to kill every last Irish native to do it."

It was a ride Maisie would never remember clearly. The world itself seemed flat, as though pressed from the leaves of a book. The only thing not black or white or gray was the blood on her hands and dress and even on the ends of her long braids that had slipped over her shoulder. She knew they rode and stopped and rode again. Stephen forced bread down her throat, and cheap wine that made her sputter. At one stop he wrapped Liadan's body in the cloak she silently offered him. Neither of them spoke a word.

Diarmid and several of his men were waiting for them three miles outside Cahir. Maisie heard the hisses of shock and kept her eyes fixed on the horizon. She would not let herself be caught by anyone else's sorrow.

But she could not avoid hearing Stephen's sharp voice. "Don't touch her."

Then she did look, where Diarmid and Stephen faced each other on horseback. The Irishman was quick enough to recognize the fanatic resolve in the Englishman's expression and did not force the issue. To fight over Liadan's corpse would be a final insult.

They rode in procession together. No one seemed eager to carry the news ahead of them to Cahir.

Even without being warned, Ailis was waiting for them. She must have had men watching from the walls. With the distance she could not yet be certain ... she would have counted the riders ... but Maisie was practically the same size as Liadan, and suddenly Maisie reached up and pulled off her hood. Let the watery sunlight catch the gleam of her white-blonde hair so Ailis would have the slightest moment of preparation ...

She didn't know why she thought that might help. There was no preparation that could matter. When they were still a hundred yards away, Ailis came running straight at Stephen. The riders pulled up and Diarmid swung down to put his arm around Ailis, which she immediately shook off. Maisie wanted to look away from her awful, stark face as Ailis realized ... but she wouldn't. The least she could do was bear witness.

This time, Stephen did not protest when Diarmid reached for Liadan. Gently, he let her down into the other man's arms. Ailis threw herself at them both so they ended on the ground, the mother stretched over her child, the peculiarly Gaelic keening that Maisie herself had produced earlier coming now from Ailis.

One of the other men helped Maisie down. She didn't know what to do. Stephen seemed in the same dilemma. He took a hesitant step toward Ailis and stopped.

This was a moment for clan only. Neither of them were wanted—or even noticed. So Maisie did the only thing she could think of to express her compassion. She walked away.

Without thinking, she ended in Liadan's chamber, where she had spent so much time. It was dreadfully, devastatingly empty. Everything was just as it had been that last night—was it only the night before last?—when Dane strode into the chamber and demanded they get up and get dressed quick and quiet. Maisie stared at the bed, the crumpled linens waiting for Liadan to return, and could not bear it.

She simply sat down where she was on the floor. There was a shoulder-height chest next to her and she leaned her head against it and began making tactical calculations in her head.

It might have been an hour later, or two, or only ten minutes when she felt something cold touch her face and she blinked herself back into her body. Stephen knelt before her, washing the blood and dirt from her cheeks. Then he moved to her hands, where the blood had cracked and dried and soaked so far into her skin Maisie would carry it with her always.

That was when she began to weep.

After seeing to the horses—not only Dane's, but those Diarmid and his men had ridden—Stephen did not know what to do. He could trace the rise and fall of the women's wailing and wanted to shut his ears or run away. Barring that, he expected to be secured in the chains left empty by Dane, but it seemed even the men of Clan Kavanaugh were lost in grief for a time. He could have left then, if he'd wanted.

Finally, he remembered that there was at least one person in Cahir as alone as he was this night. He found Maisie sitting on the stone-flagged floor next to Liadan's bed, knees hugged to her chest, still wearing the gown soaked with the child's blood. He didn't know what to do. Looking desperately around the chamber, he saw the washing bowl with water that had no doubt been sitting there since they'd vanished. He grabbed a piece of cloth and the bowl and set it next to Maisie on the floor. He could at least clean her face.

The moment he touched her, he realized she'd had no idea he was there. He was almost sorry to have broken the balance that had kept her quiet, for almost at once her shoulders began to shake. Helplessly, Stephen put an arm around her narrow shoulders and then the sobs began in earnest.

He could remember his mother holding Kit as he'd sobbed, sometimes in sorrow, other times in rage. Kit had always been extravagant in his emotions. Just like his mother had back then, Stephen curved over Maisie protectively and she ended half on his shoulder, half in his lap, as Liadan herself might have done. Stephen's own throat was so tight he could hardly swallow.

When the storm had gentled a bit, he realized there were words with her tears. She kept saying something. To him. "You called me Mariota."

She must have said it three or four times before Stephen heard and interpreted it correctly. He didn't know what to say. She looked up at him, her eyes enormous from weeping, and said, "No one has called me Mariota since my grandfather died."

Then, like the practical-minded Scots girl she was, she straightened away and Stephen dropped his hands. He still didn't know what to say.

Maisie solved that issue. "I know who you are."

"I suppose Dane gave you all the hints you needed."

"No, I meant I knew it before. From almost the first day we met."

Stephen blinked. "What are you, given to second sight?"

"I met your brother last summer at Kilkenny. His was not a face one forgets."

"Yes, I know," Stephen said wryly. "But Kit and I are nothing alike."

"The coloring, no. But the bones of your face are the same. And your expressions. You both wrinkle the corner of your eyes when you're being polite against your nature, and your jawline twitches when you're displeased. There's something about the way you both speak and carry yourselves . . . I was sure."

"And then you corroborated." Stephen let out a breath that was half laugh, half admiration. "I was warned there were questions about my present location coming from the merchant communities in London. I thought it was Mary Stuart looking for me. It was you."

"It's what merchants do," she said listlessly. "Hoard information like squirrels. For our own benefit."

"Rather like a spy."

"But you're not really a spy, are you? Not in the way you were meant to be. You might have come to the Kavanaughs for information, but you stayed for Ailis."

How had such a slip of girl so easily seen into the heart of him? Trying to deflect his uneasiness, Stephen said, "It doesn't much matter now. I'm damned either way. No doubt Dane already has messengers flying to England to tell the queen I'm a traitor. But they'll have to stand in line behind Ailis to get at me. I don't imagine she'll be satisfied with anything but my head."

"Then I would say your imagination is not very good where women are concerned."

"They're going to lock me up, Maisie."

"I know it as well as you do, and yet you came back to Cahir. Don't worry. I may not be able to defuse their anger at your initial lies, but I will be able to clear you of any involvement in . . ." She waved her hand around the crumpled, deserted chamber. "Any of this."

"Don't worry about me," Stephen said grimly.

"I'm not. Ailis won't kill you. She needs you. And I need you, too—because while I was at Blackcastle, I gathered quite a lot of information that will be useful when it comes time to attack. Men don't expect much from women, especially not young women. They let us see rather more than they should have. I've already begun calculations on the number of men Dane has on hand, the quality of their weapons and food stores, and what Clan Kavanaugh will need to beat them."

Stephen blinked. He seemed to have forgotten how to speak. Finally he managed to croak, "What?"

"It's what I do, remember? There is more to me than anyone in Ireland has guessed—including Oliver Dane."

Stephen realized his mouth was hanging open, so he shut it. But he couldn't stop staring at this girl with her cascade of silver-gilt hair so bright it gleamed in the shadows of the dark chamber. Like her own moon.

A verse from the Old Testament came into his head: *Fair as the sun, clear as the moon, and terrible as an army with banners.*

"Stephen?" Maisie peered up at him, a crease of determination between her eyes. "It's going to be all right in the end."

TWENTY

After two weeks of confinement at Hampton Court, Anabel was allowed to depart by barge for the short trip to Syon House. She thought her mother was glad to see her go. The longer the Princess of Wales remained cloistered in her bedchamber, the harder it was to keep up the pretense of a summer cold or a string of sick headaches or even female troubles. And she wasn't ready to step back into court life. She had lost weight and colour during her illness—not to mention her hair; Anabel mourned extravagantly for her beautiful hair and she hated having to wear wigs. And the terror that had seeped into her during the worst of the fever had not entirely dissipated.

The Duc d'Anjou and Esmé Stewart had been sent off to Theobalds to be entertained by Lord Burghley in his beautiful home, and from there a leisurely tour to Cambridge and the Roman city of Colchester. Anabel wondered how long they would stay in England before giving up on seeing her again. She didn't trouble herself overmuch; her mother would handle it.

Syon House was a blessed repose of beauty and quiet. She no longer needed constant nursing, and found herself irritably swatting away the hovering women who tried. At this point she could tolerate only Minuette and Madalena. Lucette had gone home with her husband. Anabel knew that Pippa was at Syon House as well. But now that conversation was possible between them, she was not in a hurry for it.

As for her household, her clerks and secretaries ran things so smoothly she supposed they hardly even missed her. Anabel knew she should care, but it was hard to summon the energy. Though the fever had broken and the rash faded without trace, she was . . . weary. Lassitude had become her constant companion, and for the first time in her life, she let herself drift without intention or effort.

The only one who brought colour to her days and a curiosity in the world was, not surprisingly, Kit. She knew that his admission to her private chambers was solely at his mother's discretion—another nursemaid would never have allowed the impropriety, now that she was no longer in danger of death. But who could complain when his own mother stayed in sight and hearing of them? Most of the time. If Minuette often drifted discreetly out of sight, who was to know?

Syon House, with all its new décor, was conducive to convalescence. Unlike other, more heavily decorated palaces, her bedchamber and privy chamber were done in a palette of muted blues and greens with liberal amounts of white and touches of silver.

In early September, Kit sat on a folding chair with an intarsia of coloured stones while Anabel reclined on a padded bench with low back and sides. The sunlight came through the unusually wide windows, illuminating Kit's bright eyes and expressive hands as he told her stories of Spain.

"Now you're just teasing me!" she protested, laughter making her throat ache. "There is *not* a woman at my father's court with an eye patch."

"I swear on my life, Anabel, I am not teasing. Could I imagine such a thing? Doña Ana de Mendoza lost her right eye when she was young, in a duel with her father's page. She's worn an eye patch ever since. And it has not in the least detracted from her great beauty."

Now he *was* teasing, and Anabel responded by sticking out her tongue. It was like they were ten years old again. "I suppose she was only one of many beautiful Spanish women. How many begged you to bring them to England with you?"

"Not a single one. For once, I was quite pleased to have no title or great wealth to offer. Made it simpler to concentrate on the essentials."

"Which were?"

He hesitated. "Do you want to do this now?"

"Talk?"

"Talk about essentials."

"I suppose I can't hide away forever." Even though the thought was awfully tempting. She sighed. "How did you find Queen Mary?"

"Insufferably pleased with herself. One would think she was the first queen in history to produce sons."

That wrung a smile from her. "James laments that. He writes that it is as though he has been erased from his mother's memory."

"James of Scotland. You have been in communication?"

"Esmé Stewart brought a letter for me from his king. It read more as a shared complaint of two children whose parents are bent on humiliating them, rather than a personal suit."

Kit nodded, and Anabel would have given much to know what he was thinking. But he merely continued with his recital. "King Philip was all that was gracious. And more at ease than I had ever known him to be. Seeing him at home in Spain was a lesson on how uncomfortable he must always have been while in England. I think you would know him better if you saw him there."

"You know I can't."

"Yes, and so does he. That does not stop him regretting it. I would guess that everything we were shown was calculated to make its way back to you, an offering of the most beautiful, most cultured aspects of Spain that are your heritage, whether or not you ever claim it."

"And how does Mary Stuart respond to that?"

He grimaced. "I don't imagine the two of you will ever meet as friends."

"As she had me held hostage to ensure her escape, I don't imagine we will." That didn't mean Anabel relished the thought of meeting the Scots queen as an enemy. At the moment, it all seemed like entirely too much work.

Silence fell between them, and as happened with increasing frequency these last days, it was weighted with tension. Anabel knew—had always known, before she even knew why—that it would be up to her to break the silence.

Despite her illness, her unaccustomed lethargy, her heightened state of sensitivity, she would always be her mother's daughter. So when she spoke, it was as direct as she could make it.

"What are we going to do?" she asked.

If nothing else had persuaded her in the last two years of Kit's feelings, the quality of his silence now would have done so. There was an eloquence to the quiet lines of his body, the familiar grace of it tensed ever so slightly in the shoulders and hands—he had his mother's long, narrow hands with fingertips that made her shiver at the thought of his touch. Anabel could not see his eyes until suddenly he raised his head, and then she could not see anything else.

"You are going to get better," he promised softly. "And when you are, I will do whatever you ask."

"Including serve in my household?"

"If you ask it of me."

"But it would not be your first choice."

She knew his answer by his wry grin. "My first choice? I think attaining my third or fourth choice is the best I can hope for in this life."

"What would you prefer to do?" Had she ever asked anyone that before? Royalty did not usually trouble with the wishes of those who served them.

"My father has suggested an intensive course of military training.

I hate to say it, but though he is your father, King Philip has his eye on war. Both his conscience and his pride cannot abide what he sees as England's heretical defiance. And with Mary at his side determined to wrest Scotland back from her own son if she can . . . before the decade ends, there will be war. I would rather not wait until it comes to be prepared."

"Well, even if you are training heavily at Tiverton, I should still see you from time to time."

There was silence. Then, "I'm not going to train at Tiverton."

It seemed he was going to make her ask. "Where, then?"

"With Renaud LeClerc. In France," he added, as though she didn't know that perfectly well.

The illness had not completely obliterated her previous temper—her first instinct was to forbid it. But she held her tongue, determined not to treat him as just another vassal. Dare she be honest?

"But I will miss my raven."

His eyes softened, and Anabel bit her lip to keep it from trembling. If he didn't move, she was going to have to . . .

With that swift grace so familiar to her, Kit knelt at her side. "Don't cry," he said, which was her first indication that she was crying.

"I'm afraid."

"Of what?"

"The future. Why cannot I just be a girl, Kit?"

"Because if you were just a girl—if you were any girl except yourself—I would not love you."

"Do you?" she whispered.

"You know I do."

"Tell me."

He cupped her face in those beautiful hands of his. "I love you, Anabel. Whatever the future brings, whatever choices you must make for England, always know that I love you. *Mi corazon.*"

My heart.

His right thumb traced the outline of her lips, and Anabel forgot who and what she was. For just this moment she was the girl she longed to be—the simple girl brave enough to lean up and kiss the boy she had loved all her life without knowing it.

Kit stilled, but only for a moment's surprise. Then his hands slipped down her throat and her shoulders to pull her against him as they kissed. As awkward and inexperienced as she was, Anabel was certain nothing could ever feel as glorious as this.

But beneath the glory beat the ever-present question she had uttered earlier: *What are we going to do?*

Not until Anabel was safely secured to convalesce at Syon House did Elizabeth attend a full privy council meeting. Dominic had made a preliminary report to both Burghley and Walsingham, condensed into written notes that had only partly penetrated her distraction. Now she could turn her full attention to Spain.

Or nearly her full attention. For the first order of business was how to graciously dispatch the Duc d'Anjou and Esmé Stewart.

"Neither man is stupid," Walter Mildmay said waspishly. "They know they were not sent away from court because the Princess of Wales had a light summer cold. We're lucky they haven't both bolted for their own countries, carrying with them rumours of her imminent demise."

Burghley's reply was more temperate than Elizabeth's would have been. Sometimes she thought that, for all she had rewarded him, there was not reward enough in all England for the burdens he carried for her. "Their graces will continue on progress for another four days before meeting the court at Richmond to bid Her Majesty farewell. They will both be invited at that time to make a private visit to Princess Anne at Syon House."

"And what will be the outcome of these private visits? We must have a decision on a royal marriage as soon as may be. If Spain moves against us before we have allies—"

"If Spain moves against us," Walsingham broke in sharply, "that will ensure England has a plethora of allies. Do not underestimate King Philip's intelligence. Spain will not move until and unless they are convinced of their overwhelming superiority in numbers."

"We are not discussing Spain just yet," Elizabeth added. "Let us deal with the matter of the foreign suitors first."

"Has either France or Scotland offered formally?" Mildmay asked.

"No. But I believe both are prepared to do so if we leave them with the appropriate encouragement."

"And which one shall we encourage?" asked Burghley wryly, for the council was split on the matter. If it ever came to a vote—which of course it wouldn't—there would be no clear consensus for either Anjou or James.

There didn't have to be. Elizabeth had crafted her own answer. One she had not discussed with either Burghley or Walsingham, though she thought the former might have guessed something of her intentions.

"The Duke of Lennox," she announced, "will return to Scotland with our royal encouragement of King James's suit. I expect the formal betrothal to the Princess of Wales can take place this winter."

There was a slight murmuring but no great surprise.

But Elizabeth wasn't finished yet. "And the Duc d'Anjou will return to France with the understanding that, when he returns to England, it will be as the betrothed husband of my own royal self."

The murmuring became dead silence, a weight of astonishment that kept Elizabeth's chin high and eyes narrowed. She was prepared to combat dissent.

She was not prepared for open contempt. Mildmay barked an astonished laugh. "You cannot be serious!"

"Have you ever known me to be less than serious on matters touching my kingdom?"

"Anjou will never agree," he said bluntly.

"He already has. Privately."

That shut their mouths, but not their eyes. Elizabeth could see the question none of them were suicidal enough to ask aloud. *Why would Anjou marry an old woman?*

It wasn't as though she hadn't asked herself that question in the dead of night. In a year she would be fifty. There was no question of more children. Why wouldn't the twenty-seven-year-old Anjou hold out for a younger woman?

Because he was ambitious. And clever. He knew how to read royal currents and was as certain as he could be at this point that Anabel would never be contracted to France. If he could not wed the young princess and sire a future English king, then why not marry the reigning English queen?

Her councilors, if disapproving and shocked, were intelligent men who could follow that train of thought. They also knew her temper. So, cautiously, Burghley spoke for them all. "This is indeed news of some magnitude, Your Majesty. It is a possibility worth considering."

She narrowed her eyes at his use of the word "possibility," but Burghley knew how to smoothly navigate treacherous waters. "Perhaps we might leave that for future discussion and turn our thoughts to Lord Exeter's reports on Spain."

With a glare that told him she knew what he was doing, Elizabeth assented. At which point Walsingham took over the reports.

"As expected, King Philip took care to impress his English guests with the most beautiful parts of his homeland," he said. "Madrid, Segovia, El Escorial . . . it was a tour designed to awe. With Spanish culture, Spanish hegemony, Spanish wealth. Their final stop was Seville, where Exeter and his family were treated to the wealthiest port city in Europe. They were allowed to explore at their leisure. No doubt the king expected them to be calculating the resources at his disposal, as well as the power of the churchmen behind him. Seville was the original site of the Inquisition. With gold from the New World and religious fanatics in the old, Spain has only to take the decision—"

"We have always known this," Elizabeth interrupted sharply. "Our daughter is our greatest asset, for I cannot believe Philip will move against her future as long as it remains uncertain."

"Agreed. Which is why, though some understanding is advisable as to her marriage, a commitment to a specific wedding date is not wise just now. Delay must be our tactic—delay and charm."

Christopher Hatton joined in. "But Exeter seems confident that there is something military in the offing. From the ships and soldiers that were not seen where they might be expected. If not England itself—"

"Ireland," Walsingham agreed. He just managed not to sound insufferably pleased at being right. "With the hundred Spanish troops reinforcing the Earl of Desmond, he has begun to strike out from Askeaton. Ormond is worried. There is expectation that Desmond's forces will march to Cork and besiege Kinsale."

"That's enough," Elizabeth commanded. "We cannot fight ghosts or fears. Bring me hard news from Ireland, Lord Walsingham, and then we can take decisions."

She did not expect that hard news to come so quickly, nor to be so shocking. That very night, an hour after she'd retired to her bedchamber to read, her ladies informed her Walsingham had arrived, eager to see her.

Eager meant highly disturbed. "Send him in." For a moment Elizabeth thought of Anabel, but dismissed her worry at once. If anything happened to her daughter, it would be Burghley who would come to her.

Walsingham's face was always dark with worry, real or imagined, but she fancied when he entered that there was a rare disquiet added to it tonight. "What?" she asked.

"Word from Ireland."

"If you tell me that Philip has landed troops in force, I may throw something," she warned him.

"It is not the Spanish. It is young Lord Somerset."

"Stephen Courtenay?" She sat up sharply. "What on earth do you mean? God help you, Walsingham, if he has come to harm in your service—"

"He is unharmed. And I am not certain that he *is* currently in my service."

"Explain yourself."

"Stephen Courtenay has been infiltrated into Clan Kavanaugh since May. We have had no useful information from him yet, but that is not unexpected. The plan was for him to take what time was necessary to gain the trust of the household."

"But?"

"Oliver Dane is claiming that Stephen's loyalties no longer lie with England. Dane was briefly held prisoner by Ailis Kavanaugh and her household. He escaped, but in doing so, Stephen's secret was revealed. When Dane managed to get him free of the Kavanaughs as well, Stephen declined to remain. He returned to the Irish household, entirely of his own will, and it is possible he intends to march with the clan when next they fight against English troops."

"I don't believe it."

"We can't afford to let sentiment guide our decisions."

"Stephen Courtenay would not turn against me. Whatever is going on, there is more to it."

"I don't care what his motives are. I care only about his experience being turned against England. Dane seems to believe the Kavanaughs will march against Blackcastle. He will not move first—he will let them come to him. But if they do, Dane will fight. No matter who is in the vanguard."

Why could the Courtenays never be simple? Elizabeth wondered. Friends, that was all she needed. Loyalty and support no matter the difficulty. Instead, they twisted and turned and used their touchy honour as a reason to cause trouble.

"I suppose Dane wants armed support?"

"Ormond will send men. But if Stephen is fighting with the

Irish . . . no quarter will be given by Dane. I think he would gladly kill Stephen."

Elizabeth shut her eyes, feeling the beginning of a headache pounding behind her right eye. These were the parts of ruling that she hated—making impossible decisions.

But one did not rule this many years without learning not to linger on regrets. "Send to Syon House for Christopher. I know the Courtenays—they will listen to no one but themselves. If we want Stephen out of Ireland, his family will have to bring him."

"Why not send Lord Exeter?"

"Dominic? I may not have sons, Walsingham, but one thing I know for certain is that they are not likely to respond well to a disapproving father. Kit is the younger brother. If we're lucky, Stephen may feel responsible enough for his safety to keep a battle from occurring at all."

Also, she did not add, just as well to get Kit away from Anabel for a little.

4 September 1582

Lucie,

I write to beg a great favour. If you read Mother's letter first, you know about Stephen. (If you didn't read it first, go read it now. I'll wait.)

The queen intends Kit to drag Stephen out of Ireland. I do not think it will be that simple. Stephen has always been the most difficult of you all to see clearly, but I do know that he does nothing lightly. If he has become entwined in this Irish household, there are deep reasons for it.

So to the begging, sister: Please will you send Julien to Ireland with Kit? He has proved that he can reach Stephen when none of the rest of us can. I do not think Stephen has been hurt—but I think disentangling him from whatever is happening will involve a great deal of pain. He listened to Julien the last time he was drowning—he might do so again. And if not,

at least Kit will not be on his own. He would never say so, but he is des-
perately worried. He worships Stephen—how will he cope if his idol has
fallen?

If Julien agrees to go to Ireland, perhaps you would consider returning
to Anabel? Mother and Father intend to stay near as well, since it is to
court that the first news will come.

Pippa

7 September 1582
Compton Wynyates

Pippa,

I seemed destined not to spend more than two weeks at a time in my
new home. Of course Julien will go. He is already packing. And so am I.
I will see you at Syon House within a week.

Lucie

TWENTY-ONE

Liadan Kavanaugh was buried in the crypt below the private chapel at Cahir Castle. Despite spending two years in a French convent school, Maisie had never attended a Catholic requiem mass; she found it almost unbearably moving. There was no monastic choir to be had, but a young boy was found to sing the Dies Irae, the haunting melody of judgment and salvation.

Stephen was not allowed to attend the requiem. He was under lock and key, enforced by a sternly justified Diarmid mac Briain. Maisie had attempted once to intervene, but Diarmid dismissed her with a wave of his hand. "He's a liar," he said brusquely. "He stays jailed until we decide what's to be done."

We? Maisie wondered cynically. It will be until *Ailís* decides. The problem was that Ailis was unreachable in her grief. How long could she stay shut away before the vengeful men of her clan took over?

But the men seemed at a loss. It was as if Liadan had been the talisman for the entire clan, and without her, no one knew what to do next. Well, Maisie finally decided, if the men weren't going to do anything, she would have to brave Ailis herself.

Maisie knew how to get her way. Getting in to see Ailis involved Bridey, Liadan's nurse who had known Ailis since she was a child. Maisie listened to the old woman weep, and told her stories of how brave Liadan had been, how proud Bridey would have been of her in her last days.

"You should tell her," Bridey said finally, wiping her eyes. "Her mother would want to know that."

"You do not think it will be worse?"

"It cannot be worse. She broods. Give her something good to think about."

And just like that, Maisie was let in. Ailis looked at her, not blankly, but entirely without interest. Bridey said nothing, just left the women alone.

There was an untouched tray of bread and cheese on a medieval sideboard, and the four-poster bed, though unmade, appeared un-slept in. Maisie had never seen Ailis look anything but fiercely pulled together; now she sat in her shift with a cloak of felted wool thrown over. Her hair hung loose, a nest of blackness.

Maisie found a carved bone comb and moved behind Ailis. Working in small sections, she began to comb the bereft woman's hair. She worked in silence and slowly she could see Ailis's shoulders loosening.

When her hair lay like a fall of black satin, Ailis finally spoke. "You used to comb her hair. She told me."

"I did." Maisie pulled a stool near Ailis and sat.

"She liked you better than me."

"She loved you. Every bit of her was focused on being like you."

"I'm almost glad she won't get the chance."

Maisie could think of no possible answer to that.

With a great shuddering sigh, as though expelling demons, Ailis closed her eyes. When she opened them again, it was though she had forcibly pulled her former self into being. "When you first came to

Ireland, I thought you nothing but a rich girl who would sit in the corner while we spent your money. How wrong I was—and gladly so. It is your mind, and your heart, that is the real wealth."

"As to my mind," Maisie said delicately, "I put it to use while I was at Blackcastle. There are things I could tell you that you might find useful."

"Useful for what?"

"For avenging Liadan."

Ailis flinched at the sound of her daughter's name. But beneath the pain, interest flickered. "Tell me."

"When you are ready to move against Dane, I will give you every advantage that my memory and my money can provide."

Ailis gave a tiny, perhaps involuntary smile. "Let us show these men what women can do." She drew a shaky breath, then added softly, "For Liadan's sake."

From the moment she assembled her council, Ailis could feel how close to the edge she stood. Beneath what had been a drowning despair, she felt a spurt of anger kindle. It cleared her head to a surprising degree, and she embraced the anger as an ally. How could these men turn on her so quickly after all she had given this clan? Her childhood stolen, her innocence abused, all the years devoted to strengthening their position—did they mean nothing? If she had been a man, her leadership would have been solidified by now.

If she had been a man, there would have been no Liadan to rip her heart out.

She took her place at the table and surveyed those here. Diarmid, looking stern and grave, but still her most devoted ally. Good. She would need him to believe in her for a little while longer. There were three of Diarmid's men as well, the most seasoned warriors, who could add their experience to the planning. All her men were competent and capable.

Also, there was Maisie.

If the men were surprised to see the Scots widow among them, they had more pressing concerns. At least Diarmid did. "What are your plans for the English spy?" he asked first.

She met his gaze coolly. "All in good time. The most pressing matter is how to answer the murder of our most innocent daughter."

"How?" Diarmid snorted. "With violence. There is no other answer."

"Agreed. Perhaps I should have been clearer—we must decide on the when and where of that violence. Maisie and I have a plan."

There were raised eyebrows at that, but the men's instinctive respect for a mother who had lost her child meant they kept their mouths shut. For the moment. Ailis nodded to Maisie.

"I saw a fair amount of Blackcastle while we were there," Maisie said, producing the carefully drawn map she had done for Ailis. "Dane could not make up his mind whether we were prisoners or guests. No doubt he expected only hysteria from females, not the ability to memorize floor plans and calculate available arms and stores. His mistake."

Next to Ailis, Diarmid whistled as the map was spread on the table before them all. A builder or military engineer could not have done better. For having been at Blackcastle just over twenty-four hours, it was a masterpiece.

Ailis, having already gone over it with Maisie, pointed out the essentials. The interior was of less concern than the courtyard and the numbers. "Stables, armory, stores," she said, pointing in turn. "Dane has mostly men in his castle—a few have wives working in the kitchens and laundry. Dane rides them hard. They're disciplined and quick. There will be no second-guessing of any orders they're given. They might have been shocked—or not—at Liadan's murder, but make no mistake, they will back Dane to the hilt. That is what the English do."

"Only English troops?" Diarmid asked. "He's been known to use gallowglass."

"Maisie didn't get any indication of gallowglass in hold. And there won't be," Ailis said decisively. "Not for this fight. It will be Irish against English."

"Are you certain?"

"I know Dane. This is a matter of pride. He wants to grind us beneath his boots—and only English boots will do."

Diarmid looked unconvinced but did not dispute the matter. There was a more critical point to make. "Even if it's only his men, Dane will have more troops than we can muster. Unless you"—he nodded at Maisie—"managed to poison their food and water, we cannot match them in numbers."

"I thought about it." Maisie said it so matter-of-factly it was impossible to tell if she was serious. "But at the time, I had no reason to suppose we would not be released unharmed. It seemed silly to provoke matters. Besides, if there's anything well-guarded at Blackcastle, it's the food and drink stores. Dane knows he's always at risk of being cut off for a time. He can withstand a siege for some weeks at least."

"We will not lay siege," Ailis said flatly. "Sieges are for cold calculation, not vengeance. Liadan will not rest in peace until Dane is dead. We must draw him out for that."

"Of course he'll be drawn!" Diarmid shouted. "He can sweep through whatever men we can muster. How will that help Liadan rest?"

Ailis felt her mouth smile and knew it was as cold in appearance as it felt. "Dane will not use gallowglass . . . but we will."

"With what money? We have barely enough to feed the household through this winter. We have nothing to sell except ourselves— and even if we could, we cannot deduct one man of us from this fight."

"Then it's a good thing Finian married a rich girl," Maisie said.

In the silence that fell, hope warred with disbelief on Diarmid's face. He spoke directly to Maisie. "But your dowry money was not great, and most of it has been spent feeding us this far."

"That was only the dowry money you knew about," Maisie replied calmly. "I am not a rich girl so much as I am a merchant's girl. My brother thought he bought me off cheaply. That's because he undervalues relationships. I have a loyal faction in my grandfather's company, and my own factor in Dublin. My dowry money was twice what was reported to you—the remainder has been invested for me. One of those investments is a private company of European mercenaries."

This time the silence was absolute. Ailis might have laughed, if there was any laughter left to her in this world. The men were staring at Maisie as though they'd never seen her before—and so they hadn't. Till now she had been thought of in the same space as Liadan, young and cheerful, meant to be cosseted and otherwise ignored.

What fools they had all been.

Diarmid was the first to recover. "A company large enough to make a difference?"

"Two hundred, half of them mounted. Including their own cooks, physician, and engineer."

"Where are they?"

"Dublin. Since the spring. Broken into smaller units to guard my business interests in shipping. The English authorities could hardly refuse us that, seeing as they cannot be trusted to guard their own interests."

Diarmid laughed. "Can they get out of Dublin?"

Maisie merely looked at him with withering contempt. "They are already on their way here. Once again, in small units and as quietly as possible. A few will head here—the rest will be just within reach until the last minute. We don't want to tip our hand."

"'Our' hand?" Diarmid asked bluntly. "What benefit do *you* derive from this?"

When Maisie spoke, it was with a voice of fire and threat. "You think vengeance is solely an Irish virtue? I rode back to Cahir with Liadan's blood on my hands and in my hair. I will have vengeance for that."

Ailis took charge once more. "So we are agreed to accept the offer of mercenaries?" She waited for each of them to assent. "There is one condition—Stephen Courtenay will command the mercenary company."

She expected a fight. But again, perhaps her grief was useful to remind them that she was only a woman and of course would act from her emotions. In any case, only Diarmid spoke. "Is this your condition? Or hers?" He jerked his head at Maisie.

"It is ours, and it is absolute."

Even a proud Irishman could swallow the distasteful when necessary. If using one Englishman would allow them to destroy Dane, so be it.

The meeting broke up, and only Maisie lingered. "Will you tell him?"

Ailis had not seen Stephen since he'd lowered her daughter's body down from his horse a week ago. She wasn't looking forward to seeing him now. "You can do it if you like."

"He needs to see you." Maisie hesitated, then added, "I think you will find him a compassionate listener. You should talk to him."

"About what?" *My blindness, my failure, my damned pride for which Liadan paid . . .*

"You both need absolution," Maisie said gently. "I think you will understand each other."

Maisie left her then, and Ailis stood alone. Could Stephen absolve her? Did she want him to? He had sins of his own to count, sins against her as well as the clan . . .

But at the very least, he would have to be told about the mercenary force and Maisie's requirement that he lead it. She would begin there and see what happened.

Stephen's second imprisonment at the hands of Clan Kavanaugh was an entirely different experience than the first. Diarmid chained him, for one thing. No one ever talked to him, for another. But mostly, the hell of it all was inside his own skull. Rather than planning and practicing his cover, preparing to worm his way into the trust of a household he didn't know, Stephen was mired in a familiar guilt. It was similar to the torture he'd passed through in the months after the prisoners' slaughter. This time, though, there was no alcohol to dull it. Perhaps that was a good thing—but it didn't feel like it in the darkest hours of the night.

As a ghost, Liadan was even more effective than Roisin had been. The child was a constant memory both waking and sleeping: her swift footsteps, her lightning smile, her ever-present curiosity and straightforward manner of speaking. The world was a poorer place without her in it, and if Stephen had hated Oliver Dane on Roisin's behalf, he now loathed the man with an intensity that curdled his stomach.

He didn't much care what the Kavanaughs did to him, just so long as they took out Dane first.

When the door opened, he expected the unsmiling Diarmid or one of the two guards who brought him food daily. But it was Ailis.

Stephen jerked to his feet, brought up short by the chains he'd forgotten he wore. He noted the pallor, the hollows carved in her cheeks, the dark rings around her eyes that spoke of sleepless nights and agonized days. All he wanted was to put his arms around her and pretend he could ease the grief.

Instead, he did the only thing he could. He apologized. "I am so sorry. I have failed you."

"By not delivering my daughter as you promised? Or by lying to me in the first place?"

"For all of it. This is my fault."

For a minute she looked as though she meant to agree, but then the edges of her face crumpled and she looked nearly as vulnerable in her distress as Liadan ever had. Stephen felt as though he were seeing Ailis as she might have looked when Dane had so casually used her in Kilmallock. He bit down hard on the surge of rage. This wasn't about him.

"Oh, Stephen, there is fault and enough to go around. I have hardly had time to count your sins—my own are too pressing."

"You have no fault here."

"I have every fault! I command here, Stephen. My voice gives the orders. Father Byrne was my most loyal supporter for years. He might have argued with me—rarely—but he would not have acted against me. Not in secret."

"Father Byrne let Dane go because Peter Martin came to him with a plan." Stephen felt a stirring of unease. From far away, he thought he could see where Ailis was going, and he didn't want her to go there. He didn't want her to say it.

"Yes, Peter Martin acted for English interests. Father Byrne only ever acted in my interest. He let Dane go because I told him to."

"What?"

"He came to me with Martin's plan. I nearly threw Martin into another cell to rot alongside Dane when I found out—but then I considered that if Dane escaped, I could hunt him down on the road and kill him in the dark. That would be legitimate. So I told Byrne to go along with the plan."

"Why not tell someone?"

"Because you were both right! But I didn't want to admit it. I didn't want to back down. My pride ... that was what killed my daughter. I should have known Dane would always win."

"Not always, Ailis. Dane cannot win the coming fight. Liadan will be avenged."

Ailis must have read his longing to touch her, for she came forward and unlocked his chains. The same chains from which Dane had been freed ten days ago. But once freed, Stephen was afraid to move. Afraid to do or say the wrong thing.

Ailis moved for him. She had never kissed him like this— desperate, hungry, as though trying to lose herself in him. The only thing to do was respond in kind. Until she began to untie his lacings.

"Ailis, stop. You're not thinking."

"For the first time in days! I don't want to think, Stephen. I want to forget."

"This isn't the way." He felt himself a hypocrite even as he said it. Everything in him was shouting for her. He was shaking so hard it took force of will to hold himself apart. But the last time he'd let his desires dictate, Roisin had died.

"What is the way, Stephen? To lie your way into my bed? To make me believe that, just maybe, there was one Englishman in the world who didn't deserve an excruciating death? You owe me. This is my payment."

He would have had to hurt her to stop it—and he didn't want to do either one. It was hard to tell which of them was more desperate. It broke Stephen's heart to see how thin she was as he removed skirts and shift, her collarbone and hip bones sharp beneath his hands. He laid her down gently on the pallet (clean, at least), and Ailis pulled him with her. There were tears mixed with gasps, and Stephen was fairly confident that, for a few moments at least, her grief was swamped by her body's joy.

She slept for an hour after, and Stephen watched her breathe. He imagined sleep had been hard to come by for her and hoped the pain of waking would be tempered rather than worsened by what had passed. He had no idea what would come next. Ailis might easily chain him up once more, or put him on trial. But he had an idea of his own, and when she finally stirred, he put it to her while her defenses were still low.

"You should hold me for ransom," he said bluntly. "You will need money to take down Dane. Take it from the English."

"What if your queen is not minded to pay to get you back? She is notoriously tightfisted, and if she's heard some version from Dane of your betrayal? Elizabeth won't fund her own soldiers in Ireland—she won't make the mistake of funding mine."

"The queen doesn't come into it. You said it yourself—I'm heir to the wealthiest dukedom in England. My own lands of Somerset could bear a significant ransom, and I do not think my father would balk overly at paying in of himself. Set your terms, Ailis, and let me make what amends are possible."

"I don't deny the thought of using English gold to pay troops to destroy Dane is enticing . . . but it's not needed. Maisie has anticipated us both. The girl secretly held back half her dowry and invested it through her own business factor. Her investments include a European-trained mercenary force. They are already making their way to Cahir to join us in attacking Blackcastle."

Stephen stared at her blankly, then was seized by a desire to laugh. All those letters Maisie had written and received? He'd thought them nothing but the everyday outpourings of a young girl far from home. She had completely and thoroughly surprised him, and he thought his sisters would be impatient with him because of it. Hadn't he lived surrounded by clever women? And here he'd fallen into the simplest of errors—assuming that because she was young and female and not strikingly beautiful, that Maisie must also be useless.

"Well done, Mariota," he murmured admiringly. "I'm glad of it, Ailis. You are planning to attack, then?"

She stirred and sat up, hair falling over her shoulders to veil her breasts. "We are planning to attack. Maisie has demanded you command the mercenaries and I have agreed."

"Why?"

"Because I think the story you told me about Dane killing an Irish girl you cared for is more or less true. One can feign desire and friendship and love . . . but I've never found anyone who can effectively feign hatred. You hate him. And I need a commander in the field who hates him for his own sake and not merely for Liadan. It will make you reckless."

"You make me reckless," he whispered. When he kissed her, he could taste a desire equal to his and felt a ridiculously male pride that he'd succeeded in teaching her pleasure.

As she pulled him down, her body finally warm beneath his hands, Ailis whispered back, "I will break your heart, Englishman."

Stephen didn't care.

TWENTY-TWO

D ominic Courtenay had to be forcibly persuaded not to go to Ireland after his son. Kit had the distinct impression the queen threatened him to prevent it, though he couldn't imagine with what. Whatever their conversation, Dominic had refrained from sailing, though he'd ridden to Bristol with Kit and twenty-four of his own handpicked soldiers.

"You brought Stephen back once," Dominic told him grimly. "Do it again, son."

Shouldn't it be the other way round? Kit wondered. He'd always thought of himself as the irresponsible one, the one more likely to need rescuing by the impatient, ever-dutiful oldest son. But these past two years had begun to teach him that people were more complicated than could fit in a few chosen words of description.

He had Julien with him this time, and was glad of it. His brother-in-law had ten years' experience on him, and a physical presence that shouted competence and authority. Kit didn't mind at all taking direction from Julien—probably because they hadn't grown up together. Why were brothers so damned difficult? He almost asked that question aloud as they stood on deck watching the Irish coast-line appear . . . before he remembered that Julien had killed his own brother.

Things could be worse.

But not much worse. Waterford was tense and hostile, refugees from Desmond's vengeful attacks huddled against the city walls. The small English party left as soon as they landed, into a landscape much worse than any Kit had seen before. His previous time in Ire-land had all been spent between Dublin and Kilkenny, the strongest holds of the English Pale, and he was shocked speechless by the emptiness. As though the English were determined to destroy every living thing in Ireland. The only thing in abundance were hares, run wild in a place without people.

The Earl of Ormond had sent a dozen of his own men and a guide to bring the English party to Templemore. When they saw the Rock of Cashel in the distance, their party skirting it to the north-east, Kit wished he could simply swoop in and pluck his brother away. He knew Cahir Castle was not far . . . but it might as well have been a hundred miles. With fewer than forty men, they could not threaten even the smallest of Irish holds. They would have to go to Templemore.

The Earl of Ormond himself was at Blackcastle. He met the party as they rode through the gates, and quickly pulled Kit and Julien away with him. When they were behind closed doors, Ormond turned on them a face like thunder. "Oliver Dane is the most hard-headed man in Ireland—and that's saying something. He admits killing the Irish girl, but will not even consider negotiating."

"What Irish girl?" Kit asked.

Ormond grunted. "I don't suppose that was part of his report to England. He escaped the Kavanaughs with a child in tow—*his* child, he admits freely. And then he killed her. Elizabeth has no love for the Irish, but even she would hesitate at one of her captains stabbing a child to death in cold blood."

"Tell me from the beginning," Kit ground out.

It was a sordid, disturbing story. Kit and Julien eyed each other when Ormond was finished, then the Frenchman said what they were both thinking. "A man like that isn't going to want us to negotiate Stephen out of Irish hands."

"No," Ormond agreed. "He seems to have taken a distinct dislike to Stephen. Dane wants his blood."

"Too bad. The queen wants Stephen alive," Kit retorted. "She's furious with him, and will no doubt punish him—but she sent me here to bring my brother back to England in one piece."

Ormond sighed. "I don't think negotiation is even a remote possibility. The Kavanaughs are preparing to move against Dane. It will be a disaster of the first order. I have no wish to raze their clan to the ground—we should be turning what English forces we have against Desmond, not wasting them in lesser squabbles. But if you want your brother, I suspect you'll have to pluck him from the battlefield. Before Dane can get to him."

"How many men do you have?"

"Not enough. Dane clearly wants the advantage to lay with his own men so he can do what he wants. I've got thirty here. With the thirty-five you marched in with . . . it will not be easy."

"Since when are siblings easy?" Kit asked. But despite his light words, he felt hollow. Was it really going to come to this—he and Stephen on opposing sides of a battle? But if he didn't fight, then nothing would keep Dane from killing Stephen.

Damn it, brother, Kit thought furiously. If this is about a woman, she had better have been well worth it. And if you really have gone over wholeheartedly to the Irish, then I hope Elizabeth claps you in prison until you come to your senses.

Once Stephen and Ailis emerged together from his cell, there was no repeat of their few, passionate hours. That was probably the only thing that saved Stephen's life—Diarmid would gladly have killed him if he'd had to endure an obvious love affair. As it was, Diarmid barely tolerated him, and that was purely for vengeance's sake. Ailis kept them apart—Diarmid was busy drilling his men while Stephen worked with Maisie's mercenary company.

They were mostly Flemish, with a few Italians and Germans thrown in. Stephen did not meet the company as a whole, for they had been prudently split into six smaller units to travel swiftly and anonymously and then camped within a day's ride in various directions around Cahir and Templemore. Stephen was kept busy riding back and forth, using every skill of leadership he'd learned from both his father and Julien to make sure the men would work with him.

When at Cahir, he spent time with Maisie, poring over her maps and notes and memories of Blackcastle. They also discussed what Dane was likely to do. Maisie was in agreement with Ailis that he would wait for the Kavanaughs to come to him. "It's his pattern," she said. "Like a duel on a larger scale—when affronted, he will answer the challenge. We took him prisoner, he answered by killing Liadan. Now it's our move. But make no mistake, he will be waiting and prepared."

"How did a Presbyterian-born, convent-educated, merchant Scots girl learn to read the mind of a villain like Dane?"

"It's not reading minds, it's simply a matter of looking at information in the right way. There are patterns in everything. One has only to order them."

"I think you would like my sister Lucette."

She tilted her head thoughtfully. "Is she the one who plays chess?"

"I don't—" He broke off, then laughed. "You caught that near-slip, did you?"

"You covered neatly. But by that point I was fairly certain of who you were, so I knew you had siblings. They must be worried about you."

Stephen brushed it off, for he was not ready to deal with that emotionally charged subject. "What of your brother, Mariota?" Ever since Liadan's death, when she'd cried that only her grandfather had called her Mariota, Stephen had continued to do so. "Does he know what you're up to in Ireland?"

"Rob? He doesn't know what his own business partners are up to. Which works out well for me. If he thinks of me at all, which I doubt, I'm sure he imagines me spending my days sewing or some other feminine pursuit. He never did know me very well."

Stephen hesitated, not wanting to insult her, but there was a favour he'd been wanting to ask and he didn't think anyone else in this household would help him. "But you do know how to sew?" he asked awkwardly.

She furrowed her brow. "You have some shirts that need mending?"

With a laugh, Stephen said, "No. I was wondering if you would make me a banner and surcoat."

"To march with? Are you sure about that? Queen Elizabeth might be able to overlook many things, but she can't overlook one of her earls raising his banner against another of her men."

"I'm sure," Stephen said grimly. "I want Dane to know who's coming for him."

Four weeks after Liadan Kavanaugh's murder, her clan marched in force from Cahir Castle. They knew Dane's spies were watching, but they only had a third of the mercenary company with them at this point, dressed to blend in with the Irish so as not to raise alarms. The point was to let Dane think he knew what he was going to face. They took two days to cover the distance, spies of their own riding ahead to report on the English state of readiness.

"They're waiting for us," was the consensus. "If they wanted, they could lock themselves behind the walls for a siege."

"They won't," Diarmid said confidently. It was one of the only things upon which he and Stephen agreed—Dane did not want a siege. Dane wanted to punish them for their pride, to crush them, to water the soil with their blood.

The second night, they camped two miles from Blackcastle. They

had timed their arrival for the dark of the moon, and in that darkness the remaining men of Maisie's mercenary company made their
way almost noiselessly to join them. Before dawn they were ready,
and when the faintest hint of gray lit the eastern sky, they marched
to claim their vengeance.

The sun had just slipped above the horizon when Blackcastle
came into sight. Diarmid and Stephen rode ahead together to survey
the field—which Maisie had drawn and mapped with a surprising
degree of accuracy—and confirm their areas of command.

The two of them were watched by Dane's soldiers on the battlements, but the English did not waste arrows shooting at two men
beyond their reach. This was a professional matter, at least for the
common soldier. As Diarmid and Stephen made a last sweep of the
field before falling back to issue final orders, the banners were lifted
on the walls above them.

Dane's aggressive boar in red and gold, of course. And it was no
great surprise to see the three gold cups quartered with the azure
and gold crowns of Thomas Butler. They had known the Earl of
Ormond was there, but their reports said with only a few dozen men
at the most. In the miserable days of his stay at Kilkenny, Stephen
had managed to grasp the fact that Ormond did not care for Oliver
Dane. But he was a committed queen's man, so here he was.

There was one more banner, at the very end of the battlements, a
flash of gold that caught Stephen's eye. He stilled, and Diarmid followed his stare. The wind stirred the fabric and it unfolded enough
for careful eyes to see the red and blue torteaux that were echoed in
quartered form on Stephen's banner.

"Shit!" Diarmid spat. "They've sent your father himself."

Stephen knew it wasn't the fact that Dominic was his father that
upset Diarmid—it was the fact that Dominic Courtenay was a better
commander with one hand than any other man with two. His own
stomach lurched in panic, but his eyes were quicker than his brain
and had already caught the slight difference in the coat of arms.

"No," he said flatly, turning his horse back toward their own men.

"It's not my father. Did you not mark the bar of cadency that signifies younger sons? It's my brother, Kit."

Damn it, Kit, what the hell are you doing here? An Irish battlefield was no place for his little brother. How was he supposed to focus on Dane when part of him would be instinctively watching to make sure Kit wasn't hurt?

Only one thing to do—throw himself into the fighting so fast and furious that Dane would be swept down before anything else. Then he would have to get Kit somewhere safe, for he had no illusions about Diarmid's men. Maisie's mercenary company would follow his orders. But the Kavanaughs? They wanted English blood—and they wouldn't care whose they spilled. Being Stephen's brother would not be a shield for Kit; it might actually make him a target.

Stephen swallowed down the peculiar mix of nerves and excitement conjured by the battlefield and offered a silent prayer. *Let me kill Dane, and let Kit be safe.*

Right up to the last moment, Kit hoped against hope that everyone was wrong and Stephen would not be with the Irish. When the alert went up shortly after dawn that the Kavanaugh forces were approaching, he dashed up to the battlements to scan the horizon for himself. The Irish were still too far to see clearly, but two of the men detached themselves from the rest and rode forward to survey the ground. They prudently stayed out of reach of arrows but were close enough for Kit to grind his jaw in frustration. He would have known Stephen anywhere, even if his brother wasn't flaunting a crudely done version of his coat of arms on a surcoat over half-armor.

Did the idiot want to get himself killed? He was marking himself for Dane, like the red cloaks to the bulls in Spain. Damn, damn, and damn again.

So caught up was Kit in the personal disaster of it all that he hardly had time to realize that he was about to engage in his first battle. Stephen had been in several light engagements against Scottish reivers on the border even before he'd come to Ireland last year, but Kit had been more sheltered. It was hard to disentangle his emotions, but he thought he was mostly furious with Stephen rather than upset about the imminent prospect of killing men.

In the three days he'd been at Blackcastle, Kit had taken his own violent dislike to Dane—no surprise—but also had developed a grudging respect for the quality of his command. He had his men split into three groups, two of which moved out in quick but orderly fashion, while the third had camped outside the walls all night. He had tried to order Ormond and Kit to stay within the castle walls, but he could not force Elizabeth's most powerful Irish earl to obey him. "We'll keep our own men out of your way," Ormond had said gruffly, "but they stay under our command."

Dane did not come straight out and say that he planned to kill Stephen himself, but he didn't have to. His contempt was clear. He knew why Kit was here, and Kit would not have been surprised to learn that some of Dane's men had been told to keep an eye on him and harry him away from Stephen.

But though Kit had not fought in the field, he had been trained by one of the finest commanders in the last thirty years and had learned to ride under the tutelage not only of his father, but the best masters the English royal court could provide for their princess. And he had under his command men from Tiverton who were prepared—because of his name and his childhood among them—to follow where he led. They had their orders, and Kit waited with pounding heart for the clash to begin.

At his side, helmed and lightly armored, Julien said, "Remember, this is not a battle—it is a mission. Your only task is to get to Stephen. Our task is to allow that to happen."

"If Dane's men are harrying me too closely," Kit reminded his brother-in-law, "then Stephen will be your task."

Julien flashed that quick, Continental smile that Kit supposed his sister found attractive. "Don't worry. If anyone's going to knock Stephen's head in today, it will be the two of us."

There were more than three times the number of men they'd expected to be facing, a fact that became crushingly apparent within minutes. As did the realization that the bulk of the troops were not Irish, but highly trained and deadly mercenaries. And their objective was obvious—to clear a path to Oliver Dane. Stephen was in their midst, and Kit, in the chaos, saw flashes of beauty in the way his brother was leading them.

Dane's forces shook under the sheer mass and reckless bravery of the onslaught. They had expected to fight only against swords and axes, but the mercenaries carried guns as well. Kit could not have imagined the noise of battle—clashing steel, grunts of shock, cries suddenly cut off. He set his jaw and his mind on one single purpose, and led his men to the left to come at Stephen from the side.

It was the hardest thing he'd ever done. His envy of his brother had never been based solely on emotion, but also on the simple fact that Stephen was very gifted. If his brother knew that he was there—and he must know, he'd have seen the banner—Stephen ignored him. Which meant, Kit realized, that he was highly likely to get injured if not killed trying to fight through the mercenaries around his brother.

Except he wasn't. When the third soldier veered his horse away, Kit realized Stephen must have given orders to the men not to touch him. Instantly and irrationally, it made the old jealousy flare up. *I don't need your favours, brother.*

Stephen was elusive, but not infallible. The mercenaries nearest to him, in the tight knot cleaving their way through Dane's forces, didn't aim to kill Kit or his men, but their blows fell harder the closer they got. Soon enough someone was going to die. "Stephen!" Kit shouted, but if his brother heard him, he paid no mind.

And then, all at once, there were Irishmen around him, four men surging into Kit's view, and he knew they would not spare a single soldier on the English side. One of his men went down and Kit wheeled his horse in a tight, frantic circle, deflecting blows. Only one of the Irish was mounted—the other three were using the mounted soldier and his horse as a shield and thrusting pikes into men as though they were tossing hay.

One thrust caught Kit's right arm and ripped through cloth into flesh. He was wearing half-armor, but if he lost his seat he would be trampled as easily as speared. Kit swore, but kept his grip on his sword tight. One of the Irish had seen the blow land, and using his pike as a club, the man battered the wound so that Kit's arm blazed and his fingers went numb. He dropped his sword.

And then Stephen was there, not fighting the Irish but shoving them aside with his horse and his voice. "Leave him!" he commanded, and Kit had never heard anyone sound so much like their father.

As there was bloodshed enough to spare, the Irish swept away into another wave of it, leaving the brothers momentarily face-to-face. "Get out of here, Kit."

"Not without you."

Stephen turned his horse's head. "Go home."

In that brief exchange, Julien had slipped his way in behind with one of Kit's men. At Kit's nod, the soldier seized hold of the horse's harness. Stephen jerked away, but Julien brought the hilt of his sword against Stephen's helmet. It jarred him enough to drop the reins, and a second carefully aimed blow got him off the horse.

Kit and Julien dragged him out of the thick of the fight, Stephen half conscious, and into a protective circle of Tiverton men. Kit prepared to remount, in order to make sure Ormond had seen what happened so he could move on with his own part of the plan. But Kit had only one foot in the stirrup when he was tackled hard from the side.

His skull jarred inside the helmet when he hit the ground and he clawed it off and threw it at his brother. Just as he knew Stephen's form when riding, he'd been tackled enough by his older brother to know the feel of it in his bones.

"What the hell are you doing?" they both yelled at the same time.

Kit scrambled to his feet and Stephen shoved him back. "Let me through!" he ordered.

"No."

And then it was like they were boys again, Kit an eight-year-old who resented his ten-year-old brother's title and, even more, his calm temperament, which everyone marked was so like their father. No one ever said Kit was like Dominic Courtenay.

They shoved and punched and wrestled—but they did not draw weapons. Not until Kit landed a heavy blow to Stephen's face that probably made his head ring and would certainly leave a nasty mark. Then, instinctively, Stephen drew his dagger and pointed it at his opposition.

Kit couldn't even swear that Stephen knew who he was anymore, if he could see his little brother or only saw the man who was keeping him from what he wanted. They were going to have to knock Stephen out again and then bind him if they wanted to get him off this battlefield. Julien was moving behind Stephen to do just that when there was a sudden lull in the noise of battle and one of the Tiverton men who'd been wise enough to keep watching outward shouted to Kit, "Ormond's got him!"

Kit knocked Stephen's dagger aside with the back of his hand. "You're going to want to see this."

It was even odds whether Stephen would listen. He did. The men opened a gap in the armed circle and the brothers stepped forward with Julien to look out.

As hoped and planned, the Earl of Ormond had got his man. The plan had been simple, if not easy. Kit dragged Stephen clear of the field, and Ormond took charge of Oliver Dane. Unlike Stephen, Dane had a long dagger at his throat.

Ormond had a voice built for carrying. "Draw off," he commanded equally to both sides. "Send forward your Irish leader and we will discuss terms."

Julien stayed behind, but Kit and Stephen strode forward without looking at each other. They were joined by a fiercely unfriendly Irishman who ignored Kit but glared at Stephen as though he'd gladly run him through whatever the cost. No matter that they'd been fighting on the same side.

They held their parley protected by a knot of Ormond's men, weapons readied outward to keep any ordinary soldier from disputing their leaders' discussion.

Dane's face was so suffused with furious blood Kit thought he might die of apoplexy on the spot. When he saw Stephen, he instinctively lunged forward. "This is your doing, English bastard!" he snarled.

Ormond jerked him back, reminding him of the dagger at his neck. "You're English," he said to Dane. "And shut up, this isn't your show any longer."

"What makes it yours?" Stephen shot back.

"I do," Ormond said grimly. "Now everyone who isn't Irish born and bred, keep your mouths shut." He turned to the rebel next to Stephen. "Your name?"

"Diarmid mac Briain."

"Of the Kavanaughs."

"Yes."

"I understand there has been a crime committed against your clan by Captain Dane. The murder of a young girl."

Diarmid spat. "His own daughter."

"An Irish whore's brat—"

It was Stephen who drove the words back into Dane's throat with a punch that slipped past Ormond's dagger. Kit threw himself on his brother and dragged him back.

"Is everyone here mad?" Ormond shouted. Then, to Diarmid mac Briain, "I am authorized to offer compensation for that crime. The tenancy of Blackcastle itself."

There was stunned silence, then Dane shouting, "The castle is mine!"

"On lease from me," Ormond said. "The castle and land are rightly the Butlers, and I offer them to the Kavanaughs—including all stores of food inside—if they will clear the field without further bloodshed."

"And the stores of weapons?" Diarmid asked shrewdly.

Ormond shook his head. "You know better. The weapons come with me. But along with the castle, you have my word I will not try to take it back. The lass should not have been so treated."

"And you think a castle worth Liadan's life?" It was, surprisingly, Stephen who objected so furiously. "An eye for an eye—we want Dane's head."

"The best you can hope for is what I'm offering," Ormond said. "Queen Elizabeth has also authorized me to bring Dane to England. You can both go before her and argue your rights."

Dane barked a laugh. "The Courtenays are Elizabeth's lapdogs. I have little chance of being heard."

"If I cut your throat on this battlefield, you have no chance at all."

Dane's colour had gone down and he was clearly weighing options. Finally, he conceded Ormond was right. "Fine," he ground out. "I'll call off my men."

"Call them off, and prepare to march them out so the Kavanaugh men can march in. Your soldiers will come to Kilkenny, where my men will watch them while we are in England." Slowly, Ormond lowered his dagger.

"You're going to England as well?" Dane was surprised into asking.

"To keep the two of you from killing each other along the way? Of course I'm coming. If only to watch the spectacle you make at the queen's court."

Stephen had said nothing since his protest about the girl. Kit stepped in front of his brother as the parley broke up. "I'm sorry," he said. "There was no other way. If I hadn't agreed to come, Elizabeth would have let Dane kill you in the field."

"I'm not that easily defeated."

"She will listen to you, Stephen. Make Dane pay for his crimes."

Stephen didn't look at him but into the horizon as though seeing something—or someone—else. "She had better."

TWENTY-THREE

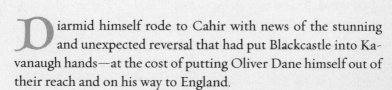

Diarmid himself rode to Cahir with news of the stunning and unexpected reversal that had put Blackcastle into Kavanaugh hands—at the cost of putting Oliver Dane himself out of their reach and on his way to England.

"It seemed best," Diarmid said defensively, and Ailis realized he was afraid of her anger. "The mercenaries were ordered to fight solely under Courtenay's command, and we gained more than we'd hoped with only a handful of losses."

"But not Dane's head."

"No."

Ailis didn't know how she felt. It was rather an absence of feeling—which after the weeks of sharp grief followed by manic preparation was almost pleasure in itself. "It is good for the clan," she found herself saying, and meaning it. "Blackcastle and Templemore have been a thorn in the Earl of Desmond's side for too long. Many will be pleased at what we have achieved."

"Are you pleased?" Diarmid asked bluntly. *Are you pleased with me?*

he meant. *Did I do the right thing? Will you ever look beyond my services to what else I can offer you?*

"My daughter is dead. I do not expect to be anything more than mildly satisfied again in my lifetime. But I am not ungrateful."

His face darkened, and she could see the struggle in his eyes. Then, abruptly, he pulled a letter from inside his battle-stained jerkin and tossed it on the table before her. "He asked me to give you this." Then he turned on his heel and left. No further explanation was forthcoming—or necessary.

Ailis,

I refrain from addressing you with an endearment not because I do not feel it, but because I doubt it would be welcome. If I am wrong, then imagine how fervently I am whispering "dearest, darling, sweetheart" to you as I write this.

By the time you read this, I shall be well on my way to leaving Ireland. Not of my own choice, but I suspect for the best nonetheless. I am sorry not to see you once more, and most sorry of all not to be bringing you Oliver Dane's head as my farewell gift.

For it was always going to be farewell for us, wasn't it? From the moment I uttered my first lie to you, our fate was sealed. And yet, if I had not lied, I should never have known you—and that, for me, would be worse. I dare not presume to expect the same regrets from you. I am English and an interloper and could never have been more than tolerated in an Irish household. Save that Liadan liked me. And you? I don't know if I hope that you are happy to see the last of me, or are touched by regret. My pride says the latter, but my better nature the former. My father told me once that to leave pain behind was the worst sort of repayment I could make to a woman. I have paid you in more than pain, and I will feel it to the end of my days.

Dane and I are both commanded to the queen's presence in London. For once in my life, I am desperately glad to bear my family's name. I will make every use I can wring out of it to see Dane executed for his crimes.

I have loved you, Ailis. Among all my regrets, that will never be one of them. May your life to come have more of joy than pain in it.

Stephen Courtenay

Ailis had hardly finished that achingly poignant letter when Maisie entered. "He is gone, then?" she asked. No need to specify who.

"He is."

"And the English queen has traded a castle for Liadan's life."

"It is a better trade than any other dead Irish child has been offered."

"I know. I'm sorry, it's just . . ." Maisie, usually so self-possessed, circled the council chamber restlessly. "What are you going to do now?" she asked Ailis.

"Ride in triumph to take possession of Blackcastle. And then, I suppose, offer our services to the Earl of Desmond. With Dane out of Ireland, my vendetta is done. I must move forward, so that Oliver Dane is followed in his retreat by the rest of his countrymen."

Ailis looked at Maisie and realized she was no longer wearing full mourning. Her gown was dark gray, but beneath the overskirt her kirtle showed pale blue. With dawning comprehension, Ailis said, "You mean to leave Ireland as well."

Maisie stopped pacing. "I stayed for Liadan. You must know that."

"I do. I suppose you will take your mercenary company with you?"

"A matter of business," Maisie said slowly. "I feel my investment will be more profitable elsewhere."

Ailis hadn't expected different. Uneasy as Scots relations were with England, it would be folly for Maisie to sacrifice a trained company to Irish fighting. But she found that it was not the practical loss that concerned her. It was losing Maisie herself.

"You will return to Scotland?" Ailis asked.

"Not just yet. I mean to evade my brother's plans to marry me off again as long as possible. I still have friends in France. And some business arrangements that would be greatly forwarded by my presence."

Ailis shook her head, a smile of respect wrung from her without meaning to. "For all my life, I shall remember not to underestimate anyone who crosses my path. Who would have guessed the formidable mind behind the child face?"

"Not such a child," Maisie said. "Not any longer."

There passed between them, almost as though Ailis could see it through Maisie's eyes, the image of Liadan falling beneath Dane's dagger. Ailis swallowed and turned away. In truth, her admiration and even liking for Maisie had been slightly tainted by the fact that the girl had been with Liadan at the end. Worse, that in the months before, it was Maisie whom Liadan had turned to over and over again.

"Safe travels," Ailis said with finality. "I expect I will hear of you from time to time."

"It is never too late to be happy," Maisie replied. "Think about it, Ailis."

There was nothing to think about. Ailis had never expected happiness—just successful vengeance. She hadn't expected it to feel so hollow.

23 September 1582

Anabel,

This may not reach you before we do, but I wanted you to know from my own hand that all is well. That is, I took only minor injuries and so did Stephen—and those we mostly inflicted on each other. He is in something of a temper; it's quite refreshing, actually, to find myself the reasonable one.

Love to my sisters, if they are still with you. Your raven is winging his way back as soon as can be.

Kit

Kit's letter found Anabel still convalescing at Syon House, though her health had improved enough for her to appear publicly twice a week. She had made charming farewells to both the Duc d'Anjou and Esmé Stewart, and was grateful for the discretion that prevailed among them all. No one had mentioned any topic so delicate as marriage, and so she was able to enjoy their last hours and thank them for the time they had spent in England.

No doubt the men had watched her narrowly for any lingering signs of illness, but she had always been able to perform well under pressure. And her mother's wig makers had provided her with a number of options that looked, if not quite as lovely as her own hair, at least adequate to the task. By spring her hair should be regrown enough to leave off wigs entirely.

Anabel was rereading Kit's letter for a third time when Madalena appeared in her privy chamber to announce that Brandon Dudley had requested an audience.

"Were we expecting the Earl of Leicester?" Anabel asked. She knew they hadn't.

"He says he hesitates to intrude, but has a personal favour to ask. He looks . . ." Madalena paused, then said, "He looks a tiny bit desperate."

Brandon Dudley, desperate? That was a sight worth seeing. Anabel laid aside the letter and said, "Bring him through."

She remained in her lovely privy chamber with its abundance of light, even in autumn, and the pale colours that so soothed her restless mind. Though not dressed for public audience, Anabel wore a presentable enough gown in the Spanish style she often chose when less formal. The stiff satin of peacock blue and gold helped disguise the loss of weight she had not yet fully regained.

Every time she saw Brandon Dudley, she was struck by his distinctively dark good looks. If he truly resembled his late uncle, then no wonder her mother still thought fondly on Robert Dudley. There had been a time Anabel had thought her mother might force a match between the two of them, but since making Brandon the Earl of Leicester, Elizabeth had dropped the idea.

Anabel knew she should think of him as Lord Leicester, but she had known him too well when they were young. "Brandon!" she said as he made his courtly bow. "It's a pleasure to see you. What have you been doing all these months since last you were at court?"

"Seeing to my estates, Your Highness. The queen has been very generous, and I would not take lightly my responsibilities. Though of course, that has kept me away from the two most beautiful women in England."

She had always thought Brandon Dudley too charming by half, but today his compliments had a slightly forced air and she could see the same signs Madalena had reported. The tension of his hands, the wariness of his eyes . . . He did look a little desperate.

Taking pity on him, she decided to skip the pleasantries. "Is there something I can do for you?"

Brought to the point, he did not hesitate. "Yes, Your Highness. I would like you to bring Nora Percy into your private household."

Of any request he might have made of her, this was the most unexpected. Anabel tipped her head curiously. "Why? Not that Nora is not always welcome, but she has no need of my household. She is a king's daughter, recognized as such, and although she may not be wealthy, she has enough to set up her own household as she likes."

"But it is not as *she* likes, Your Highness—it is as her mother likes."

Anabel leaned back in her seat. "Ah, the formidable Eleanor Percy. But Nora is—what? Twenty-eight years old? Surely she can hold her own against her mother."

"That proves how little you know Eleanor," Brandon said grimly.

"Why you?" Anabel queried. "If Nora wants aid in achieving her independence, why does she not ask me herself? We are cousins, after all."

"Because Nora is the most gentle and unassuming of women,

Your Highness. She does not believe herself worthy of any position, and thus will not exploit it. Her friends must do it for her."

"Her friends?" Anabel asked shrewdly. "Is that what you are?"

That dark skin of his could still show colour. "I am honoured to be her friend."

So Brandon Dudley was in love with Nora Percy. And apparently her mother did not approve. Sharply, Anabel asked, "This isn't merely your attempt to spirit Nora away into an impulsive marriage, is it? I would not like to be so used."

"Considering my birth, I am hardly likely to make that mistake, am I?"

For Brandon was the child of a reckless, secret marriage—between Guildford Dudley and Margaret Clifford. Not particularly troublesome, except that Margaret was of Tudor birth and her royal connections meant she could not be married without permission. Brandon's father had paid for the marriage with his life. His mother had been married off again to a much older man, and then died unhappily some years later.

Anabel spoke gently. "But you do love her?" When Brandon looked prepared to protest, she added, "I warn you, I will only help if I am convinced I am being told the truth."

He stared at the floor for a long minute, and when he raised his head he hardly needed to speak. For all his good looks and surface arrogance, there was something genuine at heart about Brandon Dudley. "I love her, Your Highness. Of course I hope that one day we can marry. But if not, I will still do all I can to ensure her happiness. And she is more likely to have that in your household than with her mother."

How could she possibly resist that plea? With her own heart so precariously happy for the moment, of course she wished to ensure that for others. "I shall be glad to have Nora with me. She is a skilled musician, I know. I will gladly make use of her talents if she is willing to share them."

Relief brightened Brandon's eyes. "Thank you, Your Highness. You will not regret it."

I might, though, she realized. I'm not sure my mother will approve of me interfering with her royal niece.

Elizabeth drew a deep breath—not quite of satisfaction—when informed that Stephen Courtenay and Oliver Dane had safely landed on English shores.

"They came without protest?"

"Without requiring undue violence, at least. So Ormond reports." Burghley and Walsingham were both with her—Walsingham making his report first. The court had temporarily moved to Richmond, but were planning a quick return to London. For now, Elizabeth enjoyed the crisp autumn air as she walked with her two favourites in her privy garden full of the roses Minuette had always been so fond of. There were still a few blooms among the hardier varieties.

"My dear Black Tom," Elizabeth said fondly. "At least, out of all this mess, it will give me pleasure to see him again." She looked at Burghley. "Dominic and Minuette have arrived?"

"In London, yes. They have leased a house in the Strand."

"They refuse our gracious hospitality?"

Burghley knew how discontented she was and phrased his reply with care. "I think they do not wish to be a burden at a politically sensitive time."

"You mean they are angry with me and decline to be reconciled as long as their precious son is at odds with my throne." Even as she snapped, Elizabeth knew she was being unfair. It was such an uncomfortable feeling that it demanded to be swamped by her temper.

"Your Majesty," Burghley said, using a tried and true technique of switching to another topic. "We should prepare to make an official announcement about Princess Anne's marital future."

"The council are prepared to endorse the Scottish marriage?"

"They are prepared to endorse a formal betrothal. The time is ripe to announce England's intentions for the future . . . with the awareness that the future is fluid. Still, a betrothal at this stage will with near certainty lead to marriage. I do not think King James will be dissuaded once your daughter's hand is promised."

"Anne knows what she must do," Elizabeth said firmly. "But you have not spoken of the French marriage."

Burghley's breath hitched and he shot a quick glance at Walsingham. Elizabeth ignored them both and sailed on. "When we bring the matter of Anne's marriage before the public, we will also bring forward that of myself and the Duc d'Anjou."

There was a ringing silence, and Elizabeth narrowed her eyes at her two most trusted councilors. When neither showed signs of breaking the silence, she said with an elaborate show of patience, "You have comments?"

She was fixed on Walsingham, for she knew where her true opposition lay. He looked uncomfortable, but his strict Protestant conscience would not let that stop him from speaking. Better, she thought, to let him air his discontent in private and get it out of his system.

"Perhaps we should not have this discussion in the open air," Walsingham said.

Which only reinforced that he intended to be unpleasant. Elizabeth narrowed her eyes, but led the way to the door that opened on her privy chamber. There were three women within—Elizabeth dismissed them and took a seat.

Only then did she speak again. "Well?" she asked with elaborate patience.

It seemed Walsingham was more than discontented; he was furiously, adamantly, opposed. "You cannot do this, Your Majesty," he said flatly.

"Cannot do what? Direct my own privy council? Obtain their approval as their monarch?"

"You cannot marry France. The council will never allow it."

"Am I queen or am I not?"

"You are a queen subject to the advisement and guidance of your council! Unless you mean to turn tyrant like your father or brother—"

"How dare you!" Elizabeth rose in a swirl of skirts, temper pounding behind her eyes. "I will not bear insolence from any man, whomever he may be. Mind your tongue or I'll mind it for you!"

Burghley made an attempt to moderate. "He means only that the council is concerned about the tenor of the public. There is uneasiness about Your Majesty's autonomy. Being so recently separated from Spain, why rush to replace it with a French loyalty?"

"French loyalty? Is that what my people think—that when I was Philip's wife, I was also Philip's slave? Have I not proved myself firm in my loyalties to my people above all else, including my own happiness?"

"Your Majesty—"

"Enough, Burghley! I will not be spoken to like a child who must needs be coddled for temperament's sake! How much have I sacrificed for England's good? How much must I still sacrifice? Am I to be denied the most common of comforts, to have a companion who pleases me?"

"Yes!" Walsingham shouted. "You were not born a common woman, Elizabeth, and if you wanted anything approaching common comforts, you should have taken care to ensure your brother survived his last battle!"

The words rang through the chamber and into Elizabeth's head like weapons. Burghley hissed, but otherwise it was just the two of them staring at each other: the queen and her intelligencer.

From the first time she'd met him nearly thirty years ago now, Elizabeth had been struck by Walsingham's refusal to be intimidated by her. Over the years, he had often teetered on the edge of honesty, without ever falling over into insubordination. For all that time, he had been one half of her most trusted duo: Burghley with his careful statesmanship, Walsingham with his intelligence and strong convictions.

But this she could not forgive. He had used her personal name and had struck at her most vulnerable spot with unerring skill. Elizabeth's voice trembled with the effort not to screech at him in her rage. "You are dismissed."

"Your Majesty, I am only telling you what others are too afraid—"

"You are dismissed from my presence and from my court."

Walsingham had never been one to show his emotions. The corners of his dark eyes tightened, but he was otherwise impassive. "I apologize for my manner, Your Majesty."

"Noted. Now get out."

She turned her back, holding herself rigid while she waited. At last she heard the soft footsteps walking away. She knew that Burghley remained, weighing how to speak to her, judging the right approach.

Elizabeth was tired of being handled. All she wanted was to give in to her passions—to throw something, to let Anjou tease her into flirtation, or simply to lay down her head and weep.

It took their disparate, discontented company weeks to make the trek across Ireland, the sea, and then England. By the time Stephen and the others rode into London, it was the end of September and the city was an assault on all the senses for men attuned to the quieter countryside of Ireland.

Ormond took Dane with him, having pledged his word to the queen for the recalcitrant captain's appearance at her bidding. Stephen followed Kit and Julien—not to court, but to a four-story brick house with high walls and open courtyard. There, he was met by the whole of his family and subjected to the sort of tactful, gentle conversation that ensured he did what they wanted—talk about Ireland.

He'd had time to rehearse the essentials and he delivered them in unsparing and unemotional terms. When he finished, it was Lucie who spoke first, with the devastating frankness she had developed during the years of estrangement from their father. "I'd like to think the queen will be moved by the girl's death, but she tends to be pa-

rochial in her empathies. Liadan Kavanaugh was not English. I fear
that will limit Elizabeth's human regrets."

"Then Elizabeth does not deserve her crown," Stephen said
curtly. "I can make her understand. I must."

He saw his parents exchange looks and imagined a shared exasperation with their son's self-righteousness. Stephen didn't care. He
was righteous because he was right. Elizabeth might be hampered by
political and religious tensions, but how could any woman, especially a mother, not be moved by the cruel murder of another woman's daughter?

The London household was rather cramped, but no one seemed
prepared to leave until Stephen had his audience. The days dragged
into weeks, and Stephen, forced to remain under a loose house arrest by royal command, began to go a little mad. Kit was preoccupied
and serious, spending more hours in study and correspondence than
he'd ever been known to do before. Pippa went daily between their
leased house and Charterhouse, where Anabel set up residence a
week after Stephen's return.

Twenty-two days after reaching London, the summons finally arrived. Stephen appeared, as commanded, at the public gatehouse at
Whitehall and presented himself with only Kit in attendance. Another caveat of the queen's. He knew it must be killing his parents to
remain behind.

They were escorted to a corridor Stephen knew well, where the
familiar figures of Ormond and Dane waited. Ormond looked exasperated, Dane insolent.

"Ready to grovel?" Dane asked Stephen.

It was an effort of will to ignore him. Fortunately, the queen did
not keep them waiting long. A page opened the door and they were
ushered into her presence chamber. In the gilded, golden space,
Elizabeth dominated on a throne set beneath her canopy of estate.
She wore a delicate crown set with pearls and a gown so crusted with
gold thread it almost had the look of decorative armor.

Usually, her presence chamber would contain anywhere from

twenty to fifty people, but today there were only two guards at the
door and Lord Burghley standing to her side. It seemed the rumours
of Walsingham's disgrace were true—Stephen wasn't sure whether
the intelligencer's absence would help or hurt his cause.

Elizabeth did not waste time in pleasantries. "Tell me why I
should refrain from locking both of you up for disturbing my peace
in Ireland." She spoke to the space between Stephen and Dane, who
stood only an arm's length apart before her. Ormond and Kit stood
gratefully behind them.

"Your Majesty," Stephen said with all the grace he'd learned at his
mother's knee, "I most willingly submit to whatever punishment
you deem fit. I know I have proved a disappointment to my family
and to your government. But please trust that it was not done from
malice, only from righteous anger."

Used to flattering speeches from men much better at making
them, Elizabeth raised a single eyebrow. "It is not intentions that
concern me, Lord Somerset, but actions. You appeared on the field
in opposition to my own royal forces. Never mind locking you up—
why should I not have you executed for that treason?"

With a voice all honeyed satisfaction, Oliver Dane interrupted.
"Well might you ask such, Your Majesty, for great damage has been
done to your cause in Ireland by the flagrant flouting of your authority by one so near to your throne. So public a betrayal should be
punished just as publicly."

From the look she turned on Dane, it was clear that Elizabeth
found him distasteful. "And for your own crime, of killing an Irish
child?"

His tone darkened, but he answered readily enough. "It was a re-
grettable incident. But the family has been compensated."

"By Blackcastle, yes. So you consider the matter closed?"

"I do. Save for the matter of Lord Somerset's involvement."

"That matter is not your concern. It is ours." Elizabeth pondered
Dane for a moment. "I understand from my dear cousin Ormond
that you are eager to return to Ireland."

Stephen moved involuntarily, and felt Kit staring at him from behind, no doubt silently commanding him to hold his position and his tongue. With difficulty, he complied.

"Ireland has been my home for twenty-five years, Your Majesty," Dane offered. "I have no remaining ties to England, save that of a subject. A role I believe I fill most profitably in Ireland."

The queen wasn't really going to listen to this, was she? Stephen shot a look at Burghley, who looked uncomfortable but resigned. The Lord Treasurer was a reasonable man—surely he would not allow Dane to return to the land and people he had ravaged and used for his own purposes all these years? How often had Stephen heard Dane in the field complaining about Elizabeth, using terms that she would have racked him for if she'd ever heard him? Dane didn't care about Elizabeth's rights—he wanted to be in Ireland for his own profit.

Elizabeth waved a single hand in Dane's direction. "You may return to Ireland to serve us, Captain Dane. For the immediate future, you will be under the close command of the Earl of Ormond. I do not care to hear of further ... irregularities in your relationships with the Irish. Prove yourself faithful, and perhaps you will regain an independent command."

Stephen felt all the blood leave his face and nearly swayed on his feet as, next to him, Dane bowed low. "Thank you, Your Majesty. You are truly wise and gracious. I will endeavour to serve you well."

"See that you do." Elizabeth turned those remote, penetrating eyes on Stephen. "As for you, Lord Somerset, you will return to Farleigh Hungerford and remain on your estates until recalled. We are displeased with your actions, but trust that you will serve us better in future."

He couldn't speak, couldn't move, could hardly even breathe. Stephen felt Kit touch him gently on the back of his shoulder as though prodding him, and he managed to swallow. There was nothing else he could do. Stephen jerked his head in perfunctory acknowledgment. "As you say, Your Majesty."

Elizabeth narrowed her eyes at his obvious reluctance, but dismissed them all with an impatient gesture.

This is not happening. Stephen felt as though he were sleepwalking. He had come prepared to be arrested, to be publicly chastised, to be stripped of all his honours and wealth . . . but he had not prepared for this. After everything, Oliver Dane had won.

Kit knew better than to try and engage his brother, but the Earl of Ormond tried, speaking low and urgently at Stephen's side. "She had no choice, boy, you must see that. With the latest victories by Desmond, our forces in Ireland are dangerously vulnerable. There are still a hundred Spanish soldiers on the ground and the threat of worse. Dane is despicable, but he is a key piece in keeping Ireland quiet."

"By sweeping away every last Irish man, woman, and child by whatever means possible? How is that English justice?"

"Justice?" The voice was Dane's, smooth and amused. He came up on Stephen's other side so that Stephen was flanked by these two men of Elizabeth's Irish service. Ormond, born and bred generations back in Ireland, but still fundamentally English. And Dane, a cynic out for his own good no matter who he had to destroy to achieve it.

"Don't fret, English lordling," Dane continued. "I doubt our paths will cross again. You have proved you cannot be trusted in Ireland—the queen will not risk you there a third time. And I have no plans to return to England. Give thanks to see the last of me and put Ireland out of your mind."

Stephen clenched his jaw. Ireland was the only thing on his mind, mostly the faces of those he'd come to know flickering behind his eyes in rapid succession: Father Byrne, upright and warm beneath the weight of his duties; Diarmid mac Briain, who led his men honourably and well; Liadan, all kinds of clever and loving, and in the end broken; Ailis, who had lost her childhood and then her daughter to this man now openly mocking the sins he'd committed.

"Perhaps," Dane mused, "I'll see if that Scots widow is still available. The queen wouldn't mind having her money available for England's use. And though she is a little older than my usual preference, she looks young enough. I'd get a few good years of pleasure out of her. And I've heard the Scots are nearly as wild as the Irish. Maisie, wasn't that her name?"

Mariota, we have to go. Blood on her hands and dress, keening over a small body, weeping alone for a child who had been nothing but a friend . . .

When Stephen moved, it was with the purpose and clarity of long-planned battle tactics. He saw every move a half second before he made it, his body in perfect alignment with his intentions. Ormond was to his left, his jewel-hilted ceremonial dagger affixed to his close-fitted velvet jerkin. One move for Stephen to swivel and snatch it with his right hand. The next move to plant his other foot and pivot back, then grab Dane's coat with his left hand. For symmetry's sake, Stephen would have preferred to cut his throat, but there wasn't time. Instead, in the manner Julien had taught him, the dagger slid expertly up and under Dane's ribs, to angle into the heart.

There was a wash of blood over Stephen's fingers and a froth of bloody spume from Dane's mouth as he fell. Even as the guards lunged forward, Stephen raised his hands in surrender, the dagger still in Dane's chest.

The guards had one job—to ensure the Queen of England's safety. They didn't care who Stephen was. They forced him down with a kick to his knees and then they were on him, striking and kicking even though he made no move to fight back.

He could hear Kit shouting at the guards to stop, trying to get to Stephen through them all. One of the guards struck Kit in the side of the head. "Leave it!" Stephen called. "It's no matter, Kit. It's fine. I'm fine."

And he was. For the first time since Liadan's murder—no, from before that, from the moment Roisin and the other prisoners had fallen near Kilkenny—Stephen felt as though he could breathe.

The guards—brought to rough order by Ormond's commanding presence, with more men pouring toward them and even Lord Burghley in the distance, hastening to see the commotion—jerked Stephen to his feet. As they twisted his arms behind in order to march him away, he sent a thought winging west to Ireland.

He's dead, Liadan. You can rest now, sweet lass.

TWENTY-FOUR

It was a full two weeks after Stephen's shocking arrest for murder before Anabel saw any member of the Courtenay family. The princess hadn't even seen her mother—the queen coped with emotional difficulty by flinging herself into intense political efforts, those things she could control. The firsthand account of what had happened came to Anabel from the Earl of Ormond, who courteously came to see her at Charterhouse when she sent him a message.

She listened to Ormond's story and asked only one question. "Did the man deserve it?"

He was too experienced to fall for such simplicity. "The question of punishment was the queen's to decide, not anyone else."

But Stephen Courtenay wasn't just anyone else. Anabel sat isolated at Charterhouse, waiting, and wondered how much her mother's harshness had to do with her earlier fury with and banishment of Walsingham.

Pippa finally came the second week in November. Anabel took her straight through to her bedchamber and commanded her other women not to disturb them. Then she sat her friend down and demanded, "Tell me."

"There isn't much to tell. My parents have been allowed to see Stephen in the Tower. He has not been charged with any crime, and there is no indication that he will be in the immediate future. Lord Burghley thinks it likely the queen will simply leave him there for some time to let him think about what he has done. No one seems to believe there is any chance he will be tried and executed."

"What do you believe?"

"I keep looking at my parents and seeing the shadows that have always been on the edges of their lives. There was a time, I expect, when no one thought there was any chance of the two of them falling from grace with the last king. Monarchs are capricious creatures."

She said it with a detached air that made Anabel grasp her hand. "Pippa, my mother is not the same as her brother or her father. She is furious, yes, at the insult to her pride and the assault made so near to her presence. But all she is doing is making a point. She would never harm Stephen."

Pippa closed her eyes, looking weary. "There is more than just Stephen. Two days after his arrest, Lucie miscarried a child. Nearly four months along . . . it was a girl."

"I'm so sorry," Anabel whispered. "How is she recovering?"

"She is in no danger. Just desperately grieving. As soon as she can travel, Julien will take her home. They have hardly been there since they were married. She doesn't want to leave Stephen, but there is nothing she can do here that others cannot do as well."

"And the rest of you?"

"My parents will remain in London as long as Stephen is in the Tower. Kit will have to oversee things at Tiverton and Wynfield Mote and Farleigh Hungerford—he will spend the winter on horseback bearing a responsibility he once craved. But not at this cost."

Anabel put Kit out of her mind. There would be time later for that. "And you?"

Pippa smiled, swift and sad. "Do you not want me with you?"

"Of course I do! I did not know if you would care to be associated with me."

"Oh, Anabel. You are not your mother. Where do you mean to spend the winter?"

"Not London. They do not think it would be good for my health. Ludlow, perhaps?" She saw the queer expression on Pippa's face and asked sharply, "What? Do you have a better idea?"

"Have you ever thought," Pippa said slowly, "of going north? It has been generations since an English royal has spent significant time in the North for other than military purposes. Richard, Duke of Gloucester, was the last royal to make his home in Yorkshire, and it was those ties that allowed him to take England's throne, even if only for a short time."

"You want me to become a Yorkist?"

"I want you to be an effective leader. Your mother's example is brilliant, but she cannot be everywhere. Why not extend yourself in a less crowded arena?"

"Why do you want me in the North, Pippa?"

Her friend had that familiar, disconcerting, otherworldly look that had always half frightened and half intrigued Anabel. Pippa sounded like a prophetess when she said, "Because the North is going to need you—and you will need them. War is coming, and when it does, England will need to meet it in united fashion, Protestants and recusants together. The North will love you, Anabel. You will have the power to command them. And also . . ."

Anabel finished that final thought. "And also, it is near to Scotland and James."

Pippa nodded.

"You hinted once," Anabel said, looking down at her clasped hands, "that I might have a husband of my choosing."

"Choices are made for many considerations, Your Highness."

Anabel closed her eyes and sighed, allowing herself one regretful memory of Kit's caresses. Then she opened her eyes. Firmly, she said, "I will speak to Lord Burghley. He will know how best to broach the subject with the queen."

15 November 1582

Dear Kit,

I begin to regret not leaving London with you. It seems wrong to flee to Anabel every day, but in truth I'm not at all certain Mother and Father notice me when I am here. Father is as silent as the grave and Mother spends her days in a whirl of letter writing and making personal calls on anyone in London whom she might charm. There has been some debate as to whether that latter should include Francis Walsingham. It has been more than a month since Elizabeth sent him away in a temper—the longer she does not call for him, the more entrenched I fear she will become. If there is one thing our queen cannot bear, it is being forced to admit she is wrong.

I can feel your continuing turmoil as easily while you are on the road as when you are in the next chamber. I shall do what I can with Anabel, but your guilt about stepping into Stephen's shoes you will have to deal with on your own.

Pippa

23 November 1582

Pippa,

I leave Tiverton tomorrow for Farleigh Hungerford. I am sure it will be as unnecessary a visit as this one, for both Stephen and Father have capable agents running things. I am merely the figurehead. And yes, I am uncomfortable. Be careful what you wish for—I am learning the truth of that in spades. I will be delighted to hand these responsibilities back as soon as Stephen is freed.

Anabel writes that you have encouraged her to go north. What do you know that I do not? (And don't say "many things"—you know what I mean.) If you can feel my turmoil, then I can feel yours. When we were three years old, I would wake whenever you had a nightmare. When we were seven and you fell down the tower steps at Tiverton, I had bruises to match yours all down my left side. And when we were fifteen, I knew the first—and the last—time you kissed Matthew Harrington. (Which is a subject for another day, twin mine. I will not forget.)

The point is, I know that you have not been sleeping well. I know that your heart is twisted every hour you're awake and that the muscles in your face hurt from presenting a serene expression before the world. And it is not because of Stephen or Mother and Father or Anabel or me or even Lucie's miscarriage . . . you are working very hard to keep something from me. There is no need. I may not have your insights, but I have fully as much love as you and a burning desire to do something!

Your not wholly useless brother,

Kit

1 December 1582

Kit,

If you know me so well, you know I have never thought you useless. Everyone seems to think that you need me to be your anchor—but the truth is, I need you even more. For courage, for confidence, for love.

There is still no word on Stephen's future. Bless her, Carrie has arrived from Wynfield. For the first time since Harrington's death, she is something like her old self. Carrie is always at her best when needed.

The queen's privy council met yesterday. No doubt you will soon have word, wherever you are, that the official papers of betrothal between King

James and Anabel are to be signed the day before Christmas. As soon as the holiday season is over, I will travel with Anabel and her household to Middleham Castle. The marriage date is still somewhat fluid. Not in the next year, at least.

And the queen, despite vociferous opposition from her councilors, has invited the Duc d'Anjou to return to England next spring and formalize a betrothal between them. The atmosphere in London is strained.

Still no charges laid against Stephen, or indication that there soon will be. Mother has reached the end of her patience. I believe she means to confront the queen as soon as Elizabeth will consent to see her.

I wish you were here to make us all laugh.

Pippa

Stephen's confinement in the Tower of London was not especially onerous. He was housed in Constable Tower, two chambers plainly but adequately furnished and warmed thanks to his parents' money. He was allowed paper and ink and he exchanged detailed letters with his steward at Farleigh Hungerford. His parents were allowed to visit several times in the first few weeks, but then the visits stopped.

But if his family no longer came, neither did anyone else. Not even Walsingham. Stephen supposed the Lord Secretary's disgrace must be running very deep if he dared not take up the cause of one of his intelligencers. Not that Walsingham would have any reason to aid him. The Lord Secretary was probably even more disgusted than the queen by his betrayal.

On second thought, probably not. Walsingham was a cold-blooded creature ruled, above all, by his refusal to trust. He must always be half expecting to be betrayed. Which is how he'd kept the queen safe all these years.

Stephen had no attendants, which meant he had no one to talk to save the guards who delivered food and occasionally passed a few words with him. Through November and December, he grew increasingly impatient for news. Even letters from his family were being strictly rationed—no more than one every two weeks and then only from his parents. Strangely enough, it was Kit whom he most wished for. During this last long journey back from Ireland, Kit had shown himself to have grown up in a manner that surprised Stephen. He'd always considered his little brother the lucky one, to have no responsibilities and thus the freedom to say what he liked and make his choices without weighing how they affected others. But Kit had been nothing if not ferociously responsible in staying by his side during the trip with Dane.

From the guards, Stephen was reminded when it was Christmas. He wondered if his family had returned home for the season. The Courtenays had always jealously guarded their privacy, and he had many memories of Christmas at Tiverton, of gathering holly and ivy, the men searching out the Yule log on Christmas Eve, the scents of baking for days in advance, the children making up plays to perform . . . Stephen missed all of it.

The slit windows in his outer chamber showed twilight's early descent that Christmas day when his prison door was opened unexpectedly. Stephen looked up from the table—where he was not writing so much as fiddling with a pen and daydreaming of mincemeat and sugared almonds—and saw the lieutenant of the Tower himself. Stephen got to his feet, heart pounding. Was this Elizabeth's Christmas gift—to finally charge him with murder or treason? The thought of being released he dared not entertain.

There was another figure behind the lieutenant, so small and slight that a head could not be seen, only the edge of heavy skirts and a fur-trimmed cloak.

"Visitor," the lieutenant said unnecessarily. The man looked slightly stunned, as though not certain how this had come about. Then the visitor stepped around him and Stephen felt a comparable shock himself.

Maisie. All five feet of her, the heart-shaped face and sea-coloured eyes unchanged, wearing velvet and silk, her abundance of light hair contained in a jeweled net, looking as at home and unflappable as she had wearing wool in an Irish household.

"Mariota," Stephen said stupidly. "What the devil are you doing here?"

"The question," she retorted tartly, "is what are *you* doing here?"

He refrained from answering until the lieutenant had withdrawn. Then he asked, "You know that Dane is dead?"

"Oh yes. It's quite the story in London. How the most favoured son in the realm's most favoured family committed violent murder not five hundred paces from the queen's own presence. The betting is running high against you in the city that you'll be beheaded by spring."

"Plan to make some money, do you?"

"Make money? Yes, of course. But not by betting against you. I know you rather too well to take that risk."

Belatedly, he pulled out a seat for her. He could not stop staring. He had never thought to see anyone from Cahir ever again. "How is . . . the household?"

How had he ever thought her bland and unremarkable? One simply had to know the tricks of her expression. There was a tilt to her chin and a pitying gleam in her eyes that told him she was not at all fooled by the vagueness of his question.

Not fooled, but prepared to humour him. "They know of Dane's death. I was still with them when the news came. I left Cahir a week later. The day after the wedding."

That wasn't humouring him—that was eviscerating him. Stephen asked, even though he didn't need to. "Wedding?"

"Ailis married Diarmid. As she always knew she must."

"Is she—"

"Happy? I do not think happiness has ever been one of Ailis's aims. She is contented with the gains they have made. She will never cease to mourn Liadan. Her marriage to Diarmid will ensure she remains in control of a significant power in the region. That has always been her aim."

Stephen sat motionless, fighting the urge to jump up and pace. He didn't want to show how strongly he'd been affected by the news.

As always, Maisie knew how to choose her moments. She rose. "The lieutenant allowed me only five minutes. There is one more piece of news I thought you might like."

"That is?"

"Word reached London two days ago—a Spanish fleet of fifty ships has landed all along the south and west coasts of Ireland. There are more than five thousand soldiers on board, provisioned for a long stay. This is no quick feint to see what happens, no raiding party to simply aid the Irish. It is a statement: Spain wants Ireland and will spare little to achieve it. You may be sitting in this prison for some time, for I doubt your queen has much thought to spare for one prisoner just now. This is the first shot in the war to come."

She didn't wait for a response. From inside her cloak, she produced a letter, flimsy and well-traveled. "For you."

Only when Maisie had gone did Stephen realize he hadn't even said goodbye, or offered thanks. He didn't know what her plans were or where she was going next. All he could do was stare at the thin letter, his name in painfully neat letters confronting him.

The sun had fully set before Stephen at last broke the wax and read the few words enclosed.

I told you I would break your heart, Englishman. I did not know that you would break mine in turn. On my part, the death of Oliver Dane is worth that price.

Ailis

On the last day of 1582, Elizabeth waited alone in her privy chamber at Hampton Court for Minuette to appear. By rights she should be at Whitehall, but in the wake of the disastrous news from Ireland, Elizabeth had wanted to retreat to her favourite palace. It had worked in a limited fashion—her headaches subsided to the point where she could work more than an hour at a time without having to retreat to vomit from the pain. But her fury still burned bright, so fierce that Burghley had only once dared to suggest she send for Walsingham. After her violent and, she admitted, profane response, he had not raised the subject again.

She heard the door open, the murmured "Lady Exeter" from the guard, then the closing of the door that meant she and Minuette were alone. As they had been so often for so long. In all her life, there was no one who knew Elizabeth the way her oldest friend did. Even those who had known and worked with her before she was queen—men like Walsingham and Burghley—did not know Elizabeth's secrets in the same way.

She had guessed that Minuette would force her to speak first. From stubbornness as much as anything. Elizabeth obliged, keeping her back to the chamber, staring out at the Clock Court where once she had kept watch for Robert Dudley. "Here to beg my forgiveness?"

A weighted pause before Minuette said evenly, "You are not the first Tudor monarch to ask me that. The begging did me little good then—why would now be different?"

Elizabeth whirled. "I am not my brother!"

"No. Will had the courage to confront me in his vengeance."

"This is not vengeance, this is ruling. Your son betrayed his title and his oath by taking up arms against my own soldiers! Do you expect me to pat him on the head and send him running along home merely because you ask me to?"

"I have not asked that."

"Then what is it you do ask?"

"One question, that's all I have," Minuette said softly. "Elizabeth, how did William die?"

For an awful, piercing moment Elizabeth was back at Hatfield the autumn of 1558, in a delicate, dangerous conversation where what was unspoken weighed far more than what was.

"What does your wide view tell you, Your Highness?"

"That the king will ride to battle . . . and that misfortune awaits kings who fight from a position of despair rather than hope."

"A battlefield is a messy place. It would be best to be prepared for all ends."

She blinked and met Minuette's eyes—not accusing, not threatening. Simply asking. Elizabeth asked in turn, "Why?"

"There is not one of us on this earth who has not made choices others might not understand. Stephen's enemy was Oliver Dane, not you. Now that the man is dead, my son is no threat to your government or your person. You know that, Elizabeth." Only the last words revealed the mother behind the diplomat, and Elizabeth was reminded of her own terrible days when Anabel had been held prisoner.

But she did not govern from sentiment. "He opposed me openly in Ireland, which just now is in great danger of being overrun by the forces of my former husband. You must know there are factions in England perfectly willing to exploit the opposition of one of my own earls against me. As long as he is locked away, he is safe from that."

"So you're protecting my son?"

"From himself, mostly. But I cannot leave his crimes unpunished."

Minuette's expression flickered. Was that fear? "But not at the cost of his life."

It was so nearly a question that it hurt Elizabeth. Did her friend really think her as cruel as Will had been? Or her father?

The hurt of it made her brusque in delivering her decision. "I shall keep him in the Tower through the winter. It will not hurt him to ponder his actions in some measure of discomfort."

"And then?"

"He may have his life, but neither his title nor his wealth. The estate of Somerset is forfeited to the crown."

Relief swept Minuette openly, for the Courtenays did not greatly care for money. Easy for them to disdain it—they did not have to equip a government and protect a kingdom.

But Elizabeth had not quite finished. "I understand Christopher intends to go to France to train with and serve Renaud LeClerc in the spring. Stephen may go with his brother. In point of fact, I will require Stephen to go with him."

"You are banishing him?"

"If I must make it official, I will. I would prefer for him to go voluntarily."

They faced each other, two women who had been children and girls and young women together. They had never—truly—been opposed to each other. Elizabeth would regret it if they became so now. But she would not relent.

Kings don't have friends, her little brother had thrown at them once, furious and despairing. And if kings could not afford friendship, then even less could a queen who must in all things be twice as good as the men who had preceded her if she were to keep hold of her power.

Minuette executed a perfect curtsey, straight-backed as Kat Ashley had taught the two of them so long ago. "Thank you, Your Majesty, for my son's life. I will not forget this."

Elizabeth watched Minuette leave, wondering if that last line had been spoken with gratitude or sarcasm.

INTERLUDE

February 1583

Pippa Courtenay walked through the corridors of Greenwich Palace on her way to visit Dr. John Dee. Unusually, most of those she passed along the way did not try to engage her. Pippa was accustomed to fending off constant attention from those who wanted to exploit her influence with the Princess of Wales. But ever since Stephen's arrest, a bubble seemed to have formed around the Courtenay family. Either people respected their desire for privacy or, more likely, did not want to risk being associated with a family in decline.

Of the Courtenay children, John Dee had always been most associated with Lucette, as a tutor and mentor. But Pippa had spent some time with him over the years, benefitting from his wide experience of the world as well as his intimate knowledge of astrology and mysticism. In his presence, she had always maintained a detached air, as though the subjects were of only scholarly interest to her.

As though that would deceive a man like John Dee.

In the last three years Dr. Dee had asked her the same question five times: "Are you prepared to ask me for a star chart yet, Lady Philippa?"

She had declined each time. Until now. Two weeks ago she had finally recognized that the time had come when she needed to consult with someone whose gifts were similar to her own. Someone who could counsel her dispassionately. Someone accustomed to the remote wisdom of the stars and the stark beauty of fate. She had at last asked for her star chart, and tonight he would present it to her. It seemed fitting that today was also her twenty-first birthday.

Whenever John Dee came to court, he kept his chambers as far removed from the center of things as comfort—and the queen—would allow. At Greenwich this meant an upper floor of one of the narrow towers that appeared plain in the corridors but opened into a warm and inviting space that reminded Pippa of Wynfield Mote. Not in design so much as feel, that here was a place one could be at ease.

That is, if one was not awaiting a pronouncement on one's fate. Pippa fidgeted in the chair Dr. Dee had pulled out for her, her eyes skipping over the homely clutter: from books to astronomical instruments to opened chests spilling over with paper. The one place she did not look was at the portfolio before Dr. Dee.

"Lady Philippa," he said gently, "there is no need to be frightened."

"I'm not frightened," she answered scornfully. It might have been more convincing if her voice had not wobbled.

"Do your parents know that you asked me for a star chart?"

"No. Why?"

"Did you know that I once read their charts? Long ago, when the queen was a princess and the king was in love."

"With my mother." Silence, since there was no need to confirm the obvious. "What did their charts say?"

He smiled at that. "You know better than to ask. A star chart is private, and made only at the request of the named individual. Although once . . . one time only did I make a chart for someone who did not ask it of me. But that has no relevance to you. I did this at your request, Philippa. If you ask, I will burn it unread and unexplored. The choice is always yours."

"The choice to know—but not the choice of what will happen."

"Ah, the arrogance of the young, so certain that their lives must be marked out in indelible paths." He leaned on the desk, fingers laced together. "I will tell you what I once told Queen Elizabeth—I do not make the stars. God alone knows what paths you will walk. I endeavour merely to shed light on a point or two along that path. You need not fear what I can tell you."

Pippa laughed just a little, relieved despite herself. "I suppose if that is true of the queen, it would be arrogance to assume more of myself." She nodded at the portfolio. "Tell me."

He opened the portfolio to reveal a sheet on which was drawn a large circle, divided into twelve sections. Some of the sections were blank while others contained astrological and mathematical symbols. If Dr. Dee had written out his conclusions based on that chart, he did not refer to it now but simply spoke to her.

"Do you need me to tell you that the time and place of your birth ensured you an inquisitive mind and passionate nature? The two are often at odds. Your life is a long experience of duality—pushing and pulling, not against the world, but against your own nature. Saint or sinner, realist or fantasist, mystic or witch . . . the world will never know how to read you as long as you do not embrace both sides of your nature."

"You're telling me to be more like Kit?" she teased, but only half-heartedly. What he said felt . . . true. And uncomfortable.

"Your twin's stars will be subtly different from yours, even born so near together. And I am not telling you what to do or not to do—I am merely explaining you to yourself. As you have long had occasion to explain others to themselves."

She dipped her head in wry acknowledgment, then said, "If I were to ask about places in my future . . . ?" She trailed off.

"As you are planning to go north with Princess Anne, I expect you already know the answer to that. But if you like, I will tell you anyway: You are meant to go north, Philippa. In that place, you will be a beacon of hope."

You will light the beacon, Doña Catalina had said. *But your princess will command the flames.*

For the last few years the North had called to Pippa. Yorkshire, Leeds, the borderlands of England and Scotland—she had long known that her path was leading her north. It was only . . .

Softly, John Dee asked, "What is it you fear in the North?"

Rushlight and fog, insistent hands and curious faces, melodious Spanish voices mixed with the unmistakable lilt of the Scots, the certain knowledge that she was dying . . .

"Not fear," she answered. "Not exactly."

She rose, and Dee followed, slowly. He hesitated, then said, "Is there nothing else you care to ask me? Most everyone is anxious to know—"

"How long their life will last?" She met his eyes and fixed on them. "There is nothing you could tell me that I do not already know for myself."

It hung in the balance whether he would press her. But John Dee was an English gentleman, always prepared to default to reticence. "Pippa," and his use of her nickname made tears prick at her eyes, "thank you for allowing me to sight your stars. It has been a privilege."

"If I said my only unanswered worries were about my family . . . I don't suppose you have any insight?"

"Your family was created from the strongest of loves, tested by fire and death. Love does not preclude pain, but it will heal it. In time."

She surprised them both by kissing him on the cheek. Her heart was lighter than she'd expected as she left. She was not—had never been—afraid of death. She was afraid of leaving things undone, of thinking too much and waiting too long, so wary of making the wrong move that she made no move at all.

She had taken the first step by advising Anabel to go north. Tonight had been the second step.

And third?

Matthew. She must do something about Matthew Harrington. Pippa just didn't know what.

Acknowledgments

As I began pondering this story, I picked up a book called *The Twilight Lords: Elizabeth I and the Plunder of Ireland* by Richard Berleth. Without that book, this one would be different—and significantly less. James FitzMaurice, Humphrey Gilbert, the Earl of Desmond, the occupation and destruction of Kilmallock, the practice of laying waste to the landscape . . . all burst from the pages of history with dramatic stories thrumming beneath the matter-of-fact words.

For the purposes of my story, Oliver Dane and Ailis Kavanaugh and her clan are entirely imaginary. But not, I think, terribly far from reality. Carrigafoyle, with defenses designed by an Italian engineer, Captain Julian, and garrisoned mainly by Spanish and Italian soldiers, fell to a three-siege by the English. In the aftermath, a contemporary observer wrote: "There escaped not one, neither man, woman, nor child."

The Virgin's Spy is meant as entertainment. But if it stirs curiosity into the nonalternate history of Queen Elizabeth's reign, I shall be well rewarded.

Now, as always, a very partial list of the many people to whom I am indebted. If I were in the position to require a royal privy council, the following would be my choices.

As Lord Secretary and Chief Councilor: Tamar Rydzinski. Even Lord Burghley cannot compete with my agent's calm in the face of chaos and her knack for the perfect advice at the perfect time.

As Lord Treasurer and Chief Intelligencer: Kate Miciak and the entire Ballantine team. With all the wisdom I lack (which is an astoundingly large amount), Kate shapes my writing and the team gives life to my imagination. Like Francis Walsingham, they see what I don't and safely guide me there.

As Chief Lady of the Privy Chamber: Katie Jeppson.

For so many reasons I would have to write an entire book to do them justice. So here are just three: for traveling with me, for eating with me, and for always speaking of my characters as though they were real.

As Ladies-in-Waiting: Debbie Ramsay, Concessa Shearer, Kari Whitesell, and the many kind women in Boston who wait so patiently for the rare moments I emerge from isolation.

There were times when I thought this book would never be written. I'm quite sure I say that with every book—but it feels particularly true for this one. Between lingering illness, family crises, and one hundred and ten inches of snow, my titular spy wasn't especially interested in moving quickly. But here it is. And here it most certainly would not be without, forever and always, my family.

And so, last of all, those faithful members of my Personal Household: Chris, Matt, Jake, Emma, and Spencer. No royal has ever been loved or served half so well.

THE
VIRGIN'S SPY

Laura Andersen

A READER'S GUIDE

My dear Robert,

How often I have longed for your presence these many years! And yet, I do hesitate to write so much for fear of seeming but a weak and sentimental woman. Almost I can hear your teasing words, warm in my ear: "Since when do you care what others think?"

The answer, of course, is since I became queen. A ruling queen of a divided country cannot afford even the appearance of weakness. Which is why I do not speak of you, not even to those nearest to me. And hardly do I even allow myself to think of you.

Occasionally, though, I cannot control my thoughts. And I find myself wondering how my years of ruling might have been different with you at my side. Perhaps even literally so, for your Amy died less than two years after I came to my throne. Had you lived, my sweet Robin, what temptations might have assailed me then! To have a husband not only of my choosing, but of my heart? I look now at my Anabel, at her instinctive resistance to a marriage of state, and I both understand and wonder what might have been.

It would have been most difficult, for you were hardly a good prospect even for a princess royal, let alone a ruling queen. A fifth son, a father and a brother executed for treason, already married . . . but I am remarkably stubborn. Almost, I can envision the fight I might have made. For a rarity, I suspect Walsingham and Burghley would have been on the same side in opposing me. Though I do wonder what possible marital choice I might have made that could have pleased Walsingham? Lord Burghley, naturally, supported the Spanish marriage. He

was nearly alone in doing so. Not that Walsingham or my other coun-
cilors had anyone realistic in mind to replace Philip. An Austrian arch-
duke? A Swedish prince? An Italian count? A Scottish noble? Hardly
appropriate, any of them.

It was not so much that Philip was a foreigner that informed their
objections—for they could never agree, either, on an English
candidate—but that Philip was King of Spain. They feared his power
and influence. Not that such considerations had ever been a difficulty
where queen consorts were concerned. But a queen regnant? I found it
insulting how quickly even those who knew me well assumed I would be
putty in a husband's hands.

That is one grudge I continue to hold against my cousin, Mary Stu-
art: that she set such a poor precedent for a woman ruler. True, her
French husband died before he could bind Scotland to him, and Darn-
ley was a disaster from beginning to end. But by the time she tried to
reclaim power as queen, it was too late. She had squandered her chances
with her impulsive and emotional choice of Darnley. At least Mary
had the good sense not to give him any real power . . . but was that not
also the downfall of their marriage? Few men are ever content to be
second to their wives.

I like to think you might have proven an exception to that rule.

I knew that Philip and his countrymen would desire power in En-
gland. But I gambled that a ruling king would never have quite the des-
perate, hungry edge of a Henry Darnley or an extraneous prince of a
faraway state. At the least, I could be certain that Philip would have
many other claims on his attention than me.

Why did I marry Philip? Certainly not for the reasons you mar-
ried Amy Robsart! It was not due to our mutual attraction—though
that was certainly part of our marriage, a strong and most pleasant
part. Does that bother you? Good. You deserve that discomfort for all
the times you sought out your wife and your other women behind my
back. How many women did you sleep with in your relatively short
life? Far more, certainly, than I care to count.

So, attraction. That was one point in Philip's advantage column.

But I could not afford for that to be the defining factor. Politics, then. It was certainly logical to ally ourselves with Spain at a time when England had been weakened by my brother's vendettas.

In the end, can you guess the deciding factor? Probably you can, knowing me as you do.

Pride.

You know how deeply ran the scar of losing Calais to the French. Held for so long by so many English kings . . . how could I bear the thought of having lost it due to William's reckless affections and careless diplomacy? But we had not the strength then to take it back. And the longer it remained French, the less likely we could ever wrest it free again.

Philip did it for me. And I do mean for me—he might have been glad of the chance to discompose the French, but Calais was meant as a betrothal gift for England's queen. And it worked. The day the Spanish ambassador brought us word that Calais had been liberated by Spanish troops and then promptly handed back into English control was the day I told Lord Burghley to draw up a treaty of marriage.

It took many months and much suspicion and wrangling of specific language, but finally it was sealed and the marriage date set. Only then did I panic. Just a little, but enough for me to beg the only friend I had left for help.

Minuette and Dominic would not come to me, in those first years of my reign. At least not to London. But every now and then I could persuade Minuette to meet me elsewhere. For advice, for comfort, for the purest friendship left to me. Even when she made me furious. No one has ever been able to irritate me as quickly and thoroughly as Minuette—except you, of course.

And no one, not even you, has ever been quicker to restore my confidence.

She did not tell me what to do. She did not offer an opinion on either politics or personalities. What she said was simple: "Do what you think is right, Elizabeth. You are at your best when you are sure of yourself to the point of arrogance."

Philip was not, could never have been, the husband of my heart. But I did love him. And for all the enmity we now throw at each other, I cannot wish it undone. It brought me Anabel, whom I love more than I will ever let her know. Unlike me, she is being raised to rule in her own right. You would like her, Robert. Of that, I am sure.

Do you know what I remember most often about you? It is not your eyes or your charm, not your grace or the strength of your hands. It is not even your impudence, though I do miss that more than I could have guessed.

What I remember are the last words you ever spoke to me. When I asked you to take Minuette out of England, far from my brother's reach, you kissed my hand. And you said, "I am your man, Elizabeth. To the last day of my life."

It is the one thing for which I have never forgiven Will—that the last day of your life came far too soon.

Because of that, my heart breaks a little when I see my daughter's eyes following the man she loves—and cannot have. But you, who knew me best, will know that sentiment will always come second to duty. My daughter will do what she must, as I did before her.

And one day, perhaps she will write just such a letter to the man who claimed her heart. As you claimed mine, so early that by the time I realized it, it was already too late.

Good night, my sweet Robin. I trust your eyes are watching me from heaven as always they did on earth.

Elizabeth R.

QUESTIONS AND TOPICS FOR DISCUSSION

1. Discuss the relationship between Mary and Elizabeth. Do you agree with Elizabeth's actions? How would you have handled the situation, in Elizabeth's position? How do you feel about Mary's relationship with Philip, compared to Elizabeth's?

2. As Anabel gets older, the dynamics between the princess and the queen become increasingly complex. Compare and contrast the two women. In what ways are they similar? How are they different?

3. How does the parenting style of Minuette and Dominic compare to that of Elizabeth and Philip? Is one technique more or less effective? Would Elizabeth be a different sort of mother if she weren't also a queen?

4. What do you think of the dynamic between Anabel and Kit? Do you see any parallels to Elizabeth's relationships?

5. Responsibility and honor are reigning principles in the Courtenay household. How do the Courtenay children embody these principles? Discuss the sacrifices each member of the family makes to uphold their sense of honor. Does each define honor in the same way? Do any of them fall short of their high moral standards?

6. The political and the personal are intimately entangled for Elizabeth, Philip, Mary, and Anabel. How—if at all—do these characters separate themselves from the offices they hold? Is there room for a monarch to have a personal life outside of the throne?

7. Discuss Stephen's experiences in Ireland. What surprised you the most? In what ways is he similar to his father? In what ways is he different? If you read The Boleyn King trilogy, do you see any parallels between Stephen's experiences and those of his father?

8. Discuss the importance of military training and experience for young men during this time period.

9. How do the events of this novel compare to the actual historical record? Did anything strike you as particularly plausible or implausible?

10. Do you have any predictions for the next novel in the series?

If you enjoyed *The Virgin's Spy,* read on for a preview of the
stunning conclusion to the Tudor Legacy trilogy

THE VIRGIN'S WAR

Laura Andersen's next dazzling novel featuring Elizabeth I

PRELUDE

July 1577

Fifteen-year-old Pippa Courtenay woke to the blazing sun of a late July day with a smile on her face and practically floated out of bed—then promptly fell earthbound under the onslaught of humid heat. She would have to choose her clothing with care today if she didn't want to melt before noon.

After the briefest hesitation, she threw caution to the wind and decided to forgo a petticoat entirely. No one would know she wasn't wearing one beneath her striped blue silk kirtle. Over that she laced her lightest gown of white voile, thickly embroidered with jewel-toned flowers and vines so lifelike they appeared to twine around her as she walked.

Then she tripped downstairs to Wynfield Mote's hall, humming as she went. And when she entered, he was waiting for her as promised: Matthew Harrington.

Eighteen, tall, broad, brown-haired and brown-eyed, Matthew gave her one of his rare smiles. "Shall we?" he asked.

Considering the unusual heat of this summer, they had decided on a breakfast picnic while the air was still breathable rather than openly liquid. For the same reason, they had decided to walk rather than punish horses with a ride. Their route was instinctive— eastward to the old church.

Pippa talked at an unusually rapid pace even for her. The words spilled out in a rush and burble of delight, dancing from topic to topic. It was such a pleasure to have Matthew home. For the last year he had been deep in his studies at Balliol College, Oxford, but returned two days ago to visit his mother.

Pippa loved her siblings, but her sister Lucie had been moody and difficult for the last few years and had taken to spending a great deal of time in London—ostensibly studying with Dr. Dee but more practically avoiding their parents. Both Stephen and Kit were training seriously with their father as well as riding back and forth with him this summer to Tiverton Castle, leaving even Pippa's twin with but little energy to spend time with her. But Matthew could always be counted on.

She didn't set out to make the day momentous. She rarely set out to do anything—if Lucie acted from principle, Pippa relied on instinct. Though most people found Matthew uncommunicative, with her he talked freely. In and around and over her shifting topics, he told her wry stories about his college and tutors and fellow students, making her laugh in a manner no one else did. Not even Kit.

After the slow ramble, they reached the copse of beeches that looked down a low hill onto the stone walls and spire of the old Norman church. She flung herself into the meadow grass at the trees' edge and leaned back on her elbows, staring up at the sky. Matthew lowered himself more cautiously to sit beside her, and deftly handled the domestic details of laying out breakfast: ripe strawberries, early apples, fresh bread and soft cheese. They took their time eating, letting their stories slowly wind down into companionable silence.

Eyes closed, Pippa lay down in the sweet-smelling, sun-warmed grass.

"Princess Anne is coming to Wynfield soon?" Matthew asked.

"Next week."

"And what trouble are the two of you planning to launch this time?" He corrected himself. "The three of you, I mean. Kit is the worst."

"Anabel's the worst," Pippa said drowsily. "Because *she* isn't afraid of my mother. You'll be here, won't you?"

"I've been invited to Theobalds for a month, to work with Lord Burghley's household. I can hardly say no to England's Lord High Treasurer."

Pippa's eyes flew open, the first shadow of the day crossing her sunny mood. "But I want you here!"

"What a pity I cannot learn the intricacies of English government from a fifteen-year-old girl."

He was deliberately baiting her, and she let herself rise to it. "Anabel is a fifteen-year-old girl," she pointed out. "And before too long she will be in a position to compose her own household and council. Shouldn't you be trying to please her?"

"The princess is far too practical to want advisors with no experience. Why do you think Lord Burghley is taking an interest in me? Because he thinks it likely Princess Anne will draw me into her circle. He intends me to be fit for that position."

She delivered a practiced pout, a little hard while lying flat on her back. And only halfheartedly, because it never worked on Matthew. Really, the only person it ever worked on was her father. When he simply continued to look steadily at her, Pippa huffed a gusty sigh and gave it up.

"I never could make you do what I wanted," she complained.

He made a sound between a laugh and a cough. "Do you think so?"

There was a queer note to his voice that made Pippa sit up and study him sharply. His face looked placid as always, but she caught the slightest quiver at the corner of his mouth.

"Matthew?"

All her life, Pippa had viewed the world with an awareness of shifting layers of meaning and feeling. Most often it was Kit whose emotions pressed in upon her, Kit who came to her in flashes of his present life. But just now her emotions were entirely her own. And in all that brilliant, beautiful day, there was only one thing she wanted.

So she took it.

Pippa leaned in so suddenly that Matthew startled back. She gave him no chance to speak or wonder or think at all. She simply kissed him.

It was, of necessity, inexpert. Pippa was not in the habit of kissing the gentlemen of her acquaintance. She was attractive and wellborn and wealthy, but she also had a formidable father who, rumour had it, had nearly killed Brandon Dudley several years ago after discovering him in passionate concord with Lucette. All of which meant she would have to take the initiative with any man—and with no one more than Matthew.

Almost at once, as though sparked by the touch, Pippa could feel Matthew's responses layered with her own. His first instinct was pure physical response—his second, to pull away. But because she felt it coming, she put her hands on the sides of his face to keep him engaged.

And once past his second instinct, Matthew let himself return her kiss. Having nothing to compare it to, Pippa had no idea if he was experienced or not. All she knew was that it was right. They fit perfectly, as she had always known they would.

Despite her curious double awareness, it was still a surprise when Matthew spoke. "I love you," he whispered in a suspiciously rough voice into her hair when they released each other to breathe. "I have always loved you, Philippa. But you already knew that, didn't you?"

She laughed, a little breathlessly. "Why does everyone think I know everything?"

"Only the things that matter."

And just like that, like a candle being snuffed out, the brilliant day vanished and Pippa was wrapped in a dream or vision—a very specific one that had crept into her life so long ago it seemed to have always been with her. *Rushlight and fog, insistent hands and masked faces, melodious Spanish voices mixed with the unmistakable lilt of the Scots, the certain knowledge that she was dying . . .*

It had never frightened her—until now. Because for the first time, a new element was added to the familiar litany of her life's eventual end. *"Run, Philippa. Run now!" Matthew's voice. Matthew's beautiful, beloved voice, strained with fear and anger. But she could not run, because he was bleeding and if she left him he could not live—*

Pippa gasped, the shock of it like falling into an icy Devon stream in winter. She came back to the hillside, the warm sun on her face, and Matthew grasping her hands. "What's wrong?" he asked.

She slipped out of his hold and stood up, still disoriented as to time and place. All she could think of was to get away as quickly as possible. "I don't always like what I know," she managed to say. "And neither would you. Don't follow me, Matthew."

She walked away, knowing he would not press her. Matthew's restraint always won out.

ONE

November 1584

Dear Kit,

I confess to being unreasonably envious of you just now. Would you believe that it snowed here yesterday? Yes, it melted by morning, but when I think of you and Stephen in the temperate Loire Valley I want to board the first ship that will take me away from Yorkshire.

And yes, I know, I am the one who counseled Anabel to take up residence this far north. But do you not remember Madalena's Moorish grandmother telling me that I am by nature contradictory? Who am I to gainsay such a wise woman?

I am not the only contradictory female in Yorkshire. I suppose you know from Anabel that Brandon Dudley and Nora Percy married suddenly last month. Not, despite what the gossips say, because there is a child coming too soon—no, for all its apparent suddenness, this wedding has been looming for some years. I am only surprised that they waited this

long. Nora is already thirty and has been in love with Brandon forever.
But her mother did not approve—probably because Eleanor Percy hoped
one day her daughter would learn to be as cynical at manipulating men as
she is herself.

Not that Eleanor's manipulations have been particularly successful
lately. The Earl of Ormond proved willing to be her lover, but not her
husband. And with the dangerous situation in Ireland, he has finally bro-
ken with Eleanor for good and sent her back to England. She was not in-
vited to her daughter's wedding.

Nor was the queen informed in advance, despite Nora being her niece.
Anabel is a little tense, awaiting her mother's response.

I wish you would write more often. To me, not just to Anabel. It has
been surprisingly lonely being apart from all my siblings. At least you and
Stephen are together, and Lucie has Julien. Still, there is little time to in-
dulge in self-pity in this household. Anabel is almost as ferocious a ruler as
her mother, and Matthew . . .

Pippa Courtenay broke off writing. For a woman who had often
been told she never lacked for things to say, she could not find the
words to finish that sentence. How to explain her current tenuous
relationship with Matthew Harrington, a man she had known since
birth? At the age of fifteen, she had allowed herself one reckless moment with him—and had spent the last seven years ensuring they
never again crossed the boundaries of simple friendship.

Twice in the last eighteen months Pippa had attempted to explain
to him the wisdom of her decision, and persuade him to look for his
future happiness elsewhere. It had not gone according to plan.

Which seemed to be the theme of the Courtenay family these last
two years. Her older brother Stephen had spent five months confined to the Tower of London. He'd subsequently lost his title and
estates as Earl of Somerset, then been unofficially banished from
England. Now he and Kit, Pippa's twin, were training in France and
serving with the men of their father's old friend, Renaud LeClerc.
And Lucie, the oldest sibling, though gloriously happy in her mar-

riage to Renaud's son, Julien, had suffered three miscarriages in the last two years.

Hands came to rest on Pippa's shoulders and the Princess of Wales said teasingly, "Run out of things for which to scold Kit? I can provide you a list if you need it."

"But then what will you write to him?"

Anabel took a seat next to Pippa and gave a small, secret smile. "Don't worry about me. I have no shortage of things to write to Kit."

Pippa put aside her unfinished letter and decided to change the subject from emotional entanglements to something less fraught. Like politics. "How is the news from Dublin?"

Anabel pulled a face. "It continues disastrous. With the fall of Waterford, only Dublin and Cork are open to reinforcements, and that's presupposing we have any to send. No one thought the Spanish troops would remain this long, but success breeds willingness, and King Philip has had little difficulty rotating men in and out without losing the advantage."

King Philip being also Anabel's father. She had not referred to him as such, not even to Pippa, since the Spanish fleet had landed ten thousand soldiers to oppose English possession of Ireland. He was the enemy now, or at least well on his way to becoming such.

"I suppose Mary Stuart continues to crow about it in her correspondence all over Europe."

"Certainly in her correspondence with her oldest son. James's letters to me are three-quarters rants about his mother and one-quarter demands that England do something about it. Not that he's offering any material help."

The courtship of King James VI of Scotland and England's Princess of Wales had thus far been conducted entirely at one remove. Pippa couldn't help teasing, "Leaving no space for a single word in any of those letters about his most cherished bride-to-be?"

"I am quite happy to escape fulsome and insincere compliments, I assure you. I am less happy when he presumes to criticize my mother and Parliament for not sending more aid to Ireland. I pointed out in my last letter that Scotland is also a Protestant nation and perhaps they would be interested in lending us money or men for the fight in Ireland. I imagine that will shut him up for a bit."

Pippa laughed. "This is quite the most amusing courtship I've ever witnessed."

Anabel sobered. "Just as long as James remains content to be betrothed rather than pressing for a consummation of the treaty."

She didn't have to add the obvious, that she continued to hope the marriage might never take place. Anabel was stubborn and passionate and hardheaded and romantic all in one. As long as she remained unwed, there existed the smallest hope that she might be allowed to marry the man she loved: Kit Courtenay.

The course of true love never did run smooth, Pippa thought mordantly. But this is beginning to be ridiculous. For all of us.

"The Queen of England will not be kept waiting by a rebel Irish countess!" Elizabeth Tudor snapped. It really wasn't fair to snap at Burghley, who did no more than deliver the message that Eleanor Fitzgerald was running late. But he'd had thirty years of serving royals and knew fairness was not something to be expected.

That didn't mean he wouldn't make his own retorts from time to time. "I could hardly burst into her bedchamber and drag her out half clothed."

"Oh, she's fully clothed, mark my words. This is a tactical move." Elizabeth, who knew all about tactical moves, let her ruffled temper smooth into glass. "She thinks she is announcing Ireland's independence. Truly independent rulers do not have to make such petty shows."

It was a further five minutes before the pages proclaimed the arrival of Her Ladyship, the Countess of Desmond. Arrived in England as emissary for the rebel earl, her husband, the only reason Elizabeth had agreed to meet with Eleanor Fitzgerald at all was to impress upon the woman the might and power of the English court.

Elizabeth had never been to Ireland, but she had read plenty of accounts and knew that the Irish nobility—saving perhaps those such as her cousin, the Earl of Ormond—often lived in worse conditions than even her own middle-class merchants. Just because she was finding it difficult to fund a sufficient force of soldiers to beat back the Spanish didn't mean the Irish had any chance at all in the end. Indeed, without Spain, the war would have long since been over.

A point Elizabeth did not hesitate to make when the tardy countess arrived and made a barely adequate curtsey. "I thought the entire point of Desmond's rebellion was resistance to foreign interference. We English have been part of Ireland for more than four hundred years, and yet we are accounted more foreign than the Spanish, who share no heritage with you at all?"

Eleanor was not easily frightened. "They share our faith. And we have less quarrel with foreign soldiers than we do with men who take our lands for their own and pretend they belong."

"As did the Fitzgeralds," Elizabeth pointed out waspishly. "Not all that many generations ago."

"Long enough ago that we have earned the right to govern our own lands."

"If you believe the Spanish will allow you that, then you are being willfully blind. It is just possible that King Philip is willing to commit troops on principle's sake—though I doubt it—but Mary Stuart wants much more. Surely you have heard the rumors that her youngest son will be proclaimed Prince of Ireland in the coming year."

"The boy is two years old. We are not afraid of a child. Not the way we are afraid of men who have determined the best way to rule Ireland is to murder every last Irish soul, thus leaving a clean slate for the English."

Elizabeth waved a hand in disdain. "I am not impressed by melodramatic statements based on hysteria. If you want the fighting in Ireland to stop, the answer is simple: evict the Spanish. When you have done that, then England and Ireland will have something to say to one another. Until then, go back to your husband and tell him I have no place for traitors at my court. You will be escorted back to your ship tomorrow."

She almost thought the woman would respond, for she had a very Irish glint to her eyes, but protocol won. When Eleanor Fitzgerald had left, Elizabeth looked at the one man in her government sure to have even more disdain for the countess than she herself. Francis Walsingham despised Catholics and the Spanish in equal measure. Long an advocate of a swift, harsh end to Ireland's rebellions, he was even more fiery now that they were supported by Philip's troops.

"Well?" she asked pointedly.

Those hooded eyes had never grown easier to interpret. "The Spanish won't go. Not until they've made a serious play for Dublin."

"Dublin will never fall."

"Perhaps not, but it might be starved into submission. If the Spanish decide to blockade the port—"

"Then they will be committing to open warfare against all our forces," Elizabeth snapped. "Philip isn't prepared for that."

"Yet." Walsingham let the syllable hang ominously, but said no more.

Elizabeth would like to have believed that her Lord Secretary had learned discretion during his banishment from her court two years ago, but she doubted it. Walsingham was who he was and she valued him for it. Even if sometimes she wanted to kill him as well.

Of the two of them, Walsingham did not hold grudges. And though Elizabeth did, she knew the difference between wisdom and vanity. He had hurt her pride with his opposition to the French marriage, but she could swallow that for the greater good. Especially since there was no chance of the fight resuming, for Francis, the Duc d'Anjou, had died earlier this year of a tertian fever. It was just as well Elizabeth had thought to take Anjou for herself and tied Anabel to James of Scotland, or else England would be doing some rapid maneuvering at this point.

"Keep an eye on the Netherlands," Elizabeth reminded Walsingham unnecessarily. "If Philip begins removing troops from the Low

Countries, then we can begin to worry about Dublin and our own shores. For now, he is stretched thin on the ground."

Lord Burghley cleared his throat.

"Yes?" she prompted.

"Sir Walter Raleigh has been making quiet inquiries into the Somerset estates. He would be most willing to buy Farleigh Hungerford from the crown. If the crown has decided to sell, that is."

"The crown has not so decided."

A long silence. "As long as it remains in crown control, Your Majesty, there are those who expect Stephen Courtenay will be reinstated to his titles."

"They can expect whatever they like. But I promise you one thing—as long as I live, Stephen Courtenay will never again be the Earl of Somerset. Spread that news, if you like."

It hurt her to say it, but not because she had second thoughts. Stephen had committed treason. Any other man in her kingdom would have paid for those crimes with his head. But Stephen was Minuette's son. So he lived—but without title or lands or even his home. He had been in France for nineteen months now. As far as she was concerned, he could stay there indefinitely.

And if he helped keep his brother, Kit, out of England as well? All the better.

Maisie Sinclair had never been to Yorkshire before. Indeed, she had never been in England at all until a week ago. Despite her birth and childhood in Edinburgh, so close to the border that there always seemed to be alarms about whether the English were coming, Maisie's travels had taken her seemingly everywhere save her nearest neighbor. After her short-lived Irish marriage, she had turned to the Continent. Since 1582 she had spent time in Antwerp, Bruges, Germany, Italy, and France. Now, at last, she was on her way home. Three and a half years after sailing from Scotland as the fifteen-year-old bride of an Irishman she'd never met, Maisie was prepared to make her play in Edinburgh.

But first, this visit to Yorkshire. Amidst her voluminous business correspondents was the household treasurer for Her Royal Highness Anne Isabella, Princess of Wales. Maisie's small but successful business interests had profited the princess in her investments, and the treasurer had issued an invitation to meet with him in person in the cathedral city of York. She had considered for ten seconds—six seconds longer than it usually took her to make a decision—before agreeing to sail to Hull and riding the remainder of the way north.

She had not anticipated feeling nervous. *We are Sinclairs*, her grandfather had often drummed into her. *We do not grovel before anyone.* But when Maisie approached the Treasurer's House in the shadow of York Minster and saw the royal banner of the Princess of Wales flying from the roofline, she very nearly turned on her heel and ran away. She had not been told that the princess herself would be here.

But her training held—all of her training, from her grandfather's hardheaded business principles to the nuns' strict codes of conduct—and probably no one noted the slight stutter in her step. One advantage of enormous skirts. She had with her a Flemish secretary she had hired in Bruges on the recommendation of one of her bankers and who had proven himself a hundred times over to be both astute and loyal. His name was Pieter Andries, and though she thought of him as a boy, he was a good ten years older than her. But where Maisie viewed the world without illusions and with the cynicism of a Scots business owner, Pieter had a boundless faith in humanity and a wide-eyed joy in the world that made her watch out for him as though he were a naïve spaniel.

Pieter looked up at the banner and grinned. "This should be interesting."

All right, so maybe he had learned her trick of cynical understatement during their time together.

They were met by pages and a soft-spoken, black-haired woman who introduced herself as Madalena Arias. She had the faintest of Spanish accents. "Mistress Sinclair," she said, for Maisie had insisted on returning to her maiden name after her brief marriage, "if you will follow me, Matthew Harrington is waiting for you in the reception hall. I hope you do not mind if Her Highness joins the meeting?"

It was a disingenuous question, but Maisie thought it well-mannered to pretend to ask. "It will be an honour," she replied truthfully.

Pieter trailed behind her, looking suitably clerkly, and Maisie was glad she had dressed with care. The blue-green of her gown was a unique dye done in the Low Countries, trimmed in lace as fine as a spider's web at the collar and cuffs. Her hair was coiled in a pearled snood attached to a small velvet cap, and her earrings were tiny matching pearls. Perfectly correct and suitable for a wealthy merchant's granddaughter.

When they entered the two-story hall with its black and white checkered floor, Maisie's eyes went directly to the red-haired princess. She was unmistakable, not only from her well-known coloring and elaborate gown, but from the indefinable air of power draped around her. She was taller than Maisie—most everyone was—and beautiful beyond merely the trappings of her dress and position. If she had been a maid, she would still have been ravishing. But combined with her position, Anne Tudor would always command the breathless attention of all who met her.

And she was as charming as she was gorgeous. "Maisie—may I call you Maisie?—I hope you don't mind me sitting in. Matthew sings your praises to such a degree that I simply had to meet you myself."

Maisie made a serviceable curtsey. "It is a great pleasure, Your Highness."

An exceptionally tall man took a step forward. "Matthew Harrington," he said unnecessarily. "It is good of you to go out of your way to come to York."

He spoke as he wrote, with economy and quiet strength. He had the build to support his height, with brown hair and dark brown eyes that assessed her steadily.

"And this," Princess Anne said, drawing forward the other woman present, "is someone most eager to meet you for herself. Philippa—"

"Courtenay," Maisie interrupted, then flushed. "I apologize, Your Highness. But she is very like her brother."

"Stephen?" Philippa Courtenay asked quizzically.

"I meant your twin, Christopher. I met him once in Ireland, on the way to my wedding. But yes, you do have something of Stephen about you as well."

The allure, she meant, but would never say. *The trick of looking at me with such focus that the rest of the world fades around the edges.* Anne Tudor might be the center of her world, but the Courtenays took self-possession to an entirely new level.

"I had hoped," Philippa Courtenay continued, "to have some talk with you of Stephen later. When you are finished with the business of high finance. He writes to you, I understand."

"He does."

"Why?"

This was not a woman to be parried with a soft answer. "Why me and not you, do you mean? Because I was in Ireland. Those who have passed through trials together can understand one another in a manner others cannot."

To her surprise, Philippa smiled, genuine and open. "True. You will not mind if I ask you about my brother later on?"

"No, my lady."

Princess Anne had managed to subtly hold herself in the background, a trick Maisie imagined she didn't often employ, but now firmly took back the authority. "Let us sit and discuss my money. And when we are finished, I shall turn Pippa loose on you. If you are as wise with your words as you are with finance, it will be quite the conversation."

Maisie drew a slightly shaky breath and took the seat Matthew offered her. Discussing money was simple. It was the thought of discussing Stephen that made her pulse flutter.

The hour that followed was more exhilarating than any Maisie had spent in a long time. Despite her polite protestations, the Princess of Wales had an astute business mind. She and Matthew Harrington between them grilled her thoroughly and by the end of the hour they had several new investments planned.

And then, with apparently artless ease, the princess took Matthew with her and left Maisie and Philippa Courtenay alone.

"Lady Philippa," Maisie said warily.

"Call me Pippa. Everyone does."

Since she couldn't quite bring herself to do that, Maisie simply nodded as though in agreement while silently vowing not to call her anything. And waited to be asked uncomfortable questions.

"Is Stephen ever going to recover from loving his Irish woman?"

Well, that was rather more uncomfortable than even she had bargained for. "It depends on how you define recovery."

A flash of amused respect from Lady Philippa. "I define it as not needing to turn to hard drink or easy women to salve his pain."

"Surely your twin can give you more accurate information than I can, seeing as how they are together in France."

"But Kit never met Ailis Kavanaugh. You were there. You watched it all happen. And before you tell me that you were far too simple and innocent to understand what was going on ... don't bother. Your pose of childlike blandness does not fool me in the slightest."

It had been a long time since Maisie had met an adult who bothered to look behind the masks she wore. Stephen had been the last, and that only briefly and in flashes between his obsession with Ailis. It was something of a relief to shrug her shoulders and answer bluntly. "Stephen is not a man to be broken by anything save his own conscience. He loved Ailis very much. But any chance they might have had vanished the moment her daughter was murdered. It wasn't his lies or their different religions or political aims that ruined them—it was Stephen himself. He will never forgive himself for Liadan's death. I think he believed that walking away from Ailis was his penance."

"That doesn't precisely answer my question."

"He will not take refuge in alcohol." She didn't dare think about women. What did she know of how men eased their pain in that way? "He will not retreat from the path he has laid before himself—to serve where he can to the best of his ability. It is your queen's loss if it is not to be in England."

"That sounds rather cold."

"You asked for honesty, not comfort."

Lady Philippa smiled, but there was something sad to it. And piercing. She seemed to be looking deep into Maisie's own cold comforts as she said, "You are not wrong, but I do not think you see the whole of my brother. There is more to Stephen than duty, and a heart with room for more than one love. I do not think passion has finished with him quite yet."

Rudely, Maisie stood up first. She had no experience with passion and no desire to discuss it with this self-possessed woman who also happened to be Stephen's sister. "My business is with numbers," she said with finality. "I shall leave passion and penance to those better equipped to recognize it."

Lady Philippa rose with a grace Maisie envied, and her smile grew mischievous. "Thank you for your honesty, Mistress Sinclair. I will not forget it. Or you."

Maisie couldn't decide if that were a promise or a threat.

ABOUT THE AUTHOR

LAURA ANDERSEN is married with four children, and possesses a constant sense of having forgotten something important. She has a B.A. in English (with an emphasis in British History), which she puts to use by reading everything she can lay her hands on.

www.lauraandersenbooks.com
Facebook.com/lauraandersenbooks
@LauraSAndersen

Chat.
Comment.
Connect.

Visit our online book club community at Facebook.com/RHReadersCircle

Chat

Meet fellow book lovers and discuss what you're reading.

Comment

Post reviews of books, ask—and answer—thought-provoking questions, or give and receive book club ideas.

Connect

Find an author on tour, visit our author blog, or invite one of our 150 available authors to chat with your group on the phone.

Explore

Also visit our site for discussion questions, excerpts, author interviews, videos, free books, news on the latest releases, and more.

Books are better with buddies.
Facebook.com/RHReadersCircle

RANDOM HOUSE

RANDOM HOUSE READER'S CIRCLE ®